MW01009027

PRAISE I
CAROLINE KELLEMS

A compelling insight into modern life in Guatemala filled with love, lust, family drama—and danger! Highly recommended.

— THE WISHING SHELF

The Poppy Field beguiles from the beginning and doesn't miss a step as the direction of the Whitehalls' journey changes with each chapter. Caroline Kellems has written a winning story about how faith, love, and family can be tested in a trial by fire. This is a first-class effort from start to finish.

— THE BOOK REVIEW DIRECTORY

A heartfelt meditation on desire and responsibility... Kellems' rich portrayal of Guatemalan culture, foods, traditions, and everyday living provides authenticity to the story, and her skillful handling of Katherine's clash of desires and duties creates tension and moral ambiguity throughout her journey. A textured and layered human drama.

— THE PRAIRIES BOOK REVIEW

The Poppy Field by Caroline Kellems is one of the best books I have read in a very long time. I can't praise it enough. It's a tale of a new life in a lesser-known country, and besides being an adventure story, it highlights the missionary's character in viewing life through rose-colored glasses.

— LUCINDA E. CLARKE FOR READERS'
FAVORITE

Sincere and deeply absorbing, the novel beautifully delves into the repercussions of choices made in pursuit of personal happiness, emphasizing how these decisions impact not only a person's life but also their loved ones. Raw and authentic.

— THE BOOKVIEW REVIEW

The book is a potent exploration of resilience, the impact of choices, and the strength required to navigate a world where survival often demands more than we're prepared to give.

— K. C. FINN FOR READERS' FAVORITE

... a solid entertainment choice for libraries and ... book clubs...The exquisite marriage of suspense, revelation, and marital-and-extramarital relationship snafus lends to a riveting story that's hard to put down.

— D. DONOVAN, SR. REVIEWER FOR
MIDWEST BOOK REVIEW

THE POPPY FIELD

THE POPPY FIELD

A NOVEL

Caroline Kellems

Grand Canyon Press
Tempe, Arizona

Book Cover design by Grand Canyon Press. Illustrations via Adobe Stock by Nick Taurus, AlaskaJade, Наталья Евтехова, and DariaBer; via Shutterstock by TheTravelStoryz

Names: Kellems, Caroline, author.

Title: The poppy field / Caroline Kellems.

Description: Tempe, Arizona : Grand Canyon Press, [2024] | "Fast-paced women's fiction about family secrets and survival."

Identifiers: ISBN: 978-1-963361-00-1 (paperback) | 978-1-963361-02-5 (hardcover) | 978-1-963361-04-9 (hardcover with book jacket) | 978-1-963361-01-8 (ePub) | 978-1-7320787-9-6 (Kindle) | 978-1-963361-0302 (audiobook)

Subjects: LCSH: Hispanic American families—Guatemala—Fiction. | Women—Guatemala—Fiction. |Secrecy—Fiction. | Drug traffic—Guatemala—Fiction. | Man-woman relationships—Fiction. | Missionaries—Guatemala—Fiction. | Survival—Fiction. | Resilience (Personality trait)—Fiction. | LCGFT: Romance fiction. | Thrillers (Fiction) | BISAC: FICTION / Family Life / Marriage & Divorce. | FICTION / Hispanic & Latino / Family Life. | FICTION / Political.

Classification: LCC: PS3611.E4235 P66 2024 | DDC: 813/.6—dc23

Printed in the United States of America

For Eduardo

...always the agenda
the missionary plans

and like the others
you will insist on exile

— DEBORAH PAREDEZ

CHAPTER
ONE

Steaming volcanoes peek through puffy clouds, and wisps of vapor stripe the sky. Caught up in the excitement of her family's adventure, Katherine peeks through the aircraft window. She had always hoped to join the Peace Corps, to make a difference in the lives of needy families. Now, with the church's backing, they will be missionaries. Next best thing!

As the plane descends, an orange haze tinges the slopes of the Valley of Ermita, and Guatemala City's buildings rise into the late afternoon sky. She closes her eyes and leans back, hoping to calm her fluttering heart.

"Mommy, look!" Exuding a twelve-year-old's excitement, Katy pulls on Katherine's arm and points downward. Banking sharply, the 737 soars past skyscrapers and descends to a runway beyond a neighborhood of shanties. Brakes screech as the plane skids onto the tarmac at La Aurora International Airport.

Katherine pulls her carry-on from beneath the seat and rummages for a breath mint, then she brushes out her hair and fastens it with a plastic grip. Auburn strands stick out like frayed copper wires. It has been a long day.

The Whitehall family rushes through immigration and to the carousel, where they collect their suitcases.

"Do you think we'll learn Spanish quickly?" Katy asks her father as they queue to hand papers to the customs agent.

"If I know you, pancake, you'll be speaking Spanish *and* the Mayan dialect before the year is over."

Justin slouches in disagreement. Since learning of their new post, he has resisted all attempts at familial enthusiasm. Fourteen is an age when a kid wants to fit in with his peers, and moving away from friends isn't easy.

The customs agent asks Phil about their numerous bags.

"We're missionaries and are on our way to San Marcos to start a new life," Phil begins eagerly in brushed-up Spanish. "We don't know how long we'll be ... "

The bored agent waves them through without a glance. "*Pase, pase.*"

They step into a throng of people waiting outside in the exhaust-laden air for friends and loved ones. Tour operators and hotel representatives bark their services in broken English, and legless beggars on skateboards extend filthy hands toward the new arrivals. Taxi drivers reach for their bags, but Phil shakes his head "no." He has been warned to keep a tight grip on their belongings. Phil's assistant is to meet them and take them to a hotel. After a good night's sleep, they'll make the trip to their new mission posting.

"What if he forgot about us?" Katy asks.

Justin's face lights up. "We can always turn around and go home."

"Not so fast, kiddo. Give him a chance," Phil says, optimistic that Jerónimo just got the time confused. Phil could have called, but he didn't have a contact number. Katherine had managed to throw it into one of the boxes that went into storage. Just like her to be scattered, he thought. Anyhow, he had more important things to worry about.

When the crowd thins, Katherine points to a husky, dark-skinned man holding a sign that reads WAYTAL in misshapen block letters. "Do you think he might be waiting for us?"

Phil approaches him. "Are you looking for Mr. Whitehall?"

"Sí, sí, Waytal. ¿Usted es Pastor Felipe? Yo soy Jerónimo." He grasps their hands heartily, his thick palms rough and callused. He wears a friendly smile and a soiled, untucked polo shirt that barely covers his ample belly. He hoists the largest of the bags to his shoulder and gestures for them to follow.

They enter a parking lot jammed with buses and taxis and stop at a battered twelve-passenger Volkswagen Microbus. While Jerónimo digs through his pockets for a key, Katy and Justin peel off layers of clothing.

Phil had sent money ahead for a car. He'd explained that the car didn't need to be fancy, only reliable. Phil sees that dust coats the van's scratched sides, and there is at least one dented fender. As the door slides open, a stench of mildew emerges from the faded interior. The four rows of seats sag like hammocks.

"This is our car?" Justin asks. "Can it even survive the trip?"

While Jerónimo stuffs their bags into the back, Justin inspects the interior. He had hoped for a Jeep, something cool to ride around in while he made new friends. This car smells like a barn.

"Dad?" Justin says.

"Look at it this way, son," Phil says. "We'll have plenty of space for our things." After all, he is the head of the family. Traveling to the unknown, he must trust in God and receive whatever difficulties come his way with a spirit of acceptance. The

Lord is his shepherd and won't let them down—his current personal mantra.

Jerónimo boosts himself into the driver's seat. They scoot in and push open the windows. As the sun slips behind a volcano, the balmy afternoon dims.

After nudging through the endless rush hour traffic, they approach the city's center. Ornate churches decorate corners, reminders of a colonial past; the garden of an old theater boasts a permanent audience of statues.

Phil can almost envision the city in its former glory, buildings erected in a time when workers carved figures on cornices and each structure was a work of art. In his contemplation, Phil thinks of Europe and photographs he's seen of glorious buildings. He fails to notice the weeds that sprout on tile roofs and in the cracks of narrow walkways or the windows boarded up like blindfolded hostages. Balconies tilt precariously over sidewalks, threatening to collapse on unsuspecting passersby.

By the time the Microbus pulls up to their hotel, the *avenidas* are silent and empty. Dusk has obliterated all vestige of color on the street, and an occasional streetlamp casts a dull glow over the desolation.

Clothing unbuttoned and barely clinging to his emaciated body, a barefoot drunk staggers along the street. Curled together in a stairwell, two bag ladies cover themselves with newspaper. Phil stares at them for a moment, thinking he could find a similar scene in any city, anywhere. Perhaps Guatemala won't be as different as he had expected.

Jerónimo unloads their bags on the curbside, and the kids duck into the entrance, where the word HOSTEL is painted in plain, black letters, the only thing that distinguishes the front door from identical doors on the block.

"Tomorrow, I come. Six in the morning." Jerónimo eases back into the driver's seat.

Phil watches with faint unease as the taillights disappear down the dark street. What will happen if Jerónimo doesn't return? If that happens, then Phil will just have to put his faith in the Lord.

After they slip inside, a guard with a shotgun slung over his shoulder secures a heavy wooden door behind them: a single lock, a bolt, and a large padlock. For good measure, he slides a wooden bar across the frame.

"Like prisoners," Justin mutters.

Phil stares at his son and tries to lighten the moment. "Hey, at least we're free from danger." He regrets the last word as soon as it slips from his mouth. Negativity draws evil, and danger is a possibility Phil refuses to acknowledge.

A cobblestone courtyard, open to the sky, is bordered with potted plants and flickering candles in glass jars. Doors line four sides of the atrium, and stairs lead up to the second floor. Off to one side is a mahogany counter where a man with a silver-toothed smile greets the family. "Welcome to Guatemala."

"I guess this is the lobby," Phil says, letting his suitcase drop.

Katherine rolls her eyes. "Do you think?"

"Are we really going to stay here?" Katy says.

"Dad says we need to be good sports," Justin says.

"I'm trying," Katy says.

"There, there, kids," Katherine says. "Look around. This place has a kind of old-world charm, and I'm sure we'll be perfectly safe."

CHAPTER
TWO

An alarm buzzes. Time to get up already? Katherine's night was restless, filled with images of barred doors and unfamiliar places. She has been sporadically excited and anxious about the trip, about their posting in Central America and potential hazards. One of her friends told her she should investigate the security situation of the country more carefully, but she couldn't be bothered, figuring that Phil had already taken it into consideration. Perhaps she had been naïve.

While they were dating, Phil, an Indiana boy, had talked about wanting to travel, but he'd never gone any farther than Chicago, certainly nowhere international, not like the other college kids who were traipsing around Europe with their backpacks. Given that they had two children and not a lot of money, maybe mission work should have seemed like an obvious choice, but what astonished Katherine was the way Phil said he'd received the message. He had an accident before they married, then a vision during the three days he was unconscious. An angel had appeared to him and said that his time hadn't come, that there was work to be done for the Lord. Katherine did her best to keep an open mind, but, never having received a direct message from God, she was skeptical. It could have been a dream, a hallucination. After all, hadn't he been on medication while he was in the hospital?

They married soon after the incident. He gave up his former life (and his rock-and-roll band), went to seminary, became the assistant pastor of their hometown church—his passion for Christ increasing week by week. Thinking—no, hoping!—his zeal would rub off, she presided over the Christian women's society and taught Sunday school. While attending church, Phil passionately took notes. Sitting next to him, she let her mind wander to the unfinished chores at home and items for their suitcases.

And now, they are here in Guatemala. Phil's goal is to build a church in the village, a place with an already established but tiny Evangelical following, and to grow community involvement. He had heard about the opportunity on an internet posting and had worked diligently to get their paperwork together. Katherine has come because she wants to help the poor. She envisions a life of service that will give meaning to her own. After all, if she is to stay with him, she must find some way to make her values align with his.

She disengages herself from the scratchy bedding and glances out the window. Though darkness still blankets the city, spring's dawn blushes in anticipation of a new day. Light seeps through the window and silhouettes her husband's sleeping form. He snores softly, and she feels a twinge of resentment at his tranquility.

"Phil," she hisses. "Wake up."

He pulls the pillow over his ear and turns his back to her. "I only fell asleep a minute ago."

"Jerónimo will be here soon."

"All right, all right. Just another minute."

Across the room, her children sprawl on a bunk bed. On the bottom berth, Katy sleeps beneath a rough woolen coverlet that dangles toward the worn, red tile floor. Above her, Justin, tossing on the thin cotton pallet that passes for a mattress, lets out a barely audible groan. The kids are going to be grumpy, but just looking around puts her in a bad mood, too. A freestanding wardrobe lurks in the corner, and a metal floor lamp hovers over an ancient wooden table. Splotchy whitewashed cement walls permeated with dampness lend a musty chill to the air, and the room smells vaguely of cigarettes and the stale sweat of former occupants.

"Time to get moving." She nudges the children awake and points to the door. "Jerónimo will be here soon, and I want everyone to shower before we leave."

They protest and rub their eyes. Each carries a threadbare towel as they trudge down the hall.

Justin's rusty hair sticks up in a cowlick. She wets her fingers and tries to smooth it.

He twists away. "Are you serious, Mom? Communal showers? What kind of hotel is this?"

"Keep it down, son. We're the only ones awake. Besides, the stalls are individual."

By the time they are showered and dressed, the city has sprung to life. Airplanes roar overhead, horns blare, people shout, and buses zoom past, shaking the foundations of the small hotel so thoroughly that Katherine wonders if these are the earthquakes her grandmother had mentioned.

Dressed and repacked, they stumble down to the lobby. Phil exchanges a small amount of cash, and Katy carries her bag to the entrance. A square opening in the door looks out onto the street. "I'll watch for our ride," she says.

In the center of a marble-topped table, a small, curved cage imprisons an unhappy bird. Like gaudy eyeshadow, its black eyes are outlined in emerald.

"Keel-billed toucan," Phil announces to no one in particular and nudges a bony finger into the cage. The bird glares at the offending appendage.

"You'd think he'd topple over from the size of that beak," Justin says.

Katherine watches Phil open his mouth. What comes next will be a lesson on the bird's beak size and weight.

"Jerónimo's here!" Katy calls.

"Remember you need to call him *Don* Jerónimo, honey. That's polite. It's like saying mister."

"That's just wierd, Mom. It's like all the men in this country have the same name. What if his name was Don?"

"Don Don." Justin chuckles. "Who's there?"

Katherine grapples with her duffle bag and turns to her daughter. "And the women are *Doña*. Don't ask why, just remember. Grab your bags and let's go."

Guatemala City traffic rivals that of any metropolis, with an added element of disorder. Motorcycles, cars, trucks, and buses dart back and forth in narrow lanes and pass on the left-hand side. Signaling other cars, drivers slam their horns or dangle their hands out windows. Some wave their thanks; others plead to be let into the line of traffic or insult neighboring vehicles that cut them off. As the van jerks through this madness, Katherine grabs at the seat in front of her and warns her family to snap on their seat belts, but then she discovers there are none. The car is that old.

Skyscrapers brush the clouds; buildings of glass and steel rise like modern forests. Bronze statues of long-dead generals guard urban parks, and pedestrians flag down overcrowded buses.

"This is crazy," Justin mutters. He can't help contrasting it with their orderly town in Indiana. "Nothing like America."

"It *is* America, Justin," his father says. "*Central* America."

Heavily armed soldiers patrol the city's center. Armed guards station themselves in front of businesses, gun-toting men (many of whom don't look any older than Justin) jam pickup beds, and policemen on motorcycles weave their way through the bumper-to-bumper traffic. Katherine's stomach lurches as she stares at all the weapons, but what scares her most is that no one else seems to notice.

Jerónimo finally turns onto an avenue that appears as though it might take them out of town.

"Where are the houses?" Katy asks.

"People live in *colonias*," Jerónimo says. "Gated places. High walls. Sharp glass. Razor wire."

Suburbs with razor wire? Katherine shakes her head, her worst fears confirmed. Perhaps Phil didn't do the requisite investigation after all.

"What about us, Dad?" Katy asks. "Are we going to live somewhere like that?"

"Pancake, we will be far away from the city. Life will be quiet and safe."

Justin always names the family cars. He dubbed the old Impala from home Irma. When they left Indiana, he swore it was one of the few things he wouldn't miss, but he hadn't yet seen their new vehicle. He sits back and ponders possible names. When the perfect moniker occurs to him a short time later, he nudges his sister and whispers in her ear.

"The Missionary Marvel?" Katy throws him a sour look. "Are you out of your mind?" Katy gazes out the window. "Leave me alone. Mom, tell Justin to stop bothering me."

Justin plasters his forehead against the glass and out of sheer boredom asks the inevitable. "Are we almost there?"

"Yeah, Dad," Katy seconds. "How long is this trip supposed to take?"

Phil twists back and breathes deeply. "We're headed for San Marcos on the border with Mexico. It's a full day's drive, so why don't you kids lie down and try to get some sleep."

Justin stretches out along the back bench, while Katy curls up catlike on the seat. A few minutes later her strawberry-blonde head pops up. "I have to pee."

Phil consults with Jerónimo, who says, "Chimaltenango. Very soon."

Whitewashed homes flash by, roofed with red tile and nestled in fertile fields. Residences scattered like windblown seeds cohere into a town. They pull into a Texaco station with a convenience store. Katherine and Katy jump out in search of a bathroom, then linger to buy sodas and snacks.

Back on the two-lane highway, cars and buses careen along at top speed, passing on blind curves and swerving to avoid potholes. Justin leans over the seat. "This is crazy. Don't people have to pass driving tests in this country?"

"No tests," Jerónimo says. He rubs his thumb against his forefinger to indicate money exchanging hands.

"I guess licenses, like a lot of things down here, are bought and sold," translates his father.

Justin considers the convenience of buying himself a license in another year and a half. "That's so cool."

But he doesn't think it's cool a minute later when an approaching bus pulls out to pass a car. Jerónimo swerves, and the vehicle lurches into a crater-like hole. The impact thunders like a gunshot and Justin's head smacks against the window. "Ow! Dad, tell our chauffeur to watch where he's going."

The car veers to the right. "Quiet, son, I think the tire exploded."

The Missionary Marvel limps to a halt.

Justin hops out to inspect the damage. "Flat as roadkill," he reports to his mother and sister.

Phil circles the van and inspects all the tires. "We'll change it in a jiffy and be back on the road in no time." The hatch yawns open as they attempt to retrieve the spare. Nothing. They move things around and check for hidden compartments. After looking underneath, Phil begins to panic. "Shit."

Roused by Phil's uncharacteristic swearing, Katherine sits up. "What's the matter?"

"There's no spare."

They find the jack and tools and pull off the tire.

"No worry," Jerónimo says. "I take to Tecpán for repair. Stay inside. Lock doors."

Phil looks skeptically at the ruined tire.

Unconcerned, Jerónimo flags down a crowded bus and squeezes in. The red-and-yellow vehicle drives off, the flat tossed on the roof amid an assortment of wooden crates and baskets of fruit.

As soon as the bus is out of sight, Katy says, "It's too hot. We can't stay cooped up here. We'll asphyxiate."

Justin adds, "Seriously, Dad. Katy's right. We can't stay inside until Jerónimo comes back. We don't even know how long that will be."

"You heard what he said. We need to keep the doors locked."

"Let's turn on the air-conditioning." Katherine leans into the front and feels around. "He did leave the key, didn't he?"

Phil searches hidden niches in the dashboard, checks the

pockets of his pants—just in case—and then shakes his head. "He must have taken it."

"At least let's open the door. Come on, it's not like anyone could steal the car, even if for some reason they'd want to," Justin says.

His reasoning makes sense. It doesn't seem conceivable they'll be held up in an old car with three tires in the middle of nowhere. But just to be safe, Phil stows passports, extra cash, and credit cards underneath the suitcases where the jack is stored.

Katherine slides the door open and hands out drinks. Phil pulls out his dog-eared King James Version of the Holy Bible, stretches out in the front seat, and leans against the driver's door.

Justin squirms. Already their car time has stretched into eternity with endless hours still to come. "Let's find somewhere to sit in the shade, Katy. The wait could take a while."

"I don't think you should leave the van," Katherine says. "Didn't you hear what Jerónimo said?"

Justin is already scoping out possible areas to explore. "I can't understand a word of what he says. Besides, what does he know? He doesn't even live around here. What could happen?"

Katy grabs her daypack. "Don't worry, Mom. We'll stay close by."

"Seriously, you can trust me," Justin says. "I'm responsible. I'm a teenager."

"That's why I worry," Katherine says.

The kids scamper up fifteen feet to a treed area at the top of a small ridge. When she scans the escarpment, Katherine can't see them, and she tries not to let panic leak into her voice. "Kids?"

Justin pokes his head over the edge. "We're right here with a great view of the highway. Seriously, why don't you join us?"

She declines in favor of staying with her husband and their

belongings, but as the car heats up, the invitation sounds increasingly appealing. She searches through her bag for something she could use as a fan and then looks up to see four men sauntering across the highway toward them. The swagger in their walk suggests danger. She stares and blinks hard. What could they want? Her heart rate increases, and she glances up to where she last saw her children. Thank God they're out of sight.

"Phil! Phil!" Katherine hisses. His eyes are closed piously, or perhaps he's napping. She shakes his shoulder. "Look!"

Two men flaunt canvas jackets that partially cover holsters. Phil sizes up the situation. "Don't worry. It's probably just some young men come to help." He puts on a friendly face. "Señores, buenas tardes. Somos misioneros. Tenemos problemas con el carro."

The leader's lips curl into a sneer. He scans the suitcases and nods slightly toward the others, who take that as a sign to start searching.

He reaches for Katherine.

"What? What are you doing?" The men have definitely not come to assist. Her chest tightens and her heart thumps in her ears. Her mind freezes in shock and disbelief, and she waits for her tilted world to right itself. This can't be happening. Four armed men haven't actually come to hold them up, have they?

The first of them grabs her arm, and she feels the grip of his hands, fingernails digging into her pale flesh. The pain detaches her from reality. He pulls her from the van, and she stumbles. With a jerk, he has her on her feet, her shoulder wrenched.

Time fractures into frames like a slow-moving film. She hears a thumping and realizes it's blood pounding through her veins. Her vision blurs, and she can't make sense of what is happening.

He puts a gun to her head.

A gun? "This is so wrong! Why are you doing this? We're here to help, to create projects in the communities, to preach and spread the word of God." Katherine isn't sure if she calls out or pleads in silence. Either way, the men pay her no heed. Paralyzed with fear, she couldn't have run if given the chance.

They drag Phil from the car, frisk him, empty his wallet of cash, and toss all but the bills in the drainage ditch by the side of the road. He tries to explain in brushed-up Spanish that they are only missionaries, but his words drift in the air, unrecognized and ignored. Phil resists and grabs at the money. The thief cuffs him with a gun and knocks him against the van. After deciding that Phil poses no danger, the thief shoves him back into the car and slams the door.

Panic forces Katherine's words out in breathy puffs. "Please, please don't harm us. Take whatever you want." Her biggest concern is for her children. What if they are discovered, or if they lose their parents in the middle of nowhere, unable to even communicate? She refrains from looking up for fear she might give them away and prays her son doesn't try to play the hero.

The men laugh at her terror.

A thief dumps Katherine's purse and stuffs her wallet into a bag. She stares in morbid fascination at a tattoo that runs from his clothing up his neck: a fire-breathing apparition straight out of Dante's *Inferno*. He turns to the others and spits derisively. "Estos no son turistas, vos. Son misioneros."

The guard jerks Katherine around and the cold metal of a gun strikes her forehead. The pain catches her unaware, and she reels. With great effort, she stays on her feet and tries to focus. Form a plan. Escape. Flag down a passing car.

The thieves are speaking in Spanish, and though she doesn't understand the words, the vulgar tone is universal. Dread tightens like a noose, and her stomach heaves. The thug's eyes lower from her face until they rest on her breasts. They haven't found much worth stealing in the car and expect something for their efforts. A fair-skinned redhead.

No! She jerks away, but his grip only tightens. She steels herself for the worst and flinches when rough hands rip at her shirt. The two top buttons pop, exposing her bra and part of her pale breast. She focuses on a place in the distance where pine trees meld into the calm blue sky, a place where the men cannot find her and none of this can be happening.

Suddenly, Phil springs from the car. Like a marionette powered by some ethereal force, he thunders, "Satan, I command you to leave," taking everyone, even Katherine, by surprise.

The men look at each other in uncertainty and glance sideways at Phil. Katherine feels the grip on her arm relax.

"God protect us through the blood of your Son, Jesus Christ," Phil chants, his voice increasing in volume as he sees his words having an effect. The men hesitate and look to their leader in confusion. The men are not familiar with this kind of resistance.

"Este hijo de puta está loco. Vámonos."

Katherine's spirits lift. In a pious country, the evilest of men can be brought down by invoking the Lord. Phil, you are brilliant!

The men glance at each other and tilt their heads toward her husband, evaluating his power, or maybe his sanity. The prize of Katherine is momentarily forgotten as a search for the car key ensues, and they notice the missing tire. The leader shakes his head. He gives her one last look, runs his tongue over his lips, and hesitates as though deciding whether to take her with him. She stares at him and reads his intentions. No! You cannot take me. She braces herself. His companion shouts to get moving, and the thought passes. He turns reluctantly and follows as the others disappear across the highway.

After the men leave, Phil enfolds his wife in his arms. "Sweetheart, are you all right?"

Broken sobs choke forth, and her voice eludes her. Has the menace gone? She gathers her strength and, in a quavering tone she scarcely recognizes as her own, calls out, "Justin, Katy, where are you?"

The children stumble down the dirt slope and into their parents' arms. They cling to each other and pray silently, each thanking the Lord that the danger has passed. Phil steps back and searches his wife's face. "I'll understand if you want to go back to the States."

There is nothing she would rather do. Such a threat could never occur at home, she thinks, and tries to slow her trembling. But was it fair for her to make them leave after one small setback? Their things are in storage. They gave up their rental. Perhaps if Phil had not offered, she might have insisted, but surely from here on out, things could only get better.

Phil leads his family in prayer. "Praise you, oh merciful Lord. You sent the thieves away. You gave Katherine your protection and me the wisdom to hide our documents and to call upon your power. You sent the children out of harm's way. We take this as a sign that you are watching over us. We are humbled by your mercy."

As they pray, doubt, that ever-present scoundrel, creeps into Katherine's mind. If they are so protected, why did they get held up in the first place?

THREE

T en minutes later, a turquoise-and-red bus, draped in multicolored streamers and plastic garlands, slows on the other side of the highway, and Jerónimo jumps off. The bus driver's assistant, the *ayudante*, scrambles up the side, hops between wooden chicken crates and baskets of tropical fruit to the newly repaired tire, unties it from the roof rack, and tosses it down.

Farting black smoke in its wake, the chicken bus rumbles down the road toward the capital. Like a gymnast, with the assurance that comes from practice and the fearlessness that comes from working for a decade on public transportation, the *ayudante* swings down into the open door of the moving vehicle.

Jerónimo breezes across the highway, rolling the tire. His expression changes to concern as he sees family members comforting each other and luggage scattered outside the van. Phil greets his new assistant with funereal solemnity and tells him about the holdup.

"¡La Banda de Los Churruneles!" Jerónimo asserts with

authority, as if he had seen the gang himself. He sizes up the Whitehalls as though suspecting they had somehow provoked the attack. "I say lock doors."

When Katherine suggests they go to the police station to file a report, he moves his head slowly.

"Police, no. Take the money. No do nothing."

Phil drapes his jacket around his wife protectively.

Jerónimo's new revelation starts another round of trembling. Grateful for the comfort of Phil's goodwill offering, she tries to clear her mind and focus on God's presence. All she gets for her effort is a throbbing headache.

"The Lord is looking out for us," Phil says, "and I'm confident that he will continue to protect us. No real harm was done." They had taken few things, and his wife is safe. He prides himself on keeping an optimistic attitude. What is the point of obsessing on what might have happened?

Katherine glances down at her shirt where the top buttons popped off. Maybe she is safe, but the brush with danger had been close, too close.

She envies her husband's simple faith. It isn't that she doesn't believe, but in the private depths of her being, she harbors a seed of doubt about religion. In the end, she blames herself; she is a pragmatic sort and wonders if her seed of doubt is a mountain-sized obstacle.

With the luggage stored, the tire mounted, and everyone back in the car, Phil explains what happened in more detail to their driver. Katherine cringes at what sounds like boasting. If she didn't know better, she'd think he was elated.

"The Lord worked through me, Jerónimo. I felt His divine power. I cast Satan out of those evil men, and they left."

Jerónimo nods as he drives. Katherine can't assess his reaction, or whether he even understands the rapid flow of words spewing from Phil's mouth.

She was there and saw it happen, but it still annoys her that Phil's new power—through Jesus Christ, of course!—has allowed him to glamorize the ordeal.

"Look!" Justin shouts. "Mayan ruins. Iximche." He points at a blue sign with an arrow showing the ruins to be five kilometers down the side road.

"Sorry, son. We are already behind schedule. I'm sure there'll be something closer to our destination. Somewhere we can visit from our new home." Phil consults with Jerónimo, whose expression is indecipherable. He shrugs noncommittally.

Katy slips into the seat next to her mother and rests her head on Katherine's shoulder. "I want to go back to Indiana," she whispers. "We never should have left."

Katherine is at a loss. How should she answer? God may bless Phil with a clear game plan, but He's never done the same for her. She searches for the right words, words of comfort. She wants to convince Katy as well as herself that another such ordeal will never occur. "We have to be positive and trust that everything else will go smoothly, that all the evil that might befall us has already come to pass." She can't help but think those words might be Phil's, and wishes she shared his certainty. For her daughter's sake, she tries her best to make it seem like she does.

Katy's face shows skepticism, and she slips back into her seat and curls up with her sweater under her head.

After the two kids nod off, Katherine clears her throat to attract her husband's attention. Phil sighs. He doesn't want to hear what she has to say, but she can't just let it drop.

"You told me we'd be safe."

"Once we get to the highlands. Roadsides and cities are

never safe. Random violence is endemic. What happened earlier should reinforce our belief in divine protection."

Trying to dislodge the lingering doubt, she shakes her head. How can Phil be so sure? She can still feel the thief's fingernails as they raked across her breast. Maybe God did save them this time, but what if He can't, or decides not to, the next time? Remembering what Katy said, she tells Phil, "Maybe we shouldn't have come."

Phil turns and looks back. "He will be there when we need Him."

Faith is intangible and unseen. Phil's faith is solid, or so it seems to Katherine, while hers is fleeting. Never has it felt less anchored than now, in this scary place where armed men pillage and threaten to rape roadside victims. Without faith, Phil could never have stood up to those men, but is that enough of a foundation on which to base her beliefs? She thinks it should be, and yet wonders why it isn't.

She remembers the gut-wrenching decisions, weighing the pros and cons. "Didn't you have any doubts about coming, Phil?"

"This is our dream, what we've always talked about doing."

"Maybe we should have waited until the kids were grown."

"We're here, so let's make the best of it."

Katherine is tired of his patronizing tone. "We left a comfortable life so that you could live your missionary dream. I decided that the benefits of this trip would outweigh whatever negatives there were, but I had no idea of those negatives until today. Today has been the most terrifying day of my life. I'm not sure you understand that."

He leans toward the front windshield and stares at the road ahead. "Have faith," he says.

His single-mindedness frustrates her and leaves her wishing he were more like most husbands: men who watch Monday night football, drink beer, and play catch with the kids in the park. Well, maybe drinking beer and watching sports wasn't ideal. But why did she end up with a man whose dream is to take his family and spread the gospel to indigenous people in the middle of nowhere? She sighs and tells herself that it was once her dream, too, helping the downtrodden, but those men on the road trampled on how she had expected their story to unfold.

The van careens along the highway, and Katherine's stomach roils. She opens the closest window for fresh air and adjusts her position to watch the road.

At some point, she drifts off to sleep, and their ominous welcome to Guatemala weaves its way into her dreams. She pictures the mission home, forested mountains in the background, distant fields quilted with crops of corn and beans. Beyond the cinder-block house, dark-skinned villagers settle under a tree. Phil preaches at a Sunday service while the rest of the family lounges on the grass. Halfway through the sermon, a red-faced man with crazy eyes and two bumps on his forehead appears and taunts them in a strange language. Masked men in camouflage ready their guns. Click-clack.

She gasps and opens her eyes. The van has just gone over a series of noisy speed bumps. She glances at her watch. Three o'clock. "Where are we?"

Phil consults with Jerónimo. "A little more than an hour away."

They have been traveling on a volcano-dotted, pine-forested highland plain that forms the northwestern part of the country. Their destination is a village nestled a mile and a half up in the rugged, evergreen mountains, in a valley between Tacaná and Tajumulco, volcanoes on the Mexican border.

Justin slips into the seat beside her. He puts his hand on his father's shoulder. "The thieves took my knife. The one Tom gave me before we left." His prized possession.

"I'm sorry, son." Phil searches for the right thing to say, then slips into a standard pastoral response. "Sometimes that's the way God works. You need to lose everything to find Him."

Justin had hoped for sympathy, not preaching. Without meeting his father's eyes, Justin moves back to the seat in front of where Katy is sleeping and nudges her. "Wake up, sis. I'm bored."

Katherine frowns. "Justin, what's the matter with you? Don't bother your sister."

Katy opens one blue eye, then the other. They move to the back and speak quietly. Katy nods at something Justin says and stares out the window.

"We're way out in the boondocks, aren't we?" Katy says.

"It won't be that bad. We still have each other—unfortunately for you." He pokes her in the ribs. Standard fare for cheering up a little sister.

She giggles. "Stop it, Justin!"

Phil turns in his seat. "Keep it down back there. Katherine, can't you keep them under control?"

"No, I can't. Change places with me if you're so interested in quiet. Every time I take my eyes off this winding road, I want to puke."

Phil mumbles and makes no attempt to change places.

Along the road, youngsters lug weighty bundles of firewood on their backs, straining forward from the effort. Like the men, they wear forehead harnesses to counterbalance their heavy loads. Women stroll gracefully, taking short steps while balancing clay jugs or heavily laden baskets on their heads.

Katy points toward a lady with a container on her head. Her

head is cushioned by native handloomed fabric. "I wish I could carry stuff on my head and walk down the road like that."

"No, you don't," Justin counters. "Look how short the women are. The weight on their heads keeps them from growing."

"Really?" Her eyes widen, then her expression changes. She gives her brother a push. "That's not true."

"Think you hurt me? Think you hurt me?" he taunts.

Katherine glances back for a second. "How are you kids doing?" Damned if she's going to shush them. Let Phil change places if he's worried about noise.

"We're okay, how are you?" Justin answers.

"Car sick." She raises her voice. "Can we stop soon to stretch our legs? I don't feel well."

"I could pee again," Katy offers.

"And I'm hungry," Justin says.

Phil answers, "We need to buy food and supplies. We are approaching the last town before we arrive at our post."

Katherine reluctantly nods to herself. No doubt her chore. Grocery shopping with sign language.

Billboards sprout like cornstalks, getting denser as town nears. Plastic bags, empty bottles, used disposable diapers, and a sea of nondegradable garbage litters the ditches along the roadside. Skeletal strays snarl and snap at vultures competing for tidbits.

Jerónimo slows the Missionary Marvel as they veer down narrow streets. He parks in front of a *tienda*, rolls down the window, and points toward the open-air market. Blue and black tarps stretch for two blocks, shading street stands that sell everything: fruit, vegetables, personal care supplies, clothing, and sundries. Her first time shopping, she hopes for Phil's help. At least he has rudimentary language skills.

The children climb around her and slide open the door.

"Have fun," Phil says.

"Aren't you coming?" she says, stepping down.

"We're going to the gas station to check the tire pressure and radiator. Meet you back here in a half hour."

"Fine." She slams the door.

Vendors are packing their goods for the day, and the stench of rotting fruit lingers in the air. Seeds and garbage slick the shiny pavement. Unaccustomed to seeing foreigners in these isolated mountains, people on the street openly gawk. Katy covers her face with her forearm. "Mom, why are they all staring?"

Though the Whitehall family stands out among the locals, Katherine and her children can scarcely tell one villager from another. Like some strangely attired militia, the indigenous women, all short and stocky with waist-length hair, are clad in handwoven, embroidered tunics: *huipiles* of identical design. The waists are cinched by embroidered belts. Men wear buttoned shirts and baggy work pants, held up by belts or rope.

"I'm sure they don't mean to be impolite," Katherine says. "They'll get used to seeing us around." She hopes she's right. There are many things in this country that are alien, such as teenage boys with guns, children with bundles of firewood on their backs, and women balancing pots on their heads, but it had never occurred to her that the Guatemalans might find *them* objects of curiosity.

She trades a few coins for a plastic basket. They buy bread from a baker, eggs from a vendor, fruit from a nearby stall, then pick up a few other essentials such as toilet paper and coffee. Katherine decides to enter a large cement building that appears to be part of the market. As they approach, the unpleasant odor of raw meat assaults them.

"Can we stay outside?" Justin asks, crinkling his nose. "We'll wait for you here."

Katherine shakes her head at her son, not wanting to let the children out of her sight in this unfamiliar place. The farther they journey into the maze of the indoor market, the worse the stench becomes. In the center are butcher shops and places to eat—*comedores*, she will soon learn—that don't look appealing or sanitary. They stop in front of a stand where the carcass of a carved pig, speckled with flies, dangles from the rafters. A container brims with chicken feet, organs, and strange cuts of meat. Blood leaks onto the counter. Katherine fights to keep her stomach under control and Katy gags.

Sensing a potential disaster, Katherine steers Justin toward the door. "Take your sister to the exit and wait for me there. And be careful."

She looks around. What can she possibly buy that her family might eat? Seeing a stand selling packaged food from a refrigerator, she points toward ham slices.

When she steps outside, the stench of vomit overpowers the stink from street garbage. Katherine covers her nose and mouth with a tissue and sees Justin and Katy on a nearby bench. The greenish tinge of Katy's skin gives her away. A barrel-shaped woman smiles and gestures toward her in a conciliatory manner.

"Let's get out of here," Katherine says.

"Mom, this place is just gross!" Justin kicks at a mango seed in the street. "Please don't tell me this is where we'll be doing our shopping."

Phil waves to them from the corner. His hair sticks up on one side, his shirt is half untucked, and his pants stained with grease. The Missionary Marvel—buried beneath layers of ochre dust—idles on the corner, the front windshield a streaky mess following Jerónimo's efforts to clean it with the wipers.

Phil sees his daughter's pale face and glassy eyes. "Are you okay, pancake?"

"No," she whispers. "Can I have some water?"

"Daddy will fix it." Phil disappears into the small store and returns with a bottle of water for Katy.

Katherine can't believe he hasn't considered getting something for everyone and snaps at him. "Justin and I would like something to drink as well if you don't mind."

Her husband slinks back into the store. A few minutes later, he hands his son and wife a bottle, plus a bag of sweets for Katherine to share with the kids. A peace offering.

Katy narrows her eyes and focuses on her father. "I hate this place. Why did you have to bring us here? It isn't at all like you said it would be."

Phil rests his hand on his daughter's shoulder. "Hate is a strong word. It's been a long and trying day, and we've had some unfortunate setbacks, but we'll be home soon."

Unfortunate setbacks? The words echo in Katherine's mind. Is that all it was to him?

"Home?" Justin questions. "How can you call this place home? Our home is Indiana with clean streets and familiar people. This place could never be home."

Phil sighs. It has been a disappointment so far, but surely things will be worthwhile in the end. He looks toward heaven. The sun slips below the clouds and evening approaches.

As they settle into the car, Katy closes her eyes and leans into Justin's protective arm. Katherine stares straight ahead and wonders what else could await them on this adventure from hell.

The two men in front confer quietly. "The town we're leaving is where we'll be doing our weekly shopping," Phil announces. "Today, Thursday, is their market day, the day all the vendors bring fresh produce and other items to sell."

"Lovely," Katherine murmurs.

They turn off the highway and up a dirt road. The Missionary Marvel bounces and pitches. Brush and trees scratch the vehicle's exterior. Outside the filthy windows, dust cakes the shrubbery. In several places, the van scrapes bottom.

"Are you sure we'll make it with this old rattletrap?" Justin calls from the back. "We should have a four-wheel drive if we'll be traveling this road very often."

"Get me the money, son, and I'll be more than happy to buy one." Phil tries to find a positive spin to put on their vehicle. "Look at the bright side. When you get your license, you can drive this car."

"Drive it? I'll be lucky if I don't have to push it."

They approach a cinder-block house in the center of a clearing, the first they've seen on the road. A cement sink rests under a corrugated metal roof supported by a wooden frame. Scattered throughout the yard are an assortment of building supplies in various stages of deterioration. A shelter that appears to be a large storage shed juts from behind the building.

"Here is it," Jerónimo says. "Home for you."

Phil stares out and sighs. Yet another challenge in a very disappointing day. As the head of the family, he searches for positive attributes but can't find any. He has reached the bottom of his well of exuberance. He gathers his remaining optimism and manages to slap on a smile as he announces, "Here we are. Our new home."

Disappointment renders Katherine incapable of comment.

Already close to tears, Katy lifts her head from her brother's shoulder. "This is where we're going to live?"

CHAPTER
FOUR

Jerónimo unlocks the door but doesn't open it. He gestures and chats away in agitated Spanish, but he might as well be speaking Mam, the local Mayan dialect, as none of them have the vaguest notion what he's saying.

With the kind of patience reserved for small children or the mentally challenged, Phil says, "Más despacio, por favor. No entender."

Nodding, Jerónimo gives the door a tap.

It swings open, and they peer into the gloom. Jerónimo steps inside and points to an empty fixture in the ceiling. "No light. Tomorrow. ¿Sí? ¿No?" He shrugs as though to wriggle out of any possible guilt.

Neither Phil nor Katherine comprehends his meaning, and they wish he'd let them know they needed light bulbs back in town, but Jerónimo strolls to a cupboard and pulls out several flashlights and candles. He pries open a drawer and extracts matches. He is so prepared they decide that the lack of electricity must be the problem.

Through a dirty window, the last of the afternoon's sun casts eerie shadows into the meadow, and darkness pulls its covers over the mountainside.

Katherine helps the men unload the van. After the bags are in the house, she explores their new home. She wonders if Jerónimo purposely forgot to have the electricity connected so they'd be less alarmed by the state of the house.

In the center of the living room is an unvarnished wooden door, complete with hinges, balanced on "legs" of stacked brick. This "coffee table" is surrounded by a shabby, once-crimson sofa and matching chair. Newly lit candles flicker on the table's flat surface, and shadows are ghostly ballerinas twirling across the wall. A woolen rug, green-edged and gray from the filth of disuse, has soaked up moisture from the cement-slab floor and smells like a wet mutt.

Three metal doorways flank a dusty hallway. Door number one opens into a room featuring a double bed and unfinished pine nightstands. Rough pine planks cling to a cement wall, awaiting books and other personal items. Several wire hangers dangle from a rod spanning one corner.

Door number two features a metal desk, a chest of drawers, and twin beds separated by a ragged hemp mat. Katy appears and plops down on one of the beds, forcing a billow of dust into the air, visible even in the dim light. She looks up with tear-filled eyes. "Mom, we can't live here. This place is awful."

Grimly, Katherine pulls her daughter off the bed to continue the inspection. Door number three must be the one with the grand prize, but it's locked. She hopes it leads to the bathroom, but it seems more likely an exit to the backyard.

In the cubbyhole of a kitchen, tired wooden cabinets sag against dingy walls. A small table with three chairs—only three!

—accompanies an ancient refrigerator and a rusty gas stove. No sink. No indoor plumbing.

No wonder this house was available, Katherine concludes. Who would want it?

Justin stumbles in from outdoors. "This is it? We do have a bathroom, don't we? Or will I have to take a leak in the woods?"

Katy swirls around. "We might not have a bathroom?"

"Oh, I'm sure there's one around here somewhere," Katherine assures them while thinking how far their standard of living has fallen. "We'll ask Jerónimo."

"I want to sleep in the Marvel," Katy announces. "There's no way I'm going to stay in this horrible place."

Katherine silently agrees with her daughter, but tries to keep a united front with her husband. Besides, she doesn't imagine he will allow Katy to sleep outside.

"I'll stay with her, Mom. I don't mind. We'll stretch out on the seats. We slept fine on the way. It's pretty comfortable over-all." He nods his head vigorously as though enthusiasm will convince her. What sounds like an adventure to them sounds like danger to her.

"I don't know, kids. I'd rather we kept together."

"Then join us," Justin urges.

Phil butts into their conversation as though someone asked his opinion. "I don't see a problem with them sleeping outside, Katherine. The two of them can sleep in the van if that's what they want." He turns to them. "Just remember, kids, you'll be right outside the house, so if you need anything, anything at all, just give a holler."

With the descent of darkness, unfamiliar noises fill the air. Cicadas, frogs, and crickets burst forth in melodious song. Owls and other nocturnal creatures play harmony. Already, evening chill and eerie fog engulf the mountain, and Katherine shivers, only partly from the cold.

Phil consults with Jerónimo. "Is there anything to worry about, safety-wise?"

Jerónimo opens his arms wide. "Safe. Here very safe."

Katherine is skeptical of Jerónimo's assessment and believes he is probably only parroting what he thinks Phil wants to hear. The holdup on the highway has given her a new perspective on what is safe and what isn't. Phil can sleep alone in the house if he chooses. After all she's been through that day, she'd rather not sleep with him at all. If the children want to sleep outside in the van, so will she. With the doors locked. She has a sudden and surprising desire for a gun.

"Where's the bathroom?" she asks their driver, no longer concerned whether he might find her bluntness rude, because if there is no toilet, she and her kids are leaving as soon as possible. Maybe tomorrow.

He grabs one of the flashlights and leads her to the locked metal door. He opens it with a key he unclips from his belt and leaves dangling in the lock. Katherine follows him onto a covered pathway leading to a small cement structure. He shines the light onto a flush toilet, a sink, and a wooden slat bench. Dirt and leaves cover everything.

She points to a corner, which is not visible from where they stand. "Shower?"

"Sí." He pantomimes bathing.

Another locked door leads elsewhere. Perhaps to storage, Katherine muses, but more likely to hell, and this is the gateway.

Stars blaze in the night sky, and a faint light filters through an open area high on the wall where glass should cover a window but where insects buzz freely back and forth.

It isn't up to her standards, but Katherine still can't help feeling grateful for indoor plumbing—even if it is technically outdoors. "We do have water, don't we?"

He opens a faucet, and a stream of tea-colored liquid splashes forth, clearing moments later.

When she returns inside, Katy and Justin are sitting forlornly on the sofa, Katy's head resting on her brother's shoulder. Katherine can't help but appreciate how the horrendous day has brought her kids' disagreements to an end.

She takes the flashlight and opens cupboards and drawers. "Sheets? Towels? Where are they? They were on the top of the list of things we asked to have ready for us." Phil and Jerónimo continue their exchange as though they haven't heard. "Phil, are you listening to me?" she calls, already impatient with these men who only pay attention when one isn't speaking to them. "Excuse me, gentlemen!" She waves her arms in the air.

"Katherine, calm down. What's the matter?"

"The bedding. Sheets? Blankets? Towels? Everything should be here."

Jerónimo shakes his head and assumes a pained expression. "*Fíjese.* No towels. No blankets. No sheets." He shows his empty hands and looks down at himself as though they might unintentionally be hidden on his person.

She faces her husband and takes a battle stance. "Phil?"

"What do you want me to do?"

"Deal with it. Find out what happened to the bedding. I've already had enough trouble for one day." She glances at Jerónimo and eyes him accusingly. He edges slightly toward the door.

Does Phil understand the significance of this? Does he realize she's at the end of her rope? "Jerónimo and Rosa were supposed to have this place ready for move in. You gave them money, and they apparently didn't spend it all on the vehicle.

Everything on that list was to have been purchased already. What will we do for bedding tonight? It's too late to go back to that ugly town we passed to buy anything, even if they do sell bedding there—which I doubt." Katherine hesitates for a moment. "I'm a patient woman, but I've reached my limit for how bad I can allow things to get. How could you bring your family to this awful place in the middle of nowhere? Jerónimo made minimal preparations, and no one even thought to clean for our arrival. I must have been insane to agree to come in the first place." She stifles the sobs that come in unrelenting waves. "Now we're stuck out here in the middle of nowhere, and I swear I can't take another day like today."

"Shh, Katherine, it's okay. We'll figure this out. You're going to frighten the children." Who he worries about frightening is Jerónimo. What kind of an impression is he making on his new assistant? He searches for ideas or words to smooth over the situation, but nothing comes to mind. "I'll handle this."

He turns to Jerónimo, who is busy inspecting the cobwebs on the wooden frame that supports the zinc roof, pretending not to hear the exchange while following every word. Phil pleads with him in basic Spanish, and Jerónimo gets defensive. Phil manages to calm him, and then translates. "He says he received the money but didn't see a list as to how it should be spent. He bought the car, rented the house. Apparently this was finalized only yesterday before heading to the airport to pick us up. He made sure the important things were bought and supplied such as a refrigerator, beds, and stove. He purchased used items so there would be enough money. He wanted to wait until we arrived so as not to repeat what we already have. Katherine, he sounds sincere."

"Sincere, my ass. He may have taken our things home, hoped we wouldn't need them." Katherine's face is rife with anger. "His excuse is not acceptable. That list was thorough. Sheets, blankets, and towels topped the requirements. How expensive can essential items be way out here? Did they buy our things and just keep them, hoping we'd bring our own?"

Jerónimo hangs his head. "I bring sheets. I have at home. I borrow for you."

It isn't in Phil's hands to do more, and he knows it. "It's been a long day, sweetheart. Jerónimo and Rosa have linens to loan us for tonight. We'll figure things out in the morning."

She gives in. "Fine. But I don't like it, Phil."

"Katherine, please," Phil hisses. "We can't afford to alienate our only contact."

"Alienate him? What about alienating me, your wife, your children's mother?" Her voice gets louder the angrier she becomes. "He can loan us what we need, right. Right? You'd better ask for a copy of his budget and receipts to see how he spent that money." She glares at Jerónimo.

Phil wrings his hands. His wife rarely loses her cool, but he feels squeezed between empathy and diplomacy. "Don't jump to conclusions. He's a Christian, after all." A brief discussion ensues with Jerónimo. "He says he'll be willing to sell us sheets."

"Good price. Great deal." Jerónimo bobs his head.

"Sell us the bedding? Are you serious?" She faces her husband and ignores Jerónimo. "Now our only contact is trying to sell us property that should be ours, and very well might be. Phillip Cameron Whitehall, what did you get us into?"

He hesitates, not sure he should confess what Jerónimo also mentioned. But, for the sake of honesty, he continues, "He seems to think the extra money is owed to him since he and his wife bought the car, rented the house, and have been buying things for us. They've invested their time and energy."

"This place is filthy or haven't you noticed. They certainly didn't invest their time preparing for our arrival. They didn't even bother to get the electricity turned on."

Phil leads Katherine away by the arm. "I know you're upset, sweetheart, but we're in a foreign country, in a foreign culture where everyone speaks a foreign language. Jerónimo is our only acquaintance. I'm not even sure I could find my way back to Guatemala City without him."

She escapes his hold. "Our life has never been luxurious, but there are limits, and I've just hit mine. If it weren't such a formidable trip back to the city, I'd be on the next flight back to Indiana with both kids."

Phil heaves a heartfelt sigh. He's at a loss and doesn't know what to do or say. "Let's use their bedding tonight. Tomorrow we'll buy supplies. We'll get through this. We will."

He attempts to put his arms around her, but she stiffens and turns away. Katherine doesn't care who's to blame for the poor welcome, but the bottom line is that Phil brought them here. She has already forgotten that only the previous day, she was enthusiastic, seeing the puffs of smoke from the volcano and descending onto the tarmac for their new adventure.

When the kids walk in, the air is rife with tension. "What's going on?" Justin asks, his tousled hair dulled by dust.

Phil shrugs. "Just a little misunderstanding." There's no point in getting children involved in adult disagreements. Like Katherine, he had expected things to be made ready for their arrival, not to find himself acting in the unlikely role of mediator. Besides, he's tired, too.

Jerónimo lingers in the doorway, wondering if he will be loaning them anything for the evening. Phil slings an arm over his shoulders and, speaking in low tones, walks him back to the van. Katherine hopes her husband isn't saying not to pay attention to his crazy wife. Is she crazy? Crazy with anger—yes!

Their driver escapes in a cloud of dust and exhaust, and Phil returns, shoulders slumped from the burden of so many practical matters. He came here to preach, not to deal with setting up a house.

As they wait for the bedding and towels, Katherine and the two kids sit on the couch while Phil faces them on the chair. A cool breeze rustles the curtains. Katy closes her eyes and leans against her mother. "I'm exhausted."

Katherine's voice sounds distant even to herself. She wonders if she is even speaking or if she's channeling another voice, the one in her head that has been telling her to run. "Today was beyond horrendous. I'm not convinced we should even be here."

Phil warns her not to talk like that in front of the children, but at this point she doesn't care who is in the room. He tries to make light of their situation and accept some of the responsibility. He is, after all, the head of the family. "I should have been better prepared. I had no idea it would be like this. Things will look brighter in the morning. I promise."

Acknowledgment of his culpability mollifies his wife, and her anger cools to a dull throb. The four of them sit quietly, mesmerized by the flickering candles on the makeshift table. While Katherine isn't sure how things can get better, surely, they can't get any worse.

Phil clears his throat. "I think we should pray together now and thank the Lord for our safe arrival. I'll start, and I'd like each of you to add something of your own."

Family prayers are something they've always done and are comfortable with, so even though they are fatigued and uncommunicative, their words in prayer flow unrestrained. Katherine has learned through experience that even mouthing prayer eventually helps steer her day-to-day struggles toward spiritual peace.

They grab hands and shut their eyes as Phil begins. "Heavenly Father, we thank you for our safety this day as we arrived at our new home. For giving me courage and fortification through your power to run off the thieves. We express our gratitude, dear Lord, for smoothly paving the way for this placement."

"Protect us in the coming days, as you protected us today. Help Justin and me make new friends and adjust to our new lives," Katy adds.

"Give me courage and patience, Lord. Help me to find peace and to forgive those who might have hurt me. Help me as I struggle with gratitude," Katherine says.

An awkward moment of silence assures Phil that Justin doesn't want to continue, so he nudges his son's foot.

Justin jerks his leg from his father's reach. "Yes, Lord, thank you for safety and please take care of our family in Indiana. Bring us all safely home when this is over."

Phil ends the prayer on a positive note. "We understand the most important thing we have is each other and your protection. We send our petitions up to you in your precious name. Amen."

CHAPTER

FIVE

L ike God pouring His morning coffee, the first rays of sunlight spill through the windows of the van. Wood-peckers, robins, and hawks join with parrots, quetzals, toucans, and other tropical birds in a dawn chorus that shatters the silence. After an exhausted sleep, Katherine opens her eyes and sits up, stiff but rested. Morning chill tinges the air. Phil had promised things would look brighter in the morning, and Katherine must admit they do. She pushes her fears to one side. The stains from yesterday's disasters dim in the beauty of the sunrise and dawn's winged cacophony.

She peers over the seat at her daughter, whose breath rises and falls with metronomic precision, arms thrown over her head in a child's abandon. The borrowed blankets, smelling distinctly of campfire, are a tangled mess. Justin grumbles from the rear. She slips on her shoes and steps outside, drinks deeply of the crisp mountain air, and listens to the sounds of daybreak. A sense of joy fills her: the joy of dawn's promise, a joy she hasn't experienced in years. Maybe, just maybe, this change, this move, will all be worthwhile.

As far as she can determine, the house stands alone. Further on, the road meanders up the mountain, but they haven't seen or heard another car since turning off the highway last night. She wonders who constructed this house and why. It doesn't look as though it has been lived in for years. How close are the nearest neighbors, and where does this road end? She can't even say for certain from which direction Jerónimo appeared last night when he brought the bedding and towels.

Pines cloak the surrounding slopes, interspersed with dense stands of gnarled cypress and flowering tropical hardwoods imbuing the panorama with splashes of purple, yellow, and vermilion. Morning sun silhouettes the treetops. Majestic scenery, musical serenades, and the sharp highland fragrance. Has she judged this place too harshly? With a daybreak's perspective, she can imagine herself living here comfortably. After all, they do have one essential thing, a decent bathroom. One could become accustomed, she supposes, and they can fix things up. Paint the house, clean the yard. Plant a garden.

Dew soaks her feet as she tromps toward the bathroom, the tall grass like green hair on the earth's scalp. Though she doubts mowers are available, even if having a lawn were a priority, machetes are everywhere—the generic tool for fieldwork.

She tries the back door and finds it secured. She raps—no response—then goes to the bedroom window. Through shabby curtains, she sees Phil sprawled across the double bed. She taps on the glass. "Phil! Can you let me in?"

Startled, he lifts his head and glances about before he spies her. "Hang on, honey. I'll be right there." A moment later, clad in boxers and an undershirt, he opens the front door. "Sorry, I didn't mean to lock the door. Force of habit."

"And you were busy telling me how safe this place is?" Irritation with her husband flares again. "Just go back to sleep."

"No, no. I should be getting up," he says, unaware of her annoyance. He grabs a towel and takes a broom to sweep out the shower area. "Jerónimo said he'd be here early to take us to town."

Katherine drags her suitcase to the bedroom, then steps into the kitchen and sits at the table. Pen in hand, she adds more items to a lengthy list.

Phil steps back into the house minutes later, his arms goose-fleshed and a towel around his waist. "Ha! More invigorating than a morning cup of coffee."

Katherine takes a change of clothes to the shower area. The icy water is almost too cold to withstand, so she shampoos, soaps up energetically, and quickly rinses. She bundles up in her warmest clothing and goes back to the kitchen.

Justin is about to help his father with breakfast when she returns. "Good morning." She kisses her disheveled son. "I hope you've at least washed your hands."

He shuffles off, and the back door slams as he makes his way to the sink.

Phil flashes his wife a small smile, sensing her anger. He wishes she weren't so sensitive, that he didn't have to watch his every move and things he says. She didn't even thank him for sweeping out the shower. He waves the list. "Good thing we're going into town today. We need a water heater for the shower. I hear there are some that attach directly to the showerhead. I'm not sure I can face cold showers every morning."

Justin walks in. "I second the motion." He rubs his damp hands together. "But we probably need electricity first."

"We'll do what we can," Phil says. "Just remember it's ultimately in God's hands, not ours."

41

Katherine envies his faith as well as his ability to tolerate a cold shower and stay optimistic. He places a ceramic mug of hot coffee in front of her.

"Thank heaven for small miracles," she says, referring to the full propane tank. She sips her brew, her annoyances drifting away as the caffeine hits her system. Nothing like coffee to give perspective.

"Hey, Dad. Do we have a fork for this fruit?"

Phil scoops everything out of the tableware drawer. Two plastic forks, a plastic and a metal soup spoon, and a butter knife.

"I would have thought that with Jerónimo's appetite, utensils would have been high up on his list," Katherine remarks. When they stopped for breakfast the previous day, they had marveled at how much food he put away. "Can you wash all this, Justin, please?"

Justin wraps the utensils in a dishcloth to take to the outdoor sink.

"The closest town is twenty minutes away, and Jerónimo says that Thursday, which was yesterday, is market day and other days don't have much to offer. We'll go to San Marcos, the department capital and a decent-sized city. Speaking of which, how much do we have in our personal account back home?"

"Not enough for everything we're going to need." Katherine's arm sweeps the room. "Why don't we call the States?"

"I don't want to get your family involved. We received five thousand to start, not counting the initial money we wired to Jerónimo for the vehicle and larger items."

"But Phil, most of that went for our plane tickets."

"He said last night he has some cash left over."

"Good luck with that."

Katherine figures their monthly stipend should cover their

needs once they get the basics bought, but basics include a lot of items when setting up a house.

Katy shuffles in a few minutes later wrapped in a red woolen blanket. She perches on the empty chair and picks at the fruit with a plastic fork. "Are we going to buy paint today?" she asks her father. "I want to paint our room purple."

"Necessities are our priority, not purple paint. I'm sorry, but it's going to have to wait."

"Aren't you going to ask me if I want the room purple? We are roomies," Justin interjects. "Uh, not really. Purple's not my color."

She stares at him and crosses her arms. This trip is not going as promised. She's sure her father would have allowed her beau-tification strategy from the safety of Indiana. He probably would have said anything for them to agree to come to this awful place.

"By the way, Dad, I need my space. I'm almost fifteen. Too old to share a small room with my little sister."

"There's always the couch, son."

"Which of you two is next for the shower?" Katherine says.

They glance at each other and shake their heads. Justin speaks for the two of them. "Thanks, Mom, but we'll wait until there's hot water."

She purses her lips, which serves to make Phil feel guilty, and then gathers the dishes together and has Justin take them to the outdoor sink under protest. "Am I the official dishwasher in this house now?"

She ignores his protests and takes a seat across from her husband. "Tell me again. What's the plan?"

"Jerónimo should be here any time now." He glances at his watch. "He promised to help with these errands. He knows where to get the best prices."

"I bet he can find excellent deals—while getting himself a

CAROLINE KELLEMS

commission at the same time." Her voice drips with sarcasm, a relapse into the previous night's bitterness. She pulls back the curtains and scans the driveway. "Are you sure he's coming? It's almost nine-thirty."

"He'll be along. He's kept his word so far."

"Phil, we don't know what all he's kept so far."

They unpack their bags and finalize the shopping list.

"He's coming," Phil assures his family.

Ten o'clock comes and goes. Katherine begins to wonder if she was too hard on Phil's new assistant. Maybe he decided not to come back at all. A half hour later, they hear a commotion. Katy races to the open door. "Justin! Mom! Dad! Come look!"

The Whitehall family gathers outside. Several dozen people, carrying assorted items, parade toward the house behind Jerónimo and a plump indigenous woman. She approaches, introduces herself as Rosa, and embraces Katherine. "We bring gifts. We greet you."

She hugs each family member. Four-foot-ten, she is shorter than Katy, her black-and-steel-streaked hair braided and twisted up on top of her head. When she finishes greeting everyone, she steps back, smiles, and her face lights up. They instantly like her.

"Please," Jerónimo says with a pained expression. "Keep the bedding, the towels. Our gift."

The villagers meld into a disorderly queue. An elderly woman looks them over and hands Phil a bag of mangoes. A child of about nine brings a container of eggs, then scurries off. A young man unloads a sack of dried black beans from his shoulder onto the doorstep. He backs away. A barefoot, wizened woman advances. Her eyes twinkle with intelligence and humor as she looks them over. She bows, hands clasped in front. From deep pockets of her frilly lavender apron, she retrieves a lumpy plastic bag and hands it to Katherine. A gift of garlic,

44

onions, yucca, and other tubers, still covered with moist, spongy soil.

"Gracias," says Katherine.

In accented English, the woman replies, "Welcome." They aren't sure if she is welcoming them or saying "You're welcome."

The villagers bring their offerings in turn: vegetables, strange prickly fruits, corn, beans, eggs, and even live hens with their feet tied.

What will we do with the hens? Katherine wonders.

Then, there is a woven tablecloth, a skillet, and a large pot, along with a shovel, a pickaxe, and a machete. Some villagers shake hands; others are too shy to make eye contact.

Gratitude mingles with shame, and Katherine's eyes brim. Here she has been complaining bitterly since her arrival, and the villagers bring to them what little they have to offer.

Jerónimo waits until everyone is quiet, then introduces the Whitehall family to their new congregation. "Pastor Felipe, Hermana Caterina, Catty, y Yusti."

"Yusti? What kind of name is that?" Justin whispers.

"Not as bad as Catty."

"¿Yusti es Fofo?" a boy asks.

Jerónimo tells Justin that Fofo is an *apodo* and points to Justin's red hair. Later, Justin looks up the word in an English/Spanish dictionary. It means nickname. Fofo is short for *fosforo,* or match head. Not much different from folks back home calling him Rusty. The Whitehalls surmise that Jerónimo's *apodo* is Chomo. That's what everyone calls him.

The villagers gather in groups and shuffle their feet. Thinking they expect a speech, Phil clears his throat and begins thanking everyone for being such a wonderful group of brothers and sisters in Christ. As he warms up and readies to launch into a sermon, Katherine hears humming in the distance and sees a cloud of dust coming their direction from up the mountain. All heads turn. Phil stops mid-sentence; no one is listening anyway.

A gold Hummer, looking as out of place as an alien space-craft, glides toward the house and comes to a halt near the sink. The family stares in astonishment as the door opens and a lanky, well-built man, impeccably dressed in black jeans, a polo shirt, and shiny alligator-hide boots, steps out. He acknowledges the crowd with a celebrity-like wave.

The mystery man slips off his Oakleys, showing his hazel eyes, smiles with gleaming white teeth, and says in fluent English, "Mr. and Mrs. Whitehall. Justin and young Katherine. I am pleased to make your acquaintance. I am Alfonso."

Momentarily at a loss for words—where did he come from?— Phil returns the greeting, and Alfonso takes his hand in a hearty shake. He gallantly kisses Katherine on the cheek, and she blushes, not accustomed to being greeted thus by such an attrac-tive man. He shakes Justin's hand and squats down to speak to Katy. "Young Katherine, I presume?"

She giggles. No one has ever called her young Katherine.

He stands and explains, "Chomo came to my villa early this morning and told me of your arrival. He asked all the villagers to extend a welcome. I am your closest neighbor and your landlord. I will take you to town so you can buy whatever you need. I hope we can become good friends."

He turns to the gathering, thanks them for coming, and tells them to return home. At his order, the crowd disperses as if by magic.

CHAPTER

SIX

P hil climbs into Alfonso's vehicle, amazed at the far reaches of the Lord, providing them with a Hummer to compensate for yesterday's trouble. A reward for good faith. Praise God!

Katherine and the children sink into cream-colored leather in the back seat.

"Hasn't Dad always told us never to ride with strangers?" Katy whispers.

"Shh, he's our landlord." Katherine agrees with her daughter, but the entire morning has been slightly detached from any reality Katherine has ever experienced. She still doesn't know what to make of this man's presence or his aristocratic, formal English and expensive clothes. The entire situation feels surreal.

Phil takes in the Hummer's technology—wireless dashboard. "This is a remarkable vehicle. A great family car. Do you have children?"

"I dote on young people but have none of my own. It is

unfortunate for me and one of the big disappointments of my life."

"But you are still young," Phil says, thinking they must be close in age. "Aren't you married?"

"I was once, long ago." His eyes grow misty. "I prefer to think that I am married to my work. Perhaps someday another woman like my Mari will come along." He glances back at Katherine and smiles.

As the ignition engages, the engine purrs. The air-conditioning cushions them in comfort. Alfonso points to the controls and explains how to adjust the airflow. He jockeys the car into gear, and, as if in a hovercraft, they glide slowly down the road, not noticing the ruts, perhaps floating above them. They are so out of their element that anything seems possible.

Admiration shines in Phil's eyes as he watches his new landlord. "What exactly is your line of work, Don Alfonso?"

"Please, please, call me Alfonso."

"Then you must call me Phil."

"Very well, Phil. I am an agricultural advisor."

"And you work in this area?"

"I work in the countryside with rural farmers. My home is here, but I travel a great deal, taking care of business. I am Mexican, you see."

Phil doesn't understand why his being Mexican has a bearing on anything but figures he must transact business in his native land as well. "You seem to do well for someone working in agriculture." Satisfied his interrogation hasn't offended, he continues, "Who do you work for?"

Alfonso chuckles. "I come from a wealthy family. My father owned a chain of department stores." He crosses himself and kisses the tips of his fingers with a flourish. "He passed away many years ago—may God rest his soul—and I was his only heir."

"I'm sorry for your loss."

Alfonso waves his hand as if to push aside any sadness. "It was a long time ago. I was studying agriculture at Monterrey Tech. I was never attracted to commerce, so when I received my inheritance, I sold the family business and moved here to follow my dream.

"I bought a sizable piece of property to develop for my residence. Your house was built for an employee and his family and used only for a short time. Later I decided to have everyone live within the compound where my home is, leaving the little house empty."

"Why did you choose to settle in Guatemala?"

"Why Guatemala, indeed," Alfonso muses. "Much the same reason you are here, no doubt. The need. While there are plenty of peasant farmers in Mexico, they are better off than the indigenous Guatemalans. I do what I can to help the villagers improve their lives." He takes a deep breath and tips his head back. "Once I came, I was hooked. I love this mountain air. Why would I choose to live elsewhere?"

Phil harbors a twinge of unanswered doubt but decides to take his landlord's words at face value. After all, his appearance is a blessing, and who is he to question God's blessings? He watches the scenery, which looks greener and fresher through a clean windshield.

After a few minutes of silence, Alfonso asks about their errands.

"We need to visit the power company," Phil says. "According to Jerónimo, the electricity was promised for yesterday but still isn't connected."

"I can help you with that. After all, it is my duty as your landlord. I will speak with the regional manager, with whom I am well acquainted. His men helped us install a hydroelectric plant when the villa was built. In this country, it is important who you know."

"You have a personal hydroelectric plant?" Katherine interrupts.

"Unfortunately, the lines do not extend far enough to be useful for your house. It is small, but along with supplementary solar power we generate enough energy for our services within the compound."

"Is that customary, to generate your own power?" She's heard of people using solar for energy needs, but never hydro-electric.

"It is not uncommon for the private sector in the interior of the country to produce energy for its use where there is a serviceable water source. Electricity from regional sources is not always dependable and was, until recently, scarce. For decades coffee plantations generated power to run their machinery. Besides, I prefer to live independently and try to be as self-sufficient as possible, for a variety of reasons."

Silence reigns as Katherine and Phil absorb the information.

After a long pause, Alfonso begins, "I am sorry for monopolizing the conversation. What are your other errands?"

"We would like to get a cellular phone. I may need a co-signer for a plan. At least that's what Jerónimo said."

"Please, please, I have more mobile phones than I need. Do me the honor of accepting one from me. In fact, take several. My contract gives me twenty phones at a fixed rate." Their astounded expressions amuse him. "I have many people who work for me, and that is how we stay in contact, but they are not all in use."

"We couldn't do that," Katherine protests.

"Why not?" he asks. "You accepted gifts from the poor who have fewer means. I am in a better position to help you."

"What can we give you in return?" she wonders aloud. "Our rent money is not much. Not enough to cover cell phones and favors."

"Do not insult me." His features stiffen. "The rent money is a pittance. I mean to waive it entirely, now that you brought it up. All I ask for in return is friendship. It is lonely living way out here without stimulating conversation." His face relaxes back into a smile as he glances into the rearview mirror.

THE TWO HOURS to San Marcos sail by in unmatched comfort, and soon they are cruising down narrow cobbled streets, searching for a parking place. They edge into one in front of a business that says HELADOS GITANOS. Teenagers, licking cones, stand beside the door. Katy claps her hands softly when Alfonso, signaling to the person inside, suggests Katherine and the children stay and enjoy an ice cream while he and Phil visit the electric company.

Heat from the freezers blasts them as they approach the counter. A rotund woman in nurse's white and netted hair offers samples of *guanábana*, *maracuyá*, and *tamarindo*, flavors never offered back home.

Phil returns as they finish. "Katherine, can you believe it. Alfonso walked in and demanded to see the regional manager. He gave the order to turn on our power immediately."

"I've never met anyone like him," Katy says. "He's like a movie star."

Katherine agrees with her daughter. He does have a certain debonair quality, yet there's something beneath the suave exterior that she can't quite pinpoint. An element of danger, perhaps? Sexy, whatever it is. "That's wonderful. That's a big something to cross off the list. Shall we shop for kitchen items next?"

"Let's get the water heater and tools. Alfonso said he'd meet us at the hardware store."

When they approach the counter to pay, the woman tells them that Alfonso will take care of the bill.

"We shouldn't take advantage of him," Katherine says to her husband. "He's already waived our monthly rent and was kind enough to take us to town. We can at least get the lunch tab. Remember, there's four of us and only one of him."

Phil pays little attention. After all, the Lord is behind this: the new wealthy neighbor is, no doubt, part of some greater celestial plan. Maybe he will be interested in funding a church, the purpose of their coming. Praise you, Almighty God! Getting their house set up will put his wife in a better mood. Now for the hardware store.

Brushes and rainbow-colored cans are painted on the outside walls, depicting items for sale to an illiterate population. Katherine stares at her list as they enter. So many things. She scans it for priorities. When she catches Phil's eye, she says, "We'll never be able to afford all this."

"Maybe we don't need as much as you think."

"How can you say that?" Her scrawled list covers an entire page.

"I'm just saying. Try to be more optimistic." He takes the sheet from her. "Okay, spatula, tableware, pots and pans. Those things should be inexpensive. I saw them for sale in the outdoor market yesterday. I'm sure linens aren't as pricey as what you'd find in a department store at a mall in Indiana. After all, they are necessities."

She admits that he may be right. They haven't started checking prices yet.

He knows she'd like to call home and ask her mother to wire money for their startup expenses. "Let's wait and see what we can get first before we think about loans from family members." Phil picks up some paint, nails, a hammer, and a hose and takes them to the front. "So far things are much less expensive than back home."

"Why are you buying paint, Phil? That's not even on our list."

"We need to fix up the house. Our Christian home should be a model for the community."

Katherine isn't convinced. He'd told Katy that paint isn't a priority, so why is he spending their dwindling cash?

"Have you found what you need?" Alfonso comes from behind, startling her. "Take your time. I do not mean to hurry you. I hope you know I will be paying for home improvements. I have not been there for several years, and I am ashamed to think things might not be, how do you say, up to par. I did not realize that my assistant had spoken to Chomo about renting it until this morning."

Katherine stammers in confusion. "Thank you, but it isn't necessary. You have been more than hospitable." She sees her husband's discontent and gives in. "Well, if you insist, but I wish we could properly thank you. Your contributions are so generous. So unexpected."

"I am happy to be of service." He bows slightly.

Phil asks at the counter about showerhead heaters, and the attendant strides toward the back. Moments later, they approach the *caja* where a man in an enclosed cage rings everything up. Alfonso pulls out a wad of cash to cover the supplies and then, with a nod, hands the Hummer's keys to the clerk.

"What other things do you need while we are in town?"

Alfonso inquires as he opens the door for Katherine. He catches her eye, and color rises to her face.

"We need to open a bank account. We have a check to deposit and would like to change dollars to quetzales," Katherine says.

Alfonso moves his head from side to side. "It is a good thing you have me here to guide you. The banks in this country keep foreign checks frozen for thirty days. I imagine you cannot wait that long. Am I right?"

Phil's forehead crinkles. "Thirty days? From U.S. banks? Are you sure?"

As if affronted by their doubts, he says with exaggerated effort, "Because they are from U.S. banks. Such is the way in Guatemala. I can help you if you wish. I keep plenty of currency at the villa and will be happy to cash a check for you."

Katherine hesitates. "Thank you, but perhaps we should work with the bank."

"Suit yourself. Please excuse me." He jogs over to greet a middle-aged man stepping out of a Range Rover.

The Whitehall family watches Alfonso from the sidewalk. "Katherine, what's gotten into you? We can't wait that long for our check to clear. What are we going to live on?"

"Don't you think it's too much? We don't know anything about our neighbor, and frankly his helpfulness seems excessive."

"He's our landlord and we are missionaries."

Katherine raises her eyebrows and says nothing.

"We should be praising the Lord for this abundance of blessings."

"Maybe you're right. Maybe it is an abundance of blessings." She doubts it, but she might be mistaken. If what Alfonso says about the banks is true, they have no choice but to accept his help. "I guess you're right. Let's set up an account, make a deposit, and let him exchange currency for us. Just this once."

Katherine watches their neighbor embrace his friend, slap him on the back, and return. "I didn't mean to sound rude, Alfonso. You've been so generous I hardly know what to make of your generosity. We'll deposit a check into an account at the bank and take you up on your offer as well."

"Of course." He nods amiably, as if never doubting they would accept. "Please go ahead. Ladies first."

As they file down the narrow sidewalk, the clerk from the hardware store races up, holding something in his fist. "Señor Alfonso, your keys." Alfonso takes the keys and hands him a twenty.

"As I was saying, there are several banks in town. I recommend this one, in particular. I do most of my banking here."

Guards with shotguns protect the entrance of a brick building. When Alfonso pulls open the heavy glass door, refrigerated air wafts out.

A young woman hurries into the manager's office when they enter. A heavyset, loose-jowled man steps out and greets Alfonso warmly.

"My friends, the Whitehall family, are here to set up an account. They are missionaries, new to Guatemala, and neighbors."

Hands shake all around. "Any friend of Don Alfonso is also a friend of mine. Please, let me have the honor of setting up your account myself." He ushers them into a wood-paneled room with frosted glass on two sides and brings in extra chairs so they can all sit.

"We need to open an account with a check in dollars," Katherine tells him, and searches her purse for the checkbook.

"Not a problem." The banker slips on reading glasses and shuffles through papers.

"How long before the money we deposit is available for our use?"

He peers over the frames. "Thirty days. That's standard in this country."

She tries not to show her disappointment as she stares at the large calendar behind his desk and calculates how much money they'll need for the next month. Most of their currency was taken in the holdup, and they are reduced to credit cards until the check clears. An idea pops into her head, and she looks up hopefully. "Are there ATMs nearby?"

"Of course," the banker says and adjusts his glasses. "There are two in town."

Her eyes light up. "Can I pull out cash using my credit card?"

"With a local card. Don't worry, once your check has cleared, we'll supply you with one."

Katherine's stomach tightens, and she nods her head in acknowledgment.

After a half hour of paperwork, they get up to leave. Alfonso guides them to a restaurant where steaks sizzle on an outdoor grill.

A doorman ushers them through the building. Linked sausages hang from a wood frame, and a suckling pig rotates on a spit. A stairway in the center sweeps up in a curve to the second floor. Off to the side, several women pat out corn tortillas and place them on a clay platter to cook over an adobe stove.

A waiter in embroidered knee-length pants seats them at a patio table fashioned from a varnished tree slab. He deals out their menus like cards.

The tantalizing aroma of grilled steak draws a crowd of

urchins who peer at them enviously through the foliage. Every so often someone from the restaurant shoos the children away.

They stare at the menu in Spanish, and even Phil doesn't understand the local names. Alfonso insists on ordering for them.

Half an hour later, the waiter brings grilled steaks with *pico de gallo*, fried black beans, guacamole, grilled sausages, and tortillas. Lots of tortillas. The food is slightly greasy but tasty, with plenty of fresh coriander. After the meal, they order coffee and dessert.

Alfonso turns to Phil. "What are your first impressions of this lovely country, apart from your initiation into its violence? Chomo told me of yesterday's unfortunate holdup."

Phil isn't sure how to react, whether to expand on what happened there—that they were in direct protection of the Divine—or to answer the question. He opts for the latter. "It's a beautiful place. Haunting, with so much need. I'm looking forward to beginning my ministry."

Alfonso's eyes sparkle with secret amusement. "Ah! It is a place of contrast, a place not only of beauty but of great need, rampant corruption, and very little hope for its people. It is a place where someone like you and someone like me can make a significant impact."

CHAPTER
SEVEN

K atherine fidgets with her spoon and pulls the list from her pocket. Alfonso takes this as a sign to stand. "Ah. Many things remain to be purchased. Where shall we go next?"

"Can you show me where I can buy kitchen supplies and pay with a credit card?" He indicates a store up the street and offers to accompany her. She declines and takes Katy, not wanting to take a chance on him paying for their eating utensils as well.

Inside the shop, rows and rows of tall shelves store dusty merchandise from China. Among woks in flimsy boxes, hibachis, and chopsticks, Katherine locates tableware, pots, skillets, knives, and other essentials. Wheeling a rusty shopping cart that veers to the right, she fills it with items from her list. The woman at the checkout line rings up her purchases and accepts her card.

Burdened with shopping bags, she returns to the central square, but Phil and Justin are nowhere in sight. Alfonso appears to be texting on his phone, but leaps to his feet when he sees them. "Mrs. Whitehall, let me help you."

"Thank you, Alfonso, but please call me Katherine." She flashes him a grateful smile.

"I should have gone with you. We could have loaded this directly into the car." He puts her things down on a bench. "Is there anything else I can assist you with," he pauses, "Katherine?"

"I know you're probably anxious to return, but is there an internet café nearby? I'd like to send an email to the folks back home and let them know we arrived safely."

"I am in no hurry, and I wish to invite you to the villa on our way back. You may use one of my computers." When she starts to protest, he raises his hand and stops her mid-sentence. "Please, it is no trouble at all. I understand you have had a difficult arrival. Relax and enjoy the afternoon."

Phil and Justin return with cans of soda and pass them out. They sit and watch people stroll past, young lovers promenading under parents' watchful eyes.

An enormous tree dominates the center of the square and envelops most of the park in its shade. The massive trunk measures eight feet across, and gnarled roots bulge, raising brick walkways and throwing benches off kilter. Its rippling base, like fingers of a hand, clutches Mother Earth. Long vines dangle from dense foliage, and mossy growths cling to the branches, reminders of a dense jungle, a time before people organized cities and towns into neat squares. As the afternoon cools, grackles, screeching at each other and haggling over choice perches, gather on branches overhead. Bird droppings litter the ground.

"This is a *ceiba*, the national tree," Alfonso explains. "Central squares in all towns across the country have one. The Mayan people believe that the *ceiba* is at the center of the universe, connecting the terrestrial world with the spirit world. According to their beliefs, these vines allow the spirits to ascend into heaven."

"What is the English word for *ceiba*?" Justin asks.

"Kapok," Alfonso says. "It is a very soft wood. Traditionally, it was used to fill mattresses, pillowcases, and dolls."

"Dolls!" Katy looks up at her mother.

"Probably rag dolls," Katherine says.

When they finish their drinks, Alfonso stands. "Come to the cathedral with me. You will find it quite unique."

Katherine hesitates, wondering if they will drag along her purchases, but when Alfonso snaps his fingers, a grubby boy about Katy's age appears. He speaks to the boy in rapid Spanish, then sits him down next to the bags.

"Do not worry," Alfonso assures her. "No one will touch them."

A Catholic church with an ornately plastered front faces the park. Two-foot-thick walls encase the church in a tomblike silence, and its stone steps are indented from five hundred years of foot traffic.

Phil and his family step into the musty air of the chilled narthex. Each footfall echoes in the gloom; it is unlike any church with which they are familiar.

Alfonso bows slightly and makes a sign of the cross. He turns to his guests. "This chapel is centuries old. Please look around on your own. I must speak with Padre Chus." He strides to the front near the wooden confessionals, his boot heels striking the hard tiles like gunshots. A boy in white vestments spots him and rushes to the back to summon the priest.

Flower petals and twigs are strewn down the aisle. Candles and scant light seeping through the warped stained glass create a warm glow inside the cathedral. Long needles crunch underfoot, and the scent of pine rises and mingles with taper smoke.

Antique dolls encased in glass crowd niches in the thick adobe walls. When Katherine sees her children looking at them, she says, "They represent saints." Then she points to a wax-coated table in front of a small chapel honoring the Virgin Mary, where a woman adds her candle. Over the years, dribbled wax has formed colorful stalactites that hang toward the piled drippings. "It's beautiful, isn't it?" Katherine whispers. "The drippings represent layer upon layer of longings and desires. Prayers to God."

In the front, the priest sprinkles Alfonso with holy water. In pews, a scattering of worshippers kneel in prayer.

Phil shudders at a large painting of a bloody heart. "This place gives me the creeps."

"Hush. People are praying."

He lowers his voice. "It's sacrilegious. They aren't praying to God at all. They pray to saints. To the Virgin Mary. Look at that cross in front. They worship a crucified Jesus."

"We worship Jesus," Katy says.

"Ours is a hopeful religion. An empty cross, a risen Christ. These Catholics," he struggles to find the right words, "they worship pain and suffering." He thinks of all the grief and death the Roman Catholic Church allowed in the New World. Priests who enslaved the native populations to build their monstrous churches and enforced religious training to subdue them. Over the ages, people have used religion to manipulate, but Catholics have been the biggest offenders. He can't understand how they can even call themselves Christians.

Katherine shakes her head. She never did buy into the idea that one religion was superior to another, especially among Christian sects. Wasn't the Catholic Church responsible for bringing Christianity through the Dark Ages? Sure, Martin Luther reformed the church, but the roots of their religions were identical.

Alfonso joins them. "Is it not thought-provoking? Do you see how the indigenous people mix Mayan worship with Christian principles? Look at the incense, the flowers, the pine. Centuries ago, Catholic priests allowed the Mayans to worship in this way to preserve their heritage. To transition to Christianity, so to speak. In this way, the two religions have melded. The saints have new names and have taken on characteristics of Mayan gods. Many of the original cathedrals were built over indigenous places of worship."

Phil bristles. Transition into Christianity? One is either Christian or pagan. He decides to speak his mind so Alfonso will know where he stands. "I never believed that the bastardization of Christianity was a good idea," Phil says and turns toward the door as if to say he is no longer interested in pursuing the conversation.

Alfonso raises his brows as though amused. "But which is the truest form of religion? The ancient or the modern? I venture to say early Christians worshiped very differently than you do, and early Christianity was the basis of the Roman Catholic Church. Everyone has their own opinion about which is the proper way to revere God, and who is to say which is correct or even better than another? I see you find this offensive, but it is the culture. You are merely a visitor and should respect indigenous ways."

"I'm not here to admire cultural differences. I'm here to show them the way of true worship."

Alfonso steps forward and locks eyes with Phil. In a calm and steady voice, Alfonso says, "I hope to live in harmony with your family, but you must respect my beliefs, and I, in turn, will respect yours."

Phil doesn't say anything, but his hands clench and unclench as he walks stiffly out of the church. Katherine is mortified by her husband's attitude. In an attempt to smooth things over, she falls into step with their host. "Don't mind Phil. He thinks there is only one way to enter the kingdom of God. He isn't very flexible."

Alfonso smiles tightly. "I am not easily offended."

They leave the church, gather their purchases, and return to the car. Lulled by gentle music, Katherine and the children doze on the way home.

Phil sneezes several times and asks for a tissue.

"In the glove compartment," Alfonso responds.

On top of papers, a travel case of Kleenex, and other miscellaneous items lies a semiautomatic revolver. Phil stares for a moment. "Why do you have a gun?"

"For protection, of course," Alfonso says as though it is the most natural thing in the world. "I do not venture anywhere unarmed."

At the mention of a firearm, Justin rouses and peers over his father's shoulder. Back home, he frequents his grandfather's gun and ammo store. He thinks he recognizes the make. "Is it a Glock?"

"Excellent guess."

"Can I see it, Dad?"

"No, it's probably loaded."

"What would be the point otherwise?" Alfonso says. "Do you like guns, Justin? I have a collection at home. Perhaps I can show you sometime."

Justin shifts in his seat and decides not to reply. His parents don't approve of weapons.

Alfonso takes the gun from the glove box and casually tucks it under his thigh as he continues driving.

Phil helps himself to several tissues and closes the compartment. The rest of the family dozes off again. They wake when they hear him exclaim. "This is where you live?"

"Home sweet home. I hope you will be frequent visitors."

EIGHT

K atherine expected his home to be luxurious—even a mansion—but the place in front of them is a fortress. Triple rows of razor wire coil across the top of a twelve-foot-high perimeter wall encircling the property, and an occasional spark twinkles on the needle-sharp barbs when an insect flits too close. Two armed guards posted at the entrance jerk to attention as the vehicle passes through the gate. Motion detectors follow their every movement.

Phil whistles through his teeth. If it were five hundred years earlier, the place might have had crenellated ramparts with armed soldiers at attention. Now, modern technology served as a protective barrier. "Is this really necessary?"

Alfonso contemplates his answer. "Chomo told me about your experience on the roadside. Having been exposed to this country's dangers may help you understand why people with money live behind high walls and take security precautions. In your country, feeling safe is a squandered luxury. We are willing prisoners inside our own enclosures." Alfonso smiles at their expressions. "I see you think it excessive, but it is amazing how one can let down his guard within the compound. I help the villagers, but there are those who resent my wealth." He waves a hand toward the villa. "This is what is necessary when one has much. A result of the disparity between the handful of rich and the legions of poor. The few I am able to help is but a drop in the bucket compared to the need."

Katherine frowns. Phil promised it would be safe in the highlands. "What about us? Should we be concerned?"

Alfonso shakes his head absently. "Not at all. Why would anyone rob missionaries? Besides which, you are on my property and therefore under my protection."

Flaming red, orange, and fuchsia blossoms cascade over walls in a blaze of color, and flowers border a lush green lawn punctuated by trees laden with fruit. Within this Eden, gardeners carry rakes and hoes like weapons of war.

The driveway winds through the manicured landscape and circles a gurgling fountain where a marble cherub holds his water-shooting penis over a circular pool. Katy giggles and nudges her brother. A servant waits at the front door, dwarfed by columns that skirt the entrance and sustain the sloping red-tiled roof of the two-story concrete mansion. Off to the left, under corrugated zinc roofing, a fleet of vehicles is neatly aligned: Range Rovers, Avalanche pickups, and two sports cars. The vehicles shimmer as the afternoon sun slants over them.

Justin points to the cherry-red convertible in awe. "A Maserati?"

"I brought it over from Italy a few months ago."

Justin is skeptical. "How can you drive a sports car on this road? Our van scrapes bottom practically the entire way."

"When I go to the coast, my men roll it onto a trailer and tow it behind a larger vehicle. The freshly paved coastal road is ideal. Perhaps you can join us some time."

Alfonso shuts off the motor and snaps an order. Several men race to open the doors. They scurry away and return moments later with rags, wax, and a handheld vacuum cleaner.

Nearby, a lime-green parrot on a perch nibbles fruit. When she notices their approach, her pupils dilate furiously, and she cocks her head to one side. "¡Hola! ¡Hola! Me llamo Poppy."

"Poppy enjoys a proper introduction," Alfonso explains. "This is Phil, Katherine, Justin, and young Katherine." The parrot marches back and forth along the perch, and as Alfonso nears she flutters onto his shoulder and digs in her claws.

Noting her yellow cheeks and the red spot just above her beak, Phil mumbles, "Primrose-cheeked Amazon parrot."

"Excellent," Alfonso applauds. "You recognize the local feathered fauna."

"I studied up on Central American ornithology before we came," Phil says proudly. It was one of the many ways he'd prepared for this trip.

"Come, and I will show you the grounds," Alfonso says. "Please follow me."

"Speaking of the grounds, how large is this compound?" Justin asks.

"Diez manzanas," he says.

When they stare at him blankly, he adds, "About sixteen acres within the enclosure."

The house is near the front of the property. To the left, past the garage and along a wall some distance from the villa, wooden structures come into view. They turn out to be horse stables.

Alfonso asks his guests if they ride.

"My parents have a small ranch in Indiana," Katherine

replies. "My sister and I practically grew up on horseback. The kids also ride."

"My animals are at your service should exploration of our backcountry interest you, or we could venture together into the countryside someday. The mountains are full of trails, ideal for riding."

He directs his conversation at Katherine, and she thanks him with a smile while pinching her arm to remind herself she is a married woman. Damn, that man is attractive!

A mare pokes her head out from the door of her stall. Alfonso introduces her as Luna Bella and softly strokes her silky muzzle.

"What about the other horses?" Justin asks, seeing a half dozen other stalls.

"They are out to pasture. We like to give them a break from their enclosures. It helps their diet and disposition. Luna Bella is about to give birth. We keep her in the stall so that we can look after her."

Luna Bella nudges Alfonso's arm, demanding his attention. He pulls a cube of sugar from his shirt pocket, and the mare nuzzles him. As he continues to caress her, she whinnies softly. From her swollen belly, she looks like she will foal soon.

They continue their tour of the grounds. Behind the house, colorful mosaic tiles line a kidney-shaped pool. Alfonso gestures toward a private gymnasium; it looks out onto the pool area. Justin cups his hands and stares through the darkened windows. Free weights line one wall. A treadmill, Stairmaster, and stationary bicycle face a flat-screen TV.

To one side, two choppers, like birds poised for flight, perch on helipads. The smaller is a four-seater while the other accommodates eight passengers. Alfonso makes an inclusive gesture toward the rugged terrain. "I often travel by chopper. As you have surmised, vehicular travel to this part of the country is quite tedious, especially if one journeys back and forth to the capital with any frequency. But let us not forget what we came for. Please follow me."

After encircling his entire home, they walk past the fountain to the main entrance.

"Mom, this is as big as our shopping mall back home," Katy says.

"Not quite, sweetheart," Katherine replies, but she is awestruck, too. The house alone has to be at least ten thousand square feet.

Alfonso returns Poppy to her outdoor perch. As they head toward the house, she bobs up and down in response.

An elaborate door, etched with Mayan designs, opens into a cathedral-ceilinged foyer. Somber oil paintings adorn the walls. A mahogany stairway curves up from the gleaming tan-and-rose-colored marble tiles that glitter with the reflection from dangling chandeliers. "Over this way," Alfonso says, gesturing to the left, "is the library, and beyond that the formal dining room and kitchen. On another occasion I will give you a more complete tour, but I believe you are under certain time constraints."

They follow Alfonso to the right and across thick Persian carpets to an open door; eight computer monitors are lined up and connected to scanners, printers, and hard drives. To one side, a guard watches several screens as they stream live videos of the grounds.

"Oh, I don't want to intrude," Katherine says.

"Do not worry." He dismisses the guard. "Take all the time you need."

"Are you certain? I can write another day."

"Please feel free to come here when you feel the urge to communicate with the outside world. There is always someone on duty, but you will become accustomed to it." Alfonso claps his hands, and a man wearing a white apron appears to take beverage orders. "We have soft drinks as well as beer and wine. Hard liquor if you prefer."

Katy and Justin order sodas. Phil replies with a shake of his head that expresses his distaste for alcohol. "Ice water will be adequate for my wife and me."

Ordinarily Katherine would prefer water. She and her husband have never been drinkers, but today a glass of wine sounds appealing. It annoys her that Phil assumes what she might or might not want. Trying to be a good Christian wife, the "good" part referring to submissive, she has slipped into the habit of allowing him to make the decisions. She turns to Alfonso. "I'd like a glass of Cabernet, please."

The waiter acknowledges the order with a slight bow, and Phil purses his lips. Katherine ignores him, sits, and writes a note to her family. Her face is drawn in concentration as she puts the adventures of the past few days into words, glosses over the ugly parts, and enhances the nicer ones. The servant returns with drinks and a tray of cheese and crackers and places the glass in front of her. She stops occasionally to sip her wine.

Phil's initial antagonism over Alfonso's hybrid-Catholic sentiments has been replaced by awe at the surroundings. "This is unbelievable. A mansion in the middle of nowhere. I can't get over it."

Alfonso chuckles. "What is money for? I derive pleasure from helping people and I employ many. I enjoy being—how can I say?—comfortable." He pauses and stares out the window toward the pool. With a start, he remembers the purpose of their visit. "I almost forgot. How much cash do you need, and do you prefer U.S. dollars or Guatemalan quetzales?"

Katherine clicks the mouse, sending off the note through

cyberspace to friends and family. "Do you have enough quetzales to exchange a six-hundred-dollar check?"

Alfonso steps into the hallway and calls for Pancho.

A teenage boy appears and looks at them with frank curiosity. He doesn't strike them as an employee, yet doesn't resemble Alfonso in any way. He has the physical appearance of the Mayans. His thick, dark hair is slicked back with gel, and just a few strands hang over his forehead. A white Abercrombie shirt strikes a contrast against his dark skin and accentuates muscular arms. Leather flip-flops slap the floor under fashionable, wide-legged designer jeans, frayed at the bottom.

When Alfonso orders him to bring five thousand quetzales from upstairs, he pivots and bounds up the staircase.

"The exchange rate is seven point eight to the dollar, but I'll round it up."

Katherine protests. "The official rate is more than fair. You're doing us a big favor."

He waves it off.

Pancho returns with money in an envelope, and Alfonso peels off two one-hundred-quetzal notes for him and gives Katherine the rest. Pancho slips the money into his pocket.

"Thank you, Alfonso. It was so kind of you to take us to San Marcos today, allow me to use the computer, and exchange money. I don't mean to be abrupt, but we really must be going. We don't know if the electricity has been turned on yet, so I'd like to be home before nightfall."

"You are most welcome." He steps aside and ushers them out of the room. "I also have certain commitments, but it was an enjoyable day for me." He bows slightly. "If you will excuse me, my assistant will take you home."

A swarthy man with a crew cut, a bulldog face, and the dense, muscled build of a middleweight professional boxer appears. With a deadpan expression, he says, "I am Chato. Follow me."

As they walk toward the door, Pancho shouts after them in perfect English, "Wait! Your cell phones." He hands over a small bag with four phones and their chargers, then leaves.

"I thought Alfonso didn't have kids," Justin remarks.

Chato glances at him coldly. "Su ahijado."

Phil translates. "His godson."

"What's that?" Katy asks as they walk toward the garage. After her father explains the Catholic tradition, she bubbles with enthusiasm. "Do you think he could adopt me as a goddaughter? Maybe I could live here, too."

"Katy, that's enough," Katherine says.

Justin rolls his eyes. "Yeah, sis, dream on."

Their purchases are transferred to a double-cab Avalanche. They climb in, and Katy kneels facing backward, staring at the villa as they hurtle onward toward their humble abode.

Phil reels with astonishment. Who could have expected a neighboring mansion tucked away in this remote place? He ponders the many scenarios where a benefactor like Alfonso could help his ministry. If only the man weren't Catholic.

Light shines from the kitchen window of the little house when they pull up, indicating that the electricity has been turned on. Though it doesn't look as bad as it had when they arrived, by comparison with Alfonso's villa, it's downright dismal. They unload their purchases and wave goodbye to Chato, who doesn't even glance their way. The truck peels out of the driveway in a cloud of dust.

"He probably figures anyone who'd live in this dump is not worth waving to," Katy says with a pout. Then her face brightens. "Can we visit Alfonso soon? He says we're welcome at his house, and he lives close by."

Katherine struggles for an answer. They would all love to spend time at a place like the villa, especially since their own home is so meager by comparison, but she fears it might be a mistake. Children should be satisfied with their own family's economic reality and not covet what they can never have. "We'll see, Katy."

Katy's face crumples in disappointment. She knows a negative answer when she hears it.

The refrigerator overflows with the gifts of food, and someone—Doña Rosa?—has left supper on the stove: black beans mashed into a paste, rice, and warm tortillas wrapped in cloth. The beds are made, the floors scrubbed and mopped, and the bathroom scoured. Still far from luxurious, but livable. "Praise the Lord," Katherine says as she looks around. Or maybe Doña Rosa.

After dinner, they gather in the living room to reflect on lessons learned since their arrival. Phil is keen on this type of family feedback. He believes that valuable lessons can be found in all experiences, but if they aren't talked through, these lessons might be disregarded. If looked at with the correct perspective, even the worst mishaps can yield spiritual advancement.

Justin slouches over to the sofa. He hates family evenings and asserts that his father drives the teachings home so hard that by the time he is finished, they are no longer worth pondering.

Phil watches his son's sullen expression. "Justin, you need to think about it, too."

The boy almost answers "about what?" before remembering the task. Lessons learned. He fastens his gaze on the spiderwebs woven into the roof beams and relives the past few days in search of truths. He thinks of all that's happened and all the things he wishes he hadn't learned.

"Justin?"

"Lesson number one. Don't ride around in old cars with no spare tires."

Phil's eyes flash. That isn't the kind of example he is looking for, and Justin knows it. Katherine comes to her son's rescue. "You have a point. We do need to keep our vehicle in good working order and always have a spare. We should look into getting a new tire next time we're in town."

Phil ignores his wife and calls on Katy to come up with something she learned.

Prompted by her brother's answer, she says, "Never use public bathrooms."

Katherine laughs. "I think that's a safe conclusion based on what we saw at the market." Water everywhere but in the sink, doors that didn't close, used tissue piled on the soaking floor. "What do you think, Phil? What teachings would you like to share?"

Annoyed at his wife for taking over his reflection time, he stares at the whitewashed wall. Hoping the ruined lesson can still be saved, he asks God for help with his answer. "Well, we learned that the Lord answers prayer." He stops himself and quickly adds, "Of course, we already knew that, but it was reinforced once again. We prayed for the bandits to depart, and they left without harming us. We prayed for help, and it came."

"Do you mean help from the neighbors or from Alfonso?" Katy asks.

"The neighbors all came to welcome us. We doubted Jerónimo's goodwill, but we were proven wrong. Every one of those people who came this morning gave something of themselves, according to their capabilities. We witnessed the extreme generosity of the poorest of the poor. Alfonso's gifts appear to be the most valuable simply because he has more to give. If we look at how much the people have according to what they gave, the one who handed us the eggs, for example, might have made the biggest sacrifice. Remember Jesus at the temple ... " He stops when he notices his family staring into space. "What about you, Katherine? What kind of lessons have you taken from our initial days here in Guatemala?"

She resists dwelling on the horrors of the previous day, so she recalls the present day's events. She was struck by differences in the way people behave: the way that Alfonso enlisted help from the townspeople, the woman praying at the church. "I learned that people from other places have different ways of doing things. Since we are to be living in a country that is not our own, we need to be tolerant and accepting. The way we've always done things at home may not be the way to do things here."

"Do you mean the market?" Katy asks. "It's way different from Safeway."

"The market is part of it. There are many things we've seen that are different. The way people dress, the way they speak, their customs, even the way they worship."

"I'm not sure I follow you," Phil begins. "Remember we are here as missionaries. We are not supposed to tolerate their religion as much as enlighten them."

"But, Phil, just look at the way Catholicism and Mayan customs have melded. Spirituality is the goal, a deepening understanding of God and his inherent goodness. You can't tell me those people lighting candles and praying in the church— praying to our same God—are pagans."

"You know nothing about it." Has she forgotten why they've come?

She holds his gaze in challenge and tells the kids to get ready for bed and say their evening prayers. She knows a discussion with her husband will ensue.

CHAPTER

NINE

"These people are pagans."

"Some are Catholics. Surely you don't believe Catholics are pagans. They may have different customs and traditions, but they read the same Bible, worship the same God. If they recognize Christ as the Son of God, they're Christians." Katherine tries to keep her voice calm. Even though the temptation to match and overpower Phil in volume is enormous, she tries to bear in mind that sometimes those who speak softly are more likely to be heard. "You don't really expect to convert Catholics."

"You think what we saw earlier is Christianity? You heard what Alfonso said about how over the years Mayan paganism and Catholicism have blended. Something new and very wrong has been created, a religion where pagan gods are worshiped as saints. We need to show them how to pray, not to saints or the Virgin Mary, but directly to God, the real, divine God." Though the tolerance she mentions goes against his official beliefs, he sees her point in some small and insignificant way but refuses to give it credit. He is silent for a moment, then adds in a lower tone, "Besides, this is what I signed on for, and it's too late to back out now."

Katherine wishes she had examined in more detail what the missionary society expected of them. She had hoped to provide an opportunity to help people out of poverty. Hers would be an aid worker's approach, every person helped a drop in the bucket of a suffering humanity. What difference does it make in the end, how their spirituality is developed, so long as their lives are improved? Phil just doesn't understand that working toward tangible results is the best way to provide credibility and influence.

He brought her here under false pretenses. Since the very beginning, things have gone awry, and she should have recognized it as a sign. Had Phil explained that he only meant to evangelize, she might never have agreed to come, and she would not have experienced the roadside horrors. Now there is no easy way for her to return.

"Phil, this is not what I expected. If things don't improve, I want to go home. Nothing has gone well since we arrived, and I'm not sure things will get better."

"Didn't we talk about this already? Three months. I told you to give it three months and if things haven't improved by then, we'll leave. Meanwhile, keep yourself busy." Exasperation leaks into his voice. "Of course, changes are difficult initially, but that's only to be expected. After all, Rome wasn't built in a day."

She dislikes his tone. He isn't the one who almost got raped, the one who deals with complaining children, the one who will stay home all day without anyone to talk to besides the kids.

~

As DAYS PASS, Phil immerses himself in visits to subsistence farms, and he attends events in nearby villages. Jerónimo introduces him to the locals and translates for him. Phil's work is a relief, an escape from home and his complaining wife. He doesn't remember her being like this before.

As Katherine awaits the arrival of homeschooling materials, she fills her time with home-improvement projects. The job of painting the exterior of the house takes the kids two days. Next, they set about cleaning the spacious yard and planting flowers in the soft, spongy soil. Above their front steps, a frame holds up the roof. Katherine decorates it with a rainbow of cascading flowers. They put in a pathway from the driveway to the front door, recycling a stack of old bricks found in the yard. They haven't seen Alfonso since that first day, though she thinks about him more often than she would ever like to admit, and she secretly hopes he will be impressed with her landscaping.

Every night the couple falls into bed exhausted, and Katherine thinks it's just as well. Her sex life, which used to be a highlight, has fizzled to an annoyance—a dull, mechanical action that only serves to keep her from needed sleep. Passionate kisses have morphed into perfunctory pecks.

Sunday is a break from the weekday monotony and strenuous gardening. Morning services are held in the backyard under the encompassing branches of their own *ceiba*. The mysterious door in the bathroom, opened that first Sunday, yielded a multitude of white plastic chairs and a simple pewter cross. Vases of wildflowers are placed on a cypress altar built by Jerónimo.

Katherine and Phil argue about how to spend their scanty income. Phil wants to save any extra cash for the construction of a new church, while Katherine stands firm on making their lives more comfortable. Phil's goal of having his own church will require the flow of contributions to increase from a trickle to a gush, something his wife is skeptical about.

"You know, Phil, this piece of land is not even ours. If you expect to build a church, we first need to buy property, and we have no idea how much that will cost."

"Alfonso isn't doing anything with this property. Perhaps he can let us have it or at least a connecting piece."

She shakes her head. "Don't push him. We're lucky to be here at all. He doesn't buy into our evangelization."

"Just because he doesn't want us proselytizing him doesn't mean he disapproves of our efforts in the community."

As neither of them has any idea what Alfonso thinks, the discussion fizzles out. They haven't seen any sign of him since that first day. When Katherine asks, Rosa says that Alfonso comes and goes. His being away for several months is nothing unusual.

Pentecost Sunday falls on the eleventh of May, a month after their arrival. Phil proposes an idea to encourage attendance. "Because it's a special Sunday," he says, hoping to ease her into his plan, "we should provide lunch for the congregation."

"Lunch will definitely bring people in," Katherine agrees. "Rosa says the crops have been sparse. But I don't want to be responsible for the meal. It's enough to have to figure out how to feed our own family."

"The Lord always provides."

Katherine tries not to show her irritation. As far as she can tell, they will be providing and she will be cooking. "I don't know if they'll want manna from heaven," she says with sarcasm, "but I guess I can donate some of those hens that were given to us."

"Every gift given for God's purpose will bring a blessing from Him."

She frowns. Why does he always fall back on pious-sounding sayings to have the last word? She can't believe he honestly thinks these things. Or does he?

Much to Katherine's relief, local women volunteer to prepare the meal. They arrive early Sunday morning and twist the necks of the old hens. They clean, pluck, and toss them into a large pot as effortlessly as she could throw a cellophane-wrapped chicken into a shopping cart at Safeway.

The pot hangs from a frame over a roaring fire for hours. Popping to the surface of the broth through a quarter inch of grease are immature, shell-less eggs, along with chicken feet. The slapping of tortillas fills the air.

Plastic chairs transform the yard into a church. They set out all forty chairs, and a few people sit in the grass.

Phil is thrilled with the turnout—double the average attendance. He wears a suit and tie while the congregation dons its Sunday best: men in pants of indeterminate color and thin, much-laundered long-sleeved shirts, the work boots on their feet the only shoes they own. The women are clad in matching *huipiles*. Beaded necklaces dangle from their thick necks, and braids wrap their heads. They wear *cortes*, skirts made of straight pieces of handwoven fabric, cinched at the waist with a woven belt. They are either barefoot with splayed toes or wear clear plastic jellies. Women, both young and old, tie children to their backs with shawls of the colorful fabric. It's impossible to tell siblings from mothers or grandmothers.

Initiating the service, Phil intones, "Praise you, most merciful Lord and Savior. Let us feel your power and presence here today. Show us your Holy Spirit. Work through me, and may the words I speak be pleasing to your ears. In Jesus' precious name I pray. Amen."

Thunder rumbles across the valley. The parishioners lift their heads and look about. The effect is not lost on Phil. He marvels at the Almighty's presence, once again come to his aid. "Praise the Lord!" He shouts in Spanish. "He is here with us today."

The crowd begins to murmur.

A member of the congregation drops stiffly to the ground. Don Santiago Chico's son kneels next to him and stretches him out. A second commotion draws everyone's attention to another section of the audience. Lucinda Valverde, an elderly woman in traditional garb, crumples like a wilted flower, much to the astonishment of her daughter and son-in-law.

People rise to their feet nervously. Fearing they might bolt like cattle in a thunderstorm, Phil shouts, "Do not fear! The power of the Holy Spirit has come upon them."

Immediately, the two parishioners begin to shake. Another drops. It's Doña Rosa.

Phil looks out at the congregation and cries, "Hallelujah! Praise the Lord." He can barely contain his glee. This is truly a Pentecostal Sunday!

Don Santiago stiffens and begins making guttural noises.

"Translate. Who can tell us what he said?" Phil shouts.

"He says the Spirit of the Lord walks among us. To not be afraid," someone shouts from the back.

"Another!"

From Doña Lucinda, Justin hears, clear as day in perfect English, "Beware of the evil one who comes dressed as a lamb. His aims weaken what was once strong."

Astounded, Justin looks around to see if anyone else heard

the message. Just as he gets ready to shout out the communication, Doña Rosa begins speaking in tongues. Everyone's focus shifts, and the second translation is forgotten. Phil calls for an interpreter.

An old hag enveloped in a shawl gets to her feet. "Always look to the light and turn from the devil. The evil one's temptations are hard to resist."

When the three regain consciousness, Phil and Katherine lead the congregation in song. Jerónimo and his sons pass a woven basket. Women reach into their bras and search for their money purses. By the time the basket is handed to Justin to take into the house, it overflows with the largest offering to date.

Phil speaks of how the Spirit of God descended on the apostles the day of the first Pentecost. He preaches that anyone who knows Christ personally can claim that power for his own—the same power that knocked the parishioners over and gave them messages from above. The crowd is mesmerized—everyone wants to receive direct communication from heaven. New faces approach the front to accept Jesus Christ as their personal savior. Phil and Jerónimo lay hands on them as they kneel at the wooden altar.

The number of villagers has multiplied once again by the time the sermon finishes and lunch begins. Katherine fears there won't be enough food for the crowd, but with everyone taking four or five pancake-sized tortillas each, there is just enough. When the last of the food is gone, the crowd quietly disperses.

THAT EVENING, the Whitehalls gather to discuss the day's events. Katy curls up on one corner of the sofa and Justin sprawls at the other.

"What did you think of today's sermon?" Phil asks with obvious satisfaction.

"Amazing," Katy says.

Even Justin looks to his father with admiration. "I've never seen you do anything like that before, Dad. It was impressive."

"Amazing and impressive is the power of God, Justin. I was only acting as His instrument. Real faith goes hand in hand with the ability to channel His glory. Remember how the thieves left that day." Phil pauses, and his mouth puckers in thought. "No one translated that second message."

Justin reveals what he heard.

"Are you sure, Justin?" Katherine questions. "You wouldn't kid us about something so serious?"

"I heard it plain as day." He looks at his parents, both with doubt sketched on their faces. "Geez, it's not like I wanted to."

"Why do you suppose Justin was picked?" Katherine asks her husband later that evening.

"As far as I know, God's choosing of the speaker and the translator are random."

"Do you really think God's choices are random?" Katherine asks, thinking that doesn't sound like something Phil would say.

Phil shakes his head distractedly. "You can't take these things too literally. God speaks in generalities to groups. It's unfortunate that Justin didn't share his communication earlier. God's words mean different things to different people. That's why Christ spoke in parables."

Katherine wonders. Justin was so sure this message was sent specifically to the Whitehall family. Could it somehow be a warning about Alfonso? She assures herself not; he has not been a part of their lives since that first day. Even so, she has a distinct premonition that their daily routine will soon be ruffled beyond recognition.

CHAPTER

TEN

Katherine stands at the counter, chopping vegetables for the day's lunch. She listens to intermittent bird whistles and the rustle of leaves, then she hears a buzzing. The sound seems to be approaching. She wipes her hands with a dishcloth and looks up as a motorcycle stops in front. Visitors are scarce. It has already been two months since Alfonso took them into town and then vanished as mysteriously as he had first appeared. Her heart thuds unexpectedly.

She misses having an adult to converse with as Phil isn't much fun when he returns tired from the field. Seeing that it isn't Alfonso, her disappointment is tinged with relief—after all, a mysterious millionaire living in a fortified compound in the middle of nowhere is more than a tad suspicious.

This visitor turns out to be a deliveryman. Leather bags hang from either side of his bike, and a cardboard box is fastened to the back rack.

"Familia Weete-all?" he asks in a deadpan voice. When Katherine nods, he unfastens the parcel, thrusts a paper and pen toward her, and gestures that she should sign for it. Expression-less, he hands over the bulky package.

From where they are gathering rocks for a garden border, Katy and Justin watch the motorcycle leave and hurry back to the house to see what came.

The corners of the box have been crushed in transit, but packing tape has saved it from destruction. Katherine slits it open. Books and papers burst out. When the children realize their school materials have finally arrived, their faces crumple with disappointment. It's not like they've been having fun, but at least they haven't had the torment of schoolwork. Evidently the mail workers had been disappointed as well. The box's contents had been opened and rifled through.

Justin reminds his mother that they will need more than just those materials. "How can we have any kind of education without a computer and Wi-Fi? I feel like we're living in the wrong century."

But a computer isn't the only thing missing from their daily lives. School friends and school activities are also noticeably absent. Katherine worries about the children remaining so disconnected from the outside world, but whenever she voices concern, Phil adamantly argues for the greater experience of living so near to nature with no modern gadgets. He also makes it clear that his is the final decision in the family. Katherine wonders again how she let herself be so swayed by her husband. Sometimes she even wonders why she married him. Where is the sense of humor that she loved, his spirit of adventure? He changed from a carefree young man to a pedantic pastor.

Most mornings, before they've eaten breakfast, Rosa arrives with her two youngest in tow. For fifty dollars a month, she scrubs their clothes in the outdoor sink, sweeps and mops the cement floors, and cleans the bathroom. She washes dishes and often cooks as well.

Occasionally one or two of her teenage sons wander over. Julio is the boy closest in age to Justin. Together they delineate the boundaries of a soccer field with painted rocks, and the boys kick a ball from one end to the other. Julio brings a locally made hacky sack and teaches Justin how to use it.

Rosa's only daughter, María Rosa, is a year younger than Katy. Lack of a common language doesn't hinder Katy. Katherine often wonders if her daughter is even aware of the barrier as she chats away.

With Phil absent most days and the rest of the family busy grappling with a new schedule, memories of Alfonso and the villa fade into an unlikely dream. Katherine adjusts her expectations to their limited options and piles into the van every Thursday morning with the kids for shopping and the few pleasures the town provides.

Among the compulsory stops is the internet café, located on a corner of the central plaza. Ancient desktop computers are the town's salute to technology, and amazingly one or two are usually working. Justin and Katy use them for school assignments and occasionally for social media. Katherine writes weekly messages to friends, family, and especially to church supporters. She keeps an eye on her kids as they wander the street stands, staring at pirated CDs and DVDs, counterfeit Ray-Bans, or whatever else might be featured at the market that day.

Marvin, the awkward young man at the counter, and Katherine strike up brief conversations, limited by his English and her scant Spanish. He always saves the best computer for her on Thursdays, one with a view of the square so she can keep an eye on her progeny.

Marvin rings up the total, and she hands him fifteen quetzales. "Nice to see you again, Mrs. Waytle."

She wishes him a good day and he bows.

Across the paving-stone street, the kids sit on a cement bench, tossing cracker crumbs to waddling pigeons. "Do we have to go already?" Katy asks. "It's so boring at the house."

"Next week we can stay and watch a movie, but your father's coming home for lunch. Doña Rosa is coming late and won't be there to fix it." She thinks of a way to placate her children. "Maybe we can all take a walk this afternoon."

The van shudders to life when the key is turned. They jerk and bump up the dusty road toward home. When they bring in their purchases, Phil is at the table waiting. "It took you long enough. I'm hungry."

She wonders why she feels guilty as she pulls out the fresh bread and prepares sandwiches. Phil wasn't so helpless before, and it irks her to have to justify her time. "I had letters to send to our supporters."

After lunch, Phil gets up to go and grabs his pack. "I might be home a little later than usual. Jerónimo wants to introduce me to a new family."

"Can't you stay for a while this afternoon? The kids and I want to take a walk. I thought maybe you could come with us."

"I've got commitments," he says. This is another example of how she doesn't appreciate the work he does or its importance. But when he sees her shoulders slump, he realizes he was too stern, and he adds, "I'd love to, but I promised the Yok family I'd be there by two-thirty. Jerónimo is already on his way. Rain check?"

If it were up to him, she thinks, they would never go

anywhere or do anything, but she's not going to let him dissuade her from the walk. "Come on kids. Get your hats."

They jump up. Justin's body burns with the urge for activity, and his sister has been feeling cooped up at home. Katherine worries about letting the kids explore without an adult along, but Justin's sense of direction already exceeds her own. Surely, if the three of them stay together, they'll be fine, even without Phil.

"Dad, can I take your binoculars?" Justin calls as his father gets into the van. Phil signals his approval.

A few minutes later, they start off. The sky shimmers blue. Puffy clouds play hide and seek with the sun.

Pines and cedars brush the heavens with uneven strokes, and wildflowers line the path as though a gardening God has personally tended to them. Something catches Justin's attention just off the trail. He picks up a porous rock that has been fashioned into a flattened face with distinctly shaped eyes. "Look, Mom. You can't say it's just a coincidence." He turns it over in his hands. "I bet there are Mayan ruins near here. Julio said there were undiscovered archaeological sites all over the country." Justin slips the evidence into his pocket.

"Let me see, Justin," Katy demands.

"Find one of your own." He turns away, not ready to share.

Katy looks to her mother, hoping she'll interfere on her behalf, but not wanting to ask. Katherine seldom gets involved in the children's arguments. Growing up, she experienced how parents can cause strife between siblings by not allowing them to work out their own issues.

The carved stone rattles in Justin's already full pocket. He is a collector like his grandfather, whose den is a scrapbook of his life, cluttered with tickets, brochures, and tokens from every trip he's ever taken.

Justin's pre-Guatemala memorabilia—rocks, fossils, and

stickers—are packed in boxes and stored back in Indiana. Katherine wanted to trash them, but he put up such a fuss, she just threw them in with boxes of books, lamps, and kitchen items into their storage locker.

Justin leads them down a path that meanders through a meadow and ends in a steep slope. Trails stripe the mountains; vast, treeless plains stretch below; and cattle—mere specks from this distance—graze on the thin grasslands.

"Look over there." Katy points to a strangely lumpy hilltop across a narrow valley. Wisps of smoke circle into the sky.

"Don't get too close to the edge," Katherine warns.

Justin mumbles and lifts the binoculars to his eyes. "Check it out, Mom." He hands her the glasses, and she sees several dozen villagers leaving the site, fanning out in different directions. "What do you think they're doing?"

Katy giggles. "Having a wiener roast?"

Katherine turns. "We should go back now."

"I want to see what's going on," Justin urges. "I bet they're leaving a Mayan ceremony." Impulsively, Justin plunges down the incline, ignoring both his mother and the zigzagging path. He slides through brush and trees on the loose gravel. Katy watches him for a few seconds and then follows.

"Wait! Didn't I tell you we were going home?" Katherine races down the pathway in futile hopes of catching up.

Katy loses her footing and tumbles. She grabs at the brush and anchors herself to an outcropping where scraggly roots provide handholds. "Justin! Mom! Help me."

A cloud of dust appears at the edge of the trail, and by the time Katherine arrives, Justin is already kneeling next to his sister. She struggles to stand, her arm slung over his shoulder, but her foot can't bear weight. Tears trickle down her smudged cheeks.

Katherine drops down to look at her scraped knee, and Katy sobs, "Mom, it's my ankle!" When her mother tries to rotate it, Katy screams. Justin suggests she hop on the other foot with their support, but the trail is too narrow to walk three abreast. In the end, Katherine and Justin take turns piggybacking her home.

As they approach the house, Rosa, worry furrowing her brow, comes running out. "What happening to Catty?"

"She tripped," Katherine answers dully, weighted with guilt. What will Phil think of her, not able to control her children? But then, why should she care what he thinks? He's never around.

Rosa clucks out misgivings and shakes her head.

The ankle is discolored and tight with swelling. Rosa crushes ice in a towel while Justin applies it to the injury. Hands shaking, Katherine fumbles with her cell phone. "Phil, hurry up and get home!" she says. "Katy may have sprained her ankle. We need to get her to the hospital."

As they wait for the van, seconds pass like minutes, and she wonders what it would be like in a dire emergency.

Katy lies with her eyes closed and her foot elevated on the arm of the couch. Whenever Rosa shifts the ice pack, Katy whimpers. Twenty minutes later, the van pulls up.

Phil steps into the house. "What happened, pancake?" he croons.

"I was following Justin down the mountain, and I tripped. The gravel was loose."

Phil's stomach tenses. He should have gone with them. If he had, none of this would have happened. He turns to his wife. "And you were where?"

"Before you blame me," she bristles, "remember I wanted you to come on this outing. I'm not saying you're at fault, but when they get something in their heads, they don't listen to me."

"You baby them. You lack authority," he says.

Each word jabs like a stiletto. She opens her mouth and feels blood drain from her face.

"Come on, little one. Let's get you to the hospital." He gathers Katy in his arms while Justin trails behind, holding the dripping ice pack. Like an uninvited stranger, Katherine slinks into the van.

They jerk along the dirt road toward the highway.

"Ow!" Katy says.

"Can't you slow down, Dad?" Justin asks. Her injury is his fault. After all, he was the one who led her down the hill.

They arrive at the hospital, where several rusted old cars are parked alongside an ancient ambulance. Inside cement-block walls, Katherine sees a large room with twenty occupied beds, separated by thin blue curtains. Off to the side is an emergency room for triage and two surgical units. They hear the shrieks of a woman in labor.

In the waiting room, they sit on brown vinyl benches. While Katy's ankle is being x-rayed, Phil fidgets. Why does he always feel compelled to put his ministry before his family? He looks at the villagers waiting to see a doctor and sits up straighter. It's because of them, he reasons, justifying himself. The souls he needs to save. Maybe the events of the day were, in some inscrutable way, part of God's plan.

Watching Justin stare glumly at the yellow and black floor tiles, grungy and pitted from age and foot traffic, Katherine laments wandering off so far in the rugged hills. She regrets coming to Guatemala. They should have waited until the children were grown. She thinks of all the dangers from which she must protect her children and reckons she is not doing as great a job as she would like. How will she ever be able to allow them to go off to college?

Phil leaps to his feet when the doctor appears.

"No fractures," she says in English, "but it's a bad sprain. I'm going to put a boot cast on to immobilize her."

"Thank you, doctor," Phil says, taking a deep breath.

Twenty minutes later, the doctor brings Katy out in a wheelchair. "Remember to keep your foot elevated for the next few days. Stay off it as much as possible for the next month." She holds out some old crutches, discolored from use. "I can loan these to you for now." She puts the padded areas under her own arms and demonstrates how to walk. "You won't need crutches if you're just around the house, but if you go out, you should use them." She pats Katy's head playfully. "No mountain adventures for a while, young lady."

CHAPTER

ELEVEN

Rainy season slips into place in a matter of days. Every afternoon, with the regularity of church bells chiming in town squares, clouds fill the sky, sponge up moisture from the atmosphere, and then burst like water balloons from heaven. Big, fat drops of water clank on tin roofs, splatter dirt trails, and drench Katherine's brand-new garden.

Phil watches the driving rain as it plummets to the saturated ground. "I don't see why Alfonso would object to having a church on this property. He's not using it, and it's not as if we aren't already conducting services." Obsessed with the idea of building, Phil is confident the comfort of an indoor church will draw the villagers in and his teachings will encourage them to stay. Their chapel will be the ideal place for people to congregate, a focal point in the community. He already imagines carpeted floors, wooden pews, and a simple cross behind the altar. "We can raise the money ourselves."

"Do you really think he's going to want to build a church that will convince villagers to convert to our way of worship?"

It annoys him that his wife is always so sensible, but he reminds himself that they make a good balance, and, besides, what can he lose by asking? As if called by Phil's thoughts, a helicopter flies over the house and lands in Alfonso's compound.

Two days later, several vehicles pull up. Large men in suits and ties open the doors of the first black Range Rover. Alfonso and Pancho step out. Two more guards emerge from the second car and station themselves around the area. Though Alfonso told them he often travels with bodyguards, this seems excessive, even for a wealthy man in a violent country.

"Is everything all right, Alfonso?" Katherine asks, eyeing the accompanying men.

"We had threats, so it was suggested that I take extra precautions."

Threats? The word hangs heavily in the air.

"I see you enjoy gardening. You have done an excellent job with this yard. It looks like a different place entirely."

Katherine smiles with pride. She wants to ask him where he recommends buying fertilizer, something she's had trouble procuring from the nearby town, when Katy interrupts from behind. "Hi, Alfonso! Look at my foot." She points to her cast.

"What has happened to you, young Katherine?"

Katy giggles. She marvels that he calls her Katherine as no one else has done. She tells him about her fall in the mountains, and concern shadows his face. "Perhaps you should not be hiking in that area. It is very steep and dangerous."

"But Mommy was with us."

His words pierce Katherine with remorse. Anything could have happened, and she hadn't even thought to leave word of their itinerary. What was she thinking? Here they are in a country where danger lurks in public roadways and who knows where else, and she and her children go hiking in a deserted, mountainous area without taking necessary precautions.

Alfonso turns to Katherine. "My dear, you must not feel bad. Children are prone to accidents, and you need not fear the villagers," he says, as though divining her thoughts. "Everyone around here knows you are guests on my property."

He gazes into her eyes, and she feels her self-possession ebb. Smooth hands grasp hers and he strokes her fingers. Mesmerized, she is unable to pull away. Time slows and seconds seem like minutes.

"You are a beautiful woman, Katherine."

She glances down at her faded jeans and button-up sleeveless shirt and suddenly wishes she wasn't dressed for gardening. Heat rises to her face. "Um ... thank you."

He steps back and releases her. The intimate moment passes, and he is all business once again. Her body trembles with anxiety. Had her children seen the flush that passed up her neck and into her cheeks?

Alfonso turns to Pancho. "This is Mrs. Whitehall, Justin, and young Katherine, known to most as Katy." He rests his arm affectionately on the boy's shoulders. "Pancho is my godson. I apologize for not formally introducing you at the villa. I was distracted that day."

Katherine pulls herself together and extends her hand to the young man.

Katy stares at him with frank curiosity, then turns to Alfonso. "Does he live with you?"

"Pancho's parents were friends of mine. Colleagues, you might say. When he was baptized, I agreed to be his godfather.

Three years ago, when his parents were killed in a terrible accident, I became responsible for him. Now he is like a son to me."

The boy's face is devoid of sadness, or of any expression at all. The conversation might as well have been about someone else entirely.

"I'm very sorry for your loss," Katherine says.

He shrugs and looks away. "Alfonso is my family now."

Katherine's stomach flutters when she looks up and sees Alfonso smiling at her. She wonders if she's ever felt such strong attraction. She determines to harden herself against his charm. She shifts her attention to Pancho and inquires about his schooling.

"I go to the American School." When she looks blank, he explains, "It's a bilingual academy in the capital."

"So you live in the city during the week." She directs this statement toward Alfonso.

"I have been away these past few months on business, it is true. But Pancho and I generally travel back and forth in the helicopter. We are on our way to town now to pick up a few things, and I thought to stop by to see how you are faring."

Phil strides up the hill from the opposite direction. As he approaches, a smile spreads across his face. "Hello there, Alfonso. I've been hoping to run into you. There's a little something I've wanted to discuss." He glances at the well-dressed guards. "Are these business associates?"

Alfonso laughs. "They are my security. A necessary evil."

Phil nods as if familiar with the need for bodyguards.

Alfonso checks his watch and nods to the men guarding the perimeter. "We are in a bit of a hurry to get to town. The real reason we came by is to invite you to the villa next Saturday afternoon if you are available. It is Pancho's sixteenth birthday, and we will have some people over for a small get-together.

Nothing fancy, just a poolside party. Bring your swimsuits and come over at one."

He turns toward Phil. "We can speak then."

❧

KATHERINE PONDERS her meager wardrobe and settles for a casual skirt to go over her two-piece swimsuit, along with a green-and-yellow-flecked blouse she's been saving for a special occasion. Squinting into a tiny compact, she dabs on eye shadow and tries not to smear the waterproof mascara.

Phil whistles in appreciation as she walks out. Their low-fat diet, which includes black beans, corn tortillas, and garden vegetables, has made the entire family leaner and trimmer. Katherine is pleased that her skirt no longer stretches tightly when zipped.

When it's finally time to leave, they pile into the van and head to the villa. The guards at the gate scratch down their names and confer with someone over a radio before waving them through. They see no other visiting cars.

"Are we early?" Katy asks.

"Could be, pancake," her father answers. "Guatemalans seem to have a different concept of punctuality."

As they round the corner, guest helicopters come into view, queued up like birds on a power line. When they heard air activity earlier, they assumed the villa's own helicopters were picking up forgotten supplies, never imagining the guests would be arriving by chopper.

Justin sums up their thoughts: "I thought people in this country were poor."

"Obviously not Alfonso's friends," his father answers, and

his eyes gleam as he considers a captive audience to whom he can appeal for money.

Boisterous noises filter through plate-glass doors as a butler ushers them through a back entrance. They admire the formal living area with Mayan stelae as they follow the butler's long strides. Outside, uniformed servants bustle back and forth from the poolside to the outdoor kitchen and bar with trays of hors d'oeuvres and drinks. A dozen young people splash in the pool, and several lounge in deck chairs. Poppy marches back and forth on a large wooden perch as though supervising the activity.

Alfonso engages three tables of adults. He rises as the Whitehall couple approaches. As he introduces them, Katherine and Phil shake the other guests' hands.

Justin and Katy glance around at a loss. When Alfonso notices their discomfort, he stands. "Pancho! Where are your manners? Introduce Justin and young Katherine to your friends. Now!"

Pancho climbs from the pool with barely concealed sullenness, water dripping from his black swim trunks. He leads them to where the teenage boys are congregated without even looking their way. Under his breath, he says, "Thanks for getting me in trouble with Alfonso, assholes."

Justin stares at his feet, and Katy colors in anger. When they get close enough to the pool, Pancho says, "Everyone, this is Katy and Fofo."

The boys glance up and nod before returning to their laughter, leaving the two self-conscious and even more at a loss. Katy grabs her brother's arm and leads him to the other side, where younger siblings throw a ball back and forth. They deposit their clothes on an empty chair and sit at the edge.

Katherine feels like an outsider as well. The people at her table are speaking Spanish, and her language skills are insufficient to join the conversation. Phil engages the man next to him in a discussion about the Bible. The man's face is masked with a veneer of politeness, and he answers in monosyllables. When Phil pulls out a modern translation in Spanish, the man glances over at another table where a couple motions discreetly. Watching the exchange, Katherine's face burns in humiliation. Why would her husband ruin Alfonso's party by proselytizing the guests?

The woman on Katherine's left attempts to converse, but beyond a few comments about the weather, they are unable to kindle a conversation. Discouraged, Katherine gets up and finds a seat near the pool with the excuse of rubbing lotion on her kids' pale backs.

Justin and Katy sit at the shallow end of the pool. Katy's right foot dangles in the water, and her left, with its plaster cast, languishes dangerously close to the edge. The doctor had warned her not to let it get wet.

Katherine holds up a tube of sunscreen. "Come over here, you two. I'm going to slather more of this on you."

Justin protests mildly, but his mother perpetually preaches that they can never have too much sun protection. As she works the lotion in, Alfonso saunters past and stops.

"Put your swimsuit on, Katherine. Relax and get in the pool. I am sorry you did not feel comfortable at the table with my other guests. If you worry about sunburn, I will be happy to rub lotion on your shoulders."

Alfonso's long, slim fingers are like those of a piano player; the nails trimmed neatly, almost manicured. They don't resemble the hands of a farmer or someone who works the soil. Katherine imagines those elegant hands on her bare skin and wonders why he would even offer. She isn't sure whether she should be flattered or offended.

"Thank you, but Phil already took care of it."

Alfonso pulls off his black polo, exposing a jungle of chest hair and a tattoo of a Z on his upper arm. His muscled shoulders and torso belie the softness of his hands. He casually tosses the shirt on a nearby lounge chair and asks, "Who would like to swim with me?"

The table where the missionaries were seated has emptied, and Phil ambles over, unbuttoning his shirt, his gaunt, pasty back contrasting sharply with that of his host. He jumps in with a splash, sputters to the surface, and treads water until his breath returns. Alfonso dives in and surfaces near him. "Do you like to swim, Phil?"

"I'm not a swimmer." His eyes are already bloodshot from the chlorinated water.

"First thing in the morning it is as refreshing as coffee. I regularly swim when I don't visit the gym. I like to be comfortable in all the elements."

"Water is definitely not my element."

"Not a water sign? You must be earth, or perhaps fire. I know. I bet you are a Virgo." Amusement sparkles in Alfonso's eyes.

Phil grabs the edge of the pool and stares at Alfonso uncomprehending. Alfonso clarifies, "I am Aquarius."

Clueless regarding the astrological horoscope, Phil isn't sure how to answer. He turns to Justin and pulls him in the water. "Come on, son. Time to get wet. No use being at a pool party if you only sit on the sidelines."

"Come in, Katherine," Alfonso urges. "The water is pleasant."

She sheds her outer clothing and self-consciously drapes her skirt and blouse over a chair. With her arms folded across her middle, she hurries to the pool.

Alfonso and other men have their eyes riveted on her. She senses that attention and wonders how long it has been since she felt so desirable. She dives into the deep end of the pool and swims underwater toward her family. When she resurfaces, she pushes back her hair and finds herself facing Alfonso. Appreciation gleams in his hazel eyes. She feels the need to say something to break the silence. "The party is lovely. Thank you so much for inviting us."

Alfonso flashes white, even teeth, the kind familiar with years of orthodontia. "You must come more often. Do you need to use the computers? Think of this as your second home. I expect you will be here more often in the future?" He says the last sentence as though it were a question.

Katherine wavers between wariness and fascination. "You were away. We didn't want to be a bother."

He waves off the suggestion and edges closer. "I am home now."

She glances around to see if her family saw or heard the exchange. She stands in the water near the pool's edge, but Alfonso blocks the way to her kids and husband. Katherine wonders how she can politely escape. She thinks she hears Alfonso whisper, "You look fabulous." She can't be sure; maybe he just transmitted the thought.

A smile forms at the corners of his mouth. "Are you afraid of me, Katherine?"

Her expression must have given her away. "No, no. Of course not."

"You have the body of a swimmer. If I did not know better, I would think you never had children."

Her response catches in her throat. "I used to be on the high school swim team."

"Another reason for you to come more often. A beautiful pool like this and it gets so little use. A pity."

She doesn't say anything. If she's smart, she thinks, she'll stay far away from the villa and its mesmerizing owner. The spell is broken when Alfonso turns to Phil and slaps him on his pink speckled back. "You are a lucky man."

Phil has no idea what his landlord is referring to but decides to use the opportunity to spread the Word. "There is no such thing as luck. The Lord provides for all that trust in Him. Luck and fate lose their meaning within the context of God's provision and answer to prayer."

"I guess you would see it that way." Alfonso exits the pool and grabs a towel.

"Alfonso?" Katy interrupts from the pool's edge. "Why aren't Chomo, Rosa, and their kids here? Aren't they friends with Pancho?"

"I am unaware of any friendship between Pancho and the local youth." He studies the tables filled with guests as he considers his words. "This is a classist society, young Katherine. They would have been uncomfortable. They could not have politely refused the invitation, and it would be awkward for everyone. It was best not to invite them. People from the wealthier classes do not socialize with the poor. It would be gauche."

Katy's face contorts as she grapples with the words. She has a surprising vocabulary for her age, yet wonders if she understands him accurately. "But you work with poor people, and so does Daddy."

"It is a very different type of relationship."

Justin interrupts from the other side of his sister. "Hey, Mom, I'll race you to the end of the pool and back."

It's a close race, but Katherine lets him edge ahead.

She climbs from the pool and retreats to a partially shaded lounge chair while Alfonso and Phil rejoin the adults at the tables.

A thirteen-year-old with wavy brown hair and braces comes forward and introduces herself as Patsy. She invites Katy and Justin to toss an inflatable ball from one side of the pool to the other, while Katherine stretches out on her towel and shuts her eyes.

Patsy likes to practice her fluent English. The kids can barely squeeze a word in through all her chatter. "This is the third time I've been out here. I think Alfonso is the best! He's good friends with my parents and my brother is Pancho's best friend at school." She waves her arms toward the other children. "Most everyone here is from school or friends with Alfonso. How did you guys get invited? Where do you know him from?"

"We live down the road," Justin says, cautiously. She stares at him as though waiting for him to continue. "Our dad is a missionary."

A sandy-haired boy who looks about seventeen pushes himself through the water toward them. "Mormon missionaries?"

"No, we're Evangelicals."

"Really? I'm Rodrigo." He holds his hand out for Justin to shake. "Did you say you're Evangelical missionaries? That doesn't sound like the Alfonso I know. He's Catholic and I hear he's interested in Mayan religions. Not to be rude or anything, but why would Alfonso invite you?"

"He's our neighbor," Justin clarifies. "Our landlord."

Katy crosses her arms in a determined stance. "And our friend."

The boy stands with his feet apart in the water, as though

firmly anchored in reality. He regards the two of them, eyes narrowed in thought.

"Have you known Pancho long?" Justin asks to defuse the tension.

"Three years, I guess. I met him when he showed up at our school. After he became Alfonso's ward. You know, after his family was murdered."

THE BUFFET LUNCH is flown in from the capital and catered by the Westin. At five o'clock the guests gather their things to leave. Engines fire up, and wind from the rotors whips the pool into whitecaps. Tufts of cottony fog float up the mountainside.

"I guess we'd better be going too," Phil says reluctantly when Alfonso returns from escorting several people to their choppers.

"Do you not have something you wish to discuss with me?"

"It can wait. It's been a long day and we're all tired."

Alfonso motions for him to be patient. "Let me say goodbye to the remainder of my guests from the city. Then we may speak in private."

When the last person is gone, Alfonso returns and motions them inside.

"We'll stay out here and wait," Justin says. He and his sister have wrapped themselves in bright towels and hug their knees against the brisk air. Justin has Poppy off her perch and is stroking her underbelly with his finger.

Katherine opts to stay with her children by the poolside. She doesn't want to be associated with pecuniary supplications. Phil's business, not hers.

THE POPPY FIELD

PHIL FOLLOWS his host into the library, where tiers of shelving contain hundreds of volumes, and wonders briefly whether Alfonso is a reader, like Katherine, or one who studies texts, like his brother. He fancies that he isn't judgmental, but since he accepted the Lord Jesus as his savior, Phil concentrates his literary endeavors on the Bible and books related, anything else being a waste of his time.

Again, Phil is overcome by the villa's opulence as he admires the paintings (not prints!) hanging on the wall and the sculptures on the table. He tears his eyes from a full-figured nude about two feet tall, unsure whether to admire the lovely, simple lines or to be shocked by its nudity.

"It's lovely, isn't it?" Phil jumps at Alfonso's words. "There is nothing more beautiful than the female form."

Phil is unable to think of a comeback, so he remains silent.

"Have a seat." Alfonso indicates a crimson leather sofa and settles into a seat opposite. "What can I do for you?"

An unusual twinge of nervousness seeps into Phil as he ponders how to phrase the request. Though he's gone over a speech in his mind time and again, he wants to make sure he doesn't either ask for too much or for too little. He begins by giving a brief summary of his projects and explains the ultimate goal, to have a church in which the villagers can worship.

"A commendable project," Alfonso says. "How many people have you in your young congregation?"

"On an average Sunday, we have twenty to thirty adults, but when we have special events such as the Pentecostal service the community of worshippers doubles in size." He finds himself exaggerating the numbers but tells himself it isn't a lie, only a projection on where the young church is headed. "I believe we will grow if we are able to have a meeting house of our own, especially since the rainy season has arrived." He hopes Alfonso can

105

take a hint, that he can offer a permanent place or at least a piece of land, but his host patiently waits for him to state his business. "I was wondering, I would like to know," he stutters, "if you can section off a piece of land adjacent to our home for this project."

Alfonso raises his eyebrows. "Deed you a piece of property, you mean?" He cocks his head, waiting for Phil's response.

"Loan it to us. Lease it to us. We are a small body of believers, and the villagers have scarce money for offerings." Now Phil wishes he had exaggerated the congregation's numbers in the opposite direction. He squirms under Alfonso's steady gaze.

"Very well. I will let you use a piece of the property. You are not paying rent on the little house, so why would I make you pay rent on land for a church building? I will have an engineer draw up the plot that you may use."

"The members of the church will be most grateful. I will tell them of your generosity." Emboldened, he continues, "There is one more thing."

Alfonso waits, and, by the manner that his eyes move toward the door, Phil can tell he is becoming impatient. He decides to blurt out his last request. "We need money to build. I know you are not a believer, at least to our way of thinking," he adds quickly so he won't offend, "but you are an excellent person." He says it quickly, all the while with a sinking dread that he might offend; Alfonso might even cancel the initial agreement to loan the property.

He sighs deeply. "How much are we speaking of?"

Phil senses that Alfonso is tiring of him and wonders how much he should ask for. A partial sum, the minimum for building, or enough for a generous-sized church, one they could grow into?

He decides to be somewhat conservative. "Fifty thousand

quetzales." Enough for something basic. They can build onto it in the future.

Alfonso gets up. "Excuse me for a moment." He leaves the room, and Phil wonders whether he has offended. His palms begin to sweat, and he has an urge to get out of the chair and pace. He wills himself to relax, to control his breathing. He stretches his wrists, his ankles. Takes a deep breath. When he is about to return to his family in great disappointment, Alfonso returns with a bag. "This is what you want. Take it."

Phil glances into the bag to see packets of one-hundred-quetzal notes. Stacks of them.

"Fifty thousand. You are in luck. I have not had a chance to deposit this in the bank. It is easiest to work with cash when building. Everyone prefers it."

With a question in his eyes, Phil looks up, and Alfonso smiles back at him. "I believe in choices. I know you may not agree, but ... " He doesn't finish his thought and shrugs. "People are happiest when they have choices. Come next week with Katherine and we can plan the building. You should be able to start construction when the rains end."

Holding the bag of cash, Phil staggers out of the villa in a daze. Like a worn-out pair of jeans, the sky has faded from vibrant blue to gray with patches of white.

Katherine doesn't see Phil right away. She appears to be arguing with Poppy, who flaps her wings at her in anger.

"What's the fight about?" Phil asks. He leans over toward the parrot. "Hello, girl."

Katherine hugs her sweater to herself against the fog. "I guess she's not crazy about me."

They climb into the van, and Phil strains to see through the vaporous blanket cast over the ground. "It's a good thing those choppers left when they did. The visibility is terrible. Ten minutes later and they would have been grounded."

"I'm sure there's plenty of space at the villa for overnighters," Katherine says. "How did your petition go?"

"He is loaning us the property. He gave me the money I requested." He throws the sack to her. "I should have asked for more."

Katherine peeks into the bag. "What? Cash? Why would he have so much money lying around?"

"He hasn't made a bank deposit. We were lucky, because it's more convenient to use hard currency for construction projects. He would know."

Katherine's face shows disbelief. "Why, Phil? Why would he do this for us?"

"He says he believes in giving people choices."

"Choices? What on earth does he mean?"

"What does it matter? We get what we want, and in his own strange way, he gets what he wants. We shouldn't analyze too hard when the Lord is backing us. This is just another piece of evidence. Before long Alfonso himself will be attending our church."

"Phil, Poppy has wings but that doesn't make her an angel. Alfonso must have an agenda." She regrets her words when she sees his stricken face. She puts aside vocalizing her misgivings and attempts to support her husband. She stretches her arm across the seat to pat his shoulder. "I guess you're right. What could he possibly want from us? Maybe he does just want to help us out and give people 'choices,' whatever that means."

CHAPTER

TWELVE

L ater that evening, Katherine pulls out her sewing kit, wishing she had the Singer she'd left back in Indiana. Now she's down to a needle and thread. Tired of seeing her son in high-water trousers, she is finally getting around to lengthening them.

Phil wanders in and puts his arms around her. "Do you know what day today is?"

She looks up at him. "Of course, silly. It's Saturday."

"Tomorrow is our anniversary. Can you believe it's been sixteen years?"

Like most mothers, Katherine judges time by the growth and ages of her children, so, yes, looking down at her son's pants, she can believe it.

"I made reservations for the two of us at a hotel up in the Chuchumatanes for our anniversary. It's a three-hour drive from here."

She looks down at the pants and thinks about the clothes, the computer—hopefully—and the other necessities they will need to buy in the coming year. "Can we afford it?"

"Can we afford not to? We need to have some time away from the kids. How long has it been since we've been able to relax and enjoy each other's company without interruptions? This is the perfect opportunity."

She concedes. Maybe they can get back what they once had. She isn't sure it can happen, but she should make the effort. Her parents have been married for forty years, her in-laws almost as long. She never thought she might want to leave her husband and isn't ready to think their marriage is beyond hope. "What about the kids?"

"Rosa agreed to stay with them while we're gone. It's only for two nights."

THE NEXT MORNING, Phil follows her in to wake the children. "Time to get up. Rise and shine!" he bellows.

"Dad? Mom? What's the big deal? Why are you waking us so early?" Justin's voice croaks with sleep.

Phil's style is nothing like his wife's. She is a nurturer and is forever trying to keep the peace. Her morning wake-ups are quiet and allow the sleep-to-wake transition to happen slowly. She softens her husband's abruptness by sitting on her son's bed and stroking his hair. "It's a special day today."

Katy looks over from her pillow and rubs her eyes. "What's so special about it?"

"You mean besides it being the Lord's Day?" Phil puts his hands on Katherine's shoulders. "Today is our sixteenth wedding anniversary."

"Oh, okay. Happy anniversary." Katy turns over and pulls the covers over her head.

Justin leans on his elbows, his face creased by the pillow. "Yeah, congratulations. Can we go back to sleep now?"

"After church your mother and I are driving to a hotel in the mountains north of here to spend two nights. We'll be home before you know it on Tuesday morning."

"What about us?" Katy asks, suddenly awake. "Don't we get to go?"

"Doña Rosa has agreed to stay with you."

The covers fly off. "Can't we stay with Alfonso?"

Katherine frowns. "I know he said you're welcome at the villa, but your father and I think it best you stay here."

"We won't be any trouble. He's got lots of space and he won't even notice us. He likes us. I know he does."

Phil sees himself reflected in his daughter's enthusiasm. "Maybe another time, pancake. We spent almost the entire day there yesterday. You and Justin need to do some schoolwork."

"Sit with me, Daddy." Katy pats a place on her bed. "Tell us the story about how you were inspired to become a pastor."

Phil loves to talk about the time when he was young and confused. When God spoke to him, revealing his future. He smiles and his eyes crinkle at the corners. "You don't really want to hear that old tale again, do you?"

Justin shoots a look of annoyance at his sister. He doesn't want to hear it again, thank you. It's been told so many times that it's become a family legend (and joke). The family has listened to Phil's versions time and time again, ears tuned for the truth, but with each repetition, his stories grow into bigger versions of themselves. Katherine suspects he might believe the growing fabrication. Katy is the only one who will listen, but only if she wants a favor. Phil never catches on.

Phil's face lights up as he begins. "We were seventeen and planning to marry after graduation. I had just dropped off your mother and was on my way home when my cousin Barney waved me down. His parents were away, and he had friends over. My curfew was one, but it was only midnight. When you're young, an hour can seem like plenty of time.

"We stole some drinks from his father's bar. Remember, Justin, I'm not condoning the consumption of liquor or being sneaky. It's a lesson. When I glanced at my watch, I knew I was in trouble. You know how strict your grandfather is, and he was even worse back then. I was tipsy and driving fast. The next thing I remember is waking up in the hospital. Everything was white. I thought I'd died and gone to a snowy heaven."

"Tell us about the dream, Daddy." Katy looks at Justin, who is showing her the whites of his eyes. She suppresses a giggle. This is the part that varies according to Phil's mood and the message he wants to impart. "An angel came to me and told me I was to spread the word of the Lord, just like what the apostle Paul directed in the Bible. That's when I turned my life around. I took the exam to get into seminary and stopped drinking. Your mama and I were married soon after that."

He smiles a loving smile at Katherine, and she can't help but return it. She's glad he didn't mention the part about the angels with glowing swords who appeared at his bedside to heal him. She has some faith, but not that much.

"You see, the Lord has plans for me. For all of us." He tickles Katy until she doubles up in laughter. "And here we are. In Guatemala, doing God's work. It's all part of a grand heavenly scheme."

~

AFTER CHURCH SERVICE, Doña Rosa prepares the noon meal for the kids while their parents take care of final details.

Katherine stands over Justin and Katy. "Remember, I left lesson plans for the next few days."

"Do we really have to do schoolwork while you're gone?" Justin complains.

"You'll have plenty of time to get ahead since I won't be here bossing you around."

"That's some comfort," he grumbles, but he is happy to have a room to himself, even if it is only for two nights. Rosa will sleep on the couch, and he has dibs on his parents' bed.

Rosa pushes a small bag of snacks toward Katherine. "For the trip. Please take."

"You didn't need to, Rosa, but thank you. We're planning on having a late lunch along the way."

"The way is solo. No many places to eat."

After hugs and waves, they throw their bags in and start off. Soon the vehicle winds through jagged mountains. An occasional trickle of water flows down sheer, rock-faced precipices and across the road, where it picks up sand and other debris in its race to the canyon floor a thousand feet below.

At each blind curve, the horn's blare echoes off the cliffs. Katherine keeps her eyes riveted on the road. The drive is so frightening that her right foot reacts against an imaginary brake pedal every time she thinks they should slow down.

Along the roadside, children laden with firewood trudge toward stick-and-adobe homes. The urge to help hastens to the forefront of Katherine's thoughts, and she remembers how she had hoped to have projects in place by now. Where had that dream gone? Almost three months into their stay and she rarely leaves home except on market day.

"Maybe you should try a different approach to your ministry,

Phil. Help people with the day-to-day stuff. Hygiene and nutrition. Family planning and the importance of boiling water. I'd love to help, and there is so much we could teach them."

His jaw sets. "My job is to prepare people's hearts so they'll have a beautiful home in the afterlife."

What if there is no afterlife? Katherine thinks. What if it's only now? He knows how much she's been wanting to work with the villagers, yet it hasn't happened. She argues her point once again. "If you assisted them in other ways, they might be more receptive to the Lord's word."

"I know you feel that it's appropriate, and I never said you can't have projects of your own. In fact, I think it's an honorable thing to do, but don't get me involved. I've got enough on my plate."

AFTER AN HOUR'S drive on the desolate highway, an outdoor restaurant appears at a wide spot along the road.

"Finally," Katherine says. "I'm starved."

A covered patio furnished with a dozen plastic tables extends around the side and into the back of a small cement home. Though deserted, the place has an inviting appeal, possibly because it's the only *comedor* in the area and they're hungry. From the door, a thick-bodied indigenous woman makes her way down several steps, wiping her hands on a greasy apron.

"Pasen adelante."

They sit. She tosses down sticky menus that offer nothing they can translate into English. Katherine points to something on the menu and Phil to something else while they hope for the best.

Katherine watches the birds soar over the canyon. "It's so

quiet here. So isolated. We've hardly seen a half dozen cars since we turned onto the highway."

"This road is mostly used by locals, and few of them have vehicles."

They sit in companionable silence, the screeching of the hawks the only audible sound aside from a light kitchen clatter where their meal is being prepared. A few minutes later, the woman brings their plates on a tray. *Carne adobado*, Katherine's lunch, turns out to be a reddish-orange pork with a distinct vinegar flavor. Phil is served *revolcado*. Neither recognizes the meat. Phil decides that it is preferable not to know its origin. He eats out of hunger and a lifelong commitment to finishing whatever food is put in front of him. He pours on a hot chili sauce to tone down the flavor and gulps his drink.

Katherine gazes about. Just as she says, "I can't imagine they get many customers," a large vehicle with darkened windows pulls up alongside their van, and three burly men with guns at their waists get out. The waitress hustles beer and chips to their table, and their raucous laughter destroys the serenity of the setting. When Phil and Katherine finish, they pantomime writing in the air with an invisible pen to get her attention so they can pay and leave.

Another vehicle appears, and several men exit. One raises his eyebrows in greeting and nods slightly when he catches Katherine's eye.

"Ya era tiempo, Julio, hombre." The speaker points at his watch. Julio puts up a hand in warning, reaches into his pocket and punches some numbers into his cell phone. He glances at the missionaries once more before putting it to his ear.

Katherine feels his eyes on them as they depart. "Strange, isn't it?"

"What, dear?"

"Those men meeting at such an isolated spot. Wasn't the one who just arrived, the one called Julio, the same fellow that Alfonso greeted our first day in San Marcos?"

Phil shrugs. "Could be. It's a small country. And speaking of isolated spots, I'm taking you to one right now where, hopefully, we won't be disturbed." He winks. "It's been a long time since it's been just the two of us."

BY THE TIME they pull into the parking lot, the late afternoon sun is dropping below the surrounding mountains. Constructed of rough-hewn logs, the hotel has the familiar odor of moss and damp earth, like a garden after a rain shower. It clings to the side of a cliff and looks as though a minor tremor could shake it loose and send it crashing into the ravine below.

Plastic plants with hanging vines decorate the dim lobby, and trophies of goat-sized tropical deer hang on plank-pine walls. A stuffed jaguar crouches near a corner fireplace, and books and board games are stacked on the mantel. "This is kind of creepy," Katherine says.

He doesn't meet her eyes, doesn't want her to know it's all they can afford. "It's recommended for cozy getaways. The rooms should be fine."

Katherine is skeptical. To have driven all the way out here to stay somewhere sleazy?

The desk clerk registers them and gives them a single key attached to a wooden totem. He explains how to get to their room.

They exit the lobby and walk toward the back. Inside the room, two chairs surround a small table, and a swath of vibrant fabric hangs in a canopy above the double bed. Four-foot-tall rectangular windows face the mountainside opposite the hotel.

Katherine shivers at the isolation. It feels like not hours but worlds away from their children and everyday lives. Perhaps Phil is right. They do need to spend time alone. She begins to relax.

There is no entertainment besides an outdoor spa, but they haven't come all the way out here to watch TV. She finds herself listening for the familiar "Mom?" in the silence. Then Phil's phone rings.

"I should have turned it off," he grumbles. "Hello?" His face shows confusion and he collapses on the lumpy bed. "What are you doing there?"

Katherine scoots closer and puts her ear next to the phone.

Katy and Justin are at the villa.

"Doña Rosa's uncle was rushed to the hospital in another town," Justin says. "They couldn't take us with them, so they called Alfonso to have someone come pick us up."

A vague sense of unease settles over Katherine, and when Phil hands her the phone, she tries to speak calmly. "Don't worry about anything. We'll be back as soon as we can. I'd like to speak to Alfonso if you can pass him the phone."

"He and Pancho went out for a while, but they'll be back soon. Katy and I are watching a movie. You are the one who shouldn't worry. I just called to check in."

"Can you have him call me when he's back? Thanks, sweetie."

"Sure, Mom. Whatever."

Katherine hands the phone back to Phil and he plugs it into the wall to charge.

"I don't like it."

"Like what? What are you talking about?"

"I don't like that they're already at Alfonso's house and we've only just arrived."

"Katherine, be thankful there was a backup plan. Wait here. I've got a surprise for you." He gets up, car keys in hand, and heads for the door. A few minutes later, he returns with an ice-cold bottle of champagne and two fluted glasses. Phil realizes that their marriage is in a rut and after considerable soul searching has decided he needs to bend to keep things alive. He knows his wife has been unhappy and he spends too much time away. Often, the little things he tries to do backfire, like when he brought her starter plants for the garden; she saw it as him trying to keep her busy and too tired to complain. He was half-afraid of taking home the sack of fertilizer he found for sale in a nearby village.

She smiles. "Where did this come from?"

Pleased that she is responding to his efforts, he says, "Ha! I've still got a few surprises up my sleeve."

She attempts to refocus on their time together. When was the last time Phil had a drink? It must have been since before the accident. He even toasted with nonalcoholic champagne at their wedding. His stodginess at one time had felt solid and genuine to her, like a steady conviction, though lately it had only felt dull. A glass of champagne on an anniversary may seem like an ordinary thing to most people, but it strikes Katherine as a major stride in the right direction.

They open the door to the outside deck. The wind has settled to a steady breeze, and coppery clouds dance slowly overhead, struck with faint sunlight from the sinking sun.

Phil pops the cork and fills the glasses. "To my beautiful wife." He lifts his glass. "To the sixteen happiest years of my life."

Katherine loves Phil, of course she does, but she could never in all honesty make that kind of a statement. Of course, there have been good times. Times when they laughed together, laughed until they cried. The children, yes, the children. The children have been the best part of their time together. But there have also been difficult times, times when she wondered why she stayed with a man with such a singular vision of life. Those times have been a trial.

The champagne slides down, and Katherine's mind returns to her children. What are they doing in the villa right now? Are they safe? Despite her physical attraction to the mysterious neighbor, she suspects there is a sinister side to him as well. She has no proof, but isn't all that security enough to merit suspicion?

"Relax, Katherine." Phil watches her expression and knows her mind. He pours her another glass. "The kids are having a great time. Katy was dying to stay there, and Justin didn't sound too upset either."

Is it just coincidence, she wonders, that the children were lured to the villa as soon as they left? But as long as they're safe, there is nothing that can be done. She knows Alfonso will care for her kids as if they were his own. After all, he does seem to have an affinity for young people. Look at all he's done for Pancho without more than a scanty moral obligation.

"Check out this view." Phil gestures toward the craggy mountains. Katherine smiles, not because of the view, but because of his efforts to distract her. Hills and peaks, evenly spaced, ascend into the heavens. Dirt roads resembling animal trails crisscross the valley. From several huts, wisps of gray like smoke signals rise from cooking fires.

Katherine tries to put her worries aside. A few days alone with her husband might make a difference in a marriage that has begun to turn stale. "Let's take a walk before it gets too dark."

He takes her hand, leads her past the car and down a steep

staircase to a trail lined with whitewashed stones. Christmas lights, draped on wires, illuminate the pathway, and spongy earth cushions their feet as they make their way over roots and past outcroppings. When darkness falls and they can scarcely discern the trail, they return.

Dinner is served in a small dining area off the lobby. The only other guests are a young couple from Denmark with whom they exchange cordial nods. Afterward they relax in the Jacuzzi, drinks in hand. A sliver of moon hangs in the vast night sky, and the stars are crowded for space.

"Thank you, Phil. This is lovely."

They return to their room, wrapped in towels. Phil reaches for her, and she slips from his grasp, giggling like a girl half her age. "Come here, you!"

Resentment, disagreements, and the general busyness of their lives fall away, and they are again the two teenagers who fell in love all those years ago. What had Katherine been thinking when she noticed her eyes straying toward their neighbor? They make love gently and slowly like they had when life was easier, when it was just the two of them. Katherine snuggles into the warm nest of her husband's arms and whispers, "We need to do this more often."

The cell phone interrupts. Phil picks it up. "Hello. Yes, yes, and thank you very much. Here she is." He passes it to her.

She wonders who might be calling at this hour, so detached she feels from her life. "Hello?" The question in her eyes is answered when she hears Alfonso's velvety voice.

"Katherine, I am very sorry to disturb you at this late hour. I just returned home and Justin told me you wanted to speak with me."

She gathers her wits and replies coolly. "I just wanted to

thank you for having the kids over tonight. I hope they won't be a bother."

"It is my pleasure. I told you before that your family is welcome at the villa anytime. We have more than enough space."

"Phil and I will be there to pick them up midmorning tomorrow." She knows her reply sounds stiff but prefers it that way. She needs to keep her guard up around this man.

"As you wish."

THE NEXT MORNING, they rise early to pack. Phil's disappointment is palpable, and he tries everything to discourage their anticipated departure, especially since they'd made such progress improving their marital relations, but Katherine stands firm. Her dreams were haunted by frightening images of her children at their neighbor's house surrounded by men with automatic weapons.

The van pulls into the villa promptly at ten, and the kids are chatting at the poolside with their backpacks next to them. Katherine jumps out of the car when she sees them.

"Relax, Mom. It wasn't a big deal," Justin says as he scoots into the back seat. "You and Dad were supposed to stay another day and enjoy yourselves."

"Change of plans. I decided to come right back, and look how I find you. All alone!"

Justin shakes his head. How could they be alone when there are probably fifteen permanent employees at the villa?

Her relief at finding her children safe at Alfonso's is tempered only by her desire to see their neighbor again.

CHAPTER

THIRTEEN

"I don't know why you had to come back early. We were having fun at Alfonso's. You should see the room where I stayed. There are two beds, and not to share with Justin, but to have a girlfriend stay the night. They even had canopies!"

Katherine decides not to point out that there are no girlfriends here to visit. No one for either of the kids, unless you counted Pancho, and he didn't seem like the kind of boy Justin would ordinarily have chosen as a friend. "What about you, Justin? How was your stay?"

"My own room. So cool. And a bathroom I didn't have to share with anyone." Katy raises her hand and interjects that she had her own as well.

"What did you do?" Katherine asks.

"We watched movies with Pancho," Justin says, "and had dinner in the game room. Mom, they even have a game room. Alfonso has everything."

"Pancho tried to teach us how to play pool, but we weren't very good."

"He has a Wii," Justin adds. "He plays *Guitar Hero.*"

"Sounds like you two had a great time," Phil says, and glances at his wife. All that worrying for nothing. He and Katherine could have stayed another night, but he knows better than to cross her when the children are involved. Things between them had begun to improve. Another romantic night might have made all the difference.

"Yeah, you guys don't need to worry. Whenever you go somewhere, we prefer to stay at Alfonso's." Justin gives a thumbs-up. "Oh, I almost forgot, Pancho invited us to go horseback riding on Saturday. We can go, can't we?"

THE NEXT MORNING at the breakfast table, Katherine serves her husband coffee and sits across the table from him. "I've thought about what you said. I want to start going out with you to see what projects I can undertake."

"I'm going to Don Faustino's this morning. Why don't you come with me?"

Full of apologies, Rosa arrives at eight. "*Lo siento,* Hermana Caterina. I stay with Fofo and Catty as I tell you, then I go." She makes a gesture with her two palms facing up and brushes one over the other. "Someone call. They say my uncle—his heart—it was attacked." She puts her right hand on her chest and mimics a heart attack.

Katherine stifles a smile and reassures her. "It's okay, Rosa. You did the right thing. Is your uncle better now?"

Her face clouds with confusion. "When we get there, he

okay. Home with family, no hospital." She shrugs. "Un milagro. Por la bendita gracia de Dios."

Katherine's thoughts are interrupted by a shout from Phil. "Honey, let's go!" Phil calls from the van. "I can't wait all day."

"Okay, kids, we'll be back this afternoon and until then you're on your own. If you need anything, ask Doña Rosa."

It's a glorious morning. As the day warms, steam rises from the shrubbery; the previous night's raindrops glisten from every leaf and flower. Birds flit through trees and the forest ripples with song. Phil pauses several times, puts his binoculars to his eyes, and takes a feathered inventory. He calls his notebook the Backyard Bird Book, but the birds are not strictly in his backyard. "I'm up to sixty species, Katherine. We've only been here a few months, and I haven't even had time to devote to birding."

"Impressive," she says without enthusiasm. Birding bores her.

"If I'm lucky I'll have at least two hundred by the end of the year." He smiles to himself as he puts the pad away.

They turn off the path and wade through a trickling stream under the cover of massive tree ferns. Traversing a damp meadow, they stomp in mud-laden boots through fields of corn with meter-high stalks.

This man Phil's going to see, this Don Faustino, has been particularly receptive to God's word, and Phil considers him one of his successes.

"Hey, wait up." Katherine hurries to catch up from where she had stopped to tie her bootlaces.

He points toward an adobe hut that blends into the hillside. The hut's baked clay has melted away following years of torrential rains and scorching sun, and the stick framework of the house shows through like skeletal remains. Don Faustino resembles his home. A scarecrow of a man, with patchwork clothing, he looks up from where he sits under a tree, sharpening his machete. He wears a straw hat from which strands of peppered hair burst through. He bows with his hands clasped together. "Pastor Felipe, señora, pasen adelante."

He waves them through a rickety wooden gate toward a mango tree where weighty fruit dangles like heavy earrings. Katherine perches on an upended log and scrapes sticky clay from her boots.

After propping the machete and file near the door, Don Faustino enters the shack and brings out a Bible. Carefully taking the worn, dog-eared book from a plastic bag, he hands it over, his eyes gleaming with anticipation, and urges Phil to read a passage.

Phil turns to Katherine. "Don Faustino and his wife live here with their daughter. None are literate. The Bible is his prized possession. On my visits, I read from it and we discuss Scripture."

In an outdoor kitchen, a tiny woman works over a wood stove. A goiter on her neck bulges like an unformed limb, and her dress is threadbare and colorless from years of scrubbing on river rocks. Katherine rises and approaches Don Faustino's wife. In beginner's Spanish, she invites the woman to join in, but the tiny woman, with the high cheekbones and ready smile of Mayan women, shakes her head. Thinking the woman didn't understand her gringo accent, Katherine rephrases the invitation, but the woman puts up a hand to hide her face. Does she not speak Spanish, Katherine wonders, or is she embarrassed by the goiter?

Katherine returns to her stump, and Don Faustino's wife quickly brings over a rickety wooden chair and motions for her to sit. Then she continues preparing something over the fire, turning to her guest several times, unsure what to make of her company.

She concocts a coffee-like beverage from roasted corn, sweetens it with a block of unrefined sugar, and offers some to Katherine in a chipped pottery cup. She puts a hand in front of her mouth while she smiles, an effort to hide missing front teeth. Then she eases herself onto the stump and glances at Katherine shyly as they sip the hot brew.

Soon a lumpy girl with dull, slanted eyes lurches over. Her mouth hangs slack; an oversized tongue protrudes. Her mother pours her a mug of the hot drink and sits her down on a wooden bench that leans against the hut's wall. The girl mutters something in Mam, and the woman replies sternly. From her tone, Katherine surmises she is telling her not to be a bother.

Katherine points at herself. "Caterina." She asks their names in gestures.

"Catalina María Poyuk Xoj." The woman smiles at the similarity in their names and motions toward her daughter. "Madelena."

Catalina prepares *masa* for tortillas. She urges her guest to join her; she gives Katherine a ball of corn dough, and shows her how to pat it, turning it in a circular manner to keep it round. When the raw tortilla sticks to the palm of Katherine's hand and rips, they laugh. That which is so instinctive for one woman seems almost impossible for the other. For a moment, they have found a common ground, and differences in culture, language, and origin are temporarily forgotten.

Katherine places her misshapen creations next to the perfectly round ones on the clay platter, which rests over a wood fire. When several dozen are cooked, Catalina picks them off the *comal* with her heat-inured hands, wraps them in a ragged cloth, and puts them in a basket.

Madelena serves the men bowls of black bean broth along with the stack of tortillas. When they finish, she takes the dirty dishes to the *pila* and washes and dries them. Then the three sit down at a wobbly pine table, and Doña Catalina whispers something to her daughter, who closes her eyes tightly and puts her hands together. She mumbles a prayer and finishes with *amen*.

Katherine wants to help these people who haven't even enough bowls to feed more than three at a time. Where to start, where to start? She glances around the yard. A wheelbarrow and a shovel lean against the hut, along with a hoe and a half-empty bag of fertilizer, but there are no animals—no dogs, no chickens, no pigs rooting in the soil. "¿Animales?" she asks, and pantomimes a hen, using her arms to represent wings.

Catalina shakes her head sadly and shows her empty hands. When Katherine asks Phil to translate, he listens to Faustino and explains, "There was an epidemic, and all their layers died. They don't have the money to replace them."

Katherine thinks this might be the perfect place to initiate a project. Henrietta, the last of the hens given to them as welcoming gifts, can have a home where she is needed. Eggs will be an essential supplement to their diet, and the hen will be a special meal when she is too old to produce. She can bring a few chicks in the future. With enough poultry, they could start a small business, or at least improve their diet.

Phil explains their need to return home before the afternoon rains come. After patting their shoulders in farewell, Doña Catalina holds out a straw bag filled with mangoes and urges Katherine to take it.

Thunderclouds send them scurrying up the trail. They reach the van just as fat drops of rain begin to fall. By the time they settle inside, sheets of water slam against the van with such force that visibility drops and their vehicle shudders, making leaving impossible.

"What did you think of the family?" Phil asks as the rain eases.

"It's unfortunate their only child is mentally handicapped."

"They were unable to have children of their own and found Madelena abandoned as an infant. They took her in and raised her."

"Abandoned?" She looks out at the dirt road.

"Forsaken at a fork in the trail, wrapped in rags and placed in a basket."

"How strange it would be to watch your daughter grow up as a member of someone else's family. What a difficult decision that must have been." Katherine imagines the scenario: too many children and not enough food, burdened with a new member who would never be able to contribute her share. An infant rejected by necessity.

It is proof of God's goodness that the same child is a blessing and joy to another couple.

The rain lightens to a drizzle, and they clunk down the road and park in front of the house just as the second half of the storm sets in. Lightning flashes from the sky and driving rain pelts the van's roof like pebbles thrown by an enraged god. They wait in the car for the rain to cease and watch as Doña Rosa turns on the lights and goes through the house closing windows. The intensity of the storm increases until the thunder and crashing rain is all they hear.

CHAPTER

FOURTEEN

The next morning, the sky breaks into blue and white puzzle pieces, promising a warm, sunny day. Katherine makes pancakes for the kids and talks to them about working with the villagers. "I hope you won't mind being more independent."

"We'll be fine, Mom. I'm glad you have something of your own," Justin says without enthusiasm. He's happy for the extra freedom but isn't sure he wants others to have as much stake in his mother's time and energy as he and his sister do. "Remember that Pancho invited us to go riding on Saturday. So, ahem, don't make other plans."

Katherine nods absently. She hadn't remembered. Besides any possible danger, she worries about them getting too familiar with the neighbors. She glances at Phil for his input.

He reads doubt on her face. "Why not, Katherine?"

"To start, our daughter is wearing a cast, in case you haven't noticed. She won't be able to use the stirrup on that side and it might throw off her balance."

"Alfonso is not going to put the kids on spirited animals."

"Don't speak to me in that condescending tone. We have no idea what Alfonso may or may not do. We barely know the man, and that in itself is reason enough to decline the offer." Her feelings about their neighbor are mixed, and the thought of her children riding horseback through the mountains fills her with dread.

"What if there's a downpour?" she asks. "Can he be trusted?"

"Must I remind you that he's our landlord? He's been nothing but generous with us, and he's not going to put our kids in harm's way. While Katy and Justin are gone, the two of us can speak to him about plans for the construction of the church."

She had forgotten their commitment to talk to him and lowers her voice so the children can't hear. "He's helped us too much as it is. What's in it for him?"

"What do you mean, 'what's in it for him'? People could ask the same thing about us. The only thing that's 'in it' for us is God's love. Alfonso gifted us money for a church with no strings attached. That's good enough for me and it should be good enough for you. It's all to benefit God's kingdom."

Yes, it furthers God's kingdom, but who gets the credit for building the church in the end? She may not be able to change his mind, but that doesn't mean she shouldn't try. "I wonder about him and his money. Doesn't his lavish lifestyle and all the security seem suspicious?"

"He's a wealthy man. A local benefactor. Everyone I've spoken to respects him. What more do we need to know?"

"He must have an agenda."

"Does everyone have to have an agenda? We are the ones who should know that isn't true. Our agenda, like his, is helping others. He thinks everyone should have religious choices. This isn't about his backing one over the other."

"But you don't promote religious choice. You promote our way of worship. It's different."

"In the restaurant he said we weren't so different. We were all trying to help others."

"There's something else. Rosa said her uncle wasn't in the hospital at all. It was a false alarm, and next thing you know, the kids are over at the villa."

"What are you talking about? You make it sound like the kids were lured over with evil intent. Someone called in a prank and, given the circumstances, Rosa and Jerónimo made the best choice they could. Look at the kids. They're fine. They had a great time at the villa." He gestures toward the kitchen table where Justin is dealing cards. Katy glances over, her face a question.

"I mean, what if he's a drug kingpin?" There, she'd said it.

"Why would a drug lord fund a church?" Phil takes a deep breath. Alfonso's wealth does seem a bit much, but surely God has a hand in all of this. "Without money how can we build a church? Without a church, we'll never have a steady congregation, and if we don't have a congregation, what are we doing here?"

AFTER PARKING their car in the garage, they walk toward the mansion. Alfonso strides back and forth across the cemented area near the pool, arguing with someone on his cell phone. He gestures in anger with his free hand and barks out parting words, slips the phone back into his pocket, and adjusts his expression.

Tooled leather saddles straddle the backs of a roan mare and an Appaloosa as they await their young riders. Katherine assesses them, still apprehensive about letting Katy ride. The horses are superior to any she's been on, but one should err toward caution with unknown animals. She wonders if it's too late to change her mind.

Alfonso notes her concern. "You need not worry. I have selected the most docile animals for your children. Even if they do not ride well, the horses will follow Pancho's stallion."

Alfonso's authoritative manner demands compliance, and who is Katherine to doubt him? Even Pancho, surly teen that he is, would not purposely set out to anger his godfather. That's become obvious even in the short amount of time they've spent together.

Justin mounts the mare, and Phil helps Katy onto the Appaloosa. Her face is aglow with excitement. Alfonso gives them a refresher lesson in guiding and handling the horses.

Pancho grabs the reins of a mottled Spanish stallion and swings himself up with practiced ease as if born to the saddle.

Katherine's imagination dashes ahead. Why should she be sending her children on horseback into the remote mountains with Pancho, a young man only slightly older than Justin? Although Alfonso has assured her that Pancho is trustworthy, he appears anything but. Adding to her misgivings, she wonders why his parents were murdered, and what relationship those parents had with Alfonso.

She steps toward Katy's horse, ready to change her mind, when Alfonso motions toward her. "Please. Ride with your children. It will be much more enjoyable for you. Phil and I can talk finances while you are gone."

"Come with us, Mom," Katy urges.

She is baffled by their host's unfailing regard. He anticipates her desires before she can express them. When she looks to her husband for guidance, he shrugs as if to tell her to do whatever she wishes.

It's an easy decision. A discussion about money with Alfonso or a horseback ride in the hills with her children. Besides assuaging her worries, the latter sounds fun. A stable hand brings out a saddled horse for Katherine. She hadn't planned to ride and looks down at her ankle pants and sneakers. No matter. During the long summer days of her youth, she and her sister rode bareback, often in shorts, through fields and valleys back in Indiana. She wishes her children could experience some of that freedom, but such carefree times are in the past. Today's world, even in rural Indiana, is filled with danger. There's no way she could let her kids run free anywhere, least of all here.

She smiles a thanks as she mounts. The horse tosses its head and prances.

"She is spirited but gentle. Her name is Noblesa." Katherine pats the mare by way of introduction. Alfonso takes the lead rope and winds it into loops, which he attaches to the saddle. He puts his hand on her leg companionably and leaves it for a moment too long. Then he slaps the horse's flank and moves away.

Confused by the familiarity, she glances at Phil, who is oblivious to his landlord's attentions. She shakes her head in frustration. It has been said that the church is the bride of Christ, but there are times when she feels that the church might as well be the bride of Phil. She would like a little of his attention as well. As his wife, isn't she at least entitled to that?

But maybe her life will change for the better soon. The visit to Faustino's has only served to whet her appetite, to give her a taste of what life might be like if she threw herself into development work. Phil told her that Alfonso has ongoing projects including rural health centers and has been making improvements to the local school. Perhaps she can assist in some way—at least with Alfonso involved, funding won't be a problem.

～

PANCHO'S STALLION leads them down a dirt path toward a side gate. The trail widens, and Katherine moves up alongside the young man. "You seem very comfortable on horseback. Do you often ride?"

"Yeah, I like to ride. At the end of the school year, Alfonso takes me out with him. Says I'm apprenticing. The farmers he works with reside way out in the sticks. When there's no road, we go on horses. When it's too far away, we stay the night."

"Really?" Justin asks. "Camping?"

"Whatever," he says dismissively. "We take a tent, but people live there. We don't go inside. The houses are like caves. Talk to them in the yard or in the field while we look at their crops."

"They live in caves. That's really cool." His voice implies that he would love an invitation to join them in the future.

"Don't think they're cooler than they are. They aren't really caves. They're adobe shacks with tin roofs, but they might as well be. All dark and creepy inside. Wood smoke, fleas, and lice. Bats at night."

Katherine drops back so the boys can chat, but not so far back that she can't eavesdrop. Pancho's disrespectful attitude toward the poor irritates her. Although Pancho is not much older than Justin, he has a maturity beyond his years.

When the trail along the forested hillside narrows, they ride single file. Suddenly, Katy cries, "Look! Mom! Justin!" She points to the hilltop above. It is the place they saw the day she fell and sprained her ankle. From this viewpoint, partially excavated pyramids, still garbed in earth and weeds, are silhouetted against the morning sky.

When they reach the trail, they tie the horses to a tree and start toward the ruins. Justin races to the top, but Pancho and Katherine stay by Katy to assist her as she limps along the stony path.

Guarding the entrance are several stone sentinels. Pancho leans against a nearby mound and watches while Katy and Katherine struggle to regain their breath after the steep hike. "The altitude wears ya out if you aren't used to it," he drawls. Lost in thought, he gazes down at the valley below. "We're at nine thousand feet. Brought the altimeter once, just to check. Oxygen's gonna be a little thin at this elevation."

Justin sits on stone steps and turns to his mother and sister. "I told you there were Mayan ruins up here." He faces Pancho. "Was this a city?"

"Alfonso thinks it was a holy area. A power place where special ceremonies were performed. The highest center of Mayan life or some crap like that. No one really knows. But they did astronomy here. Dates from the calendar past, present, and future. It's all in the construction of the temples, the way the light enters through temple windows, falls on rocks or whatever. They were probably some kind of astronomy monks." He kicks at a rock as though somehow embarrassed by his knowledge. "Villagers have always used this area for prayer and festivals."

Katherine once again finds herself wondering about Pancho's family. Is he originally from here? "Are the ruins being restored?" She gazes at a place where someone has scraped soil and brush from the original structures.

"That's Alfonso's project."

What kind of project? she wants to know, but Pancho doesn't elaborate and she doesn't ask.

"It's not a known site, is it?" Justin asks. "I looked them up before we came and didn't see any ruins in this area."

"There are plenty of ancient landmarks around that aren't officially on the maps. Cuts down on looting." He stares ahead. "Maybe you'd better not mention that I brought you."

Poking around, Katherine sees three pyramids hidden by brush. A fourth is still hidden beneath the soil. Certainly no one would stumble upon this place by accident, and yet, clearly, it is still in use. Melted wax from colored candles coats nearby rocks and suggests an altar. There are rose, scarlet, and white flower petals. Also, pine needles and ashes. Feathers are scattered on the ground. "Do you come here often?" Katherine asks.

"Alfonso comes once or twice a week. I join him when I'm home. We meet farmers here. Discuss agricultural practices. Pray for good crops."

Prayers at the Mayan ruins? If Phil thinks the Catholic church is bad, Katherine shudders to think what his opinion of this will be.

"But isn't Alfonso a Catholic?" Katy asks.

"Sure, and so are most Mayans." Pancho's tone indicates that, at least in his mind, one would not necessarily preclude the other.

The tiring climb has made them hungry, and they break out Katherine's sandwiches. "It must be awesome going back and forth to school by helicopter," Justin says, his underlying tone indicating a mixture of envy and admiration.

"It's kind of a drag. I leave Monday morning and come back Friday afternoon. I get to stay for the weekend some-times. Alfonso lets me if he's in the city, or if he happens to be out of the country. It's not like I'm there alone. There're all kinds of other people. Hired help. Maids, a cook, a gardener, a chauffeur. Alfonso makes me come back either Friday afternoon or Saturday morning. He's training me to take over the business."

Katherine wonders if the boy chose the wrong word—probably Alfonso is teaching him how to help the farmers—but she refrains from putting her young host on the spot.

They start back to the spot where the horses are tied, then make their way down the trail. How silly she had been, a worry-wart and all for nothing. Pancho hadn't taken any risks, and he'd brought them safely back to the pool.

The men are seated at an outdoor table, conversing companionably.

Alfonso takes the reins from Katy. "How was the ride, young Katherine?"

"Wonderful! Thank you for loaning us horses." She beams at him, her dimples mirrored apostrophes.

"You are most welcome."

Phil approaches Katherine, pets the mare's velvety muzzle, and holds the reins while she dismounts. "How was it, where did you go?"

Pancho speaks up. "We rode up and down trails in the hills. Found a scenic place to eat lunch. The sandwiches Mrs. White-hall brought were delicious."

"You should have seen the incredible view!" Katy says and winks at her mother.

Alfonso sweeps his arm in the direction of the pool. "We have prepared refreshments for you."

Pancho feigns an excuse about a school project and leaves. A house servant appears at the sliding door and signals Alfonso. "Excuse me," he says. "There is something I must attend to."

Phil slips into step with Katherine. "Alfonso had a plan drawn up. We are going to build a modest church that will comfortably seat forty."

"Did he say anything else, dear?" She isn't sure exactly what she's fishing for but would like some clue as to his motive.

Phil shakes his head absentmindedly. "Wouldn't it be strange to have so much money that decisions like this could be made in an instant? What would you spend money on if the cost weren't an issue?"

She isn't sure what her answer would be, but the fact that Phil even voices the question disturbs her and makes her wonder what he is thinking. If it were her money, she wouldn't be spending it on a church. Not when there is so much other need.

CHAPTER

FIFTEEN

The aroma of roast beef wafts out the open window next to where Justin and Katy are playing hacky sack. Justin peeks in. "Smells delicious. What's the occasion?"

The occasion is their three-month anniversary in Guatemala, and Katherine believes it deserves celebration. It was the goal they had agreed on, but she no longer yearns for the American Midwest and has begun to feel that her missionary life has value: homeschooling the children, running the household, and her charitable projects. Her face has taken on a glow of satisfaction for a small triumph she doesn't wish to discuss.

"I hope you aren't celebrating the anniversary of our arrival," Justin says, divining her expression. "Because that's nothing to celebrate." She gives him a warning look, which he pointedly ignores. "I don't know why I listened to you guys. I should have stayed with Grandpa. I could be going to football games with my high school and playing on the baseball team." He makes a face.

"I could be doing almost anything back home, but, no, here I am, trying to keep from being bored."

"Justin, that's enough," his mother interrupts. "You listened to us because we're your parents, and as part of this family, you are obliged to stay with us."

Phil puts his paper aside. "You'll look back in years to come and remember this as a valuable experience."

"Yeah, right."

Phil picks up the paper again, signaling that the discussion is over.

LATER THAT EVENING, a rapping at the door interrupts family prayer time. "Hang on, hang on," Phil stumbles to the door.

An angular-faced Mayan in his late teens stands at their doorstep. Large, damp eyes look out from a face furrowed with worry. He shifts his weight from one foot to the other. When he sees Phil, he hesitates. "Pastor Felipe?"

"Come in, come in," Phil urges, recognizing him as Pedro Tomas, a member of his fledgling congregation. Pedro steps through the doorway and hesitates, mumbling that he doesn't wish to interrupt.

"Pase, por favor." Phil swings his arms inward.

Katherine herds the children to their room and follows them in. "You kids really need to straighten this up," she says when she closes the door and leans back against it.

"Mom, it's too small. I have no space," Katy whines.

Justin has used pebbles to divide their area and has taken the larger portion. "Do you really think this is necessary?" Katherine asks her son, pointing to the size difference.

"I'm older. It's my privilege to have more space. Geez, I have to share with a twelve-year-old, and not just that, but with a girl. Guys my age need privacy."

"Tell him to move the line, Mom. It isn't fair."

"Just clean up the mess. I'm going to take the dirty dishes out to the *pila*."

When she slips into the kitchen, the visitor is getting up to leave. "Por favor, Pastor. Solo usted nos puede ayudar."

After locking the front door, Phil collapses onto a chair, head in hands. To Katherine, it isn't clear whether he's praying, unhappy, or perhaps both. "What's going on? Why did Pedro Tomas come at such a late hour?"

Phil lifts his head in anguish. "His sister, María Victoria, has been sick, and now she's taken a turn for the worse. His parents sent him to fetch me so I can pray for her. They think I am the only one who can help."

"Haven't they been to a doctor?"

Phil shrugs. "It's one of those superstitious things. They told me that she took a fright one afternoon when a neighbor's cow confronted her on the trail coming home from school, and that's what started this illness. Frankly, I thought it was psychosomatic. Since they haven't mentioned her lately, I figured she had gotten better."

Katherine stares at him. What kind of ignorant people would believe a story like that? They've depended too much on faith and not enough on medicine. "Perhaps you should take her to the hospital. He only left a few minutes ago. You can still catch up."

Phil glances out at the darkening sky without even a moon to help light the way. Then he checks his watch. "It's already late and the trail is steep and dangerous. If the girl can't walk, we'll never get her out in the dark." He stares at the door as though deciding. "I'll pray for her and hike out there first thing in the morning."

"I'll go with you."

~

KATHERINE FILLS two backpacks with food, water, and a first aid kit. They leave the car at a trailhead and hike for almost an hour up a steep, narrow trail. Phil is so lost in thought that neither the surrounding beauty nor the tapping of a woodpecker rouses his interest.

A small hut appears on the hillside just beyond a cornfield. Hungry dogs surround them, barking their distrust.

"¡Chuchos, chuchos! ¡Callense!" The canines slump in retreat as a woman appears and rushes them into a windowless room. Light squeezes through chinks in the mud walls, and a ragged curtain separates the room from the rest of the house. Nine-year-old María Victoria thrashes about in delirium under a woolen blanket. The skin is stretched taut over her bloated face and body, and she gasps for breath. The family looks to Phil in awe as though he is a renowned physician or a miracle worker. Their last hope. "She was like this all night. I don't know how much longer she can hold out. Pray for her, Pastor," the girl's mother pleads in Spanish.

Katherine searches her husband's eyes. "She needs to be in a hospital."

Phil tries to hide his shock. He never expected to find the child this ill. "I'd be the first to take her there, but she'd die before we even got to the van. Look at her."

Perhaps the family is right, Katherine reasons. Prayer might be the only hope at this point, and a tenuous one at best.

She balances on a wooden stool at the girl's bedside in the

crowded room and watches as her husband lays his hands on her and prays. All the while she thinks how this might have been prevented. Hadn't Phil said she'd been ill for months?

Phil supplicates the Lord on her behalf, but it's too late. She heaves her last breath not long after they arrive.

He feels like he's been exposed as a phony, though he never advertised himself as a miracle worker. Amazing things have happened when he's called on the Lord, but this brings all his successes into doubt. Perhaps the Lord doesn't work through him after all. No, that couldn't be the case. All one really needs is faith.

"It isn't your fault," the father says to Phil as though divining his thoughts. "It must be God's will."

He doesn't know what to say. His singular trust has been challenged over and over since he's been in Guatemala, and he wants to believe this is another test. Somehow, in some way, her father must be right. María Victoria's death must be part of God's divine plan.

The father's comment about God's will angers Katherine. Phil doesn't actually believe that, does he? She leads him to one side. "We could have taken her to the hospital earlier."

"I had no idea, Katherine. Don't you think I would have taken her myself had I known?"

Katherine knows he speaks the truth but can't let go of her anger. "This is inexcusable. Isn't there a health center nearby?"

"Alfonso donates medicine to a small clinic where a nurse works during the week. The only other option is a private doctor or the national hospital where we took Katy."

"Did you suggest the hospital?"

"It's been over a month since I was here last. How could I have known how ill she was? I'm a pastor, not a doctor or a psychic."

She stares at him and narrows her eyes. He should have followed up.

Katherine bears her own guilt. Not a personal guilt, but a general guilt. Why did her family have easy access to a hospital and medical care when Katy's ankle was sprained, yet this child, seriously ill, went without any medical attention at all?

WOMEN from the family wash the child's body and dress her. The distraught mother weeps and wails toward heaven, pleading with an invisible God, one who has forsaken her. A neighbor pats her shoulder, embraces her, and leads her to a chair.

Don Emiliano approaches Phil. "Please stay. María Victoria was our only daughter and a believer. She deserves a Christian burial. It will be a great consolation to us, especially to my wife."

Phil and Katherine consent. At least they can comfort the living.

Katherine calls Doña Rosa and tells her what happened. "Can you stay with Katy and Justin, please?"

"Doña Caterina, I have my own *niños. No se preocupe.* They can go to the villa."

To the villa? When she agreed to join Phil on this visit, she never considered they might have to stay the night, but it is too late to object. The decision seems to be out of her hands. "Do what you think best," she says.

Family members and neighbors arrive throughout the day. Dark shawls conceal the women's bright *huipiles.* The men mumble to each other, bewildered by a God who won't heal a nine-year-old. Why would God take a half-grown child?

The villagers converse in Mam and, through gestures and limited Spanish, politely offer coffee and broth to the missionaries. Katherine attempts to comfort the weeping mother. With her arms around the woman, sympathetic tears well in her eyes as she contemplates the pain she would feel if something happened to Katy.

A dozen women stuff squares of *masa* with pork sauce, wrap them in banana leaves, and then drop them into boiling water in a soot-encrusted pot hanging over a pinewood fire.

As the endless night unfolds, Katherine loses track of time. Her thoughts are like a whirlpool in which she could easily drown. She wonders about their calling to missions. What kind of difference are they really making? Here was a child they could have helped and didn't, while Katherine's only tangible project is a laying hen and a few chicks. How much can they expect to do?

Phil scoots beside her on the wooden bench. "Death is always painful."

"She was just a child. They were counting on you to heal her."

"Don't put this on me."

"They thought you could perform miracles. You fostered that hope."

Phil gets up to join the others. "God can perform miracles, Katherine. You know that and you've witnessed it. I never take the credit."

"What if they didn't go to a doctor because they thought you could save her through prayer?" she calls after him.

At her words, he stops and turns. He's sick of her doubts and blinded by grief. "Look, Katherine, if God had wanted to heal her, it would have happened. It wasn't God's will, okay? We don't understand how it works, but the Lord is in charge." At least, that's what he'd preached. But is Katherine right? Did his sermons contribute to this innocent child's death? He shudders at the thought. Maybe he is too focused on building his church, too selfish to think of the most important thing—the people themselves. He spins around and heads for the door. He must calm his mind and find somewhere private to pray.

"And who are you to say what God's will is?" Katherine shouts to his retreating back. "Maybe it was his will for you to take her to the hospital."

CHAPTER
SIXTEEN

"Yusti! Catty! *¡Vengan!*" Doña Rosa calls.

"Let's see what she wants." Katy is anxious for a distraction. She throws her schoolwork aside and gets up.

Justin tips his chair and stretches his legs. He's not about to race over. He drags out the time, pushes back his math papers, and gets to his feet. Just as he begins to concentrate on his studies, something invariably comes along to throw him off track, but he doesn't think his mother will take that for an excuse. He must have his work done by the time she returns.

Doña Rosa has been scrubbing their clothes on the washboard surface of the *pila,* and a pile of soaking garments drowns in a plastic tub. She takes each piece, wrings it, shakes out the wrinkles, and hangs it on the line. She takes her time as she lifts the last piece of laundry, keeping the kids in suspense.

"We're here," Katy says, thinking that Doña Rosa must have forgotten about them.

Doña Rosa turns. "Your *papás* come tomorrow. Chato come for you now. Take you to the villa. I call him."

"Tomorrow?" Justin asks. Why would their parents stay the night out in the *campo*?

"Now?" Katy says.

"What happened?" Justin asks, knowing full well his mother would never allow them to stay at Alfonso's if she had a choice in the matter.

"Someone died." Rosa turns her back and punches some numbers into her cell phone.

Justin hopes it isn't anyone he knows. Like many young people, he is shocked by life's impermanence. He knocks on the wooden table superstitiously.

Katy skips toward the house. "We get to go to the villa! We get to go to the villa!" Her eyes sparkle. "Isn't it lucky we get to go to Alfonso's again?"

"I don't know. I guess it isn't lucky for whoever died."

By the time they get a few items together, Chato arrives in a white Range Rover. They say their goodbyes to Doña Rosa. She grabs their faces and kisses each cheek. Justin pulls away with a disgusted expression; Katy tolerates the show of affection. "*Mijitos*, behave," Rosa commands as they climb into the back seat and roll down a window to wave.

The vehicle pulls out of the driveway but heads away from the villa.

"Wait. Where are we going?" Justin cries.

Chato glances in the rearview mirror, his eyes cold and unfriendly. "I have business." He puts a CD in the slot in the dashboard, and Latin music blasts forth like the heralding of war. Then the music turns whiny, and the singer wails about misfortunes, broken hearts, and untrue women.

Justin shakes his head at Chato's taste in music, but it beats an awkward silence.

The vehicle turns onto an unfamiliar dirt road flanked by zinc and stick hovels. Skeletal dogs search for morsels in roadside garbage, and wastewater drains into the street. Chato jerks the steering wheel back and forth to avoid ruts, and the two in the back are tossed about like rag dolls. When the vehicle comes to an abrupt stop, they are thrown forward.

Chato gets out, glances back, and then locks the doors. They watch as he picks his way along the street and disappears into one of the huts. "He'd better come back," Katy says.

"Of course he will. He won't dare leave the car in this neighborhood for long, or it'll be in pieces and ready for the chop shop when he gets back."

Polarized windows keep the inside from getting too hot, and the kids play rock-paper-scissors while they wait. Suddenly, the car lurches as a couple of ruffians lean against it.

The kids duck down as a guy with dark-stained teeth stares at his reflection in the window and smooths back his greasy hair. His buddy has oozing zits. The two of them poke each other and call out to young women passing by.

"Eww, Justin. They're despicable."

"Contemptible."

"Loathsome."

"Disgusting."

She can't think of another good word and neither can he.

A teenage girl lugging a bucket of water and wearing cheap rubber flip-flops slogs through the muck in the street.

"Chi-chi-chi," the man with the stained teeth hisses. He throws his smoke down and approaches her. "¿Que tal, mi amor?"

She looks down at the ground and hurries past, but he grabs

her. She twists away and runs, leaving the bucket overturned and the water spilling into the gutter.

The guys congratulate each other with high-fives.

By now Katy is hunched down on the floorboards while Justin scans the area for Chato. He sees him standing in a nearby doorway with a wizened woman, who calls out to him as he leaves. Justin doesn't understand the words, but they sound like something a woman might say to her son.

"*Oye*, Chato," a thug taunts. "Why you such a mean man with your little mama?"

Chato threatens them with a hoarse growl, and they back away from the car, arms raised in the universal sign of surrender. Justin and Katy wouldn't be at all surprised if Chato took out his sidearm and shot them. Who could know what Chato is capable of doing?

He opens the door, checks to make sure the two are still in the back, and gets in.

"*¿Una propina?*" One of the toughs holds out his hand to the window for a tip. "We took care of the car."

Chato ignores them and starts the Range Rover, and they bounce out of the alleyway.

Justin leans over the seat. "Are we going to the villa now?" He regrets the words as soon as they are out of his mouth. Scary Chato's lip turns down in a sneer, and Justin collapses back onto the seat.

A half hour later, armed guards motion them through the gate, and they are deposited at the front door. Justin follows Katy to her room and plops down on the second bed.

Sun rays glint through the window and dance over the walls. On the other side of the stables, the brilliance reflects off the zinc rooftops of several single-story structures, illumining them as if God himself were pointing them out. Justin hadn't noticed them before, and Alfonso didn't point out those buildings when they toured the property. Curious, he decides to wander over later and check them out.

It's already mid-afternoon and the kids haven't had lunch. Guided by the smells of cooking food, they venture downstairs to look for something to eat. Swinging doors open to a spacious kitchen where an indigenous woman of indeterminate age chops vegetables and occasionally stirs a pot on a gleaming stainless-steel stove. The housekeeper is putting groceries away. A man— either a guard or a gardener—leans against one of the several refrigerators and chats with her. Another woman slaps out tortillas on a corner grill. The hired help appear relaxed and comfortable in this area. Justin clears his throat to get someone's attention and then calls out. "Buenas tardes."

The housekeeper straightens and brushes off her apron; a flash of irritation crosses her face. "¿Necesitan algo?"

The word for hunger in Spanish evades him so he pantomimes his request. She picks two bananas from a bunch and hands them over, then she points at a container of luscious fruit. "Mango?"

He nods. She peels and cuts them up. The kids thank her, take their bowls out to the pool, and take seats beneath a green umbrella.

Poppy flies over and perches on an empty chair-back. She cocks her head and watches them eat the way a dog might watch his human family eat a steak dinner. When Justin has only a small piece of mango and a bite of banana left, Poppy springs off the chair and lands near his plate. She attacks the fruit vigorously, and then she climbs up Justin's arm and settles on his shoulder. With her beak, she pulls a strand of his hair and licks it with her tongue. He puts her back on her perch.

Sunlight dapples through surrounding foliage, and the sky is a glowing sapphire. Justin stretches and rests his feet on a nearby chair. The cook brings sandwiches and drinks.

"I wish we lived here," Katy says. "Pancho is so lucky."

"Wish away, little sister. We don't. Besides, you don't know anything about Pancho's luck. Nothing at all." Justin sounds harsher than he means to, but he knows Pancho is an orphan and he can't imagine how it might feel if he didn't have his parents in his life. In a mature flash of insight, he is aware of the temptations of living in a place like the villa. He remembers his earlier mission and changes the subject. "Do you want to walk over to the stables with me?"

Katy shakes her head and raises her injured foot. Justin shrugs. He was just trying to be polite.

He stops by the stables on his way to the unknown buildings, and the earthy smells of fresh straw remind him of his grandparents' farm. His heart aches for home. Why did his father have to take them so far away?

The top sections of the wooden slat doors are partially open, and a small plaque identifies the Appaloosa mare. She sticks her head out in expectation of a greeting. "Hello there, Reina."

She nickers softly. Justin strokes her silky muzzle and breathes in her comforting, horsey odor. The only friend he's made so far.

A grimy boy in ragged clothes appears. He stares with his head cocked to one side. The groom's son. With downcast eyes, he motions Justin forward to another stall to see a foal nursing.

Justin leaves the stables and heads down a well-traveled dirt road, which leads away from the villa and curves through a small forested area toward the buildings he saw earlier from Katy's window. As he gets closer, the groom's son races up, shaking his head in warning. Justin understands that he must be heading toward a forbidden place. Curiosity forces him onward. He steps behind a pine tree and peers out.

A door opens. Several men with Guatemalan features— short, dark, and slightly paunchy—exit, look around furtively, and stroll to nearby motorcycles, where they say their goodbyes. The last man out secures a padlock on the door. It looks to Justin like the end of their workday. He waits until the coast is clear and approaches a window. It's too high for him to see into, so he spots a nearby crate and steps on it so he can see inside. Large vats like he saw at a dairy on a school field trip line one wall, and there are ovens on another. Now he's really curious. Is this some kind of agricultural research? Perhaps they're perfecting a new kind of fertilizer. Maybe they need to keep their work under wraps until their inventions are patented, which may or may not make sense, he thinks. Then again, he's seen in movies how companies often spy on rival companies. Maybe that is the reason Alfonso has so much money. Justin knows he's letting his imagination run wild. Probably the buildings aren't secret at all and have some mundane purpose. Still ....

He wonders whether he should mention the vats and his suppositions about the lab to his parents but decides not to. They would just tell him to quit poking around in Alfonso's affairs and mind his own business.

Any doubt about the secretive nature of the buildings is cleared up when Chato appears at his side, glaring fiercely. "What the fuck you doing here? This ain't your goddamn business." He turns abruptly and storms off, muttering just loud enough for Justin to hear, "Damn kids. Stickin' their noses where they don't belong."

Heart pounding, Justin hurries back to his sister. He intends to find out just what goes on in those mysterious buildings when Alfonso's manager, or whoever that guy is, isn't around—if there is such a time. He is about to tell his sister what happened when she puts up her hand and shushes him. "Listen. Someone's here."

The Hummer pulls into the parking area and Alfonso strolls over. "Justin, young Katherine, what a pleasant surprise." He glances around as though hoping to see someone else.

"Didn't Doña Rosa tell you?" Justin asks, though it's obvious she hasn't. "Mom and Dad are staying the night in the *campo,* so Rosa called Chato and asked him to bring us."

Alfonso smooths over his initial confusion with a slight nod. "I have given instructions to always make you welcome when you come. Pancho is in the city today, but make yourselves at home."

In the rec room, Katy parks herself in front of a fifty-inch, flat-screen TV. "Do you want to watch a movie?"

"Nah. You go ahead." He picks up the Wii guitar.

Alfonso appears with Poppy perched on his shoulder. "How are my two favorite guests? Is everything okay?"

Katy beams at him. "Perfect."

Poppy climbs down his arm and onto his finger. "Would you like to hold her, Justin? She seems to be partial to you."

Poppy hops onto Justin's finger and lets him stroke her chest. Begging for a caress, she presses her head against his hand, reminding him of the cat they left with Aunt Rose.

He hands her back and picks up the plastic guitar.

Alfonso watches him thoughtfully. "Do you play any musical instruments?"

"I took piano for years. Trombone, too." Justin remembers all the years of tortured practice and his relief that they didn't have to bring their instruments to Central America. "Katy plays the flute." He looks down. "My father used to have a guitar, but he doesn't play anymore." After the words had left his mouth, Justin was immediately remorseful. Why blurt that out? What did Alfonso care?

"Why not?"

"It's a long story. He ended up selling it. Maybe he'll take it up again some time." His father played in a rock band when he was young, before his call to ministry. When his guitar was damaged in the accident, he decided it was a sign that he should give up that kind of music. God gave his life for mankind, so at least Phil could give up his guitar for God. Justin always thought the reasoning was strange, but that was his dad. Once he got an idea in his head, who could reason with him?

Katy gazes at their host with innocent eyes. "Why do you always wear black, Alfonso?"

"It is my favorite color." He smiles and winks. "Does it make it too obvious that I am a villain?" Katy crinkles her eyes in appreciation of his wit, but Justin is not amused. There is something very strange going on at the villa, and he intends to find out what it is.

CHAPTER

SEVENTEEN

Ever since their horseback trip, Justin can't stop thinking
of the nearby Mayan ruins. The candles, the feathers,
the secret ceremonies. His parents warned him not to
go off without permission and especially not alone, but he figures
what they don't know can't hurt them. One morning when his
parents are away and Doña Rosa has not yet arrived, he seizes
the opportunity and asks his sister to make excuses for his
absence.

"Where are you going?" she asks.

"Back to the ruins."

"Why?"

"To see if I can find another carving."

"Mom and Dad won't be happy if they find out."

"Are you going to snitch?"

She shakes her head solemnly. Of course not.

It's worth the risk. With nothing else to look forward to, he
welcomes the thought of a little intrigue. How could they punish
him anyway? No television? No computer?

"What do you want me to say if they come home? What if something happens?" Katy faces her brother, hands on hips, like a miniature Katherine.

"Nothing will happen. I'll take the cell phone. Tell Rosa I went out for a walk, tell her I went to look something up on the computer at the villa, tell her whatever you want. Maybe she won't even notice I'm gone."

He slips out the back door and finds his way to the trail. He slides down the steep hillside at the shortcut, the one where Katy fell, knowing he should be especially careful but feeling reckless. His cell phone beeps about halfway down the hill, advising him a text has arrived. "R is here."

He crosses the valley and scrambles up the hill, pushing through brush and around gnarled trees. His heart sprints as he reaches the top. Excavating tools peek out from under a blue tarp near one of the pyramids, but little work appears to have been done since the previous week.

A branch snaps and gravel crunches. Justin jumps. He instinctively hides in some brush behind one of the temples. Blood pounds in his ears. Two men carrying machetes trudge up the hillside and sit down on ancient stone steps. Suddenly a beep from Justin's cell phone pierces the silence. He sets it to vibrate, but he's been detected. He scrunches farther down in the brush as the men raise their heads and look around. They mumble to each other and get up to investigate. Justin's heart hammers. Why is he so paranoid? What could they do to him: offer him up as a sacrifice? He wills himself to calm down.

A familiar voice beckons them back. Justin takes a deep breath, relieved at having escaped discovery. He peeks at his phone. "R u coming?" the text reads. It is no longer possible to leave without being spotted. "Not yet."

A crowd of villagers, both men and women, stream to the

hilltop. More than their church attracts on any given Sunday. His hands shake with anticipation. And fear.

The familiar voice belongs to Alfonso. While people mill about, greeting each other and chatting companionably, Alfonso brings his fingers to his mouth, and a sharp whistle cuts through the valley and ricochets off the cliffs. He stands on a stone mound, an altar, above the gathering, wearing a shaman's black robe with a red embroidered collar. A matching bandanna, knotted pirate-style, conceals his hair. Poppy is perched on his shoulder. In a booming voice, he offers token words of Mam, then switches to Spanish, speaking so slowly and clearly that even Justin can understand. He tells the villagers to prepare their land for the new crop that must be planted when the rains begin to slow. He takes a plastic Ziplock filled with tiny black seeds and scatters a handful.

"These seeds are uncommon. The flowers that will grow from these seeds have great power, power like this holy place where your ancestors worshipped. Like this holy place, they must be kept secret.

"These flowers will change your condition. You will be freed from poverty. Your profits will increase twenty-fold. Your sons and daughters will live longer." He holds up a long-stemmed tulip-like blossom, a virgin offering.

"This is powerful medicine, grown for centuries in ancient societies. It cures illness and diminishes pain and suffering. The world needs these flowers, yet their cultivation is forbidden. Plant them high in the mountains where no one ever goes."

Justin frowns. Why do the plants have to be hidden? Does this have something to do with the laboratory?

"Together we will work out the best places for seeding. Harvest your corn, burn the stalks, till the soil, just as you always do, but plant these secret seeds. They are your future."

158

As a dramatic finale, he launches Poppy into the air. She screeches as she veers off, and her green wings beat a course back toward the villa.

Slinging his arm around Chato's shoulders, Alfonso explains that his assistant will also be able to answer any questions they might have. "Let us pray to the gods of our ancestors." Alfonso leads the people to the ceremonial area.

The sun is directly overhead. Justin debates whether to leave or move closer when Mayan voices begin to chant. A drum beats. Thump-thump-thump. The drums or his heart?

Crouching behind a weeded, crumbling wall, he has a better view. Nearby, a tree grows out perpendicularly from the slope, an arrow shot from heaven.

The villagers gather around a fire. The glittering eyes of an old woman catch his, and he senses recognition. Frightened, he averts his eyes and slides lower, but not before he sees her lips curve into a smile. His limbs are paralyzed.

The scent of burning cedar, herbs, and incense wafts over. A man pokes at the flames, urging them higher. Alfonso plucks petals from the strange flower and several women toss them into the flames. Sparks fly like enraged insects as flames consume each petal. Alfonso sprinkles a powder around the perimeter.

The tempo increases and Justin's head throbs. A live hen is pulled from a covered basket. A man takes a bottle and forces drink down the bird's throat. A knife blade catches the sun's glare. Alfonso seizes a pulsating organ from the hen's breast, kneels down, and offers the sacrifice to the gods of the blaze. He yanks off the head and with the bloodied stump paints a red swath around the circle. Frenzied, the people tear at the carcass and throw pieces into the flames. The air reeks with the metallic stench of burning blood and feathers.

Justin is sick with revulsion. While everyone's attention

rivets on the ceremony, he gathers his courage and backs out of his hiding place. He half runs, half slides down the trail, hoping the beating drum will mask the noise of his descent.

Boulders serve as stepping stones for crossing a spring at the bottom of the trail. He exhales in a gasp, unaware he'd been holding his breath.

Smoke swirls from the hillside and mingles with menacing storm clouds that advance on the horizon. Vultures gather, attracted by the smell of death. They circle and dive into the ravine beyond the ruins.

The cell phone in Justin's back pocket vibrates.

"Where r u?"

"On my way."

"Hurry."

He crosses the narrow valley and hastens up the path. Doña Rosa is waiting on the steps when he arrives. "Where you been? I worry. Your sister says you come soon." She squints. "Why you come from there?" She points.

"I took a shortcut."

She squints at him. He shrugs and tries the opposite argument. "I took the long way."

She clucks her misgivings and tells him to strip off his dirty clothes. "I no want you dirty the house. Go wash for lunch."

Justin does as he's ordered. By the time he's at the table, his sister is halfway through her *guisado*.

"What happened?" she mouths.

Doña Rosa doesn't look their way, but he knows she is paying attention to their conversation. "I'll tell you later."

As the dishes are being cleared from the table, the Marvel clunks down the road and stops. The front door opens, and Katherine calls, "Kids, we're home."

Justin glances at Doña Rosa, pleading silently not to tell. She glances at him thoughtfully and turns to continue her work.

~

THE SCENE at the ruins fills Justin's thoughts. He shudders when he thinks about it and wishes he'd never gone. He promises himself he won't poke around anymore in Alfonso's business, but with fingers crossed behind him. Just in case.

All afternoon, he debates about telling Katy the truth or making up a story. Telling a lie. The only problem is, he's never been much good at making up stories, and whatever he comes up with doesn't sound convincing. After dinner, alone in their room, he lets the truth spill out.

She eyes him suspiciously. "Are you sure you aren't just making this up?" She wears her why-are-you-always-teasing-me face.

"I swear to God."

"Stop, Justin. Don't swear to Him. This whole thing is scary." She stares in the direction of the ruins. "What if God gets angry at us? I mean, you were there when they were praying to Mayan gods."

"It's not like anything could happen to us. Alfonso hasn't been cursed, and he's like a high priest or something."

"Okay, you have a point, but are you going to tell Mom and Dad?"

"I don't know."

"Maybe you shouldn't. What if Dad gets mad and we never get to go over to the villa again?"

"More likely, they'll ground me for life." He'll keep his mouth shut unless Doña Rosa squeals on him. Putting the decision on someone else makes it easier to live with the secret.

Katy is quiet for a moment. "I like Alfonso. Even if he does those things you say, I don't care. I wish Dad were more like him."

"There are advantages to being Alfonso's friend," Justin admits. "But Dad loves us and does the best he can. Besides, Alfonso is not as cool as you think, and he's got lots of secrets. We probably don't know the half of them."

EIGHTEEN

E vening has fallen and nocturnal birds have begun their song, only to be interrupted by an insistent ringing. Katherine reaches over to answer the cell phone. "Yes?" She pauses for a moment. "Well, thank you for the invitation. I'm sure they'd love that. I'll speak to Phil and we'll let you know."

Phil shuffles through his sermon notes at the table. He glances up. "Who was that, dear?"

"Alfonso. He and Pancho are going to the beach for the weekend and invited us to come along."

"The beach." Interest flickers across Phil's face. He's never actually been to the ocean, only to the Great Lakes. He remembers his commitments and shakes his head. "I can't be gone on Sunday."

"He says they'll bring us back on Saturday evening, so you won't miss church the next morning."

"I want to go!" Katy jumps up from where she and Justin were playing cards. "Can we? Please."

"Dad, it'll be way cool," Justin seconds.

Phil's indecision crumbles. "Hand me the phone and I'll make the arrangements."

FRIDAY MORNING, a Range Rover, the Hummer towing a sports car, and two double-cab pickups filled with bodyguards and supplies stop in front of their house. Everyone piles out. The men carry weapons, and only Pancho is unarmed. Phil and Katherine exchange glances. The security is excessive and makes them uncomfortable, but it seems too late to back out.

Alfonso emerges from the Hummer. "I understand you must be back by Sunday," he says to Phil. "Chato will pick you up late Saturday afternoon and fly you home in the helicopter."

Katy's eyes widen. She and Justin were disappointed when they heard they would have to return on Saturday, but a ride in a helicopter trumps an extra day at the beach anytime.

Katy's cast was recently removed and she walks with a residual limp. Alfonso whisks her into his arms and deposits her onto the back seat of the Hummer. "Young Katherine, at your service."

She giggles with delight.

He opens the passenger door for Katherine then turns to Phil. "Ride with the driver in the Rover. Then both you and Katherine will have front seats to better enjoy the scenery."

It should have been a request, Phil thinks, but sounds like an order.

"Why do you not join your father, Justin?" Alfonso gives Justin a light tap on the shoulder, nudging him toward the Rover. "Pancho will be riding there as well."

Phil hesitates. He'd pictured a family outing. Did Alfonso

want to separate him from his wife and daughter? But maybe Alfonso did want them to "better enjoy the scenery."

"Are you okay going with him, Katherine?"

"Katy and I will be fine," she says.

He shakes away lingering doubt and allows Pancho to guide him away.

THE CONVOY SPEEDS down the mountain, passing vast expanses of coffee bushes shaded by umbrella-shaped trees. As the elevation decreases, the vegetation becomes lush and tropical. A strange odor of industry hovers in the air where the coffee bushes are replaced by rubber trees; the deep gashes on their trunks and the cups below to catch the sap remind Katherine of maple trees and the homey warmth of maple syrup.

"This is so interesting, Alfonso. I had no idea that latex was a natural substance. When you live in the U.S., you imagine that everything is manmade."

"Manmade or natural. What is the difference? Many processed commodities have natural bases. What harm can we find in things that God has entrusted to us? Cures for diseases and unknown riches still are waiting to be discovered in remote forests. By endowing us with intelligence, God has given man the key to unlocking the earth's mysteries."

She is taken aback at his words. "Are you a man of faith?"

"Faith that God has given me powers to help as well as to hinder, yet I hope I may be of more help than otherwise."

She remembers how he had been blessed in the cathedral that day, yet he strikes her as a practical man, not one overly influenced by the spiritual. She is about to question him further when the car begins to slow. Alfonso opens his window to signal the other cars, and sweltering heat replaces the Hummer's air-conditioned comfort. They pull into a Texaco station, and several suited men emerge from the pickups to stand guard as they fuel the cars.

Katy leans over the front seat and stares at the compass on the dash. The convoy continues south. "I thought south would be South America, not the Pacific Ocean," she says.

"Guatemala's southern ocean is the Pacific. Geography is a subject not to be downplayed, especially from the perspective of a small country. Though these republics south of Mexico hold little interest for most Americans, I assume this is not the case for you."

Katy is silent. Living in Guatemala certainly hasn't stimulated her interest in geography, but she senses it might be the wrong thing to say. Instead, she tells him what she thinks he wants to hear. "Oh, yes. Geography fascinates me. It's my favorite subject."

She sees Alfonso glance in the rearview mirror and smile. Her mother turns and glances back at Katy with doubt on her face.

"My vacation home is located due south on a river delta," he says.

She leans forward. "I bet it's beautiful."

"It is a humble home with thatch roofing. I like that it blends into the backdrop of mangrove forests."

Katy doesn't believe him and neither does Katherine. Nothing they've seen about Alfonso is humble.

Along the coastal plain, a black strip of asphalt divides the crops. To the left of the road, banana plantations stretch as far as the eye can see. The ripening bunches, covered with blue plastic bags, weigh the trees sideways, and the flimsy trunks are roped to stakes to keep them upright. On the other side, plantations of olive-green trees are so densely packed that the foliage creates a murky darkness.

"These are African palms," Alfonso says. "Harvested for oil."

He rolls down his window and motions for the escort vehicles to stop. Men get out and unfasten the tie-downs holding the Maserati. As they push the sports car off the trailer, the Hummer lurches.

Pancho, with Justin tagging along, propels himself from the Range Rover and shoves the men aside.

Justin notes Pancho's confidence—pushing the bodyguards is claiming first dibs on the Maserati—and he catches his mother's eye. Maybe if he were more assertive, like Pancho, he would be able to do more.

After rolling down the window, she shakes her head and wags a finger. "Boys and fast cars. No, no, no. A dangerous mix."

"Aw, Mom. Please."

"Let them have their fun," Alfonso says. "They are only young once. I am sure that even Phil must have had some reckless fun when he was young."

Phil survived his accident a better man, she tells herself, but he almost lost his life in the process. No way is she going to put her son in harm's way. If Alfonso wants to let his godson risk his life, all right, fine. But no way is Justin going along for the ride.

Dejected, Justin turns back toward the Range Rover.

Pancho slips behind the wheel and straps himself in. The engine roars. Glancing at Alfonso for a quick okay, he speeds off, tires squealing.

The plan is to meet at Los Limones, the midway point. Alfonso explains that in the Maserati, Pancho can make it to Ocós and back to meet them.

"That's too fast. What's the speed limit?" Katherine asks. As soon as the question leaves her mouth, she realizes its futility. From what they've seen in Guatemala, laws are seldom enforced, and the few police vehicles they've seen are not concerned with highway safety.

"Maseratis are built for maneuverability and speed. It is a shame to let its assets go to waste."

Fifteen minutes after Pancho disappears, Katy curls up in the back seat and falls asleep. Alfonso touches Katherine's hand. "Alone at last."

She flashes him an uneasy smile. "I didn't mean ... " she starts. "It wasn't my intention to lead you on. I'm a married woman."

"Do not be anxious, Katherine. I have no desire to approach a woman who does not enjoy my attentions. You are so beautiful. I love that you do not know that about yourself. You remind me of someone I once knew. And cherished."

"Stop, Alfonso. Really. This is all very flattering, but please, my daughter is in the back—"

"Sleeping," he says, ending her sentence. "I did not know until I met you how truly lonely I have become."

"Don't be silly. How can you be lonely? A handsome, wealthy man. You must have women lined up in every city where you travel. Why yearn for one who is already taken?"

"Why indeed," he says to himself.

"I'm already taken," she repeats in a whisper, mostly to remind herself, and wonders what it would be like to kiss him. As if prompted by her thoughts, he leans in, but she pulls her head away.

He focuses again on the road ahead. "Maybe so, but how happy are you?"

The question hangs in the air. Katherine reviews how much Phil takes her for granted, how unappealing he can be when he pushes religion. Does she even find him attractive anymore? She remembers the weekend in the Cuchumatanes and prefers not to answer Alfonso's question. To say she is happy would not be the whole truth. To admit that she wishes for more would define the vanilla blahness of their marriage and give it shape.

"You are attracted to me, are you not?" he asks.

She says nothing but glances back at her daughter, whose eyes are closed. Her breath is even.

She wishes she could curb her desires. A pastor's wife shouldn't have straying eyes.

"I don't know how to answer," she says.

"I will take that as a yes."

"Then, maybe," she says.

AROUND A CURVE, the Maserati is stalled sideways across the road. Pancho staggers out. The Hummer screeches to a halt, and Alfonso throws open the door, jumps out, and races over. He grabs the boy's arm to steady him. Katherine jumps out, frightened and relieved that Justin wasn't in the car.

"What happened?" Alfonso asks.

"When I went around the last curve, I saw this." He points to branches that someone had placed to form a barrier across the road. "I threw on the brakes, but the road was slick, and I spun out."

Bodyguards surround them. Alfonso slings his arm around Pancho's shoulder, and they step away to allow the guards to investigate. Changing the subject, Alfonso asks, "How did you enjoy driving her?"

Pancho waves toward the car, a lopsided grin on his face.

"Other than spinning, it was great. In fact, the spin was fun, too. But scary."

The dark areas appear to be wet pavement, but on closer inspection, rainbows swirl in the splotches. A suited man kneels and swipes a fingertip across the liquid. He sniffs his finger, and then stands, scanning both sides of the road. Another guard walks up to the barricade and moves branches out of the way. Men check the perimeter and reload the red convertible back onto the trailer.

One approaches Alfonso and points to the road ahead.

Alfonso's face turns grave.

"I don't understand. Why the roadblock?" Katherine asks as Alfonso settles behind the steering wheel.

"Someone poured oil on the road. It appears that they were waiting."

"Why would someone do that?"

He shrugs. "There is no sign of anyone. It could be that we interrupted their plans with our arrival. This is the best stretch of the road to set a trap. The place where a car might accelerate after the last curve and the only place where a trap would not be visible." He glances at Katherine's startled face. "I have enemies. Someone must have thought I would be driving the sports car. I race this road when I can. The adrenaline revives me."

She can't get beyond his first sentence. "Why do you have enemies?"

He brushes away the idea into insignificance. "Running a business in this country comes with an element of danger."

Katherine's forehead pinches. It isn't the first time she's heard mention of a business, but didn't he already sell his father's business? "What kind of business do you have?"

"Like many wealthy men, I have numerous investments. I will not bore you with details."

170

A BRIDGE over a mangrove-lined estuary marks the entrance to Ocós. Passing municipal buildings painted in pastels, the convoy proceeds down a sandy street. Posters on storefronts advertise soda and cell phones. Like children's playhouses, stick-sided homes with thatched roofs rise from the sand.

When breaking waves appear at the end of the street, the vehicles veer left, past simple restaurants serving lunch to scantily clothed villagers and cantinas where rowdy men guzzle *guaro*, the cheap, local sugar-cane liquor. Naked, bronzed toddlers with rounded bellies and thin limbs play in sandy yards with pigs and chickens.

The road ends a half-mile past town at a three-story brick building with a steeply pitched roof of woven palm fronds. A wooden porch encircles the structure, and string hammocks are suspended between tall trees. On an open patio above, more hammocks, like fishnets drying in the sun, hang from hooks. In the front yard, a tropical garden surrounds a brilliant blue pool. Wood-plank pathways lead to the beach, the estuary, and around the house to an empty helipad.

Katy lifts her head in wonder. "I can smell it. The ocean." She leaps from the car as soon as it stops. "Come on, Justin," she calls to her brother in the other car. "Let's go down to the water."

They take off their shoes, roll up their pants, and let the waves lap at their feet. Katy laughs and chases crabs the size of spiders into holes in the damp black sand.

NINETEEN

"How long since you've been to the beach?" Justin asks.

Katherine has found a hammock and eases herself into it.

"Does a lake count?"

"No, a real beach."

She thinks back. "I haven't been to an ocean since my parents took my sister and me to a family reunion in Mystic, Connecticut. We were about your age. But that was nothing like this. What I remember most is the freezing water. The ocean breeze stinging with icy spray."

"Hey, come back here, sweetie," she calls to Katy, who attempts to slip past. "Let me get some sunscreen on you." She slathers them both down. "Be careful not to stay out too long. We're close to the equator. I'm being extra careful, and you should, too."

Binoculars and camera swing from Phil's neck as he strides down the passageway in his shorts and favorite Hawaiian shirt.

He watches the kids splash at the water's edge. Because of currents and undertows, they've been warned not to go in past their knees. Any swimming must be done in the pool.

Phil snaps photos of the mangrove-lined beaches near the river and the dunes farther beyond. He studies the pelicans who swoop across the breaking waves. On such a beautiful day, he doesn't want to be stuck inside playing cards. Besides, Katherine is a good woman, his wife, his partner. The fact that she's playing cards with their wealthy neighbor doesn't mean she's flirting. Besides, if he stays out on the beach, he can add birds to his list, and she can take a break from watching the kids.

Pancho sprawls belly-down on a towel. He digs holes in the black sand with his toes, adjusts his Maui Jims, and stares out at the horizon.

"Where's Mom?" Katy asks. An hour has gone by, and her mother still hasn't come out. She wants to show her the miniature crabs.

"She and Alfonso are playing cards."

"How come you're not with them, Dad?" Justin's voice cracks with accusation.

Pancho lifts his head, apparently interested in the answer.

"Your mom can play cards if she wants to. I'm taking photos and looking at the bird life."

Justin supposes his father wasn't invited to the card game, but he can't leave his mother alone with Alfonso.

"I'm going back to the house for some water," he says.

Pancho says, "I can phone and have them bring it here."

"No thanks," Justin says. "I need to pee."

Barefoot and silent, he tiptoes across the entryway's cool tile. At last, he's within listening range, ready to interrupt. He slides down the wall and sits.

"Katherine, you look sumptuous in that color," Alfonso says. "I could just eat you up."

The husky tone of Alfonso's voice makes Justin uncomfortable. He cracks his knuckles.

"Thank you," she says matter-of-factly. "But you don't strike me as the cannibal type. Your turn."

Justin is confused by his mother's reaction. Not only is she not offended, but she seems to enjoy the attention.

"What will be my prize when I win?"

"Who says you're going to win?" After a pause, Katherine responds, "Besides, I couldn't give you anything you don't already have."

"A kiss maybe, just a kiss?"

Justin hears his mother laugh. Trying to think, he wraps his arms around his knees. He can't quite figure out what's going on.

"I enjoy your company," she says, "but I won't deceive my husband."

"Phil is unworthy of a woman such as you."

Justin hears a chair scrape back.

"To give you warning, yes, I do like a challenge."

Footsteps come toward the entryway.

Should he run? Justin turns his head and sees Alfonso looking down.

"Enjoying yourself, son?"

"Yes, sir." Justin tries to blank his expression. Caught red-handed.

"Interesting place to sit."

"Um, yes."

Katherine peers around the corner. "Justin! What are you doing? I hope you weren't eavesdropping."

Alfonso extends a hand. "Let me help you up."

To demonstrate that thirst was the motivation for his presence, Justin finds the kitchen and pours himself iced lemonade.

"Come on, Justin. Let's go down to the beach. The sun is lower now," Katherine says.

As he accompanies her to the water's edge, Katherine tries to break the uncomfortable silence. "Isn't it lovely?"

"It beats our dreary house." He can't keep the resentment from his voice.

"I hope you don't think I'll fall for him."

He doesn't need to hear the name; he understands to whom his mother is referring.

"His attentions are flattering, but I would never do anything to hurt your father."

"Don't spend time with him, Mom. Please." He knows his father is no match for a guy like Alfonso. Not in looks, wealth, or status. Maybe his mother's intentions are honorable, but she should know better than to get too close to a fire. Alfonso is hot. Even Justin can see that.

He stares at the water and the crashing waves. A plastic bottle floats to the surface. As the ocean swells, the container bobs and the current sucks it back under. The wave crashes again and spits it out as the water races forward. Justin grabs it when it reaches shore. The outside is mangled, the inside partially filled with sand. He looks for a garbage can.

"Hey, Fofo!" Pancho walks over with the Frisbee. "Let's play."

Justin hurls the bottle as far as he can before joining Pancho. Katherine watches them for a while, then goes over to Katy, who presents to her the tiny crabs she's named.

The boys toss a Frisbee back and forth as the sun slips below the horizon. Like an unstopped vat of dye from heaven, colors spill onto the ocean.

By the time they return, barbecued steaks are sizzling on the smoldering charcoal of an outdoor grill. During dinner, the pink clouds darken. After the sun has fully set, Alfonso builds a campfire on the beach, and the kids toast marshmallows on wire lances. The wood crackles like fireworks and sparks fly into the star-studded sky.

～

LULLED by the hum of ceiling fans and breaking waves, they sleep soundly and awake to the aroma of coffee and bacon and the slapping of hand-patted tortillas.

"Can we go to the nature reserve you told us about last night, Alfonso?" Katy asks when they are all seated at the long wooden table for breakfast.

"An excellent idea, young Katherine. The reserve is on the island of Tilapa and is called Manchón Guamuchal."

"That's a mouthful," says Phil between bites.

Justin turns away. "You're going with us, too, aren't you Justin?" his mother asks.

"Nah. Pancho and I are gonna take a boat up the estuary."

She looks alarmed—Why doesn't he want to stay with his family?—but Alfonso places a reassuring hand on her arm. "There is no danger to them here. Let them spend time together as boys like to do."

While the others prepare for the trip to Tilapa, Pancho and Justin walk to the river dock and climb into the boat. The water is murky and coffee-colored. The caretaker unties the skiff and shoves it into the current. Pancho starts the outboard, and they zip upstream, frothy foam in their wake.

Katherine grabs her daypack from the bed and watches her son from the upstairs window. He is growing up so fast. She

wishes time would stand still, and she could preserve their innocent childhood.

Then she heads down to where a larger boat is waiting.
Alfonso masters the helm as the boat points toward the open sea
and a spot of land on the horizon. As they approach the island,
birds startle from branches. Mangroves line the estuary, roots
protruding three feet above the brackish water. Alfonso concentrates on the contours of the shoreline, and soon they come to an
inlet with a welcome sign.

PANCHO EASES himself into the cola-colored water and pulls the
boat by a rope attached to the bow. Two hundred yards in, the
waterway ends, and the boat's underside slides onto sludge.
Justin jumps out and sinks halfway to his knees in the mushy
bottom. Pancho laughs at his astonished expression. "Dude, this
is an estuary, not a river."

They yank the skiff up the muddy embankment, and
Pancho, explaining that the water rises and falls with the tides,
ropes it to a mangrove trunk. They slog barefoot through the
muck. Soon the ground becomes firm and spongy with moss.

Skeletal roots crowd the eerie swamp, and birds teem in the
branches far above. Along the shoreline, Justin recognized egrets
and herons, but there are birds he's never seen. In the swamp,
Pancho points out the nests of warblers and kingfishers.

A bright green creature about three feet long struts up the
gangly branches of a nearby tree, startling Justin. "Did you see
that?"

"An iguana." Pancho's eyes fill with mischief. "You ain't seen
nothin' yet."

The boys stop at a small clearing where wire fencing encircles a pond. What at first appear to be floating logs are half-submerged crocodiles warming themselves in the sun and cruising along the muddied water.

"What's this?"

"Alfonso's conservation project. How many can you count?"

"Six?"

"He started a few years ago with four. Now we've got fifteen. Cool, huh?"

"Why would you want to raise crocodiles?"

"If we let them go, they'll be slaughtered. The villagers would eat the meat and sell their hides. Croc steaks. Yum." He opens his eyes wide and watches Justin's reaction.

"You don't really eat that stuff, do you?"

"Naw. I mean I would, but Alfonso prohibits it. He's got a thing about conservation. Damn if I know why."

Justin sits down on a mangrove root to watch. "Do you come out here often? I mean when you come to Ocós?"

"The caretaker comes out about once a week to feed them. If I'm around, I join him. If the crocs aren't given enough food, the larger feed on the smaller. I guess that's the cycle of life."

Pancho's analogy doesn't sound like any cycle of life Justin wishes to contemplate. "Does anyone else know about this place?"

"Just the caretakers and us." He studies Justin, and his eyes glitter with malice. "This is a perfect place to dispose of bodies, don't you think? You should hear some of Chato's stories." The scenario plays out in Justin's mind. A helicopter flies overhead and drops its load directly into the pit. No telltale bodies, no crime. Suddenly the mangrove swamp gives him the creeps. The bleached roots remind him of death and graveyards.

"Why would you believe what Chato tells you, anyway?"

"Why wouldn't I?"

It seems obvious enough to Justin, but he isn't comfortable enough with Pancho to say, because Chato can't be trusted. "Because you can't believe everyone's stories. He might be pulling your leg."

"He's my uncle, and, in case you haven't noticed, he doesn't have a sense of humor. Besides, if anyone would know, it's him."

∽

ALFONSO POINTS out spider monkeys in the trees, and Phil stops, peering through the binoculars. "Birds!" he says, aiming his camera at the trees.

Katy looks up into the canopy.

Katherine follows their host down the path. He's waiting and grabs Katherine's hand, bringing it to his lips.

"What are you doing?" she whispers.

"Forgive me. I could not resist."

Phil takes out his notebook and frantically scribbles bird names.

"If you think the birds are cool," Katherine says, "check out the monkeys."

"Ah, thank you for reminding me." Alfonso disappears and returns with a bucket of fruit. The animals approach and start chattering. He clutches a stick with a small net fastened to the end containing sliced papaya and bananas. He lifts it toward the branch, and a dozen furry hands reach for it.

"Can I do it? Can I feed them?" Katy asks.

He refills the basket and hands it to Katy.

Later, they walk the shore and stop at a sea turtle project. When they leave the island, instead of going right back to the house, they turn off for lunch.

"What a great day!" Katy says. "Justin is missing everything."

~

THE BOYS RETURN to the boat, but the motor's roar prevents conversation. Justin is anxious to get back. Pancho creeps him out in a frightening and thrilling sort of way. They leave the boat tied to the dock and head for the house. The others haven't yet arrived, so they climb into string hammocks and swing themselves by kicking nearby posts.

"Has your old man always been such a religious nutcase?"

Justin tries not to be offended. "As long as I can remember."

"That's fuckin' weird. Your old lady seems nice enough. She's okay with his trying to convert everyone he meets?"

Justin doesn't like where the conversation is headed—it isn't the kind of thing he ever thought to question. "She's Christian too, and she loves him."

"Doesn't answer my question, dude, but whatever. My grandmother is a Christian nutjob like your dad. I can't hardly stand to be around her. She thinks we're in league with the devil or some shit like that. What do you think about all that churchy crap?"

Justin shrugs. Just when he starts to doubt, something comes along to snap him back into his faith, like hearing the translation at the Pentecost sermon. Besides, talking about faith with a guy like Pancho is pointless.

A servant brings them two coconuts in their husks. The tops are hacked flat, and straws stick out of round holes. Pancho asks about Katy: her age, her friends, if she is happy in Guatemala.

Maybe Pancho is inquiring about his mother on Alfonso's behalf, but why would he ask about his little sister? "What's it to you, man?" No way is he gonna let this guy be around Katy—him being too old for her is only part of the problem.

Pancho frowns but doesn't continue.

Justin puts down his coconut and kicks the post to swing the hammock higher. He's had his fill of conversation. Before long, a worker calls the boys for lunch, and just as they finish, the rest of the group returns.

"Hi, Justin." Katy flashes a smile at Pancho. "You really missed out!" Her eyes sparkle and her skin glows pink. "We went to a nature reserve. There were so many birds that Dad was going crazy taking photos, but the coolest thing was the spider monkeys. I got to feed them. We saw a *tortugario*, where volunteers gather turtle eggs from nests in the sand and protect the babies until they crawl back to the ocean. When we got back from the island, we stopped at a *comedor*. Can you believe they actually had turtle soup on the menu? All I could think about was those poor little *tortugas*."

Not to be outdone by his little sister, Justin says, "Pancho showed me Alfonso's conservation project. He's protecting crocodiles from human predators."

"Is that so?" Katherine says as she comes closer and looks over at their host.

"The people here eat them. They sell the hides on the black market. They are in danger of extinction, but, to be fair, there is so much poverty in Guatemala, that all living creatures are at risk. You saw the turtles on the menu. Even the spider monkeys would be eaten by a hungry family if they were not taken and sold for cash on the black market. Their biggest protection is the island's inaccessibility."

~

AT HALF PAST FOUR, the buzz of a helicopter summons everyone outside. The noise grows to a deafening roar as the chopper lands on the bull's-eye target and, with a final rush of air, quiets. Chato climbs out. The men in suits have changed into khaki shorts and polo shirts with shoulder holsters under light-weight vests. Chato hands one a heavy daypack and tells the others to unload the duffel bags of cargo.

Alfonso greets Chato, grasps him firmly by the forearms, and then hugs him like a brother. Speaking and gesturing, Alfonso tells him about the near accident on the road, and then they saunter off down the beach.

The Whitehalls gather their belongings, throw them in a pile, and wait. When Chato reappears, they climb into the helicopter and wave goodbye. In a tornado blast of wind and noise, the chopper lifts into the air.

Dense green forests carpet the ground, and in the distance storm clouds gather, darkening the edges of the horizon. The door remains open, and wind whistles through the cabin. A flock of migrating birds flies below them. Phil points them out, and Katy leans over her brother to see.

Twenty minutes later, they fly over the ruins. Their canary-yellow house comes into view. The van in the yard hasn't moved. As the helicopter slows and aims for the helipad, it passes above the zinc-roofed complex beyond the stables. No one but Justin looks twice.

After landing, Phil hops out and helps the rest of his family. They want to thank Chato for the ride, but after he gives orders for their bags to be put into a pickup, he turns and walks away.

CHAPTER

TWENTY

P hil and Jerónimo plan to attend a four-day mission retreat in Quetzaltenango, locally known as Xela. Phil spends several weeks taking photographs and collecting data for his presentation of the theme: evangelizing in the Mayan world. Sunday services are canceled for the weekend.

When Jerónimo arrives Thursday morning, they all pile into the car. Katherine and the kids will drop off the men and stay in town to make their weekly purchases.

Excited by the upcoming conference, Jerónimo drives full speed down the narrow streets of the hamlet, banging the horn and swerving only when collision seems inevitable. Phil wishes he'd taken the wheel.

Shortly after they pull into the bus terminal, the *camioneta* bound for Xela rolls in. Baskets of fruits and vegetables fill the roof rack, and the bus sways under its top-heavy load. As the produce is unloaded, passengers board. "¡Xela! ¡Xela! ¡La capital del altiplano!" the assistant hollers while gesturing to everyone in the vicinity to get on.

The engine idles and the bus rocks with Phil and Jerónimo making their way down the aisle. Noisy conversation competes in volume with Tropicana, the self-proclaimed hit radio station of the western highlands. Phil finds a seat next to an old peasant woman, her head covered with an embroidered scarf. When she transfers a basket from the seat to her lap, two feathered heads peer out from under a checkered cloth.

Seats in what once must have been a yellow, American school bus would comfortably fit two, but passengers squeeze three across. Jerónimo, sitting sideways with his feet in the aisle, braces himself on the bench's outside edge. People continue to board until the travelers are packed tight.

Hot sunshine streams in, painting strips of light over the passengers. The smells of unwashed bodies and wood smoke hang thickly in the air. The bus thrusts forward, the interior mass of humanity swaying like cattle headed for slaughter.

After two hours, Phil longs for the van and wishes he hadn't so gallantly left it for Katherine. Erratic driver or not, Jerónimo has always managed to get them to their destination.

The chicken bus stops every ten minutes to load and unload. Occasionally, buses coming from the opposite direction pause mid-highway, and the drivers chat until the honking from cars piled up behind them forces them to move along. After three hours, Phil begins to despair.

Sweat drips in rivulets from his temples, and his thinning hair plasters his head. There is no air-conditioning, and the few open windows do nothing to staunch the sweltering heat. When Phil's seatmate leaves, Jerónimo joins him.

"Is riding the bus always this bad?"

His assistant cocks his head as though he isn't sure why Phil thinks this experience is bad, and Phil assumes the affirmative.

When the bus enters the terminal at their destination, they

grab their belongings and disembark onto garbage-slicked asphalt to take a waiting shuttle to the convention center.

~

AFTER SHOPPING, Katherine treats the kids to lunch. They are surprised and pleased to find that even the smallest of towns have a café serving its own version of Asian cuisine. Justin fiddles with his sweet and sour pork and worries about the things he's kept from his parents: the visit to the ruins, the strange lab at the villa, Pancho's stories at the crocodile pond. To divulge secrets could get him into trouble, but he doesn't want to withhold information that might jeopardize their safety.

"Justin?" Katherine says several times before catching his attention.

"What?"

"Are you okay? You're a thousand miles away."

"I haven't been sleeping well."

"Justin's been having nightmares," Katy explains in a know-it-all voice.

Her brow wrinkling, Katherine studies his flushed face. When they leave the restaurant, she touches his overly warm forehead. "What are the nightmares about?"

"I don't want to talk about it. I'll tell you when we get home."

The Missionary Marvel wheezes to life and shudders ominously. Katy closes her eyes and settles back into the seat. A half hour later, the house comes into view with the front door standing open. Katherine stomps the brake pedal. From the back seat, Katy cries out, "Watch out. I almost landed on the floor."

Justin sits forward. "It looks like someone broke in."

"Shush. Maybe there's an explanation." With trembling hands, Katherine digs through her purse and dumps the contents onto the seat beside her. Why would this happen as soon as Phil leaves? "I know the door was locked when we left."

She picks up the phone and punches in some numbers. "¿Hola? Sí, soy Katerina ... Are you at our house by any chance? ... Did you come over earlier? ... *Gracias.*"

She puts the phone down slowly. "Rosa hasn't been here, and I'm not taking any chances. We're going to the villa. We need someone to come back with us, someone who's armed in case there's still an intruder."

A short way down the road, she pulls over to the side and calls Phil.

PHIL IS surprised by the number of missionaries. There must be over two hundred Americans, stationed in various parts of the country. He and Jerónimo sign in and are shown to an assigned dormitory with five cots, each room with its own bathroom. Thinking he might not have another opportunity when the other roommates arrive, he strips and jumps in the shower. As he finishes soaping up, his cell phone rings. He turns off the water, grabs it, and glances at the screen. Katherine. "What?" he says more gruffly that he meant to. She picks the worst times to interrupt.

"Oh, I'm so glad to hear your voice," she says. "I know you're busy, and I'm sorry to disturb you, but it's an emergency. We just got home and it looks like someone has broken into the house."

With soapy ears and bad reception, he barely understands a word she says. He thinks she says her home is broken without him. "What are you talking about?"

"Can't you come? I'm sure they'll understand. Phil, we need you."

"Katherine, I'm flattered, but I'm sure you can handle things for the weekend. We'll be back Sunday afternoon." He puts the phone down and unwittingly turns it off. She's been acting strange, but he can't tell why. Maybe he's done something to make her angry. Women are so complicated, especially his wife.

He eases back into the hot shower and rinses his hair.

KATHERINE FROWNS and throws the phone onto the floor. "Damn it."

"What did Daddy say?" Katy sits up.

"He said not to bother him. He'll be back Sunday afternoon. We'll just have to deal with it ourselves." She wanted to give Phil the benefit of the doubt, but if he isn't willing to protect his family, Alfonso will surely help.

"I think you should call Alfonso," Katy says.

"I was about to," Katherine says.

"What about the police?" Justin asks.

She doesn't answer. Alfonso will know what to do and whether it will be necessary to involve the authorities. She picks up the phone to see if he's home.

When they arrive at the villa, Katherine pulls up to the front door. The keys are in the ignition and she is shaking. It's awkward arriving like this, with Phil away, but Alfonso is waiting.

"Welcome," he says, and opens Katherine's door. "Please come into the house. You do look as though you have had a fright."

He puts one arm around Katherine and the other around Katy, and ushers them into the library. Justin follows. Feathers ruffled, Poppy watches them from her perch.

He takes them to the library, where a burgundy leather sofa and matching chairs take up one corner and bookshelves line the walls. Classical music floats softly in the air. Floor-to-ceiling windows afford a sweeping view of the garden and pool.

Alfonso claps his hands and a servant responds, waits for instructions, then disappears. He reappears moments later carrying a tray of soft drinks.

"Let me prepare you something stronger, Katherine." He takes a bottle from a bar near the bookshelves and pours a healthy shot into her drink. "This will calm your nerves. Now, please, tell me what happened."

"When we returned from town, the door to our house was open. I was afraid to go in for fear someone was there. With Phil away until Sunday, I didn't know what to do or where else to go."

"You did the right thing in coming here. You must remember, this is a violent country and you need more than just God's protection."

Katy fiddles with her cloth purse, and Alfonso takes her hand in his. "Do not worry, young Katherine. I will make sure you are safe." He gets to his feet. "You must spend the night. We have plenty of space and you can rest easy."

Katherine wavers. "I don't know. You've already done so much ... " She leaves the sentence without resolution. He does more than should be expected from a landlord. Just the thought of staying at the villa with handsome Alfonso is almost more than she can handle.

He settles back in his chair and says, "Then it is decided."

"No," she says, with sudden determination. "We must return. I need to see what shape the house is in and if anything has been stolen. Besides, I can't impose."

A flash of anger crosses his face, but just as quickly a mask of bland hospitality takes its place. "You are not an imposition. I am sorry you will not accept my offer, but just remember, you are welcome to return if you change your mind. I will send Chato back with you to make sure your house is safe and give instructions that Horacio follow later to stand guard during the night."

"Shouldn't we call the police?" Justin suggests.

"There is no point in calling the law enforcement. They would block the road for an entire day, disrupt traffic, make a report, a supposed investigation, and in the end resolve nothing. I would have curious police officers running all over my property touching things and looking into my business. It would not do at all." He reaches for his drink and takes a deep swallow.

Again the charming host, he turns to Katherine. "I hope this will not stain your view of this beautiful country."

"Honestly, we've had more than our share of trouble here. It's a wonder I still love Guatemala."

Bulldog-faced Chato enters the room as though he's been waiting for instructions. "Sí, Alfonso."

"Accompany the Whitehalls. Their home was broken into. I want you to check their house for intruders. Send Horacio to guard them tonight."

Deadpan, he clicks his heels in response.

They follow Chato to the garage where the Missionary Marvel is now parked. Katherine follows his pickup and stops a short distance behind while Chato gets out and approaches the house. His gun is drawn, and, just like in the movies, he puts his back to the wall and approaches the front door. Then he barges in.

The rooms light up in succession as he goes through the house. He checks the outdoor bathroom last, then strides out the front door and barks, "All clear." He climbs back into his vehicle and roars off, dust billowing in his wake.

"He sure wouldn't win any congeniality prizes," Katherine says.

After the dust settles, they approach the house cautiously. The front door doesn't lock. It hangs from the hinges and won't shut properly. The sofa lies on its side; chairs are toppled and papers scattered.

In the master bedroom, books litter the floor, clothing is draped on overturned chairs, and their things are spread all over. A tornado might have whipped through the house and left it in a similar state.

Katherine's eyes brim with tears. "Why would anyone go through our belongings like this?"

Justin scans the room. The bottom drawer of his mother's jewelry box hangs open and empty. She follows his glance and slumps. "My jewelry isn't the problem. There isn't much of value. What's missing are our passports and cash."

"Why would anyone want our passports? No one in this country looks anything like us."

Katherine throws her arms up. "How should I know, Justin? They must be worth something on the black market. That's the one thing they say to be careful not to lose when you're abroad. Now we'll have to go to the embassy in Guatemala City to get our passports reissued. All I can say is that it's a good thing the construction money is hidden in the storeroom. They didn't force that lock." She starts hanging clothes and putting things back on shelves. "Come on, you two. Give me a hand."

They straighten up the house and shove the sofa against the front door. The kids set the table while Katherine prepares dinner. Afterward they all take turns using the bathroom and keeping watch. The dark forest looms threateningly, and a frigid wind whips across the field.

"Why would anyone steal from us, Mommy? We don't have that much," Katy asks as they settle back on the double bed.

"There's always someone who has less, and I guess we're an easy target. The thieves must have known Phil was leaving and that we go to market on Thursdays."

"That's not too hard to guess," Justin scoffs. "Thursday is market day, when everyone goes to town."

"It's just one more thing." Katherine sighs, thinking of all the bad things that have happened to them so far. "But your father will probably put an optimistic spin on this."

Katherine suggests they pray. She pleads with the Lord for safety. She asks for strength to fight the villa's temptation, and she prays for peace. She asks for protection for Phil as he and Jerónimo travel. Katherine has found over the years that nothing calms the soul like prayer, and she feels comforted when they finish. She turns to Justin. "Now would be a good time to tell me what's been bothering you."

He stares at the ceiling. "I know I shouldn't have gone off on my own, but last week I went up to the ruins. A bunch of people arrived after me, so I hid. Alfonso was there. He told them about a crop he wants them to plant. Some kind of flower. They had a Mayan ceremony and sacrificed a hen."

"That's it? It sounds like one of those vivid dreams of yours."

He agrees that it seems like a dream but assures her that it happened.

"You shouldn't have gone off on your own, son. Remember Katy's ankle."

"It was weird," Justin continued. "He held up a red flower. Looked like a tulip, but it wasn't. He told them to plant the seeds where it would be hard for anyone to find because it was forbidden. He said the flowers would make them all rich."

"What did you think it was about?"

He hesitates. "I hadn't mentioned it, but when Katy and I stayed the night that time, I discovered a lab behind the stables at Alfonso's. I figured he was doing some kind of research."

Katherine ponders the story. Forbidden. Riches. That might translate as illegal. She goes through the list of illegal crops in her mind: marijuana, cocaine, opium. Wait, could those flowers be opium poppies? The information clicks into place like a missing puzzle piece. There's always been something about Alfonso that she didn't understand, and this could explain it all. Too wealthy, too security conscious, and living too far from civilization. It also might explain the threats and his business.

"Even though Alfonso told us he is an agricultural advisor, agricultural research doesn't quite fit." She pauses. "Well, I guess maybe it does if he's cultivating illegal drugs."

She doesn't mean to say it out loud and realizes her mistake when Justin's eyes get big. "Illegal drugs?" Justin asks.

She figures she might as well tell him. "It sounds like poppies. Opium poppies."

Katy gets to her feet, hands on her hips. "I don't believe it. Alfonso hasn't done anything wrong. What's an opium poppy, anyway? All he wants to do is help the poor farmers make money and live better. The only poppy we know about is his parrot."

"And her name should have been a clue," Katherine mutters. "Sweetheart, listen. Sometimes people do things we wouldn't believe they could. Anyway, we don't know anything for sure."

They hear a vehicle outside. Katherine pulls back the curtains and glances out the window. "Horacio's here." She scans the room as though planning an escape. Where could they go? Out the back and into the woods? "I wonder if we're in any danger," she mutters. No, she shouldn't be paranoid. She can't let her children see her frightened. Alfonso had nothing to do with the break-in. They have no choice but to trust him. She turns to her children. "We'll have to pretend we know nothing about these flowers. That's the safest thing."

She glances at Justin's still worried face. "There's more?"

He doesn't say anything.

"Spit it out. All of it."

Justin is relieved by his mother's reaction—she didn't get angry about him slipping away—and figures this is probably the best moment to let the rest of the secrets out. He knows he'll feel better when he does.

"Pancho hinted that they throw dead bodies to the crocs that are hidden in that pond out in the mangrove swamp."

"And you believed him?"

"Why do you think I've been having nightmares?"

"You and your overactive imagination. Pancho was trying to freak you out and succeeded. Let's not have any more of this talk. You're frightening your sister."

"Can I sleep here tonight?" Katy asks.

Justin stares at his sister. He hates sharing a room with her, but tonight, maybe it wouldn't be so bad.

"Of course," Katherine says and glances at her son, divining his thoughts. "You're invited too, Justin. Bring your mattress in, and we'll barricade the doors. It'll be like a slumber party."

TWENTY-ONE

K atherine lies awake listening to her slumbering children. The theft suddenly feels like the least of their worries; they're living in the midst of a poppy-growing area, and their neighbor-landlord-friend is a drug king-pin. What kind of crazy world is this, and, more importantly, how dangerous is it for them to be living here? She wishes Phil were home. Maybe now, he would consider leaving. Yes, that would be the best option—leave before things get more intense.

When she finally dozes off, noises from the forest morph into intruders. She awakens, tumbles from the bed, and goes to the window. The pale moon casts a sliver of brightness, and fireflies weave a sparkling net across the backyard.

Horacio reclines in the truck, his face illuminated by the glow of a cigarette. He opens the door and steps out. His foot-steps crunch on the gravel as he checks the perimeter of the house. Katherine slips back between the sheets, slightly reas-sured, yet in the back of her mind she can't help but wonder if he is here to provide protection or to keep an eye on them. At least now she better understands Alfonso's reluctance to get the authorities involved.

Katy sleeps with the confidence of a trusting child. Though young, she is not easily ruffled, and, like her father, she has embraced the language and the culture; however, unlike Phil, she prefers ease and comfort, while Phil is interested in money for more complicated reasons. Katherine worries that her daughter is swayed by the luxury offered by the villa. Another nagging fear she has is Pancho. She has noticed him watching her beautiful daughter and is wary of the two of them spending time unchaperoned. Katy is too innocent and trusting for a worldly boy of sixteen. And, as for Justin, the story Pancho told him is absurd. Pancho has a mean streak, and it would be completely in his character for him to tease and horrify her son.

Despite Horacio's presence, the next morning Katherine keeps them all inside and phones Rosa, telling her not to come. The kids entertain themselves with a deck of cards while Katherine inventories and organizes their few possessions, vigilant for anything that might be missing.

Her thoughts whirl. Someone broke into their home, their sanctuary; their things were ransacked; passports, jewelry, and money stolen. Alfonso has local farmers involved in illegal agriculture in a profitable and competitive enterprise. He isn't a development worker at all! Guards, automatic weapons, security cameras—of course, that's why they're needed. Judging by Pancho's close call in the sports car, Alfonso has powerful enemies. Life here just keeps getting scarier and scarier. Perhaps the villa isn't as safe as Alfonso would have them think.

Alfonso calls midmorning to check on them. Katherine croaks out a "hello" in response and clears her throat. "Excuse me, Alfonso. I'm still upset about the robbery."

"Be reasonable. Allow Horacio to bring you and the children here so I can ensure your safety."

"Thank you, but we'll be fine. Phil will be home Sunday afternoon."

Not wanting him to keep insisting, she cuts off the conversation. He always sounds polite and solicitous, but what if he's really a danger?

Justin puts his hand on her shoulder. "What if he's keeping tabs on us? Our cell phones are actually his."

"Justin, stop! Don't upset me more than I already am. He doesn't know that we suspect he's involved with poppy cultivation, and besides, we have no proof. He's right about the police not being able to do much about the break-in. Remember what Jerónimo said when we were held up on our first day?"

"I didn't say we should go to the police. I said he might think we would." His voice sounds injured by the misunderstanding.

She shakes her head. "He's given us a guard until Phil gets home, but it doesn't mean he's watching us."

After lunch, Katherine takes a deep breath and expresses what she's been tossing about in her mind. "I've come to a decision. We'll go down to San Marcos and check into a hotel."

"What will Alfonso say?" Katy asks.

"We won't tell him. It's none of his business." To get some distance from this place and its implicit danger is tempting. Just to be somewhere else for a while, somewhere safe.

She picks up the phone and dials her husband's number. When the ringing stops, a recording asks her to leave a voice message. She tosses the phone on the sofa. "He was supposed to call me today." She glances at the startled look on Katy's face. "Don't worry. I'll call him when we find a hotel."

Katherine is determined to leave and can't come up with a better plan. She can't risk the drive to Xela to meet Phil, even if she knew where to look. He didn't leave her the information, or at least she'd never find it in the mess of papers that got thrown together. Besides, what if the van didn't make it or got a flat? Once she's away from the crime scene, she'll be able to think more clearly. She stuffs a few things into a daypack and has the kids do the same. They head out to the Missionary Marvel.

"We're going into town to pick up a few items," Katherine says as they pass the guard.

Horacio immediately gets out his radio to inform Alfonso. What if he wants to join them, be their bodyguard? They settle into the seats and Katherine turns the ignition key. Nothing. She tries again. "The battery must be dead."

Katherine glances suspiciously at Horacio, then shakes her head imperceptibly. No way could he have sabotaged it. Horacio has kind eyes and a ready smile. She turns to Justin. "The danged car's been acting up lately. I guess it was just a matter of time."

They gather their belongings and trudge toward the house. Horacio questions her. She tells him the car won't start. He gets back on the radio.

She glances out the kitchen window, envious of the freedom she took for granted only days before. Her phone rings. Phil? She stares at the number—Alfonso. "Hello," she answers in a tentative voice.

"Katherine, I heard you wanted to go to town and your car isn't working. Is there anything you need that we can get for you?"

"No, but thanks. I just wanted a change of scenery. We've been stuck in the dreary house for too long."

"Come to the villa."

"You've already done so much." She hesitates.

"I insist you come. I can no longer spare a guard."

197

She considers the alternatives. They can't possibly remain alone in this house when the door won't even shut, and now they no longer have a vehicle. It's only for a few days, and it's not as though the children haven't already spent several nights there. After tossing the phone aside, she turns to her kids. "It was Alfonso. He needs Horacio and has instructed him to take us to the villa. We can't stay here with no transportation, no locks, and no guard. Grab your bags."

The palm of her hand against her forehead, she paces the hallway, trying to come up with an alternative plan. But if there is one, it eludes her. Though Alfonso may not be the angel Phil thinks he is—she can see him encouraging poppy cultivation—she also knows he does a lot of good in the community and seems to care about people.

"Even if they are illegal, the flower crops benefit farmers so much that maybe growing opium isn't all that bad," Justin says, reflecting her own thoughts.

She looks at his earnest face. "Remember, we know nothing about those poppies. Nothing at all."

Horacio opens the doors of the double-cab pickup. Katherine sits between her children and reaches for their hands, not sure if it is to give strength or to receive it, but her daughter shares none of her dread. Katy stares out the window; her excitement is evident.

Inside the compound, as gardeners clip foliage and mainte-nance men sweep sidewalks, Katherine is struck by the ordinari-ness of it. She shakes her head. Can this really be a center for drug trafficking?

Horacio parks in front and helps them with their things.

The front door stands open in welcome. Katy and Justin race up the stairs and leave their mother standing awkwardly in the foyer. She waits until the housekeeper comes and shows her to a guest room, a lovely space filled with antiques and a sliding glass door that opens onto a small balcony.

She expects to see her children, and after a few minutes, panic overtakes her. "Kids?" she calls from the doorway.

They step out of a nearby room. "Yes?"

Her hand covers her rapidly beating heart. She forces herself to calm down and manages to smile. "I just wanted to know where you were. If you need anything, let me know. I'm going to lie down. I hardly slept last night."

She reclines and stares at the ceiling. Sleep is inaccessible. After resting, she showers and gets dressed. Someone taps at the door.

"¿Sí?"

The knob turns slightly and a uniformed maid enters. The woman is carrying a tray with a glass of red wine and some hors d'oeuvres. She tells Katherine to leave the empty platter on the floor in the hallway and she'll be by to pick it up later.

Room service? Katherine checks to see that the children have been offered food. They lounge on the twin beds in Katy's room, mechanically stuffing popcorn into their mouths, eyes glued to a flat-screen television. Katy glances over and waves.

Katherine wanders downstairs, where Alfonso is reading a newspaper in the living room, shoes removed and stockinged feet resting on a leather footrest. The intimacy of his shoeless feet startles her.

"Hello, there," Alfonso says. "Please take a seat. I trust you have everything you need."

She sits on a nearby chair. "The room is lovely. Thank you for helping us." Poppy screeches from the nearby perch, an evil look in her eye. "I guess Poppy isn't happy about my presence."

"She is terribly jealous of you. She does not like to share the spotlight with another female, but enough about Poppy. I am delighted you could join us."

"We didn't have much choice," she reminds him.

"My apologies about the guard. We are shorthanded this weekend."

"I really don't mind going to a hotel."

He waves his hands, tossing aside any possibility. "I will not hear of it. We have plenty of space, and I am sure Phil will be more comfortable with his family under my protection."

"What about when he gets back?"

"I do believe you will need a place to stay once construction on the church begins."

Katherine cocks her head to one side, wondering what he means. Sure, the construction will be a mess, but there would be no reason not to go back to their home once the doors are secured and their van fixed.

"Even if you decide to stay put, I hate to have you in such a small, cramped space. It's a wonder I allowed my employees to live there back then, but again, they were only three." He shakes away the thought with a movement of his head and flashes his most charming smile. "It is my hope you will stay."

"I'm very grateful, but the situation is temporary. Once Phil returns we'll get the car up and running, and the house front door repaired. Thank you so much for your generous hospitality, but it's enough for us to stay these few days."

"Oh, by the way," Alfonso announces, as he rises when Katherine gets up. "We are hosting a formal dinner tonight. I expect you and your children to join us. Please be ready and downstairs at eight."

CHAPTER

TWENTY-TWO

Katherine, enjoying the quiet and the afternoon sunshine, leans on the railing of the bedroom's balcony. Below, the Avalanche pickup, burdened with their belongings, rumbles into the compound.

She races downstairs. "Wait! What's going on? I thought I told you we'd be leaving as soon as Phil gets back."

Alfonso, directing the comings and goings of men carrying boxes, turns to face her. "My dear Katherine, your things could not stay at the house unprotected any more than you could. They will be safe here."

"I didn't authorize you to do this."

"I do not need anyone's authorization. I do what needs to be done."

Disconcerted, Katherine sits on the bench and watches helplessly. This is one of the reasons she was reluctant to come—the loss of control. With their things at Alfonso's, she knows it will be that much more difficult to leave. Alfonso directs the men to put the boxes of kitchen items and linens in a storage shed and to take the personal items up to their rooms. Suddenly, Katherine is ashamed. From the perspective of the villa, their things look like paupers' belongings. She follows the men upstairs as their meager possessions are brought to their rooms.

"What's going on, Mom?" Justin asks. "Aren't we going back to the house when Dad gets here?"

"I don't know."

"Dad's not going to like this."

"We don't know what Dad will like. Now go upstairs and put your things away."

His puzzled expression troubles her, but then, of course, it would be obvious to him that she is allowing them to be held captive. What other choice does she have?

Too bad Phil is at his church conference, but then again she remembers how embarrassing it had been at the pool party with Phil carting around his Bible and antagonizing the guests. She has to wonder if Phil will insist they leave when he arrives, or if he will allow his family to drift along in the swift current of Alfonso's will. Somehow, she believes the latter will be the case.

On the bright side, the children will have computers and internet at their disposal, but she knows that it comes with a price, and the first installment will be tonight's party. What, exactly, does Alfonso have in mind?

Sighing, she goes upstairs to her new room and puts away her things. When she opens the closet, she sees a gown with a note attached hanging inside.

I found this in Guatemala City and thought of you. Please do me the honor of wearing it tonight.—A.

A formal evening. She had already put it out of her mind.

The gown sparkles as though tiny emeralds are embedded in the fabric. On the floor are matching pumps. She stares at the dress without daring to move, afraid it might be an illusion. Initially, she feels cheapened and angry, but curiosity takes over and she is fascinated by the allure of the dress, a gown unlike any she has ever worn. She tries it on. A perfect fit, a second skin.

She tells herself that she will certainly wear one of her dowdy Sunday dresses for the dinner. After all, what might Alfonso expect if she wore this one? To see herself from every angle in the full-length mirror, she spins around in the glowing garment. How much could such a thing cost? She's never worn anything so elegant, and she closes her eyes and imagines herself an actress strolling down the red carpet at the Oscars. If she were wearing this dress, people would turn and stare at the fiery redhead. No, she can't accept the dress. No way. But maybe she can borrow it, just for tonight.

In the back of her mind, she worries about falling into his scheme. She doesn't want to accept his overtures and is aware that he is playing a game with her. A game she may be powerless to resist.

Katy tentatively opens the bedroom door. "Mom, can we come in?"

Katherine motions her in, and Justin follows behind.

Katy, in a shimmering purple taffeta dress and two-inch heels, shakes her head in wonder. "Are you my mother?"

Justin stares. "Where'd *that* come from? It's not yours, so why're you wearing it?" His voice drips with disapproval.

Heat rises in Katherine's cheeks. What does a fourteen-year-old know about right and wrong? Then she adjusts her expression and gives them each a quick hug. "It was hanging in the closet with a note from Alfonso to wear it to the dinner party tonight. I'm sure he knows we didn't bring formal clothes with us."

Katy smiles and twirls around, the taffeta skirt crackling as it flares. "Look what he left for me! I love it!"

"Pancho brought these," Justin admits. He glances down, self-conscious in new khaki pants, a button-down shirt, and a sports jacket. "He said it's all stuff he outgrew, but I doubt it. The tags were still attached."

"He's probably got so many clothes he doesn't get a chance to wear 'em all," Katy says.

Katherine tries to convince herself that Alfonso is simply a generous man who enjoys giving gifts, and it isn't as though cost is an issue.

She leans over and holds a thin gold chain with a pearl teardrop, an engagement gift from Phil that was overlooked in the theft. "Can you fasten this for me, sweetheart?"

Katy clasps the ends together, then follows her mother into the dressing room. "Can I put on some makeup too?"

Katherine outlines her lips with lip gloss and watches Katy rummage through the cosmetic bag.

"Lipstick? Maybe a little mascara?" Katy pleads. "Remember when I used to play dress-up when I was a little girl."

"You're still a little girl," Justin says, not happy with his sister growing up too soon. "Are you guys done already? It's not like the president is showing up tonight."

"We don't know exactly who is showing up, now do we?" Katherine answers.

The gown Alfonso left for her is a far cry from Katherine's all-occasion black dress. She has never worn anything quite like it. At her wedding she wore her mother's pearl-encrusted gown. A few snips and stitches had made it a perfect fit, and she remembers the thrill of that day, the culmination of a girl's dreams, finally marrying her high school sweetheart. Her sister and her girlfriends were bridesmaids. Like all brides, she expected to live happily ever after. In the years since, she has discovered that reality seldom lives up to fantasy. She had been young then. Very young.

When Katy and Katherine are ready, the three of them go out and stand at the top of the stairs. On cue, Alfonso appears at the foot of the curved staircase. The tuxedo he wears emphasizes his narrow waist and broad shoulders, and he wears it as comfortably as someone else might wear pajamas. His hair is slicked back, and a few strands of silver distinguish his appearance.

He whistles under his breath. "Young Katherine, is that you? You are such a lovely young lady."

Dimples punctuate Katy's delight.

"I am glad those outgrown clothes of Pancho's fit, Justin. They look like they were made for you."

His attention shifts to Katherine, and his eyes linger as they wander from her head to her heels. "Katherine, you look stunning." His voice rasps in wonder.

Her cheeks are aglow, the problem of being a redhead. Whatever drama she is about to become a part of, she will share the stage with her children, and they will bear witness to any flubbed lines or missteps.

When she reaches the bottom of the stairs, she takes Alfonso's proffered arm. His body heat emanates through the tuxedo and startles her. He leads them past the internet station and into the formal living room, which until now she hadn't entered. Scattered throughout the room are the stelae taken from the ruins on the mountain, one at least six foot in height and another about half the size, plus smaller stones mounted on marble

pedestals and a few carved jade pieces. Potted palm trees decorate the corners of the room.

Padre Chus, the Catholic priest from San Marcos, is the only
one there. Like most Guatemalans, he is a small man. He walks
with a limp and wears a thick-soled shoe on his left foot. Lines
crease his face, particularly around his mouth. Instead of giving
him a righteous air like that of his namesake, Jesus, his features
seem frozen in an expression of perpetual disdain.

After Alfonso introduces them, Katy and Justin sit together
on a leather sectional. Perched on the edge of a recliner, Katherine, in her form-fitting dress, is afraid to settle back. She doesn't
want to look like an ingenue on a casting couch. Apparently
intent on being an exceptional host, Alfonso walks to the stelae, a
large one as tall as a grown man to the left of the door and a
shorter one to the right.

"You have an admirable collection of Mayan artifacts," the
priest says, strolling over to the shorter stela.

"I enjoy being reminded of all Guatemala offers," Alfonso
says, "both past and present. So often, the poor and underprivi-
leged are not encouraged to be proud of their ancestry."

"You can't relieve hunger with history," Padre Chus says.

"A sense of pride, a little hope—these things go a long way."
Alfonso points to the stone slab and explains that it depicts a
Mayan priest offering sacrifices to gods. "Incorporating Mayan
beliefs into the Catholic tradition was one of the most effective
strategies used by the conquistadores."

The priest's mouth stretches into a sneer. "Many believe it
corrupted Christianity." He glances at Katherine as if to gauge
her reaction.

Katherine makes an effort to not comment one way or
another. Phil's presence is palpable, and she can imagine what
he would say.

"I disagree," Alfonso counters. "Integrating indigenous customs made it easy for the natives to adopt Catholicism. It helped conquer the Americas for Spain and the Church. The institution was willing to give a little to receive a lot."

Padre Chus shrugs as if discussions with the laity are beneath him, and Katherine wonders if Alfonso is provoking her because she's a non-Catholic. On the other hand, maybe he just wants to know if she shares her husband's beliefs.

"I found this at a nearby site in the hills." Alfonso moves to the other side of the door and points to the intricate carving on the taller stela. "Depicted is a high priest. Elements in the figure suggest it comes from the Classic Period, between 300 and 900 AD. Note the use of quetzal feathers in the headdress." He points to the carved figure. "The elaborate costume gives the priest a commanding and impressive presence. Even back when the quetzal was more abundant, it was a feat to catch one of these birds."

The priest looks down at his simple clothing. "Surely you aren't insinuating that what a person wears is important to their spiritual purity. Clothing is merely a superficial covering. God recognizes his people regardless of their earthly attire." He glances at Katherine surreptitiously.

Alfonso smiles. "Of course clothing is important. It changes people's perceptions, their mood—if you will. Why else would women get the urge to shop for shoes when they feel down?" He thinks for a moment. "Here is a good example. Were you not wearing clerical clothing, Katherine would not take you for a priest. If you did not wear your vestments for mass, the parishioners would react differently toward you. What you wear matters. The vestments you wear for Easter, for instance, are always light and richly decorated, a beautiful symbol of Christ's resurrection. Clothing can make you feel powerful or weak, confident or self-conscious." Alfonso locks eyes with Katherine. "Do you not agree?"

She knows she's being played. She admits that she feels different in this dress: sexy, elegant, desirable—adjectives that had never before been part of her self-description. As she struggles for words, Katy interjects with her usual enthusiasm. "I love my new dress, Alfonso. Thank you! And the shoes, too. I've never worn heels before."

"You are very welcome."

He catches Katherine's eye and winks. Discomfited, she shifts in her seat. Now she sees he's played them all. What all is this man capable of?

The priest frowns as he considers the artifacts. "I hope you don't plan to take these out of the country. That would be illegal, you know."

Alfonso laughs as if the question is absurd. "Of course not. These will be donated to the National Museum of Ethnology if and when I leave Guatemala. Though I must say, I have no intention of leaving anytime soon."

Pancho, wearing a tailored suit, strides in. His slicked-back hair gleams with gel, and the scent of his expensive aftershave wafts through the room.

Turning to Katherine with disapproval, Padre Chus says, "I saw your family at the church in San Marcos with Alfonso several months ago. Why isn't your husband with you?"

Her face burns. What must the priest think of her—unaccompanied at a party in the home of a handsome, wealthy bachelor? "He's at a missionary retreat in Quetzaltenango. He'll be back Sunday afternoon."

He picks up a book from the coffee table and absentmindedly flips through the pages, but his attention is focused on Katherine. "And you are staying here as Alfonso's guests?"

"Our home was broken into and ransacked. Alfonso was kind enough to take us in until we get ourselves situated," she replies in her defense.

She never expected to be glad to see Chato. He enters the room exactly at that moment, accompanied by a short, heavyset man wearing thick, horn-rimmed glasses and a rumpled suit. His comfortably plump wife teeters on high heels. Katherine sees that she is wearing a floor-length gown, and, for a moment, she is grateful to be wearing a dress that allows her to fit in as one of the local royalty.

"Señor y Señora López, un gusto." Alfonso stands and greets them. "Señor López is the director of the local public school."

"Your husband is the missionary who works with Chomo, I presume." Señor López extends a damp, limp hand to Katherine.

"Yes, he is," she says. "I am Katherine Whitehall, and these are my two children, Justin and Katy."

"Chomo is a dedicated man and devoted parent. Three of his children study with us."

Justin speaks up, his interest piqued. "Where is the local school?"

Señor López coughs and looks around to address the inquiry. He seems slightly disoriented, giving the impression that he doesn't often converse with young people, despite being the school's director. He adjusts his glasses and focuses on Justin, bushy eyebrows raised in surprise as if just noticing the children. "Walking distance from here. Less than three kilometers away. You are welcome to visit whenever you like."

Static and indistinguishable chatter blare from the radio at Pancho's waist, indicating the arrival of more guests. He gets up and returns a few minutes later with a tall, blond bear of a man, whose presence fills the room.

"Señor Alfonso," the man booms. "*Gracias por la invitación.*

We were surprised and delighted." Next to him is a petite brunette, dressed in a short black cocktail dress.

Alfonso explains that Hans Pregel owns one of the largest coffee-producing estates in the San Marcos area.

Katy, fascinated, stares at him. "You don't look Guatemalan."

His smile lights up the room. "Ha! But I am. Guatemalans come in all sizes and colors. My great-grandparents left Germany in the late 1800s with a wave of immigrants who settled here and began cultivating coffee. My wife, María García Granados, is descended from Spanish settlers."

"I haven't seen any coffee farms nearby," Katherine says.

"It's the altitude," María says. "This is much too high for coffee. Coffee doesn't do well above six thousand feet. Finca La Providencia, our farm, is an hour's drive downhill and slightly to the north of here. Why don't you come for a visit?"

María hands Katherine a business card. "Here's our address and phone number. Next Friday is August 15, *Día de la Asunción*, a holiday in Guatemala City, so we will all be there. It just so happens that the Virgin of the Assumption is also the patron saint of our farm. There'll be food, dancing, and festivities."

"We'd be delighted," Katherine says, and hopes her husband will agree. Of course, if there's a crowd, there will be people to convert, and that is exactly what he would try to do.

ALFONSO RISES and leads the guests to the formal dining area. Warmth emanates from a fire blazing on the stone hearth. Crystal chandeliers hang like icicles from carved cedar ceilings and cast tiny rainbow reflections on the walls. Linen napkins, heavy silver flatware, and sparkling glasses are set out on a long table. Alfonso seats Katherine to his left, Chato on his right, and Padre Chus opposite.

Among these educated guests, Katherine feels perfectly safe. With this many chaperones, what could go wrong?

A full-length portrait of Alfonso working with peasants in a field, hoe in hand, hangs on a wood-paneled wall. He looks the part of a development worker, kind and compassionate, a saint or a hero, but is this the real Alfonso or the one who poses for photos that will enhance his public image? Katherine turns from the painting and sees Alfonso, eyes sparkling with humor, observing her, and again she suspects this whole evening was planned for her benefit.

Padre Chus gives the blessing, and the first course is served. After waiting for Alfonso's cue, the guests tackle the food. Señor López rises to his feet and taps a wine glass. "I'd like to propose a toast to our host and benefactor, Don Alfonso. In the name of Public School Canton Piedra Grande, its two teachers, and all its students, I thank you for donating the computers and the new desks. Piedra Grande is an impoverished community and long neglected by the authorities. If all Guatemala's wealthy gave back to the local communities as you do, many of our problems would be solved."

Alfonso nods, accepting the recognition.

"There was no place to keep the computers," his wife continues, "so he arranged for a room to be built. He also helped fathers of the students fashion a small soccer field and stands for spectators."

"Chato made the arrangement," Alfonso explains. "We had timber left over when this area was cleared and developed." He nods toward his assistant, whose eyes hold a glint of pride.

Padre Chus raises his glass. "To donate toward education is

to work toward tomorrow. The future of the country belongs to the youth."

"I agree," María adds quietly, "but we all must admit that public schools have a long way to go to be able to compete with private."

"It is true, unfortunately," Señor López concedes. "Educational funding is limited. I expect there is not enough money for the various improvement projects, and that doesn't take into account government corruption—but let's not get into that right now. We all must do our best with whatever resources we have. A few generous contributions make a world of difference."

Hans leans over and explains to Katherine that the public school system is so underfunded that only the very poor use its services. Children from more affluent families attend private schools.

Señor López, listening in, adds, "Even so, free education is expensive for rural families who struggle to purchase shoes, required uniforms, and school supplies. Most of these children don't have enough to eat and arrive at school hungry. Much of our budget, apart from salaries, goes toward providing nutritious snacks. Growling stomachs overpower teachers' lesson plans."

"In the States," Katherine says, "the National School Lunch Program provides free lunches for children in need. Is there not something similar here?"

"On paper the government promised to provide breakfast for students," Señor López says, "but in reality the food never reaches the community in its entirety. All the way down the chain, funds are siphoned off into bureaucrats' pockets. Here at the local level, we try, but there are many barriers to success, hunger being only one of them."

"The public school system works well in the United States," Katherine says. "It isn't perfect by any means, and some districts are better than others, but both my husband and I graduated from public schools, and our children have attended them. A good public system equalizes education and strives to give an equivalent opportunity to everyone."

Hans shakes his massive head. "Our school system is based on that idealized model, but in practical terms it is doomed to failure because of the huge gap between social and economic classes. Almost ninety percent of the rural population lives in poverty. To put it in practical terms, the tax base just isn't there."

Katherine turns to Alfonso and smiles. "It's wonderful of you to use your resources to help."

"That's not all Alfonso has done," María adds. "He established a number of health clinics in the area. One of them is near our farm. Alfonso put the building up and donates medicine. We heard about it from our employees and decided to help as well. We provide a full-time nurse, and once a week a doctor comes out from Guatemala City."

Katherine remembers Phil mentioning local health centers established by Alfonso. Is poppy growing a way of raising money to help people and give back to the communities? To help bring them out of poverty? Though he plainly makes plenty of money, he might have altruistic motives. Maybe she has been hasty in her assessment of Alfonso and his practices.

Under the table, she crosses her legs and touches Alfonso accidentally. The contact jolts her like a bolt of electricity. Heat spreads through her body. "Excuse me."

He smiles with his eyes but makes no comment.

Padre Chus clears his throat and straightens his napkin. "Alfonso regularly donates to a trust fund he set up for widows and orphans. Many benefit from his generosity. Like the Mayans who carved their stories in stone, Alfonso is carving a place for himself in heaven."

"Please, please," Alfonso interrupts. "You must stop now. This is embarrassing."

Hans raises a goblet. "One final toast to Alfonso."

General conversation ceases and is replaced by a low murmuring as everyone concentrates on the meal. Waiters serve course after course of food. Just when everyone marvels how much they've eaten, the chocolate mousse is brought out.

After dinner, the party drifts into the library. The two youngsters trail their mother and find themselves in front of a tall white cage where a small red-bellied, lime-colored bird perches stiffly. Tiny iridescent feathers on its head rise into a green mohawk. Its tail feathers measure several feet.

"I wish Dad were here," Justin says. "He'd know what kind of bird that is."

Pancho comes from behind Justin. "It's a quetzal, dude."

"Why stuff it? Why not a real bird?"

"Symbols of freedom and that kind of shit. They can't live in captivity. They'd rather die than be imprisoned." Pancho pokes his finger through the bars to stroke the long tail feathers.

"Hey, Justin, did you see this hot chick?" He points at the full-figured nude statue on a nearby table. "Personally, I like them slimmer, but she's got some amazing tits!"

Justin glances at his mother conversing with the guests, wondering what she would think of the statue. His father sure wouldn't approve.

Katy yawns. "Come upstairs with me, Justin. I'm tired."

He scans the room and decides there's no reason to stay. Television with hundreds of channels is more entertaining than an adult party. "See you tomorrow, Pancho. We're headed up."

"Maybe I'll see you in the gym. I'm usually there by seven."

Justin seriously doubts he'll be up by then, but appreciates the invitation.

Katherine watches as her children slip out. Stimulated by the company and conversation, she has already forgotten her previous sleepless night and hopes the evening doesn't end too soon.

Seeing her alone, Señor López approaches. "The conversation at the table must have been interesting for you."

She agrees. "Yes, in the year ahead, I'd like find ways I can make a difference."

"I hear you are also an educator."

"I substitute teach for the school district back home. I've never had my own classroom until now." She clarifies. "I'm homeschooling the children."

"They are very lucky to have you as their private tutor. If you come to visit our little school, don't be surprised if it looks nothing like American schools. Despite Alfonso's help, it is still quite humble."

She smiles and accepts a cup of coffee being passed by a waiter. She would like to see what their host has done.

The conversation on the other side of the library falls into a lull, and guests drift over. Padre Chus addresses her. "Do you work with your husband at all?"

Katherine hesitates. His question is tinged with frost, and she suspects he is attempting to goad her. "I help with music during Sunday service, and we go out together to villages two or three times a week. He regularly visits parishioners in their homes, prays for the sick, and reads Scripture. While my husband focuses on religious teachings, I have started projects of my own."

"I understand that poverty is not exclusively in third-world countries. Our mighty neighbor to the north also has its underdeveloped areas."

"It's true, I'm afraid. Many Americans suffer from abject

poverty. Though I am aware we could be helping in my own country, we elected to come here for our mission work."

The priest regards her quietly, and she senses that she has passed some type of unknown test.

"What kind of projects are you working on?" María prompts, and moves closer.

Katherine tells her about the laying hens she acquired for Don Faustino and his wife, about teaching women how to cook more nutritiously using green vegetables and herbs found in the countryside, and about teaching them to boil their drinking water.

"There are many ways to help," their host interjects, and everyone agrees. "It isn't important how we help or what our projects might be. The important thing is to do whatever we can. All of us have something to offer, a way to contribute. I have brought you together tonight to share the many ways that each of you are helping to make this country a better place."

The guests depart around eleven, and Katherine retires to her room. She is exhausted, but sleep eludes her. Perhaps it is the after-dinner coffee combined with the wine, or maybe the unaccustomed stimulation of a social evening. She tosses and turns, her head spinning with the days' events and particularly with the new image of Alfonso that has emerged.

She puts on a robe and creeps downstairs for a glass of filtered water. The house is quiet and the servants have retired for the evening. She wonders if her host is awake, and her heart beats rapidly thinking of her boldness, a woman alone at the home of a handsome neighbor, one who also finds her attractive. On her way back and not anxious to return to her room, she stops near the front door, thinking to step outside for some fresh air, perhaps a walk in the garden. She likes the feel of the quiet, empty house.

When she tries to open the door to get out, she finds it securely locked and bolted. She notices the flash of an alarm on a nearby control panel. A shadow lurks outside the door, ghostlike through the beveled-glass pane. A Doberman growls, and she jumps back. A voice comes from behind, and she swings around.

Alfonso chuckles at her startled face. "I wondered if it was you wandering around the house. I hope the dogs did not startle you. I forgot to tell you not to go out at night. I have a remarkable lifestyle, but, like everything, it comes with a price."

He reaches out as if to embrace her, but she spins around and hurries up the stairs to her room.

TWENTY-THREE

K atherine's feet, accustomed to sandals and sneakers, are blistered from the borrowed pumps, and her eyes puffy. She showers, wraps herself in a fluffy towel, and wanders toward the window. She pulls the heavy curtains back, and light slices into the bedroom, leaving warm tracks on the tile floor. Judging by the sun's height, she has slept late.

She dresses quickly and heads downstairs in search of her morning elixir. In the breakfast room, Alfonso peruses the morning paper. When Katherine enters the room, he puts it down and stands. "Good morning. I trust you had a good sleep. Is there anything I can get for you?"

"Just coffee, please."

He stands and pours a cup from a nearby thermos.

Outside, a lawnmower roars to life, silencing the chirping of birds. Familiar tortilla slapping echoes from the kitchen. She wraps her hands around the mug and turns to her host. "Have you been up long?"

"I do not sleep much and am always up by daybreak."

In workout pants and a muscle shirt, arms and neck glistening with sweat, Pancho swaggers into the room. He grabs a plate and helps himself to a volcano of scrambled eggs from the buffet on the counter.

Alfonso frowns. "Where are your manners?"

The teen glares back sullenly. "Morning."

"Next time shower before breakfast. You spoil our appetites."

Pancho takes his plate out to the patio.

Feeling awkward, Katherine says, "Really, Alfonso, I don't want to put anyone out. Please don't think you need to act differently because we're staying here."

"Correct etiquette is the key to earning a place in polite society. I don't know why Pancho has such difficulty with manners. No one wants to associate with a thug."

Startled by his comments, her eyes grow wide.

A wince flickers across his face. "Do you have plans for today?"

She shakes her head. What kind of plans could she possibly have?

"There is a beautiful, remote place up in the mountains I would like to show you. It is a breathtaking ride."

Alone? He wants to go out with her alone? "What about Justin and Katy?"

"They will be fine. There are plenty of things to amuse them within the complex. I have asked the chef to prepare a lunch for us to take."

Her sense of propriety screams "no," but he's been such a gentleman, and the ride does sound exquisite, just what she needs to nurse a slight hangover. Surely, she can control any situation that might come up. He would never make her do anything against her will. She is thrilled at the thought of an afternoon with Alfonso and at the same time is terrified by her boldness.

"I don't know." Undecided, she searches lamely for an answer. "I probably shouldn't with Phil away ... "

His eyes narrow slightly. "This has nothing to do with Phil, and I would not invite him if he were here. He tells me he does not care for horses. Please be ready to leave at ten." His voice is commanding, the statement an order. He excuses himself and leaves the room.

Katherine is stunned. She tries to tell herself that he just speaks directly and that he is accustomed to having his own way. She glances up as the clock chimes half past eight. She goes over possible excuses: a feigned illness, a problem with one of the children, but when it comes right down to it, she wants to go.

A short while later, Katy joins her. She listens as her mother explains about the horseback ride. "You're so lucky! I wish he'd have invited me."

Still conflicted, Katherine shrugs off her concern. Katy's right, of course. Why all the worry? It will be an adventurous day on horseback, nothing more. After breakfast, Katherine goes out to the pool and stretches out on a recliner near her daughter. She rolls up her pants to receive the morning sun on her pale legs.

Katy makes a sweeping gesture with her arms to include the garden, the pool, and the mansion. "Isn't this wonderful. I can hardly believe we're here. It's my dream come true."

"Well, your dad isn't here yet, sweetheart. We don't know what he's going to think about all of this. This isn't exactly how most missionaries live."

"I bet he'll love it. Can't we just live here? Forget about that horrid house."

"Honey, we're guests. This is only temporary."

Justin approaches through the sliding glass. "I was looking everywhere for you. Why did you let me sleep so late?"

"I thought you'd be glad for a few extra hours of sleep."

"Don't we have stuff to do? I don't know, schoolwork or chores, or something? We always do at home." He's mainly worried that their lives have taken a turn that might not so easily be reversed. Their previously ordered schedule was comforting in its safety and boredom.

Katherine smiles at him. "Consider yourself on vacation for a few days. We deserve it." She stands. "I'm going to change. Alfonso invited me on a horseback ride this morning. You kids stay here. We'll be back after lunch."

"Don't worry about us, Mom. Have fun." Katy shoos her away.

"Just the two of you?" Justin says and glances around the yard, as though looking for others who would join them.

"I doubt we're going alone. Alfonso rarely does." Katherine is filled with feelings that range from fear to euphoria, but excitement wins out. Her palms sweat. An inner voice tells her not to go, but she's made up her mind. Why not be daring? She's played the "good wife" to Phil for sixteen years. Anything resembling fun or excitement, he manages to ruin. Now is her chance. She'll be with the most attractive man she's ever known. Her stomach flutters, but surely, she can stay in control. What harm could come of a little flirting?

Precisely at ten, the groom leads two saddled horses from the stables. Alfonso appears with a basket and helps Katherine onto the bay mare. He hands her the reins and secures their lunch behind the saddle.

She remembers her son's concern and glances around for a chaperone. "What about bodyguards?"

"No need." He pats the holstered gun at his waist.

The black stallion dances and skitters, tossing his mane until Alfonso gets him under control. "Mil Amores was shipped to me from Spain. The mare you ride is Noblesa. You may remember her from last time."

Katherine pats Noblesa. "Hey, girl." The mare flops her ears in response and follows the prancing stallion to the gate. The guard salutes Alfonso and waves them through. She isn't sure whether to be wary or thrilled.

Turning in his saddle and raising an arm, Alfonso points out the Tacaná volcano in the distance.

"Beautiful," she says.

Like bursts of sunshine, yellow wildflowers light both sides of the road. Purple orchids, mountain laurel, and daisies are the colors of Monet's palette. Katherine's spirits soar. After a half-hour ride, the shaded, meandering trail forks at the bottom of the hill.

Alfonso stops at a hut camouflaged in the brush. "Feliciano! Hey!" Fingers in his mouth, Alfonso whistles sharply.

A small man in tattered clothing appears from behind a tree.

"Don Alfonso." He puts his hands together and bows slightly. "I am your servant."

"Take these animals and give them water. I wish to show the señora Las Piedras Sagradas."

They dismount, and Don Feliciano leads the horses away. Katherine follows Alfonso to a familiar trailhead. He steadies her over rocks and exposed tree roots. They stop where giant hand-carved stones, dumped like a child's building blocks, rest in jumbled array.

Katherine remembers that Pancho had made them swear to keep this place secret, and she pretends to be surprised. Alfonso faces her and takes both her hands in his. She tries to avoid his eyes but finds she can't.

"This is my project. My passion. I could have been an archaeologist, but that wasn't the path I chose. Instead, I work at it as a hobby."

The sudden intimacy of the two of them in this lonely place frightens her. As if wanting a better look at the ruins, she pulls away. "Is this a well-known place?"

"A well-kept secret. I have spoken to the community to keep it that way. Once word gets out, looters come. I hope to document and restore what I can. We call this place Holy Stones. When I first came here, people still used the site for prayer, but they had no *sacerdote*, no one to lead their worship, so I began to study their beliefs."

"I thought you were Catholic."

"I am. Do you not see how the two religions have melded over the years? I find all religions fascinating. It is a basic need in most men's souls to worship a higher being."

When her surprise levels off, she realizes he is still speaking. He has gone on to speak of natural skeptics, those who, because of certain personality traits, have difficulty believing in God or gods. He doesn't say outright but hints that she might be included in that category. She is taken aback. Perhaps he speaks of himself, but how can he presume to know this about her?

"Religion fulfills a basic human desire," he says. "We turn to religion to fulfill our lives. To make sense of the world and to justify happenings that are beyond our control. Whether or not we are believers in one God or many, we should not impose our beliefs on others if they are not actively seeking alternatives."

Why is he funding their church if he feels this way? She takes a step back. "How can you say that? That's exactly what Phil and I do as missionaries."

"What Phil does. It seems to me that you are more interested in helping the less fortunate."

"Who do you think you are to criticize our work?" she says. "Besides, if it weren't for people like us, how many souls would continue in darkness?"

"Is darkness having faith in something different from what Phil believes? Is that not presumptuous to think the Judeo-Christian ideals are the only valid ones?"

She crosses her arms and frowns. He has touched a raw nerve.

He looks down, regretful. "Forgive me. I did not mean to offend."

Sure, she has doubts, but doesn't everyone? Everyone, that is, except Phil.

"I can see you are a woman of strong opinions," he says, "but I did not bring you here to argue. Let me show you the ruins." As they stroll among the fallen stones, he explains the structures and their presumed functions in the ancient world.

Katherine has difficulty following his words. She is distracted by the faint scent of an unfamiliar flower. Petals are scattered in an area looking south. Candles and offerings are set into niches in a stone wall.

She speaks her thoughts aloud before she realizes. "Justin would love it here. He's fascinated by the Mayan culture."

Alfonso smiles, but anger flashes in his eyes. "Do not take me for a fool. Pancho brought you, Justin, and young Katherine here on horses and swore you to secrecy. I appreciate your loyalty to the oath you made, but your allegiance must be to me. I demand that of everyone."

"My allegiance?" She bristles. "My allegiance is to Phil."

His lips tighten. "When you are living in my home, your allegiance is to me."

Not wishing to provoke his anger, she changes her tone.

"Why did Pancho make us swear not to mention it if he was going to tell you anyway?"

"For the excitement, of course. Is not the forbidden and the secretive much more thrilling than the mundane and the conventional?"

He searches her eyes and she averts them, looking instead toward the distant mountains. The mundane, conventional husband versus the forbidden and secretive neighbor?

"I will tell you something you may not know. Justin came a few weeks later, unable to resist." He shows her where her son hid that day. "It just happened that we had a ceremony planned for that morning, and he got a good show. He believes I am unaware of his visit, but there is little that escapes my attention."

A chill runs through her at his words. He is aware that we know about the poppy crops. She wonders why he is taking her out to the distant hills. To kidnap her? Kill her? "Maybe we should turn back now. I'm concerned about my children."

"They are in good hands. Do not worry, dear Katherine. I see by your reaction that Justin informed you of what went on that day. I believe I can trust you with that information."

The statement is delivered in a matter-of-fact tone, and she isn't sure how to interpret it. She is intrigued, even though she knows to be wary. She wants to ask him why he does it—the poppies—what is his motivation, but she can't risk it. She doesn't want to bring her suspicions out in the open.

They return to the horses. Alfonso helps her mount, and they continue south for another hour, following the curve of the mountain and a stream. The path narrows and ends where a thin stream of water drops from a height of a hundred feet into a crystal-clear pool below. Wild orchids hang from trees, white, purple and fuchsia. A hidden paradise. Sunlight filters through the trees and creates latticework in the clearing. The air is warm and moist, and foliage is much more tropical at this lower elevation. Birds sing, and Katherine is reminded of the aviary at their local zoo. She thinks of her birding husband and then, annoyed by her thoughts of him, tries to put him out of her mind.

Katherine's breath catches in her throat. "This is incredible."

Alfonso dismounts and ties his horse. He holds the mare's reins and reaches up for her. "It cannot compare to you, my dear."

His closeness overwhelms her. Her pulse quickens. She should never have come. She fears what she cannot or does not want to prevent. The sun strikes the water and blinds her. She fancies God is sending her a warning, but is it too late?

The waterfall's fine spray cools the shaded air. Katherine shivers and Alfonso edges closer. "Are you chilly?" He rubs her arms briskly, then slowly and sensuously. She breathes in his musky aroma and the hairs on her arms stand upright. She feels pulsed with electricity and pulls away.

"What is the matter? Do you not feel safe here with me?" He takes out two goblets from the pack and pours from a wine bottle. "You are still upset about the break-in. I understand. This will help calm you."

"Phil is my husband. I am not at liberty to be with another man."

"You are not enslaved. You made the decision to come here with me. Do you think I will take you against your will?"

"No, no. Of course not. I just thought ... " She can't focus on the best way to finish the sentence. She fears her own reaction, but to say so is to admit her weakness.

He spreads a cover over the soft, damp ground, and they lunch on cold cuts, cheeses, and French bread. The wine is spicy, with a hint of sweetness. She can only imagine the cost of so exquisite a bottle. She sips and he refills her glass immediately. She senses that her thirst should have been quenched by water, not by wine. "I shouldn't be here with you," she protests weakly, but all her resistance has disappeared into the bottom of the wine glass.

He moves closer. "Yet, here you are."

The effects of the alcohol take hold. "I need some food in my stomach," she says, breaking off a hunk of bread. "Otherwise, I'm going to fall off my horse when we return." Not that she's in a hurry. She'd be happy to stay here all afternoon. In a plea bargain with God, she trades her body for the protection he offers her family, but does she really believe that straying from her marriage vows would protect her children? Then she consciously puts any thought of Phil and the children out of her mind and decides to enjoy the moment. It may be the most romantic afternoon she's ever shared with anyone. A pity it isn't with her husband.

With tales of his travels and plans for the future—building schools and helping poor farmers—Alfonso enthralls her. He is a man who makes things happen, and he hopes Katherine will be part of those plans. She is captivated by his dream, swept up in the vision. The allure of the place, a desirable man, a mutual dream. She feels she is in an alternate world, one not governed by the rules that have, up till now, dictated her daily life.

A twig snaps from a tree branch and Katherine jumps.

"Relax. Do not worry. It is only you and me. The birds and the animals of this place are sworn to secrecy. What happens today, stays here."

Her world tilts and her skin burns. The water droplets on the breeze freckle her fevered limbs. Damp, cool shade contrasts with patches of blinding sunlight. Gooseflesh appears on her arms. She hears his speech, but can no longer make out the words. He leans in and kisses her. Her own response startles her. Her ears thrum with the pulsing of her blood.

She feels a flame engulf her. He whispers "Katherine," and it is like the rustle of trees, water falling from hillsides. He cries her name into the forest and a flock of birds takes flight, and Katherine realizes this is real and not just some nighttime fantasy she has used to fill the void of her own passionless life.

TWENTY-FOUR

Reality breaks through her slumber. Sober and awake, she scrambles from Alfonso's arms and covers herself with a blanket. "What have we done?" She reaches for her watch, thrown aside with her clothing. "It's already four. We must leave. What will my children think?"

He props himself up on an elbow, fully at ease with his nudity, and laughs. "Your children have not even missed you. They are quite happy at the villa. I do not think it is your children that concern you."

"I never meant to cheat. I'm not that kind of person."

"This was set in motion the moment we left the compound together."

He's right. Her protests are nothing more than weak, inconsequential attempts to assuage her own guilt. In the back of her mind, she suspected this might happen, even desired it. No matter what kind of person she believed herself to be before, with Alfonso she was a willing partner. She lowers her eyes. Meet the new Katherine.

Amusement glints in his eyes. "Besides, I dare say you never enjoyed sex with him like this. Is it true that missionaries only have one position?"

She bristles. It's true, at least with Phil. She's annoyed that he knows this was the best sex she's ever had but would never feed his ego by admitting it. She keeps her tone even. "Don't make this any worse than it already is. What goes on between a husband and a wife is no one else's business."

Alfonso watches her with a half-smile. "I want you, Katherine. And I generally get what I want. I have not so greatly desired a woman for many years."

She puts up her hand to prevent him from saying more. "I'm married and have children. This can never be." Out of the question, she tells herself. A taste was fun, but how could she leave Phil—the father of her children—for him? Despite his smooth veneer, he is nothing more than a drug trafficker. She kids herself to think otherwise.

"You and I were destined to find each other. God's will, if you like."

She stands and backs away. Grabs her clothes and hides behind a tree to dress. Although she knows there is no way to win an argument with him, she is unable to stop herself. "What could you possibly know about God's will?"

They ride back in silence. Maybe he's angry, but why should she care?

Back at the villa, he hands the horses to the groom and excuses himself without glancing her way. Poppy's afternoon perch is empty.

Katherine finds her children near the pool and sits down next to Justin. "How was your day?"

He shrugs almost imperceptibly and reaches up to pull a leaf from her hair. "Where did you ride?" His words drip with accusation, or so it seems to Katherine. "You smell like alcohol."

"We rode through a forested area, and, yes, we had a glass or two of wine with lunch." Katherine's cheeks burn as she recalls how the leaf might have gotten entangled in her hair. "We stopped by the ruins."

Surprise flashes across Justin's face. "Did he say anything?"

"He knows we went with Pancho and he told me you saw a ceremony later."

"Was he angry?"

"He didn't appear to be."

Lost in thought, she scarcely listens to Katy, who rambles on about her day, swimming in the pool and playing games. "I'm going to shower. I'll see you two for dinner."

KATHERINE SCRUBS herself with a loofa and scalding water. Maybe it was the wine. A rational, practical Katherine never would have allowed this to happen. Adultery. The big A. Tears mix with water. She can't place all the blame on Alfonso.

She steps out of the steaming area and towels off. She pulls out a tee shirt and sweatpants from her things and, for the remainder of the afternoon, stares at the beige walls of her self-imposed prison. What will happen when Phil returns? She will never forgive herself if she is responsible for endangering him in any way.

At seven, the housekeeper knocks at her door to announce the evening meal. Katherine changes and heads to the dining room. The kids and Alfonso are already seated. Though she finds herself opposite their host, she avoids eye contact. Their relaxed, flirting relationship is strained.

Justin watches the interplay and nonverbal communication. He is old enough to pick up the subtle vibes. The afternoon ride changed the way his mother and Alfonso relate to each other.

"Can you join me in the library after dinner?" Alfonso asks Katherine when dessert is almost finished.

"Of course," she says, and after she has made sure the kids are settled in the game room to watch another movie, she joins him.

Like a schoolgirl in the principal's office, she sits primly on the edge of the sofa while he reclines in an overstuffed armchair, head thrown back and slightly tilted in her direction. "It does not need to be awkward between us."

"How can it be otherwise? Tomorrow my husband returns."

"You need to start thinking about making a choice."

Has it come to that already? "What would my children think if I were to leave him for you?"

His face hardens and the tone of his voice flattens as though he is making an effort to control it. "You would have to ask them, but I am sure they would come around eventually." He studies her reaction and says thoughtfully, "Marriages often lose their flavor and their meaning. You need not tie yourself to someone you no longer love. Is it so unusual for people to change partners in life?"

She scarcely knows how to reply. How presumptuous! How can he assume that she no longer loves her husband? A marital commitment is supposed to endure. She can't just run off with Alfonso because of one afternoon of fulfilled lust.

"If you are worried about custody of your children, I could always arrange for an 'accident.'"

The hairs on Katherine's arms stand on end.

"Just kidding, my dear."

She doesn't know what to think of his joke—how could he

joke about something like this?—so she changes the topic back to her making a choice. "I need time."

"I promise not to pressure you." He regards her thoughtfully. "For now."

THE NEXT MORNING, Alfonso is gone when they awake. Showered and dressed, Pancho joins them at breakfast and plays the host in his godfather's absence. "Would you like to go to the nearby public school this morning? It is closed on Sunday, but Alfonso keeps a key."

"Where is Alfonso?" Justin asks.

"He's gone to look for Poppy. We can't find her anywhere."

The kids are eager to visit the place where the local kids study. She would just as soon stay at the villa, but since she doesn't want to find herself alone when Alfonso returns, she decides to accompany them. The school's director, Señor López, had mentioned a visit only a few nights earlier. Of course, he was referring to a day during the week, but just to look around they didn't need his assistance.

They follow Pancho to a padlocked tool shed. Parked in the center is an all-terrain vehicle large enough for four. He puts the gears in neutral and pushes it out. He revs the engine, and Katy climbs onto the front. Katherine and Justin sit in the rear and hold on tightly as they bump over the path toward the exit. When the gate sentry questions him about security, Pancho pats his side where a gun bulges under his jacket, a habit he must have picked up from Alfonso. Somehow the question of whether sixteen-year-olds are allowed to carry weapons is irrelevant. The sentry checks his watch and jots a note on his pad.

"What was that all about?" Justin asks, referring to the delay.

"Security. Everyone has limited access. Well, everyone but Alfonso and Chato."

The vehicle cruises down a road overgrown with weeds that rise to a height of almost twelve inches between the tire tracks. The sickeningly sweet, humid air hangs over the lush green fields.

"How far is it?" Katy questions.

"A kilometer or so."

As they start up a hill, Pancho shifts to a low gear. The vehicle jerks, and Katherine is nearly thrown off. Once they reach the crest and the road levels, Katy clasps her knees and turns to Pancho. "Why don't you just go to this school? It'd be fun to ride back and forth and easier than traveling every week to the city."

"A school like this is for *campesino* kids. They're only required to study to the sixth grade. I go to a private academy. Big difference."

"What?" Katy says, her eyes wide.

"It's like this, Katy," Justin says. "Rich kids in this country don't hang out with poor kids. They don't even go to the same schools."

Her face crinkles in confusion, and she turns to her mother. "Are we rich kids or poor kids?"

"You are who you are. The quality of person you are to become has nothing to do with the amount of money you possess." Katherine glares at Pancho's back, annoyed with his snobbery.

Though the road has deteriorated into a rutted trail, Pancho keeps the gas pedal pushed to the floor. A field mouse runs in front of them. He veers toward it.

"Don't hit it!" Katy screams.

The creature escapes in a burst of speed, and Pancho laughs. "Scared ya, huh."

As they crest the hill, corrugated zinc roofing comes into view. Hard-packed dirt surrounds a concrete-block building with a sign on the top: ESCUELA PUBLICA NO. 237, CANTON PIEDRA GRANDE. Pancho angles the vehicle against the building and kills the engine. "Here we are. Not much to see." He unlocks and opens the metal classroom door to reveal forty new wooden desks, which face lists of words in Spanish and their verb conjugations. Colorful crayoned pictures decorate the walls. "New desks. Thanks to Alfonso." He rolls his eyes. "Computer room next door. Opens on the other side."

"Can we see it?" Katy asks, and starts out the door.

"Naw, I forgot the key." He quickly steps in front of her.

"How exciting for the students to have computers and internet," Katherine says. "I bet none of them have a computer at home."

"And neither do we," Justin mutters.

"Huge waste of money," Pancho says. "Most have never even seen a computer. I told Alfonso it was a lame idea to start with, but he didn't listen. The parents think if their kids can navigate the net, all their problems will be solved." He shrugs. "I don't get what they expect. They're all gonna be subsistence farmers like their parents in the end. As if computer skills would ever be useful to a bunch of *campesinos*. Ha!"

"It's a start in the right direction," Katherine counters. "Why should they keep lagging farther and farther behind as technology advances? Besides, they can access smartphones."

Pancho doesn't say anything, but he doesn't appear convinced.

The door to the boys' bathroom hangs lopsidedly, the top hinge pulled away from the door. Water drips from a small sink, and a stained, seatless toilet reeks of urine. The girls' room is locked tight.

When he sees them observing the facilities, Pancho says defensively, "Alfonso is planning to build new bathrooms."

"Is this really the best public school in the area?" Justin asks as he looks around.

"Absolutely," Pancho says.

"What did it look like before Alfonso got involved?"

Pancho shrugs. "Like all the public schools. Like crap." He points to a leveled piece of land surrounded by wooden bleachers on the other side of the ravine. "Over there is the *campo de fútbol.*"

"Schools here sure don't look like schools at home," Katy offers.

Pancho frowns. "Private schools aren't like this. I'd be willing to bet that the academy I attend is nicer than your school in Indiana." He shifts his weight. "Ready to go?" As he locks the classroom door, voices can be heard from the other side of the building, and Pancho motions for them to be silent.

Two voices converse in Spanish. "Hijo de la gran puta. Este candado es difícil."

Even with her elementary language skills, Katherine understands that they're trying to pick the lock on the computer classroom.

"Rómpalo como el de la casa de los misioneros."

Katy, Justin, and Katherine exchange glances. Katherine's anger flares. These must be the men responsible for her awkward predicament. She looks over at her children. Katy's eyes widen with fright, and Justin backs against the wall. They all watch Pancho, who waits, hands in pockets. When he hears a click indicating another unsuccessful try with the padlock, he draws his revolver and creeps to the end of the corridor. Katherine's heart speeds up, and she puts her hand over Katy's mouth, not knowing how her daughter might react. Will he shoot them? Pancho raises the weapon and fires into the air.

"¿Qué fue eso?" one of the men says.

"¡Vámonos!"

KATHERINE RUNS to the corner of the building just in time to see the backs of two men as they disappear into the woods. Pancho aims toward them and plays at pulling the trigger, then blows on the gun barrel. She is surprised to find herself slightly disappointed that he doesn't take another shot.

He glances at her and smiles sheepishly. "*Ladrones*. Not worth wasting a bullet."

Katy's eyes widen. "Do you always carry a gun?"

"Unless I'm with armed dudes. I mean, ya never know. Look what happened on the way to the beach. The guys coulda been hanging around, then what would I have done?

"I guess you're pretty good with it, too." Justin's remark is a statement.

"Heck, yeah. I wouldn't carry one if I couldn't shoot straight. That'd be dangerous."

Before Katherine can object, Pancho hands the revolver to Justin. She reminds herself that her father-in-law has a gun store so of course Justin has held guns before. She just doesn't like it.

He turns the weapon over. "Beretta .22."

"Careful, dude. It's loaded."

Justin hands it back and Pancho pulls out the magazine. "You wanna learn to shoot, Fofo? There's a place for target practice at the back of the property."

Justin raises his brows. "For real? That's awesome." Justin, looking for approval, turns to her.

Katherine wills the shakes to go away. "I don't want you handling guns. You're only fourteen."

"No worries, Mrs. Whitehall. I've been training with a gun since I was twelve. The best way to avoid an accident is to be proficient."

She doesn't say anything. After all, Pancho isn't her son. She doesn't agree with the way Alfonso raises him, but he did take him in as an orphan and treats him as his own.

Pancho stuffs the gun back into its holster. He nudges the holster under his arm so that his jacket hides the weapon. "Come on. Let's go."

WHEN THEY RETURN to the villa, Justin sees that the Hummer is being hosed down, and he wonders if Alfonso has had any luck finding the parrot. Justin likes Poppy, and he can't imagine the bird, so used to the luxuries of the villa, being able to survive in the wild.

Pancho lets Katherine off at the front door.

"I'll pull around back and put the ATV away," he says. "You guys can stay here if you want."

"We'll go back with you. I want to sit by the pool." Justin wants to check Poppy's other stand.

"Thanks for taking us," Katy says, stepping out of the ATV. "Maybe we can go out some other time."

"Sure," he says noncommittally, pulling the vehicle into the shed and then jumping out, the keys jingling as he heads for the house. "Hey, I gotta run. Paper due on Monday."

Justin hadn't thought about schoolwork for days. Since coming to the villa, the schedule of math assignments, history lessons, and English classes had evaporated.

"I wonder if Alfonso is back," Katy says, lingering by the diving board.

"I kinda hope he isn't," Justin says.

"Why?" she asks.

Justin has a bad feeling about his mother and their host. "I'm glad Dad's coming back today. Then things can get back to normal. Back to the way they were before."

"Don't be so grumpy, Justin. Maybe Dad will let us stay."

"Don't count on it," he says, opening the back door as if he had a perfect right to make himself at home. But this house is an illusion, part of the illusion Alfonso has created to fool the world into thinking he's a good guy. This isn't actually a life they can ever have, and Justin knows it. It's not even one he wants to have. He pauses, then turns back to his sister and says, "This dream world won't last forever, so don't get too used to it."

CHAPTER
TWENTY-FIVE

While Alfonso drives into town to meet Phil at the bus station, Katherine opts to stay with the kids. She can't bear the idea of being in the same car with both of them. When several hours pass and the men still aren't back, she begins to fret. Just as the drone of the Hummer reaches her, she hurries from the library to the front door. Phil waves as he gets out, and the kids, in their swimsuits, come running from the pool. She's torn between fear that he'll discover what she has done and annoyance that he hadn't come when she asked him to. If he had been there, she could have hidden in the shadow of his protection.

With a backpack slung over one arm, he ambles across the lawn, a lopsided smile on his face. He hopes it is a face that shows he's happy to see her.

Instead of greeting him as she usually does, she snaps, "It's about time." Her eyes fill with tears, and she rubs them on her sleeve.

"Does that mean you missed me?" Phil says.

"Phil, you put your ministry before your family. Again."

Until Alfonso informed him a few hours ago, Phil was unaware of what had happened while he was away. He thinks about what he had mistakenly heard, then how he realized at the conference's end that his phone was accidentally turned off. He was so involved in the conference, making new connections and listening to the speakers, he didn't think about home. He knows Katherine will be upset. Though being at the villa could have been prevented, things actually turned out for the best.

Hurt shines in Phil's eyes as he watches his wife. "Alfonso told me about the break-in."

Her eyes narrow. "What do you mean?"

He puts the backpack down on the gravel driveway. "We stopped by the house and there's nothing left inside. Alfonso assured me all our things are safely stored."

If he only knew. "Do you think I wanted the neighbor, our *landlord*, to be the one to comfort us? The one to solve our problems? You're the head of the family."

Phil decides not to mention the misunderstanding. It will only make him look like a fool. If he'd have known that thieves had broken into their house, he might have returned home, he thinks, but probably not. He screwed up again. He should have kept in better touch.

Katherine lightens her tone. "What are we going to do now?"

"Alfonso has generously invited us to stay." Phil watches as his wife stiffens and wonders why she seems so resistant to what appears to him to be an ideal solution. "Is that so bad?"

Is there some way, short of confessing her indiscretion, that she might convince him otherwise? Living at the villa might be the death knell for her marriage and perhaps even for her husband. She stares at him in silence, not knowing what to say without giving herself away.

"We like it here," Katy says, her eyes shining with anticipation that they will stay.

Justin stands beside her, a hand on her shoulder. "Dad, say something."

"I know it was hard for you all," Phil says, "living in that drab little house in such poverty."

"It's not that I haven't wanted to be more comfortable, but this," she gazes around the villa and its grounds, "is too much. How can we maintain a family life when we are Alfonso's guests?"

"He's only being hospitable. It's temporary. Until we are ready to move back to our own place, until we have the church built, the house and the car fixed. The Lord won't let us down. We prayed for things to improve, and Alfonso appeared. What better proof can there be that this is some kind of celestial plan?"

Once Phil gets started talking about the Lord being on his side, Katherine knows she's lost the argument. There isn't a more difficult adversary.

"Before you know it, we'll be independent again." He puts his hand on his son's shoulder. "I bet you're happy now. A room of your own and a buddy to hang out with."

"What buddy?" Justin says.

"Pancho," Katherine says.

Justin shrugs and glances at his mother. "He's only here on weekends."

"Come on, family. Let's go inside." Shouldering his pack, Phil starts toward the house. "I can't wait to take a long, hot shower."

~

ALFONSO ARRANGES for the family to eat together in the breakfast room.

"How did the conference go?" Katherine forces herself to ask.

"Better than I expected. My talk was well received." He hadn't shared the content with her before his departure, mainly because she hadn't asked and that hurt him. Again, he waits for her to ask. When the pause is long enough to ensure that they aren't going to ask questions, he continues, "Jerónimo and I plan to organize Bible study groups. I signed up to get free copies of the New Testament. They just came out with a new Mam translation. And we'll start prayer vigils, too. I have a much better idea where to take the ministry."

She strains to smile. It's not that she isn't happy for him, but it sounds like his schedule will be busier than before, and it doesn't include her in any way. "What about the things I'm interested in?"

"No problem," he says. "Since we're already here, you and Alfonso can put your heads together."

She is silent. If her husband knew he was pushing her into Alfonso's arms, he might think differently. Her ardent lover woos her while her husband rejects her. The choice doesn't seem too difficult if one were to see it in that light, but she doesn't want to be hasty. Phil is the father of her children.

"Tell me about your past few days," he says.

She mentions the formal party and how the guests toasted Alfonso for all his contributions to the community.

Phil agrees. "He's done so much for so many."

Her mention of the party reminds her of the invitation to Finca La Providencia the following weekend. She had actually forgotten about it until that moment. "I hope you don't mind that I agreed to go."

"Not at all. It sounds like a great opportunity to see more of the country."

Eyes down, Phil, noting that his wife doesn't seem to care what his weekend was like, sips his coffee. Why should he even try to explain how thrilling it had been to pray with other pastors and to glean ideas?

Katherine resigns herself to living under Alfonso's roof. Phil simply won't listen to reason. Maybe there is a way she can make her efforts part of Phil's ministry, rather than having them be part of Alfonso's philanthropic agenda. "With computer access," she says, "we can actively seek donations from people back home. We can broaden our approach to the ministry. I'd like to see our efforts reap benefits for women and children."

"A good idea," he says. "The extra income can go toward the church structure until construction is complete. After all, the church is our priority."

His priority. She would like to make him see that if they help people improve themselves economically, they won't be so dependent on Alfonso and his illegal crop. They might give Christianity a chance. But then, she reminds herself, Phil still doesn't know about the poppies. Maybe when she speaks to him in private, he will change his mind.

"How can people concentrate on their spiritual lives," Katherine asks, "when they're so desperately poor?"

"We went to the neighborhood school," Katy interrupts.

"Did you? What did you think?" Phil turns to his daughter.

"Two men on the other side of the building tried to break into the computer room. We heard them say they'd broken into our house."

Phil turns to his wife, suddenly alarmed. They'd been talking all through supper, and this hadn't come up. "Why didn't you tell me?"

She shrugs. "It was a busy weekend."

"Pancho ran them off," Justin says.

"With a gun," Katy adds. "But they were just thieves. Not interested in us."

"Pancho had a gun? Where were you, Katherine?"

"I was with them. Phil, it was an elementary school. Who would have thought?"

"Dad," Justin interjects, "if you really want us to be safe, maybe we should all go back to Indiana."

Phil inhales sharply. He shakes his head and puts down his fork. "Excuse me," he says, scooting back from the table. "I have some things I need to discuss with Alfonso."

"I don't want to be left out of any more decisions," Katherine says. "Last time I checked I was still your wife and equal partner, or has that changed as well?"

"Let's go then," he says, and waits for her to clear the plates and put them in the sink.

In the library, Alfonso motions for them to be seated. "Katherine, I was telling Phil that tomorrow we will tow your car to San Marcos. My mechanic can check it out and make any necessary repairs."

"It's probably something simple like a dead battery."

"It is better we take it in. It is more than that, and you need to buy tires as well."

"What happened to our tires?" Katherine asks.

"It's hard to believe they were taken right off the car," Phil says.

"What? The tires were stolen? Why would anyone pilfer old tires?"

Alfonso tilts his head as he watches her, a slight smile tugging at his lips. "To sell, perhaps? To use as soles for sandals? Who knows? It was inevitable. Thieves will steal anything that is not fastened down. With no one at your house, it was an easy target."

He changes the subject and turns to Phil. "I am honored to have you as my guests. As you can see, I have plenty of space. Pancho spends his weeks in Guatemala City, and I have no set schedule, so you can almost have the place to yourselves if you do not mind Chato and the servants."

Phil beams. "I hardly know what to say to such a generous offer."

"Say yes."

"For now, at least, yes."

Suddenly businesslike, Alfonso says, "Very well, work will begin on the church as soon as I can get hold of the workers. By including the existing structure, there will be plenty of office space, a room for a guard, bathrooms, and plenty of storage. I took the liberty of making a few changes to the building plan and arranged for a truckload of materials to arrive in the morning."

"B-but ... " Katherine stammers, "if we add on to the mission house, where will we live?" He can't possibly mean for them all to live together under one roof, can he?

"Here, of course. As I said, you are most welcome."

Phil senses her reluctance. "I don't know. Katherine is anxious for us to have a place of our own."

A glint of amusement sparkles in Alfonso's eyes. "What do you think, Katherine? Would it be so bad to share this space with us, or do you not find our company pleasing?"

The look on his face dares her to acknowledge the underlying meaning. She tears her eyes from his and focuses on the wall. Does he expect her to make that decision now? "I don't know what to say," she begins. "I'd hate to impose permanently."

He waves his hand through the air as if to sweep away any

thought of impositions. "I am sure something will occur in the meantime."

Katherine's insides churn at his veiled threat.

"What are you getting out of this?" Phil asks, in an unfamiliar burst of curiosity.

"Friendship. Fellowship. I have grown quite fond of your family. Remember. *Mi casa es su casa,* as Ronald Reagan was fond of saying. I want you to feel comfortable here."

TWENTY-SIX

P oppy still has not returned, and, although Alfonso says she occasionally leaves and always returns, he continually searches the trees and sky.

Katherine manages to avoid Alfonso whenever he is present, which, as it turns out, is not that often. She and the kids quickly settle into a routine and resume homeschooling. Phil continues his missionary work without her. She prefers not to leave the children at the villa unsupervised until they are better established.

Tired of constantly being on her guard, Katherine is looking forward to getting away from the villa for an overnight. Friday morning, they are up early for their visit to the coffee farm.

"Horacio will take you there and bring you back," Alfonso announces at breakfast.

"You don't need to loan us a car and a driver," Phil says. "Just take us to town and we'll catch a bus."

"There are no regular buses to Finca La Providencia. Horacio has been there before. He knows the way."

Phil consents, and they toss their overnight bags into the back of the pickup and climb in. They drive down into a valley, turn at a gas station, and bump past fields where sheep and cattle graze. Soon, the road rises into the hills. Shrubs, four to six feet high and covered with round, green berries, dot the mountains on both sides of the road. Shade trees tower above them.

Katy points to the bushes. "Is that coffee?"

"Sí, café," the driver says.

They cross a creek. On a hill silhouetted against a sapphire sky, a Catholic church with a white cross on its steeple overlooks a diminutive village with one main street and several alleyways.

"This is it?" Katy says.

Horacio points to a lovely home on the opposite hillside, then stops in the center of the village. "Un momentito." He gets out and walks to a nearby *tienda*.

Katherine rolls down the window. The hamlet is already bustling with activity. Several chickens and a hairless black sow scurry across the road, turkeys gobble, and giggling children light firecrackers along the roadside. As popping begins, the children dart away. Men set up stands and women stroll by with food on their heads: pots of tamales and *chuchitos* to be sold during the festival.

A man staggers over to the truck. "*¿Gringos?* You speaka Eengleesh?" His breath reeks of alcohol, and the fermented stench fills the car. Katherine quickly rolls up the window. As Phil leans over to lock the doors, Horacio returns. "Váyase, hijo de la gran puta." His voice is not overly loud, but his presence and the gun at his waist intimidate the drunk, who trips over himself in a hurry to get away. Horacio mumbles something in Spanish.

As they leave the village, a stream flattens and flows over the concrete roadway. Along the roadside, naked children play in irrigation ditches while their mothers scoop out water and wash clothes on nearby rocks. The car splashes through the clear water and then follows the road as it curves gracefully up to the house.

Like abandoned playgrounds, cement patios sit on both sides of the road. A wheelbarrow is flipped on its side. "What is this? A school?" Justin asks.

Horacio explains that the zinc-roofed structures with towering chimneys are the wet and dry mills for coffee processing and that the patios are used for sun-drying coffee, weather permitting.

They pull into a parking area to one side of the house and get out. María comes down the steps of the lovely hillside home to greet them, and Katherine reintroduces her to the children. "You remember Katy and Justin. And, this is my husband, Phil."

María comes forward. "Mucho gusto." She holds out her hand. "I'm so glad you could come. Hans will be right back. He went to supervise some work up on the mountain."

Horacio unloads the bags and arranges them in a neat row on the veranda. María invites him in to have coffee, but he declines, feigning haste.

Katherine pauses on the steps and looks out over the valley. "This is beautiful." She wonders what it would feel like to own a piece of property like this. An entire mountain. "Really amazing," she says.

"We like it. I come as often as I can, but our children attend school in Guatemala City, so I spend most of the time there. Hans lives here year-round and visits us in the city on weekends and holidays when we can't make it to the farm." When she sees Katherine's surprised expression, she adds softly, "It's very common here for men to manage the farms while their families live in the city. It's the attraction of the good schooling. You are lucky you can homeschool and stay together. I can't imagine taking on the work of teaching my children. Anyway, we're all here this weekend."

"Excuse my manners. Please sit down and let me get you something to drink." She leads them to a table, brings out a pitcher of natural *refresco*—soda—and glasses, then opens the screen door. "Sally, Diego! Come!"

A moment later the screen door opens, and a slender blonde walks in, followed by her raven-haired brother. "Yes, Mama?"

"Sally and Diego, I want you to meet our friends, the White-halls. This is Justin and Katy."

Diego's eyes sparkle. He races over and halts in front of them. "Hola."

Katy's face lights up.

"Diego is twelve," María says to Katherine, "and Sally is fifteen." She turns to her daughter. "Sally, show Justin and Katy where they'll be staying. Justin can bunk with Diego, and Katy with you."

The girl, slightly taller than Justin, leads the way deeper into the house and up some wooden stairs to a loft, a golden braid slapping her back as she bounces along. The adults watch them leave, and when they finish their drinks, María stands. "Let me take you to your room."

The guest room for the adults is located outside of the house, next to a foot-tall statue of the Virgin Mary ensconced in a niche in the whitewashed brick wall. Phil averts his eyes, and Katherine breathes a sigh of relief. She's never sure when Phil might say something offensive about someone else's religion. As a diversion, Katherine asks about the farm and its origins.

"It's been in the Pregel family since the turn of the century. Hans's great-grandfather carved the farm out of the *selva*. There was nothing out here then but jungle. Monkeys, tapirs, and jaguars. Things have changed considerably since then. I'm afraid we don't have those exotic animals in these parts anymore."

She turns toward the door. "Make yourselves at home. I know you probably ate before you left, but I've prepared a snack anyway. It'll be ready in about ten minutes."

The room is small but cozy. A matrimonial-sized bed fills much of it. The shower stall and toilet are divided from the room by a six-foot wall. The countertop is made from flat, varnished stones. Katherine opens their suitcase and hangs up their clothes in an old *armario* that looks like it arrived with the conquistadores.

By the time she and Phil return to the living room, the four kids have had a chance to get acquainted. Near the hearth, a sofa and overstuffed chairs surround a coffee table. Windows, starting about three feet above the floor and stretching to the wood-plank ceiling, serve as walls. Their home is spartan compared to the villa, but lovely, and this is the first time in weeks that Katherine feels her body relax.

"Please take a seat," María says.

A moment later, Hans, making his usual bearlike entry, bursts through the door. "Hello, hello. Sorry if I've kept you waiting." He settles at the head of the table. "After we finish eating, I'll take you on a tour."

"Your farm looks immense. How much land do you have?" Phil asks.

"The farm was originally a hundred fifty *caballerías*. Since then it's been split several times for inheritance, and pieces have been sold off to keep the lenders at bay. That's farming for you! I've done fairly well and have bought back some of the smaller sections. Now we have forty-five *caballerías*, but only nineteen of them are planted in coffee. The rest is virgin forest."

Katherine looks puzzled. "How big is a *caballería*?"

"Sixty-four *manzanas*." Then, as if remembering that these are strictly local measurements, he adds, "I'm sorry. A *caballería* is more or less one hundred acres."

Katherine calculates. Four thousand five hundred acres. A mountain indeed, or several. She wonders about the contrast between those peasant farmers who are lucky to have a tiny plot for their subsistence farming.

"Do you own the little town we came through on our way here?" Katy asks.

He nods. "The village is part of the estate. It's called Providencia, the same as the farm. We manage the buildings and make sure there are always supplies in the stores for our workers. There is a bus that comes in and out of the farm on Sundays if the workers need to go to town. We have more than four hundred people, including women and children, who live and work on the farm year-round. We provide them with a salary and some acreage for their crops. With the influx of migrant workers during the coffee harvest, the population swells to about fifteen hundred."

Katherine thinks about the complications and logistics of owning a company town. Hans appears to be a good manager, but life must still be difficult for the poor. Economically speaking, profit is what matters to Hans and the other growers. If the business can't turn a profit, the people must leave the only home they've known.

After a quick meal, Hans, eager to show them around, pulls a double-cab Toyota Land Cruiser up to the veranda. Phil and Katherine take the second seat. The kids climb into the back. As they drive up the mountainside for the tour, Katy and Diego stand behind and hang on to the roll bar. Sally and Justin crouch on the humps above the back wheels.

As they tour the plantation, Hans drives with one hand and

uses the other to point. From time to time, they stop to look at a coffee bush. Hans gives long, detailed explanations of the types and varieties of coffee. Though her mind wanders, Katherine tries to appear interested. She would never admit it, but she can't distinguish gourmet coffee from Folger's.

From the top of the mountain, Hans points out the threads of roads and trails joining Guatemala and Mexico. "It's impossible to keep track of the flow of contraband and drugs. By foot, by car, by truck. Major players use helicopters and planes."

"And are there a lot of drugs going back and forth?" Phil asks, for once appearing to take narco-trafficking seriously.

"You have no idea. Cocaine is transshipped through Guatemala from South America on its way to North American markets. Mexican cartels don't bother to travel to Colombia anymore. Opium and heroin are trafficked as well. Poppies are planted in remote areas of both San Marcos and Huehuetenango. Guatemala is now a major player in world opium production. In fact, last I heard, we were the third or fourth largest producers in the world. Hardly something to be proud of."

"That's so odd." Concern creases Phil's brow.

When Katherine told him the other night that she suspected Alfonso was involved in opium production, he had refused to listen, refused to accuse their host. He had never heard that there was any opium grown anywhere in Central America, so her claims were easy to discredit. Maybe he should keep his mind open to what his wife tells him. Maybe, just maybe, there is more to their host than what appears on the surface. On the other hand, as a man of God he must avoid making false accusations. "I've never seen anything suspicious in our area."

Hans and María glance at each other and look away, but Katherine takes note. She knows they are friendly with Alfonso and asks, "What do the Guatemalans think of those who grow or traffic drugs?"

"Narco-traffickers are everywhere," Hans replies. "Everyone has had to adjust and accept them. They might be our friends, our neighbors, people we see on a daily basis. Fighting them would be futile. Counterproductive. Even dangerous."

Hmm, she thinks. They know.

Hans leads them along a cobblestone path back to the coffee mills. While he explains coffee processing, Katherine's mind keeps returning to the earlier conversation.

After lunch, they saunter down the stone road and stroll onto the central plaza to watch the celebrations. The road is blocked. Food and beverage stands line the street. Men already under the influence of moonshine stagger up and tip their hats to Hans. "Hola, patrón."

They situate themselves on a reserved makeshift bleacher with a privileged view. The villagers crowd the streets for a glimpse of the action.

Diego stands and points. "Here they come!"

A local band leads the parade. Musicians in buttoned-up shirts, black wool jackets, and aged bow ties play trumpet, viola, accordion, and guitar. Phil cringes at the discordant music, but no one else seems to notice. Town elders swing metal incense boxes toward the spectators. Gray smoke billows out, filling the air with the pungent odor.

"They're purifying the crowd in preparation for the sacred dances," María explains.

Behind the marching band, six men wear elaborate costumes and painted masks. They dance forward and charge the watching throng. Like a living creature, the crowd moves as one. Then the dancers turn in the opposite direction to repeat their performance with the onlookers from the other side. The dancer representing the Gran Conquistador wears the mask of a blond-haired, blue-eyed man, his ceremonial robes brilliantly colored with tiny pieces of mirror sewn into the fabric.

Sally giggles and pulls on Justin's arm. "When I was little, I thought he was pretending to be Daddy."

Other costumed creatures join the dance: monkeys, tapirs, and jaguars. The band moves aside and dancers take center stage. A drum and a native flute play the melody as dancers leap and twirl.

"The farm workers do this dance every year for the *feria*. We encourage them to keep their traditions alive," María explains.

Soon the children become bored and leave.

During the ceremony Hans insisted on buying beer, and both Katherine and Phil are a little tipsy as they stroll up the hill. When they arrive at the house, Phil excuses himself. When he doesn't return fifteen minutes later, Katherine checks and discovers him snoring on the bed. She returns to her hosts.

While Katherine talks about their life in Indiana, María serves a heady, sweet coffee. So far, the conversation has kept to neutral topics, but one question torments her. Finally, she blurts out, "What do you think of Alfonso?"

Hans and María exchange glances. "You were there at the dinner, Katherine," she replies. "A wonderful host and perfect gentleman."

"But isn't he involved with poppies?"

"Shh. Don't repeat those words to anyone, or you could find yourself in grave danger," Hans warns. "I think I understand your concern, so let me speak in generalities. There are many types of people involved in the narco trade. I don't believe it is likely to stop anytime soon, at least not until it's legalized and controlled by the governments of countries that consume the end products." He hesitates and watches her reaction. "We should be grateful that there are those who try to make a positive impact on the local communities while they carry on with their illegal businesses. Even if it is to their own benefit."

"What do you mean, 'their own benefit'?"

"It's like this," he explains, "narco-traffickers help their neighbors, which in turn gives them loyal followers who protect them. It's a win-win situation. The farmers are making far more money growing poppies than they would be able to make with any other crop, even coffee. The traffickers have more money than they can spend, so investing in the community only makes sense. Who can say that's bad? It may, eventually, give the *campesinos* a better life. Besides, no one is forcing people in your country to consume drugs. If there's a market, there will always be someone willing to supply it."

CHAPTER

TWENTY-SEVEN

"We have the place to ourselves for a few days," Phil says when they return to the villa. "Alfonso told me he and Pancho would be vacationing this week in Mexico."

"But it isn't ours, and it isn't empty. There are at least a dozen servants and guards that also live here. Phil, we need to look for somewhere else to stay," Katherine says. Her lover and her husband under the same roof? An immoral and potentially dangerous idea. "We could always fix up the little house and return."

"Don't worry, honey. This is only temporary. But I don't think we'll be going back to the house because Alfonso plans to make it part of the church. They've drawn up plans already."

"We can find another place. Phil, this solution seems too easy, but we no longer have control over our own lives. We don't have our own vehicle nor our passports if we needed to leave." She hesitates. "I hate being relieved that Alfonso isn't here, especially since we are his guests. It's awkward. Living here just doesn't feel right. It is a lot to ask of someone to host us indefinitely."

Phil wonders himself why Alfonso is so eager to have them stay. It's not like their host is Evangelical—they don't even have common interests—but the Lord led them here and He knows what is best. Perhaps Katherine's growing friendship with Alfonso will convince their host to accept Jesus Christ as his Lord and Savior. God would never lead his wife astray.

Justin knocks at the door. "Dad, did Mom tell you about what I witnessed that day I sneaked up to the ruins?"

"Can't we have a bit of a rest from speculation? No one has any facts, and the jury is still out on what's really going on."

Justin looks to his mother to see if she tried to convince him. She nods and shrugs helplessly. "Dad, Alfonso's encouraging farmers to grow poppies in the mountainside, instead of corn and beans. I was there."

"You don't understand what you saw, son, and you don't have a good grasp of Spanish. I've been up in the mountains plenty and have yet to see any of these so-called poppy fields. I'm surprised your mother was so quick to believe you without any proof."

Katherine turns to her husband. "Don't be an ass. Remember what Hans said about opium production in the area."

"Explain to me then why Alfonso is such a leader in the community. Explain why the school director, a coffee farmer, and a priest all spoke so highly of him that night of the party, or have you forgotten already what you told me? Alfonso has been good to us. We couldn't ask for a better landlord, neighbor, or friend. Why brew up such serious charges?"

"That day I was up there," Justin continues, ignoring his father's outburst, "Alfonso was giving the farmers instructions.

259

He handed out seeds and told them to keep the crop hidden. Why hide the flowers if they aren't illegal?"

"How should I know? Did he actually say the seeds were for poppies?"

Justin thinks back. "He didn't mention it by name, just held up a flower. Called it a forbidden crop."

Phil shook his head. "I need more evidence than that. What you heard was mixed with supposition. What were you doing at the ruins again anyway? I thought your mother and I made it clear you weren't to go gallivanting around in the mountains alone."

Katherine stands, goes to the window, and then turns back. "Hans told me that narcos generously help their communities. It creates loyalty with the peasant farmers. He all but told me that Alfonso is involved."

Phil's jaw remains set.

"Okay, he didn't directly say, 'Alfonso is involved in the trade,' although I did ask. I don't suppose you'd believe it even if you were confronted with a field of poppies. After all, it isn't convenient for your missionary ambitions, is it?"

"Please. Dad, let's find another place to live."

"We'll leave when I say we leave, and I don't want to listen to any more of this. Last I heard, I was still head of this family."

Katherine's lips tighten and Justin's frustration brings him to his feet. "Fine! When things get out of control, just remember Mom and I both warned you." He stomps out and slams the door behind him.

"Nice job with that, Phil. I think it went very well with your adolescent son." Her words drip with sarcasm. "But you might consider finding new verbal weapons because your daughter will be a teenager soon and just saying that you're the head of the family won't cut it." And his authority doesn't cut it with her either, she realizes.

～

AFTER AN HOUR of flipping through television channels, Justin clicks off the power. It's a quiet Saturday afternoon with few people working. He gets up to see what the rest of the family is up to. When he goes to his parents' room, he overhears his mother asking about the car.

"It's still in the shop. Besides, where do you need to go? We have everything right here. Alfonso loans me a car and a driver whenever I ask."

She pauses and continues in a lower tone. "Have you called about it?"

"Our phones no longer work. The plan ran out and the extra phones were disabled."

"Surely there's a landline."

"I haven't seen any."

"The other issue is our passports. We need to go to Guatemala City to apply for new ones."

"I called," Phil says. "We need to make an appointment."

"Did you make one?"

"I was hoping we'd have our car before we trek back to the city. I don't feel comfortable asking that big of a favor of Alfonso. Once we have our car, we can make the appointment, and Jerónimo can drive us."

"Take initiative, Phil. Ask someone about the car. You can see how important this is to us. You speak better Spanish than we do. Can you spend a little time worrying about your family and less time devoted to everyone else's problems?"

"I resent that. Of course I worry about my family. I failed to come back early from Xela a few weeks ago, and now I'm never going to hear the end of it."

"Never mind, I'll call. Do you at least have the name and number of the mechanic?"

Phil searches through some papers on the dresser. "Here's his card."

Justin pokes his head in the door. "I know where there's a phone."

Katherine turns. "Do you always have to eavesdrop?"

"It's in the library. Come on. I'll show you."

She and Justin head downstairs. "Don't worry. It's only temporary," she tells him, knowing he'll understand she's talking about the living arrangements. "As soon as we get the construction started, we'll move back to the little house."

"You know he plans to keep us here."

She narrows her eyes. "Now, why would you say that?"

He shrugs and shows her to a corner table, past the naked woman statue in the back of the library, where a phone rests. Justin gives the statue a double take, but Katherine ignores it completely. She grabs the phone, punches in the numbers, and listens. "It's ringing."

She listens for a few minutes and finally says *"Gracias"* before hanging up. "It was the guard. He says the shop doesn't open again until Monday morning at nine."

THE NEXT MORNING, Sunday, they walk the half kilometer down to their outdoor church. Along the way, Phil waves his arms and practices a sermon to an invisible audience while the rest of the family lags behind. Justin shakes his head and says to his mother, "Do we really all need to show up? Isn't it enough that Dad goes?"

"It's called family support. Besides, we've always gone to church together," Katherine says, though she can't help but agree with her son. They barely understand the sermon, and by the time the service is over, it will be a hot walk back.

The little house comes in view, and Katy says, "Can you believe we actually lived there? What a dump!"

"Katy, watch your mouth! I know it may not seem like much compared to where we are now, but it was ours."

"Yeah," Justin snaps, "we lived better than most folks around here. Look at them." He gestures toward the approaching villagers. "Most would be more than happy to have cement floors, running water, and electricity. What makes you think you're so special?"

Katy doesn't respond.

Jerónimo and his family have already set up the altar and distributed the chairs. Julio, closest to Justin's age, walks up behind him. "*Hola,* Fofo. How are things at the villa?" He rolls his eyes. "Too much fun to arrive early?"

"It's not that fun," Justin says. On one hand, he enjoys living in the villa, but he also knows there must be talk about them staying with Alfonso. They all must know what he does with the farmers. "You take the good with the bad." Julio can interpret those words however he wishes.

"Play?" Julio throws Justin a hacky sack.

"Sure," Justin says, "at least until my dad begins."

New people are flocking to the service, people he's never seen before. Men greet each other, and women keep a watchful eye on the children.

Julio, with a twisting motion, lofts the hacky sack. They kick it back and forth several times until Justin catches the bean-filled ball and tips his head. "Let's grab a seat while we still can." From the back row he sees his dad taking one last look at his notes and then putting them in his pocket.

Phil begins by thanking everyone for their presence and leads a short prayer for the Lord to work in their lives.

"Julio, why so many people?" Justin whispers from the back row. "Is today a holiday?"

"Your family." He holds up his left index finger. "Alfonso." He lifts his right index finger, then rubs the two together. "Tight."

Justin gets it. In a small community, word travels with the speed of sound. People who were afraid to come in case Alfonso was opposed to the Evangelical teachings show up out of curiosity.

No explosions of thunder interrupt the sermon, and no one falls into a trance or speaks in tongues, but the four-day retreat in Quetzaltenango has renewed Phil's spiritual energy, and seeing the great turnout convinces him that his efforts are finally paying off. Each person sitting in a plastic chair represents a soul on its way to being saved. After the final hymn, people crowd him, all reaching for his hand. "Gracias, Pastor." "Bien dicho." "Nos vemos el próximo domingo." Thanks and compliments on the service. Just what he wants to hear.

Justin helps Jerónimo's boys gather up the chairs and put them into the storage room. They padlock the door. His mother and Katy are talking to an old woman and her granddaughter, and Katherine motions for Justin to go with his father. She and Katy will be right along.

Justin looks up at the sun. Not directly overhead, but almost. The half-kilometer walk is all uphill. Phil is lost in thought as they climb the gravel road. Justin kicks loose rocks and watches the dust fly. After only a few days without rain, the earth is dry.

Jerónimo races down the road after them. "¡Hermano Felipe! Workers start tomorrow." Jerónimo bubbles with enthusiasm.

Phil tilts his head in confusion. "What are you saying?"

"We build *mañana. A las ocho.*"

"Who told you that?"

"El maestro de obras." The lead bricklayer. He mimed laying block.

Phil has looked forward to having a church and spreading his beliefs for almost his entire married life. This dream of his is becoming reality, thanks to his own persistence and thanks to Alfonso. Especially Alfonso.

He claps his assistant on the arm. "I'll be here first thing in the morning to speak to the master bricklayer."

Jerónimo smiles and says he'll see them then.

The sun beats down on Justin's neck. He's sorry he forgot his cap. His big toe sticks out of a hole in his tennis shoe, and he can feel the rocks through the soles. The villa is as far away as Indiana, at least a half kilometer under the high-altitude sun. When the church construction begins, there will be no turning back. They won't be able to return to the little house. No matter how primitive, at least it was theirs. How to make his father understand?

"What's up, Justin? Something you want to discuss with me?"

"You don't believe what's right before your eyes. Why don't we just go back to Indiana before it's too late?"

"Respect, son. I'm your father. I've had just about enough of your complaints. This is about Alfonso again, isn't it? You heard Jerónimo. Alfonso has arranged for workers to start church construction. Why criticize a man who has been so helpful? I'd advise not to say another word without proof."

"Look how influential he is. All the people who came to the

service today. Now that they know you're all right with Alfonso, they're eager to join."

Phil stops and turns, eyes sparking with anger. "What are you saying? That people didn't come to hear my sermon? That they came thinking it was what Alfonso would want? What can you possibly know at your age? I spend four days at Quetzaltenango praying, fasting, and hoping to make a difference, and you think," he snaps his fingers, "just like that, that it wasn't God, but Alfonso who sent them to prop up my ego? What's gotten into you?"

"No, Dad, that's not what I meant. It's just that now they know Alfonso isn't opposed to your church, they are more likely to come. That's all." When he sees his father's reaction, he hangs his head. "I didn't mean to make you upset."

Phil waits for Katherine to catch up so he can tell her what Justin said.

She understands her son's point immediately. "Think about it. Suddenly more people show up for a service. Maybe Justin's right. Maybe these folks wanted to come but were afraid to cross Alfonso, especially since they know he's Catholic. You know how much influence he wields in the communities."

He stops for a moment to reflect. "Can't you believe this is just God's will?"

Her head tilts and she stares. Her eyes blaze with a look he recognizes as disdain. "God isn't the only one who makes things happen around here, Phil."

TWENTY-EIGHT

The approaching whir of a chopper wakes Katherine from a deep sleep. Alfonso and Pancho, on vacation in Mexico, must have come home a few days early. She reaches over to feel for her husband and finds his side of the bed empty. His absence doesn't surprise her. Most days he leaves at dawn and gets home late, only occasionally showing up for lunch. Of course, why would he walk back in the heat of the day just to have lunch with her? The only thing that excites him anymore is the church. She's sure he'd rather spend his lunch break at the construction site. Unlike someone else she could name.

She throws on her robe and heads downstairs. In the dining room, she takes coffee from the pot, wraps her hands around its warmth, and wanders into the library, the place where she generally meets Alfonso.

Ten minutes later, she hears his footsteps down the hall. She crosses her legs and smooths her robe, although he has seen more of her skin than anyone but her husband, so what is the point in trying to be modest?

Alfonso settles into an overstuffed leather chair. "I'm back."

"Yes, you are. And early," she says. "I'm glad."

"My dearest, I could not stay away. You missed me, I hope?"

She blushes. Is it so obvious? Still, she has her projects, the people she has been helping, but she needs some way to get around. "We need to talk about the car."

"Do not worry about your vehicle. We have sufficient transportation here. I can provide a driver to take you wherever you wish."

"I appreciate that, I do. I'd just rather not be so dependent on you."

"I want you dependent on me. Our lives are intertwined. We are dependent on each other."

"What can you possibly depend on me for?"

"Now that you are here, I am home more often to breathe the same air you breathe, to see your smile light up a room, to hear the sweet peals of your laughter. My home is with you now. You see I could not stay away from you for even a week."

A blush spreads through her body. "Please don't say things like that."

Alfonso laughs. "Do not be concerned, dear Katherine. I am quite confident that things will work out for everyone involved."

Justin has a habit of turning up whenever the two of them are together, so she is not surprised when he wanders into the library.

"Good morning, Justin. Since you are here, tell me something," Alfonso begins. "Your mother says your birthday is approaching, and I would like to do something special for you. Is there anything in particular you might appreciate?"

With no friends and his family falling apart before his eyes, the idea of a celebration depresses him. "I don't know. I guess I'd rather not do anything this year."

"Fifteen is a landmark age. You must celebrate. How about if Pancho and I come up with something?"

"Yeah, okay. Whatever." Not daring to speculate what that something might be, he looks toward the kitchen. "Where is Pancho?"

"Try the weight room. His regular morning workout."

Justin slaps his forehead with the palm of his hand. Of course.

Katy comes down a few minutes later, and when Alfonso asks her the same question, she replies instantly. "I know piñatas are mostly for younger kids, but I've never had one."

"If that is what you desire, it can easily be arranged."

LATER THAT DAY, Phil does return for lunch. As he walks through the house, Alfonso motions to him from the library. "Please enter. I have something for you."

Phil steps in tentatively. He rarely visits this part of the house, and when he walks by, he tries not to think about how often his wife is here. He knows how comfortable she is among books, but he also knows that their host spends most of his time in that room. Alfonso motions to someone in the hallway, and a servant fetches a three-foot-long box from the foyer. "I bought this in Mexico. I hope you will find it an appropriate gift." He wears a smile of slight amusement that Phil doesn't want to understand, but deep down Phil knows he's being placated—a present in exchange for his wife's attentions.

He opens the box and his eyes grow large. A hand-tooled instrument in a beautiful leather case.

"Your son told me that you used to play. I thought you might take it up again. Musical accompaniment for your services."

Phil thought about his old guitar, scratched and dinged, in no way comparable to this one. He had been good once, damned good. Maybe he gave it up too soon, on an impulse. Maybe he was afraid that he loved the guitar too much, feared his love of music could tempt him away from his calling, but he had never considered using a guitar during worship. He wasn't against backup harmony—services at home always had an organ or piano—but he had never thought of a guitar as a church instrument. Still, now that he was here, he could see that a guitar would be much more practical. The choir would benefit from accompaniment, and music had always been important in helping people open to the word of the Lord. "I don't know how to thank you."

"You already have."

Phil takes the instrument up to his room and places it carefully in the corner. At bedtime, when Katherine sees the instrument propped in the corner and asks where it came from, he explains that it was Alfonso's gift, an ideal one. "It'll be an excellent addition to the service, and with me accompanying you, it will be easier for you to teach new hymns. Maybe we can form a choir. Much better than if you just sing and hope they can follow."

Resentment fills Katherine. She had been after him to take up the guitar again for years—why waste his talent? So why does he act as though picking up the guitar again is such a novel idea? It occurs to her that she was sold out first by a church, then by a guitar.

270

~

On Katy's birthday, a staccato of fireworks awakens them at six in the morning, and music floats up from a mariachi band playing beneath her window. Justin rolls over and covers his head with a pillow, but if he thinks he can sleep again after all that going on, he is sadly mistaken.

"Justin! Justin!" Katy bursts into his room. She opens the window and waves at the musicians. "Isn't this exciting?"

She holds up a box, shredded wrapping paper hanging from it. "Look what Alfonso got me—a purse with a pink iPod Nano inside!" She hugs it to her chest.

Justin pushes the covers off and crawls out of bed. "What the hell, Katy. It's so early."

"Don't blame me for the noise." She sits at the foot of his bed. "It's part of my birthday celebration."

He staggers into the bathroom and when he returns sees that she's opening a small wrapped gift with a handmade card. She opens the card and unwraps the carved stone he'd found the first day they went exploring.

"Thanks, Justin." Standing, she gives him a hug. "Come on. I'll show you what else I got."

He shuffles down the hall behind her. Her bed is a mess of tangled sheets and blankets. "Mom and Dad came in early to wish me a happy birthday. They brought me this." She points to a colorful shawl draped over the table. On it sits an opened box of Guatemalan candy. She tosses the shawl over her shoulders and twirls. "Isn't it beautiful? Daddy bought it for me in Xela."

"Very nice." He gives her a brotherly punch, returns to his room to throw on some shorts and a tee shirt, and goes down to the workout room. Finally, he's up early enough to see what Pancho does down here.

271

Pancho wears a muscle shirt and faces a floor-to-ceiling mirror while he checks out his biceps. "Look who's awake. Birthday alarm help ya out?"

The clock on the wall indicates seven fifteen.

"Not like sleeping was an option."

But, now that he's here, Justin decides to start his workout on the treadmill. He turns it on and starts running. Wanting to show off, he sets the speed too fast and can't keep up.

"Whoa! Pace yourself." Pancho shakes his head slightly and laughs as he tinkers with the controls and sets a moderate speed. "Ya need to start slow."

Pancho gets on the Stairmaster and Justin puffs away beside him, thinking of ways to show him up. After ten minutes, he stops to catch his breath.

"You wanna lift some weights?" Pancho leads him to the lineup of free weights and hands him dumbbells. He takes a heavier set for himself. When Justin protests, he says, "I've been doing this for three years now. You need to work up to it, or tomorrow you'll be hating life."

After an hour in the gym, Justin heads back to his room. He grabs the newspaper his father absentmindedly handed him when he returned from Xela, thinking this might be a chance to practice reading Spanish, especially since he could do it from the comfort of his bed. It doesn't take him long to realize that much of the vocabulary in the newspaper is beyond his grasp, but at least he can pick up the gist. The article he's trying to under-stand is about a possible narco-war. Rival gangs. A car set on fire. Six killed, one a girl on her way to school. He puts the paper down. He showers and crawls back in bed, wishing he'd just stayed there to begin with. His muscles ache and tomorrow he's sure he'll be stiff.

The events described in the article seem unreal as he gets up again and goes downstairs for breakfast. After a bowl of cereal, Justin looks for Pancho and finds him in the computer room. "Hey."

"What's going on, Fofo?"

"Any ideas about what to do?"

He peers out the window. "Looks like a decent day. Wanna do some target shooting?"

Target shooting sounds like a good plan, just as long as no one decides to take a shot at him. The intriguing idea of target practice makes him forget the disturbing news. On one level, he believes Alfonso is involved in the cultivation of narcotics, but in the daily tedium of waking up, doing lessons, going for a swim, and then eating dinner, the possibility of anyone attacking them seems unreal. "You don't think my mother will notice the noise?"

"'Course not. The guards are always practicing out back. You probably never even paid attention. Come upstairs with me and grab the rifles."

Justin follows him up, down another hallway, and into Alfonso's suite, the one place Justin hasn't explored in his meanderings around the villa. Embers glow from an earlier fire. Wisps of smoke drift up the chimney. Two stone Mayan carvings guard the marble mantelpiece. In front of the fireplace, a small sofa and two overstuffed chairs surround a glass-topped table littered with various Guatemalan and Mexican newspapers. A navy comforter covers a mahogany four-poster, and Justin wonders if his host actually sleeps in that oversized bed. If someone told him Alfonso never slept, he'd believe it. Rules don't seem to apply to him.

Pancho opens the closet door. One side is filled with hanging suits and folded clothing. Black ceremonial gowns, like the one

Alfonso wore at the ruins, hang at the far end. Floor-to-ceiling shelves hold books and other objects. Pancho pulls at the wall of shelves and the shelves glide open, exposing a metal door with a combination lock. He moves the dial back and forth until the lock clicks and the door opens into a small room. An arsenal.

Dozens of guns in all sizes rest on shelves and hang from hooks on the padded walls.

Justin stares. A hand touches his shoulder. He flinches and shies away.

Alfonso looks down at him, amused. "I meant to show you my gun collection, but I see Pancho beat me to it."

"I ... we ... he invited me to go target shooting."

"It is quite all right. I am sure you can be trusted with this knowledge."

"Oh, yes. Of course." Justin exhales, unaware that he has been holding his breath.

Alfonso steps inside the arsenal and hands each boy a .22 rifle. "This is a Ruger 10/22 semiautomatic. You know about guns, Justin. You recognized the Glock the first day of our acquaintance. Tell me how you know."

"My grandfather on my dad's side has a gun store. He lets me hang out sometimes after school, but my father doesn't approve. He doesn't get along with Grampa Joe."

Alfonso nods in thought. "So, Phil is a rebel of sorts?"

"Yes, sir."

"Tell me what else you recognize, son."

Justin's eyes stop at a Colt M1911 semiautomatic handgun. "That looks like a collector's piece. Does it work?"

"Of course, but do be careful. All these guns are loaded."

"Isn't that dangerous?"

"More dangerous is needing a weapon and finding it unloaded."

Justin points at the Pietro Beretta, the one Pancho took the day they visited the school. "This looks like something the old James Bond used in the movies."

"Similar, perhaps, but Sean Connery used a Walther."

"And this little one?" Justin touches a .22 Magnum Derringer.

"For putting in your boot as a backup. Just in case."

Alfonso, Justin sees, has the entire collection of Glocks: 9 mm, .40, and .45; next to them are a SIG Sauer and a CZ 75. Among the revolvers, several have mother-of-pearl handgrips.

"Meet Mr. Smith and Mr. Wesson." Alfonso hands him a .38.

Alfonso makes no reference to the more dangerous weapons: Galils, Uzis, AK-47s, and M16 assault rifles with extended magazines—but he goes into great detail about the smaller weapons: their makers, their histories, their ammo. Completing the collection are 12-, 16-, and 20-gauge shotguns.

Thinking a shotgun would be perfect for target practice, Justin reaches for the 20-gauge.

"That's for bird hunting," Alfonso says, and a flash of sadness crosses his face.

"I've got rifles," Pancho says, a rifle in each hand. "Let's go."

Justin's eyes fasten onto the robes in the back of the closet.

"You have a question?" Alfonso asks.

"No, not really."

"You saw me at the ruins."

"Yes, but not the whole thing."

"What then is your question?"

Justin's heart thuds. "Why do you do that? Dress up and lead them in their service to the Mayan gods."

Alfonso gazes thoughtfully at the boy. "It is like this. When I came, the people still followed their ancestral ways with no leader. The hilltop at the ruins is an ideal place to gather. A place where no one can eavesdrop, no one can come or go without my knowledge. For what I do, this is advantageous."

Justin swallows. Alfonso's secrets are bad enough, yet, to make matters worse, he combines opium growing with worshipping false gods. "But these are pagan gods."

"The Evangelical way is not for everyone. Should the people not have options? It is part of their heritage. That is all I give them. Options. They can embrace them or not as they like."

Alfonso's words contradict everything Justin has learned at church and from his father, but hearing Alfonso explain himself so calmly and without a hint of guilt makes Justin wonder if his father's way is the only way to worship God.

"Of course, the ceremony also serves other purposes. While the farmers are gathered, we discuss crop management and production. It works well for everyone. Even for your father, who is receiving the church he so badly wanted. People have the right to choose." He pats the boy's shoulder. "Things are not always as black and white as one might wish, Justin. Life would be ever so much easier if they were."

Pancho, carrying their rifles and a box of ammo, backs out of the arsenal. When they reach the foot of the stairs, they exit the front entrance to avoid being seen by Katherine, who is reading a book under a green-and-white umbrella while Katy splashes in the pool.

Earlier that morning, Justin had heard his mother try to convince Katy to invite Rosa María over, but Katy shook her head and said that she preferred to be alone.

A horse nickers as they pass the stables. The boys follow the trail through the woods past the mysterious outbuildings. At the far end of the walled compound, a stand of bamboo shields the range from view. Surrounding the range are earthen mounds to catch stray bullets and absorb the noise. Pancho sets up targets on a bench and thrusts a rifle at Justin. He hands him protective ear plugs and puts some on himself.

Pancho illustrates how to stand and take aim. "These don't have much of a kick, but hold it like this." He braces the butt against his shoulder. They take turns shooting at cans and paper images. Pancho's bullets nearly always hit the mark. When Justin occasionally hits the target, he's surprised.

"I think you've got ability, Fofo. You just need practice," Pancho says generously. "We'll come back again soon."

After an hour on the shooting range, Justin's arms ache. He is secretly relieved when they put everything away and start back to the house. Passing the structure that he suspects is a laboratory, he says, "Hey, Pancho, what's in there?"

"Nothing. Empty."

Justin doesn't believe him, but their conversation stirs up the dogs on the other side of the building.

"Does Alfonso keep hunting dogs?" Justin asks, heading around the corner.

"Not unless it's people being hunted," Pancho says.

Penned Dobermans and Rottweilers pace their enclosures. They snarl viciously and jump at the wire fence.

"Don't get too close, dude. They're trained to attack. You do know not to leave the house at night, don't you?"

"Who lets them out?"

"Chato. He's the only one who handles them."

The boys back away.

"Been thinking about your birthday. Come with us to the city next weekend," Pancho says, "and I'll take you out on the town."

Justin hears a machete thwacking in the distance. Maybe it's hacked-up enemies that Chato intends to throw to the crocodiles. His muscles tense and his eyes dart right and left. If he had to hide, should he run to the stables or make a break for the arsenal? As they approach the house, he sees Katy, Katherine, and Alfonso taking turns hitting a piñata with a big stick. Phil is behind the camera.

CHAPTER
TWENTY-NINE

J ustin's parents are reluctant to let him go to the city with Pancho, but once Alfonso's mind is set on something, he won't be denied. In the end, they give in on the condition that he return in time for Sunday services.

Friday afternoon, Justin waves goodbye to his family and climbs into the helicopter. He imagines where they're going as a teen club. Maybe it will be like the dances held in the YMCA back home. Pancho has promised him a great weekend—talked up the city house, the discos, and the parties. "In Guatemala, fifteen is the dividing line between being a boy and being a man," Pancho says, "so we will celebrate your birthday for the important occasion it is."

Justin hears a little bit of Alfonso in those words.

Traveling by chopper seems almost normal now, Justin thinks. None of his friends back home would believe this. For their birthdays, they'd be going bowling or maybe have a sleepover. Maybe their parents would take them to the Ponderosa for steaks. But nothing even remotely similar to how cool his birthday is going to be.

The chopper swings into the air, and as they pass Lake Atitlán, clouds cover the volcanoes like a down comforter. Soon the chopper begins its descent. Justin holds tightly as they drop through a low-lying mantle of white fog and onto the tarmac at the airport. Two men run over and take their bags to a black Lincoln parked nearby—Alfonso's city car.

The chauffeur opens the front passenger door and tips his hat. He leads them to the car, and the boys climb into the leather-upholstered back seat.

Accompanied by several black SUVs and weaving through traffic, they drive across the city. Armed guards wave them through several checkpoints as they wind up a wooded hill to an exclusive residential area. Close to the top, a black wrought-iron gate opens automatically, and the car stops in front of a modern four-level house with stone and tinted-glass walls. They enter the top floor, the lower floors clinging to the mountainside beneath.

"Room's this way," Pancho says. "We'll have dinner and head out around ten."

Justin passes modern artwork and stark chrome furnishings, their footfalls echoing on the blood-colored tile floor. The fog cover has burned off, and the inky sky is cloudless. At the end of a long hallway, city lights glitter through wide windows.

Justin stops at a wall of family portraits, stunned. In one of the photos, Alfonso has his arms around a woman who looks enough like his mother to be her. On closer inspection, the woman is taller than Katherine. Her smile is slightly different. Anyone but a close family member would think it was the same woman. Farther down the wall, he sees pictures of the happy couple on a beach, waving from a car, wedding photos.

Pancho comes up behind him. "Her name's Marisol. A dead ringer for your mother."

"What happened to her?"

"Died a few years ago in the attack that killed my parents. Alfonso doesn't speak of her anymore. Took down all the photos at the villa. Come on. You can look at these later."

Pancho shows him to a room three levels below, dominated by a king-sized bed. A flat-screen television with a Wii attachment is mounted on the wall. A door opens into a private bathroom.

Justin kicks off his shoes, and his feet sink into a plush rug. What a life! He changes into slacks and a polo shirt, and then slips on his new loafers.

Pancho waits on the top level. "What d'you think?"

"You live here during the week? This is awesome."

"You should see the kick-ass parties we have. Alfonso doesn't mind. He's not in the city much anymore. At least not since you guys moved close to the villa."

At the dinner table, Alfonso pours them each a large glass of wine. "Have you had wine before, Justin?"

"No. My dad's pretty strict about anything alcoholic." But Justin is thirsty. He takes a few swallows and his mouth puckers.

Alfonso laughs. "Let me serve you something sweeter." He whispers something to the server, who returns minutes later with a chilled bottle. The beverage tastes like exotic soda. Justin's glass is refilled several times during the meal.

When he tries to get up from the table, he stumbles and almost falls. "Whatch going on?"

"Perhaps you had more wine than you should have. No matter," Alfonso says. "You are young, and it will wear off shortly."

281

Soon he is being helped into the car. Pancho's face blurs in and out of focus. "Where're we going?" he manages to say.

"K'Luna. It's the hottest nightclub in the Zona Viva."

As the driver swerves around hairpin turns, Justin, hanging onto the door, fears he might boot dinner, but the feeling passes by the time they reach the valley. The driver stops in a brightly lit part of town where young people fill the streets. Girls in spaghetti-strapped tops teeter on high heels. Guys with gelled hair lounge against walls and smoke cigarettes. From the back seat of the car, he can see a lineup of people waiting to get into a disco, and the line stretches halfway down the block.

"Is thish where we're going?" Justin struggles to say.

"This is it," Pancho says. "K'Luna."

"I'm not twenty-one," Justin says. He looks at Pancho. "You're not either."

"No worries. It's eighteen in Guatemala, but no one enforces it."

As Justin stumbles out of the car, his legs are limp and uncooperative. With Pancho supporting him, they cut into the front of the line.

"He's too young," the burly bouncer at the door says. Pancho slips him some bills. The man pockets them and steps aside.

Inside, the music pulsates. They push through the crowded, smoke-filled room and find a small table. Not only is the table the size of a steering wheel, but it rotates as well. Justin grabs onto it and pretends to be driving. A uniformed waiter arrives to take their order.

"I'll have a gin and tonic," Pancho says. "What about you, Fofo?"

Justin shrugs. He makes automobile noises in his mouth and tries to avoid invisible cars on his phantom roadway.

"Bring one for my friend, too."

Lights flash around the dance floor. Young people gyrate to a Latin beat, the lyrics in Spanish. Justin's tongue begins to lose its thickness.

The waiter places two inviting drinks on the table, and Pancho pulls out a wad of cash. The drink is served in a green-tinted glass with a slice of lime and an umbrella. The thought of a drink having a paper umbrella makes Justin giggle.

Pancho frowns. "Pace yourself, Fofo. I don't wanna have to help you to the crapper to puke your guts out."

"Maybe you could get me some water, too."

"When the waiter comes back."

Two girls join them at the table.

"Fofo, this is Roseanna." Pancho leans over and kisses one of the girls on the mouth, putting her off limits. He waves his arm in the direction of the other girl. "Her friend, Tatiana. Girls, this is Fofo."

In an effort to be polite, Justin mumbles a greeting.

Pancho turns to the girls. "Can I get you ladies drinks?"

"Thought you'd never ask." Roseanna's glossy black hair ripples halfway down her back. Her tawny eyes remind Justin of Whiskers, their old cat from Indiana. He struggles to tell her but can't seem to turn his thoughts into words. She probably wouldn't have appreciated the comparison anyway.

Pancho calls the waiter over and orders for the girls. "My buddy here is celebrating his birthday. I'm showing him a good time this weekend."

"How old are you?" Tatiana moves her chair closer to Justin. She smells of perfume and her eyes are made up like Cleopatra's. Her dark, bobbed hair, streaked with blonde, shimmers under the flashing lights.

"Eighteen, of course," Pancho says before Justin can answer.

Justin doesn't mind being eighteen for the night. Not at all.

He thinks of it as a gift to himself. He sits up a little straighter and tries to act his new age. The waiter brings out more drinks, and, halfway through them, Pancho suggests they leave and go somewhere more interesting.

They pile into the Lincoln and go to another club. Then another. Pancho and the girls smoke cigarettes and hand one to Justin. He tries to puff but ends up having a coughing fit.

For Justin, the rest of the evening is a blur of loud music, lights, cigarette smoke, and dancing. When the chauffeur brings them back to the house, he staggers down the stairs and throws up in the toilet before undressing and crawling into bed.

HE WAKES the next morning with a throbbing pain in his head and little recollection of the latter part of the evening. Bits and snatches come back, like lost pieces of a jigsaw—lights, drinks, broken glass. He vaguely recalls stumbling on the dance floor when Tatiana tried to show him how to salsa. He remembers the cigarette taste of her mouth.

Pancho cracks the bedroom door open. "Are you up yet, party boy?"

"Leave me alone," he groans, and puts a pillow over his head. "I hate life."

"You told me last night you'd never had so much fun."

"I don't remember," he says through the pillow, thinking no amount of fun could be worth this pain.

Pancho steps in and puts down a glass of water and two pills on the nightstand. "This is for your hangover. You'll feel better in a while."

Justin pops the pills, downs the water, and drags himself into the shower. In an effort to revive himself, he switches the water to cold. Then he notices bruises on his arms and legs that weren't there the day before.

Showered and dressed, he climbs the stairs to the dining area, where Alfonso and Pancho have just started eating.

"Feeling rough, Justin?" Alfonso asks.

"Kinda," he replies, and turns to Pancho. "Did we get into a fight or something? I hurt all over."

"You fell down a few times. No big deal. Wait till tonight. I've got something planned you'll never forget."

PANCHO TAKES Justin to Oak Park Mall for lunch, then a movie. Feeling better, he decides not to drink anymore—just the thought of more alcohol turns his stomach. Besides, if it is to be a night to remember, he wants to remember it.

The indoor shopping area is a glittering pedestrian city packed with people window-shopping. The difference between malls in Indiana and this mall is that few here carry purchases.

"Sure you don't want a brewski, Fofo?"

"I'm positive. And remember, you're driving."

"Couple a beers are nothing to me."

Pancho waves at several people from a distance. A tall, dark, bespectacled dude saunters over. Pancho introduces him as Juan Jo.

Juan Jo grabs Pancho's hand in an elaborate shake that ends in banging their fists together. He nods toward Justin, then meanders off toward some other teens.

After the movie, Justin climbs back into Pancho's car and straps on his seat belt, feeling a little unsure about Pancho driving after three beers. But, he seems to handle it okay. Sure, he leans on the horn, tailgates, and darts between cars in the traffic, but everyone in the city drives that way.

Back at the house, the boys plop down in the living room in front of the TV. Pancho glances at his watch. "Gotta run an errand with Alfonso. Be back in a while. You should take a nap or something, Fofo. Save your energy for tonight."

Justin stretches out on the bed and falls into a deep sleep. He wakes up when Pancho walks in carrying a phone. "I'm reserving dates." He winks. "How do you like your chicks? Dark and sultry or blonde and sassy?"

He remembers Sally. "Uh, maybe blonde."

Pancho leaves, talking on the phone in low tones.

Six o'clock. He gets up, showers again, and puts on his good clothes. He shaves the few uneven spots where growth has begun on his chin and around his cheeks. An unopened bottle of cologne sits on the bathroom shelf. He opens it and slaps some on his face as a finishing touch.

On the second level, Alfonso and Pancho are outside on the deck. The view of the city is spectacular.

"Hello, Justin," Alfonso says. "You look recovered."

Pancho glances at his watch.

"Gustav will be driving you," Alfonso says.

"I can drive," Pancho says.

"No, it's better if Gustav takes you."

They slide into the smooth leather back seat of the Lincoln. Gustav, his light brown hair in a small knot on the back of his head, observes them in the mirror with frosty blue eyes. "Where are we going tonight, sir?"

"Ecstasy, please."

He puts the car in gear, and they drive the remainder of the way down the hill in silence.

"What kind of place is Ecstasy?" Justin asks.

"The best place in the city to pick up girls. They're just waiting for us. I reserved two of the prettiest, Helga and Amber. But you can change your mind if you see something you like better."

Reserving girls? "What the heck's with that?"

"You're not wimping out, are you? I know you're a virgin. Don't tell me you've never wanted to do it?"

Justin glances out the window. The car is almost down the hill. "Of course I want to." His heart suddenly beats faster, and he shifts in his seat.

"Hey man, these girls are pros. Just go with the flow. If you're nervous, I'll buy you a drink."

"Well, maybe ... "

The car stops in front of a large house, a former mansion, where armed guards watch the street. Music blares from inside, and the hypnotic movement of colored lights is propelled out the front entrance. Gustav steps out and opens the car door. "I'll be around the corner, sir. Just call when you need me."

He waits until the boys enter the building before driving off. Justin can't help wondering how he feels calling a sixteen-year-old "sir."

They pass through the metal detector and wait while a guard waves a wand over them. Pancho walks confidently toward the bar. "What'll it be?" the bartender asks.

"The usual."

The bartender has no neck, and thick muscles bulge through his polo shirt. He could easily have been a linebacker. "And you?"

"I'll have a Coke."

"We don't allow snorting at the bar."

Justin almost laughs but catches the guy's expression. His

stony face tells him it isn't meant as a joke. "Oh, then just a bottle of water."

Nearly naked women dance slowly and sensually on a red-lit stage. Others mingle among the men. Slim chicks look like models, and then there are the blondes with boob jobs and the redheads—imported for wealthy male customers, he guesses.

Justin has a sudden urge to bolt, but where could he run?

Pancho studies him. "See anything you like, Fofo?"

"Hey, sugar." A syrupy sweet voice comes from behind, followed by a luscious blonde of about nineteen.

"Fofo, this is Helga," Pancho introduces the blonde. "I figured you liked German girls."

"Hi, handsome!" Her shoulder-length blonde hair frames her face in soft curls. How did Pancho know about Sally? Big blue eyes look at Justin with frank curiosity. "This is your first time, isn't it?"

Terrified and shaking but intrigued, he glances toward the stage and its half-nude dancers, gyrating to the music.

He can't bring himself to say anything.

Helga rubs her body against his already throbbing boner. "It's easy," she whispers in his ear. "We just let nature take its course."

She grabs his hand and guides him toward a hallway. "Don't you smell wonderful!" she exclaims.

"Wait. Do I have to pay or something?"

"Baby, it's all taken care of." She glances at him with a question on her face. "Alfonso owns the place, didn't you know?"

As he follows Helga, he glances back nervously at Pancho, who gives him a thumbs-up.

CHAPTER

THIRTY

When she hears the helicopter, Katherine rushes outside. Her son! He's only been gone two days, but she missed him more than she would have ever guessed.

Justin jumps from the aircraft, stumbles from beneath the rotors, and throws his arms around her.

"Honey, are you okay?" She tilts his face toward hers, but he won't meet her eyes. Never a good sign. "Justin? Answer me."

"Everything's fine, Mom. I'm just glad to be back. I missed you."

Alfonso steps out and greets them, his face offering no information about Justin's birthday weekend. "Has Poppy returned?"

Katherine shakes her head.

"Pancho stayed behind," he says, glancing at Katy. "Studies at his academy begin tomorrow. He'll be back next weekend."

As they walk toward the house, Katherine presses her son for details but gets monosyllabic answers. It is almost time for church. "Drop off your things and freshen up. We'll be leaving in a few minutes. Then I want to hear all about your trip."

He rolls his eyes and looks up at the second-story windows. Thinking his reluctance is about attending service, she says, "Forget it, mister. The condition for your weekend jaunt was to be back in time for church."

"Okay, okay. Just give me a sec." He snatches his bag and slouches off to the house.

She grabs the belt loops in Katy's skirt to prevent her from following her brother. "We'll be waiting for you down here. Hurry up."

Because they're running late, Horacio drives them to the construction site. The new church walls rise higher each week, and soon services will be held inside the building.

Parishioners crowd the road and spill into the yard. Soon all the seats are taken. Like books between bookends, people squeeze together between the cement columns on the half-built walls.

Phil strums hymns on his new guitar. He speaks of generosity and neighborly sharing, like when early Christians helped one another in times of need. The theme seems to be inspired by his own family's story, but Katherine can't say for sure. There was a time when Phil discussed sermons with her, when they discussed much more than just their children, but those days are in the past. It's not his fault. They are both to blame. Since her tryst with Alfonso, she doesn't see Phil with the same eyes, nor does she seek him out.

The villagers listen with rapt attention, and at the close of the service, Phil basks in congratulations. New and old attendees crowd around him. Men shake his hand and women pat his shoulder. Everyone looks up to him. Of course, he is one or two heads taller than anyone else in the congregation.

Several new members ask if he'd honor them by visiting their homes.

"Con mucho gusto," he replies.

"Bring your family," one man says. "I want you to meet my children and see my crops. I was inspired by your sermon and have a story of my own to tell."

Katherine hears them agree on a date later in the week, and, when the man leaves with three barefoot boys and a small girl in tow, he calls back, "See you Thursday, Pastor."

Thursday is Justin's birthday, and Phil says nothing to indicate he remembers. Maybe he thinks this weekend counted as the big celebration. On Thursday, maybe they'll do something low-key, something with just the family, but now that Phil has gone and made plans, there's no guarantee there will be a celebration at all.

Katherine wants Justin to have had a good time, to make up for all the attention his father isn't giving him. As they walk down the rutted dirt road, she says, "So tell me what you did, Justin. Give me details."

Justin wonders what he can tell his mother that will be somewhat neutral. Something that won't give away the truth. He attempts to infuse his answer with enthusiasm. "Alfonso's city house is a killer. You know, the one where Pancho lives during the week."

"Okay, that's a start. But what did you do?"

"We went to a mall and hung out with some of Pancho's friends. Had lunch. Saw a movie." He omits the drinking and the women. Alfonso had made it clear that what happens in the city, stays in the city.

"What else did you do?"

He shrugs.

"Did you like the city?" she asks.

"It was okay," he says. "You remember. There's a lot of traffic."

Over dinner, Phil announces that they'll be visiting Don Carmelo's farm on Thursday and that he wants all of them to go.

Katherine waits to see if Justin will remind Phil what day it is.

"Sure, Dad. That'll be awesome," Justin says absently.

On Thursday morning, Katherine wakes Justin. "What the hell, Mom? It's my birthday. Let me sleep."

She doesn't like that kind of talk but decides that the day shouldn't be one for disagreements. "Happy birthday, son." She kisses him on the forehead. "You told your father you were happy to come with us to Don Carmelo's farm. The fact that it's your birthday is even more reason to spend it with family."

"Is there any way I can get out of it?"

"Not easily," she says. "Besides, it's your birthday, and I don't want to leave you here."

"All right, then." He staggers out of bed.

A short time later they all meet for breakfast, and Alfonso tells them, "You need a substantial breakfast as it is quite a trek to Don Carmelo's place. Be careful along the way. The stream you must cross is swifter than it appears."

The assistant cook brings out plates laden with eggs, bacon, black beans, and tortillas. After eating, they load their daypacks into a pickup, and Chato drops them off at the trailhead, pointing out the way. When they ask how long it takes to get there, he says, "Una hora más o menos."

He reaches into the glove compartment, hands Phil a preprogrammed cell phone, and tells him to call when they need to be picked up.

The damp earth glistens as they follow the meandering trail. What locals call the *canícula*, a short respite from daily rains, ended the previous week. The mornings are clear and bright, and then in the early afternoon, the sky clouds up, bringing a dramatic display of thunder, lightning, and pounding rain. They must plan their outings around potential rainfall.

Morning dew quickly soaks their footwear. Wet clay from the saturated ground clings to their soles and makes the sucking sound of a toilet plunger as they trudge along. They stop several times to scrape off the mud.

When they reach the stream Alfonso warned them about, they see that water spews from the hillside and merges to form an icy torrent. Silt and debris cloud the water and conceal the stream bottom's slippery stones. They shed their shoes and roll up their pant legs. Phil crosses with Katy on his back and then returns to help his wife. While the two on the far bank tie their laces, Phil waits for Justin, who insists he can cross on his own. When his foot slips, he lunges for his father's outstretched hand and misses. Safely on the other side, he looks down at his drenched trousers. "Can I go home now? This is not my idea of fun, especially today."

"And head back across that stream? Forget it," Phil says. "You'll dry out soon enough."

A half hour later, the smoky aroma of a cooking fire announces Don Carmelo's home. "¡Buenos días!" Phil calls.

"Pasen adelante."

They open the wire-and-wood gate and stroll down the citrus-lined trail. The farm's earthen courtyard is shaded by mango and avocado trees. Much like other such homes in the surrounding area, an adobe hut blends into the earth. A half dozen little urchins peek out curiously from a partially open door.

Don Carmelo greets them and invites them to sit on crudely fashioned wooden benches.

"How many children do you have?" Katherine asks in Spanish.

"Diez." He shows all his fingers.

"And your wife?"

He opens his hands to show them empty. "She died in child-birth last year." He shakes his head sadly. "María Concepción is twelve. A good girl. She and her nine-year-old sister take care of the little ones. Conchita," he gestures toward María Concepción, "also does the cooking and housework."

"What happened to the baby?"

"*Gemelos*—twins. Praise God they were both saved. Don Alfonso heard about my troubles and provided formula, bottles, and medical help through the local health center. Including the infants, six of my children are sons," he says proudly. "The thir-teen-year-old and eleven-year-old already work the fields with me."

"What about school?" Katy cocks her head. "Don't they go to school?"

Don Carmelo shrugs. "The older boys went for a few years, but the girls haven't had any schooling. I need them here."

"But education is so important," Katherine says.

"Circumstances don't allow it. I believe in education, but what choice have I? I would have them all study if it were possi-ble." He holds out his hands with the palms up.

Katy pulls on her father's sleeve. "Why can't the girls study?"

Phil explains quietly. "He needs them to care for the babies and do the cooking. They're too poor to educate their children."

"Why can't they go to public school if it doesn't cost anything?"

He remembers Señor López's explanation. "It always costs something, even if it is only the shoes they wear or their required uniform. But mostly it takes time away from doing their chores at home, chores that are necessary for the family's survival."

Katy's eyes flash. "What do the girls think of that?"

"Pancake, they have little choice. In this culture, the father rules the family. Once a girl marries, her husband makes the rules."

"What if they leave their husbands?"

"Single mothers can't support themselves and their children, especially if they have no education. Their choices are limited."

Katy stares at Conchita with both pity and admiration, trying to imagine life from her perspective. When the girl looks over at her, she forces a smile.

"You didn't know how lucky you were to be born in the United States and have options," Katherine says softly.

Don Carmelo continues. "If my children were able to attend school, perhaps then they could get jobs and live better lives. That's why I'm so excited about Don Alfonso's project."

Katherine realizes where the visit is headed—to a poppy field. "How long have you been working with him?"

"Don Alfonso approached me soon after the twins were born." He nodded toward two toddlers being held by younger siblings. "Well, you know he helps farmers around here with their crops. Your sermon last Sunday reminded me of all he's done for us, so I thought you'd want to see how he's changed our lives." He remains thoughtful for a moment. "But of course I don't go and worship at Piedras Sagradas. I'm a Christian."

Confusion distorts Phil's face. "Piedras Sagradas?"

"The Mayan ruins nearby where he leads ceremonies."

Phil visibly pales. "Alfonso conducts Mayan services?"

"He's a *sacerdote* Maya. I thought you knew, Pastor."

"How would I know?"

Don Carmelo glances at Justin. "Your son saw us while we were there."

Eyebrows raised, eyes wide, Phil looks quickly at Justin and then turns to Katherine. "Did you know about this?"

She shrugs. "I didn't tell you because I knew you wouldn't want to hear it."

A dark-skinned nine-year-old with one of the toddlers tied to her back comes from the kitchen with glasses of lemonade. Phil struggles to recover his composure.

A boy of five runs out and stands near Justin. He smiles shyly, then touches Justin's wet pants with curiosity.

"¿Como te llamas?" Justin asks.

"Bayron Genero Chixoy Tum." He speaks softly and rapidly.

"*Hola,* Brian."

"Bye-ron," he corrects, and darts off on bare feet to join his siblings. A moment later the group of them giggle and point at Justin. The boy mimics Justin's pronunciation, provoking peals of laughter.

"I want to show you my crop," Don Carmelo says. "This project will enable my children to have enough to eat and also be able to study—luxuries I could never hope to give them before."

Katherine throws her kids a meaningful look to reinforce that for these farmers, simply having enough to eat and being able to go to school are considered luxuries.

They follow Don Carmelo as he strides along a path. The *milpas*—cornfields—offer heads of immature corn to the gods. Black-bean vines twist, snakelike, up the cornstalks.

Katherine looks sideways at her husband. No matter how

much they've tried to tell him, he has refused to listen. Now he will be confronted by the very thing he has been denying.

Beyond the traditional crops, the path curves into the mountains. They pick their way carefully through brush and over rocks. Don Carmelo turns for a moment to let them catch up. "I have an entire *manzana*. Most farmers are only allowed half as much. You see, I have so many young ones to raise. With the added income, I won't need to send my oldest girl to work in the city as a maid."

"I'm sure you're doing the right thing," Katherine says.

"My daughter loves her family. She would be terrified to leave, but she would go for our sakes. I don't want her to. She should be with her family, so with the money I will receive from harvest, I hope to find another wife. No woman would want to be part of our misery now." He spreads his arms wide. "All these children and not enough food."

As they follow, Phil keeps his head down. Katherine sees a flash of lime through tree branches. Could it be her? Come to watch them see the crop she was named for? "Look, Phil! Is that Poppy?"

He lifts his binoculars. "I don't think so. There are two of them. They must be mates."

Perhaps Poppy found one of her own species to mate with. Birds are no different from humans. Ultimately, all creatures search for the right partner.

"Why did you plant so far into the hills?" Phil asks as they trek, sweat beading on his brow.

"So the crop won't be found and destroyed. But do not worry. We're almost there."

Around the bend and through a small stand of trees, beautiful and green, is a poppy field. The immature plants rise a foot and a half high, rose-colored buds beginning to form. "All the seeds germinated," Don Carmelo explains. "We were lucky."

Phil asks, "¿Que cultivo es?"

"Amapola, por supuesto." Poppy, of course.

Phil frowns and strokes his chin. Poppies? It was true after all. He hadn't wanted to listen when he should have. He wanted to be the one to convert Alfonso, to have it all turn out perfectly. He had been deceiving himself. "Don Carmelo, my family and I must leave now."

"What about lunch?" His shoulders sag, and the animation in his face fades. "You can't leave now. We killed a hen in your honor."

"Phil, we can't go," Katherine cries. "They've prepared a special meal for us. That would be an insult."

Phil longs to be alone, to let this new information settle in and figure out what he must do. If anything. Since the family is with him, they must all leave. "Tell him to feed his children with it," he mutters, unable to focus. "They need the food more than we do."

"I'm so sorry," Katherine says, torn between her husband's agony and the disappointed farmer. Just because Phil wants to leave doesn't mean she must leave, too. "My husband has another commitment, but the rest of us will be happy to return to your farm and have lunch."

Don Carmelo turns to Phil for confirmation. Phil tries not to allow relief to show in his face when the compromise is reached. The farmer offers to show him a shortcut back to the road. When they reach the trailhead, Phil apologizes to Don Carmelo.

"Wait a minute, Phil," Katherine calls as he walks away. "What are you planning to do?"

"Confront Alfonso. Surely there's an explanation." It was

the only thing left for him to do. Perhaps they were wrong after all. All wrong.

"Oh, yes. An explanation." Angry heat flushes her skin. Asking for an explanation might not be safe. "What's Alfonso going to say, 'Phil, I thought you knew! I teach farmers to grow opium poppies for profit.'"

Phil winces. "Did I want that church so badly that I was willing to overlook where the money came from?" He looks toward the trail then back at his family, unable to meet his wife's eyes.

"We tried to warn you ... " she starts, but his face is so filled with pain that she can't continue. She wants to say, I told you so —she's wanted to say that for months—but now that the timing is perfect, she doesn't have the heart.

"You thought you were doing the right thing," Justin says. "Accepting Alfonso's help. It wasn't for you. It was for the community. For God."

Phil pushes at the air as though pushing away his family and everything he thought he understood so well. He turns and hesitates before he begins hiking down the path, his mind already focusing on what he will say to Alfonso.

Don Carmelo stands nearby, frowning and kicking at a stone.

Katherine can see by his expression he feels responsible for what is obviously an argument. The poor man doesn't understand why the pastor has gone away upset, and her Spanish isn't good enough to explain. Bitterness bubbles up inside her and bursts out in a barbed reproach that she shouts at Phil's retreating form, "We're in this country because of your divine revelation, Phil. You'd better start praying for another."

He slumps in defeat as he hears her words, then straightens

his shoulders. With a remaining shred of inner determination, he marches down the trail toward the road.

Katherine turns to her children. "Come on, kids. Don Carmelo is waiting for us."

In the distance, a feathered voice cries, "¡Poppy! ¡Me llamo Poppy!"

THIRTY-ONE

While his family gathers round to watch, Don Carmelo seats Katherine, Katy, and Justin at a table. It's disconcerting to be the honored guests and eat in front of hungry children, but Katherine knows from Phil that this is customary in the *campo*. They can't refuse without it being construed as an insult.

Thunderclouds lurk like thieves in the sky. Katherine glances up from time to time, worried about the impending walk. After the meal, she thanks their host. If they depart immediately, maybe they can get back before the storm hits.

Shortly after they ford the swift creek, thunder crashes, and the clouds burst like giant water balloons, soaking everything below. Electricity surges through the air, standing their hair on end. When lightning strikes a nearby tree, Katy screams. Rain batters the earth with furious intensity.

They huddle together under the dense foliage of a tall mango tree. Fat raindrops find their way through and leave them soaked and chilled. Every so often a mango thumps to the ground and a splatter of muddy water leaps from the saturated earth.

When the rain eases to a drizzle, they start walking. Katherine urges them to move fast to keep warm. Drenched clothing weighs them down, and their shoes squirt water with each step. They expect to find the driver from the villa waiting, but muddy tire tracks are the only trace of the vehicle.

"Can't you call?" Justin asks.

"Your father took the phone."

"Why didn't Daddy have the car here to meet us? How could he have forgotten?" Katy sobs.

Inconsiderate, insensitive bastard, Katherine fumes silently. You'd think he'd remember his family.

"Something must have come up. He wouldn't just forget," Justin says in his defense. "They're probably on their way now."

With no other choice, they head for the villa on foot. With each step, Katherine's anger grows until it becomes a monster stomping home.

Two miserable hours later, they reach the gates. A new guard doesn't recognize them and orders them to identify themselves, not believing this bedraggled trio could possibly be residents.

Katherine has lost all reason by now and tries to force her way past, but his arm holds her back. "Take your hands off me!" She shoves the guard.

"Just call Alfonso," Justin says.

The guard looks from Katherine to Justin, and then finally presses the intercom.

After he receives the okay, the guard lets them pass. Leaving her soaked shoes at the door, Katherine marches into the villa and asks the startled housekeeper where she can find Pastor Felipe. She points upstairs.

"He'd better have a good reason for not coming back for us." Barefoot, she stomps upstairs.

Katy and Justin shed their shoes and race after her. She bursts into the bedroom. "What's your excuse this time, or do you even have one?"

He is reading a magazine, one foot resting casually on the opposite knee. He jumps to his feet. Surprise turns to horror when he sees her face and bedraggled appearance. "Oh, my Lord, Katherine. What happened?"

"What do you mean 'What happened?' You kept the phone and didn't think to send Chato or someone else back for us. We walked for two hours through a rainstorm to get here. Thank heaven we didn't get lost on our way back."

"I'm so sorry. I assumed it would be taken care of, that someone would go back for you. Forgive me. I was wrapped up in a discussion with Alfonso, thinking about those poppies." He looks at the floor. "I guess I forgot."

"You forgot? Your family stranded in the mountains and you 'guess you forgot'?"

Katy and Justin stand in the doorway. "Go to your rooms," Katherine orders, and slams the door shut. "It's easy to forget about us while you're sitting here comfortably, isn't it? Easy to forget—just like it's easy to ignore facts when your family could be in danger." She pauses to ready herself for another assault. "So, Mister Missionary, what did Alfonso say? This'd better be good."

"I should have known better than to doubt him. It's all legal," he says with a satisfied air.

"Yes, of course it is ... and ... ?" Her voice drips with sarcasm.

"He has a permit to sell morphine to pharmaceutical companies, and he showed me the laboratory where the process is completed. He keeps the production concealed and secure. It all makes perfect sense! Heroin and medicinal morphine share the same opium base. He has to be constantly on the lookout for thieves."

"That's what he said?" Her voice falters. She hadn't considered that Alfonso would come up with a cover story. "Obviously you believe him. Did he show you the permit?"

"Well, no. I don't need to see it. I have no reason to doubt his word."

"You're such an idiot! You believe whatever's convenient for you. I've been suffering from misguided loyalty, and I should never have agreed to come with you to this godforsaken place and bring our children, too. This place will be the ruin of us!"

Who cares if the poppies are grown for pharmaceutical purposes or for street drugs? When she continues, her voice is moderated. "Maybe it matters to you whether the crop is legal or not, but what about Don Carmelo and the other farmers? Do you think it matters to them? Do they even think or care about that?"

"I don't know," he admits. "But surely their consciences are clearer knowing that it's legal. I mean, I feel better about it."

"We've been here—how long?—and you still don't get it! Don Carmelo has a clear conscience knowing his children will have enough to eat, that Conchita won't have to be a house servant in someone's home to support her family. That's what's important. You missed the whole damn point."

"No need to raise your voice," Phil says quietly.

"Damn you for bringing us here. Damn you for wrecking our family and our lives. Damn you for allowing us to get close to Alfonso. He's made me see that he's a far better man than you, despite what he's involved in. Personally, I don't even care about that anymore. I can justify his actions by all the good he's done. You talk about how God protects the broken and the needy.

Don't you see that Alfonso does the same?" She folds her arms and glares down at him. "And you—it's a miracle you haven't gotten us killed. You have no idea how to protect your family, and I regret the day I allowed you to convince me to come. I had some far-out idea that God would come to our rescue if anything happened. That you were saved for a purpose. We would still be a happy family if we'd stayed in Indiana. I don't know how you ever got so hung up on missions."

Turning, she strides across the room, jerks the door open, and rushes out, smacking into her son, who had his ear bent to the keyhole. "What are you doing? I told you to go to your room."

As he slinks off toward Katy's room, she calls, "Wait! I'm going to use your shower."

Ashen-faced, Phil follows her into the hall. "Katherine, come back. Let's talk about this. Please."

"Talk?" She turns around. "It's a little late for that. I've been trying to talk to you since that weekend we were robbed. And that divine revelation you had back home? It was probably just an opium-induced dream brought on by your morphine drip."

She returns to the room, grabs a change of clothes, and stalks out.

In the shower, she tries to scour away her rage. She puts on her clothes and steps into the hall, suddenly at a loss about where to go or whom to turn to. The door to Katy's room is ajar, and she stands nearby and listens, expecting the kids to notice her presence.

"She'll get over it," Justin says. "She always does."

"She's pretty mad. I've never seen her so angry."

"Dad still doesn't get it," Justin says.

"Hey, Justin, I just remembered."

Katherine, hiding in the hall, peeks around the door.

Katy pulls out a gift. "This is for you. For your birthday."

Justin shakes the package and turns it over.

"Open it," Katy says.

He pulls off the tape. It is a small plaque with fabric stretched over a frame, decorated with dried, pressed flowers. Katherine had helped her daughter make it. In cross-stitched letters it says, "To the best brother ever. Happy Birthday."

Katherine sighs, wondering how things will end for all of them, but she suspects they won't end well.

Downstairs in the library, Alfonso is reading the newspaper. When she comes in, he rises to his feet. "I was so sorry to hear what happened. Had I known, I would have sent a vehicle."

She surmises he did know, but it was Phil's responsibility to see it through. Chato sure wouldn't do them any favors of his own free will. "You win. My marriage is over."

"Do not choose me because you are fighting with Phil or because you no longer wish to be with him. You have other choices. Think about it long and hard. There will be no turning back."

She respects his words. The balance has tipped toward Alfonso now, but will it remain that way?

She excuses herself to make a pot of tea in hopes it will take the edge off her anger. Phil leaves the house and shuffles down the cement walkway toward the back of the property. Taking advantage of his absence, she goes upstairs to retrieve Justin's birthday gift and then taps on his door.

"I'm so sorry about all of this with your father. I wish you hadn't heard." She hands him a package.

With one hand he puts the package behind his back, and

with the other, he reaches around her shoulder and draws her close. His face brushes her cheek. Soon, he will be as tall as she is.

"What's going to happen to us, Mom?" he asks. "I'm afraid."

"Me too. Me too."

She leads him to the bed, and they sit on the edge in silence. She can imagine what he's thinking because the same thoughts are running through her mind.

"Do you really believe the poppies are legal?" Justin asks.

"Honestly? No," she says.

He picks up the gift and carefully opens it, smoothing the paper out as he goes. Inside is a book with blank pages of an unusual textured paper. He looks up, questioningly.

"It's handcrafted from coffee parchment," she explains. "To remind you of our visit to La Providencia and the Pregel family. You want to be a writer? Write this story."

He nods. The time they've spent in Guatemala, the things that have happened, many of them too strange to even talk about —written down on paper, perhaps the purpose of their coming might become discernible.

"Justin, I was wondering ... "

"Yes?" he prompts.

"What do you think of Alfonso?"

He wants to be honest, but still, with Alfonso, around each corner lies a secret, some his mother doesn't know. What would she think about the pictures in the city house? About the debauchery that weekend?

"I don't know," he says. "I like him, I guess. It's hard not to. But I guess I don't like what he's done to our family."

"I want you to know it's been your father's doing as much as his."

"You know, Mom, he's not the nice guy he appears to be."

"He's a complicated man. I once told you I would never be tempted away from your father, but things have changed."

"Please don't say that. Give Dad another chance."

"Come downstairs with me."

They meet Alfonso in the hallway. His gaze settles on Katherine, then her son. "I have something for you, Justin."

"Thank you, but that isn't necessary. You and Pancho have done enough already."

"Perhaps we have," he says, handing him a package, "but I would like you to have this anyway."

Justin looks at the package. He could unwrap it here in the hall. Surely, that's what Alfonso expects, what any gift giver expects, to witness the delight on the recipient's face. Somehow, Justin doesn't think he's going to like this gift. He thinks it's likely to be something he shouldn't have. Rather than disappoint Alfonso or have to fake a thank-you he doesn't feel, he takes the package to his room.

In the kitchen, Phil says grace and then eats a silent dinner, not asking what they had for lunch or if they'd had trouble crossing the stream. The children's eyes are on their plates, and they pick as if they're still full from the scrawny chicken. The long walk back ruined three pairs of shoes, and they are barefoot. The maid cleaned off the mud and washed them with a hose, but the shoes are still wet and will likely be unwearable. With no money and no transportation—without even their passports— Phil's stupidity has gotten them in a situation where the family is wholly dependent on Alfonso, and Phil, a man Katherine should look up to or at least believe is her equal, is too clueless to recognize the complicated web of lies and half-truths in which they've become entangled. Katherine's anger sparks the air with an invisible current.

Shuddering with disgust at the cowering simpleton across the table, she carries her plate to the library, not to eat, necessarily, but to get away from Phil and the things she might say if she opens her mouth.

A few minutes later, Alfonso joins her. "I want you to know I can be here for you," he says. "I would do anything for you, even give all this up if necessary." He waves his arms to include the house and surroundings. The riches.

She believes he would do many things for her, but to give up everything? She doesn't believe that. Not for a moment.

After eating, she puts her plate on the end table and opens her book. Comfortable with each other like an old married couple, he picks up the paper and tells her the latest exchange rate. As the evening wears on, she says, "I need to go upstairs with the kids."

"Stay with me tonight. I know you won't be with your husband."

"Not with my family here. The time isn't right." But it's more than timing. She still hasn't decided. Though comfortable in his presence, can she leave Phil for a drug trafficker? How far can a wife meander from her marriage before the return path is permanently blocked?

JUSTIN IS asleep in his room with the television on. She turns it off and tucks the covers around him. Her son. Fifteen already. Tossed on his dresser is a hastily opened gift, a new Swiss army knife with dozens of functions. She knows he would have loved it dearly. Had it been a gift from anyone else, he would have put it away carefully and cherished it. Instead, she can imagine him thinking the gift is a form of bribery. Perhaps he is correct.

In Katy's room, the television is also on, but her daughter is lying on her bed in front of it and kicking at the pillow.

"You're up past your bedtime, you know."

"Aw, just let me finish this program."

"Okay, but lights off after that. I'm going to join you later. I hope you don't mind."

"Of course not. It'll be another slumber party."

Too upset to sleep, Katherine sneaks downstairs for a snack, hoping, yet dreading, that she'll run into Alfonso. When she finishes in the kitchen, she sees that he has waited just outside the door. He follows her upstairs and gestures for her to sit on the love seat at the end of the hall.

If she is going to do this, leave her husband for this man, she must find out the truth about the opium cultivation. She has seen firsthand how local farmers benefit from the crop, but is it legal or not?

"Is it true then," she asks, feeling the warmth of his body and his gentle fingers stroking her hand, "what you told Phil?"

He brings her hand to his mouth and kisses it. "Does it matter?"

Currents of desire ripple through her body. She sighs. "I thought at first it did, but it doesn't, at least not to the farmer who only wants to improve his means and the circumstances of his life. As you say, you are giving people choices."

He nods. "I try to do that with every aspect of my life, but as you have seen, sometimes, it doesn't work. Poppy hasn't returned."

"I think we saw her today. With a mate."

"It was bound to happen. Perhaps I made a mistake by giving

her so much freedom. Had I caged or clipped her, she would still be mine."

"She would be a prisoner."

He nods. "You are very perceptive."

"Not always," she says.

He places her hand carefully in her lap and then stands. "I will let you rest now, dear." He leans over, brushes her lips with his, and goes toward his room.

Katherine opens the door to her daughter's room and slips into bed. She hears Katy's steady breathing and the guard dogs' occasional bark. She hears the whirr of the ceiling fan and the rattle of shutters. Outside, the *caballero de noche* warbles his nightly greeting. Phil once told her it was the common pauraque, but she prefers the translation from Spanish. Gentleman of the Night. Reminds her of Alfonso.

THIRTY-TWO

K atherine spends much of her free time with Alfonso. They stroll the grounds together, sit in the library and talk, or drive to town. He has given her extensive tours of his community programs. She can hardly believe six weeks have flown by since she first arrived at the villa.

"I would love for you to officially become the director of my benevolent projects. You have a flair for working with the under-privileged."

"It sounds like an ideal job, but I'm homeschooling my children. I just don't have the time."

"We can send them to the American School. It is one of the best learning establishments in the country. They can stay in the city during the week and come back and forth in the helicopter with Pancho. They will graduate fully bilingual and have access to top U.S. universities." He speaks as though it is a foregone conclusion that she and the children will stay with him.

"It's too much."

"I could write the schooling into your job contract if that

makes you more comfortable, at least until we formalize things between us."

"But if I do this, where's the money going to come from? Back home, I suppose I could write grants and get government money, but here? Without Spanish? I don't want to be dependent on you for everything."

She is quiet, thinking again about her impending choice, or maybe it's a choice she has already made and is just waiting to tell Phil.

"There are enough funds in my philanthropy account to make a significant impact. The three health centers could potentially benefit thousands of poor farmers, and we could build more. It is a matter of having the right person involved. Someone to take charge, someone to follow through, someone who cares about the welfare of the villagers. Until you came, I despaired of finding the right person, and I do not have enough time to manage things as they should be managed."

It's exactly what she's hoped to do, not be Phil's helpmate, there to run choir practice or show up for service, but someone with a portfolio of her own. On one level, she can't help but think this is God's work and that, in an odd way, He brought the two of them together.

Phil is right about Alfonso's character. He is an excellent person, respected by everyone with whom she has come in contact, from the poorest to the richest. Those at the dinner party sang his praises, and even when she was out of his presence, the couple who'd invited her to their coffee plantation—Hans and María Pregel—had nothing bad to say about him, only about the unfortunate effects of violence between the cartels. Here in Guatemala, the damage heroin does in the developed world seems irrelevant. After all, those in poverty have no choice, and, as Alfonso says, he believes in giving people choices.

Aren't the addicts in developed countries making a choice to use the drugs?

Later that week when Alfonso suggests they spend a day in San Marcos, she accepts his invitation. She tells the kids that she and Alfonso are going to check on the van and makes a note to herself to ask about it. "We'll be gone all morning, but don't worry. Your father will be around."

"Can't we come too?" Katy asks.

She shakes her head and uses schoolwork as an excuse, but in truth she is looking forward to spending time alone with Alfonso. He told her about a small apartment he keeps in town and wants to take her there. Would that be so wrong in light of her no longer sharing her husband's bed?

On the drive down from the villa, they pass the little building where a dozen men slap mortar between cement blocks. Phil's dream. She has misgivings about Phil staying and giving sermons just down the road from where she is getting ready to make her new home. This, too, is something she must work out.

Alfonso puts his hand on hers. "I am truly happy with you here beside me."

She sees a new life laid out for her, even better than she could have imagined. Alfonso makes her feel special, valued and cherished. Her life has a fresh purpose. Will it be as easy as Alfonso makes it out to be to let her children know? She is sure that Katy will be happy, but Justin will need convincing. Still, as Alfonso once said, many people in the U.S. get divorced and the children adjust.

An hour out of town, the phone rings. Alfonso picks up. "Hello, Justin." He pauses. "There is no use becoming angry. While I am away, you must stay inside the compound for your own security. You are living under my roof, and you must respect my rules."

"What was that about?" she asks as he cuts off the cellular.

"It was nothing. Your children wanted to go outside for a walk, but there are plenty of places to go within the limits of the villa's compound. Even while I am there, I must insist on you having an escort. These are dangerous times."

JUSTIN, with Katy close behind him, shoves the phone at the guard and stomps back toward the villa. "Don't be so upset," she says. "Alfonso wouldn't keep us inside without a good reason."

Justin whirls around. "Is keeping us prisoners an acceptable reason?"

"We're not prisoners. We're guests and he's protecting us. Besides, there're lots of places to walk inside the compound. Have you seen the hydroelectric plant? Pancho took me last week."

He raises his eyebrows. "Pancho took you? When was that? How come I didn't know about it?"

"You were watching TV or something. Come on, it wasn't a big deal."

Justin doesn't like the idea of his little sister getting too close to a creep like Pancho. He has enough on his mind already without having to worry about Katy.

Sun penetrates the thin highland air, taking the damp edge from the morning. The walk begins to calm him. He doesn't like that Alfonso has gone off with his mother while they are restricted to the compound. If it is so dangerous outside, why would Alfonso take a chance on driving to San Marcos?

His sister skips along as though she hasn't a care in the world. "Why are you so happy?" he asks. "Do you really like it here?"

"Like it? I love it! I love living in this beautiful place with a pool of our own, servants who take care of us, and horses to ride. I can't believe things have turned out so well! Don't you think it's wonderful?"

"Hold on, Katy. None of this is ours. It's Alfonso's and we aren't part of it. As for me, I wish we'd never come. There's a lot of stuff going on around here that we don't know about."

"Alfonso will take care of us. You can go back if you like, but don't expect me to. If I had my way, I'd stay here forever."

A swift stream ripples through a field, hurtling over smooth stones and glistening gravel. "This is it? It doesn't look big enough to produce much electricity."

"That's what I told Pancho. He said the speed is more important than the amount of water. See how fast it moves?" She throws a twig into the creek, and it quickly disappears into a small building the size of a latrine. "That's where the machinery turns it into electricity." Inside, belts creak and valves hiss. Current-carrying wires poke out of the tin roof on their way to the villa. A padlock bars the door.

They take their shoes off and dangle their feet in the water. Minnows nibble at their toes and Katy giggles.

"Let's put our shoes on. I'll show you where Pancho and I practiced target shooting."

The practice range is a ten-minute walk. Justin hasn't been here since the day Alfonso showed him the arsenal. When they arrive, Pancho is collecting rifles from the shed. "What're you guys up to?" He squints as though calculating where they've come from. "I hope you aren't hanging out near the creek."

Justin makes a face. "We're not allowed outside the compound."

Pancho doesn't look surprised. "Alfonso takes precautions. There've been some threats. Happens sometimes. But if there was an attack, the hydroelectric is the last place you'd want to be. If they were smart, they'd take out the electricity first. That would disable the security cameras and the electric razor wire."

"Do you really think someone might attack the villa?"

He shrugs. "Wouldn't be the first time. Why'd you think we got all that security? It's not just to be cool. My parents were Alfonso's personal guards. They gave their lives to save him. That's why he feels responsible for me, but, hey, can't complain about that!"

They hear an explosion followed by the staccato of automatic weapons, which sounds as though it is coming from the front entrance. The kids freeze. Pancho reacts first. "Hey man, I gotta go. They need my help up front."

"Don't leave us!" Katy pleads.

Pancho scans the surroundings. Nearby are the mysterious buildings Justin saw the men going in and out of that day several months earlier. The buildings are solid cement with steel-ribbed roofing. The exchange of gunfire grows louder.

"Follow me." Pancho pulls out a key and opens the nearest door. "You guys'll be safe in here. Find a hiding place and stay till I return. I gotta see what's going on." He hands one of the rifles to Justin. "You probably won't need this, but just in case." After locking them inside, he races off.

The room is dark. As Justin's eyes adjust, he sees something that looks like a restaurant oven with a glass door. There are the large chrome vats he saw that previous day. An unusual scent lingers in the air. There is a table with butcher paper, several scales, and boxes of plastic baggies. Justin opens closets and cupboards. When he finds an empty one, he shoves his sister inside and shuts the door. "I'll be nearby. We need to stay hidden for now."

"I'm scared."

"Don't worry. Like Pancho says, there's nothing to be afraid of. There's nowhere safer than the villa with all their security. He'll be back soon."

Justin steps into a utility closet and tries to believe his words.

THE PHONE RINGS. Katherine sees from the screen that Chato is calling. Alfonso generally doesn't take calls when he is with her, but this time he picks up and listens. "Ahorita voy," he says tersely, ending the conversation.

He spins the car around, tires squealing, and they head back.

"What is it?"

"There is trouble at the villa."

"Is my family okay?" Alfonso focuses on the road and doesn't reply. She stares at his profile and knows better than to disturb him.

Trees and scenery fly by. They pass cars, pickups, and buses. Alfonso concentrates on the road, his knuckles tight on the steering wheel. He races up the dirt road toward the villa.

Katherine hangs on tight. He hasn't said so, but somehow, she knows the villa is under attack. Why did she think she could leave her children for an afternoon with ineffectual Phil?

A pickup truck barrels down the hill toward them, and Alfonso swerves to avoid a collision. Bullets slap the Hummer and ricochet off—praise God for bullet proofing!—and when she looks in the side mirror, she sees a man with a bandanna covering his face firing in their direction. Alfonso grabs the gun under his thigh, then decides against it and picks up his cell phone, speed dialing someone at home. If he is concerned, he hides it well. He drives one-handed and listens, nodding, yes, yes, okay.

He hands her the phone. "Do not fear. The villa was attacked, but, evidently, the attackers are now on the run."

As they reach the open gate, several guards are investigating an abandoned Jeep. Others drag heavy bundles wrapped in tarps —bodies?—and heave them into the back of a pickup.

"What's going on?" she asks.

"We will know soon enough. I must get you inside."

"Where are my children?"

"I don't know. Go to the library and I'll find out."

He slams the Hummer into park and jumps out, running for the front gate. "Quickly now."

She steps down onto the running board, tempted to follow.

"Katherine! Katherine!"

She turns and sees Phil peeking from behind the front door. "Are the kids with you?" he calls.

"No," she says. "I left them in your care."

"I don't think they're in the house."

"Don't you know where they are?"

"Actually, I think they might have gone for a walk."

"A walk," she says. "A walk where?"

Phil closes the door. "A walk, you know. A little stroll. I don't think they've left the compound."

"Could they be with Pancho?"

"Let's hope not. Pancho was in the middle of the action," Phil says. "I saw him out front with the guards. He was shooting. I tried to go out, but they wouldn't let me."

"Then where are they?" she asks.

THE GROUNDS ARE WRAPPED in an eerie silence. Katy unfolds herself from her hiding place. "Is it over?"

"Shush," Justin says. "How would I know? Be quiet."

The door key turns. "You guys can come on out now. Bandits are gone. Ran 'em off. Told ya it'd be fine."

Justin opens the door of the utility closet. "What happened out there?"

Pancho looks at the rifle. "Let me take that."

Justin hands it over.

"Is it safe to come out?" Katy asks, joining them.

"Yeah, we ran them off," Pancho says.

"But what happened?" she said.

"It was just another attack on the villa. They didn't even plan it well. Shows they're not too smart. Coulda tried from both entrances at the same time—tactical advantage, but no, they wanted to stick together. Stupid for them, lucky for us. They'd have never made it anyway. No one can get into this fortress." He smiles with pride.

"Were you in the action?" Justin asks with wonder.

Pancho shrugs. "Whaddya think all the target practice is for? Winged one of them. He'll be hurting I bet. Only wish I'd had a bigger gun."

Eyes wide, Katy looks at him. "Weren't you scared?"

"Naw. I wouldn't be living here if that kind of stuff bothered me."

Justin catches Pancho's swagger, his attempt to show off, and decides to take advantage. "Hey, Pancho, what is this place anyway? It looks like a chem lab."

"Or a giant laundromat," Katy suggests.

Pancho hesitates, and Justin imagines him torn between self-importance and what he knows is a well-kept secret. "I shouldn't be showing you, but you'll probably find out anyway. Besides, you've been here for an hour already. I could always say you discovered it on your own."

He flips on the lights. Industrial chrome vats line one wall. A series of control panels and gauges embellish another. A white powder trails off one of the shelves and creates a path to a locked door.

Justin overheard the discussion between his parents the day they saw the poppy field, but he wants to hear Pancho's version.

"This is the most state-of-the-art heroin lab in this hemisphere," he says arrogantly. "And one day it'll be mine."

The two stare, waiting for him to continue. "Alfonso wants to do it right—not in makeshift labs or any of that shit. High-quality smack fetches the best price. We only do business with the best."

Heroin, not opium. "So you produce heroin here?"

"You deaf or something? Why else would we encourage farmers to grow poppies? The real money is in the processing and trafficking."

"But Alfonso told my dad they processed morphine for pharmaceutical use."

"Yeah, right," Pancho sneers. "No offense, but it's fuckin' easy to fool your old man."

Justin's knees go weak, and he staggers.

Katy grabs his arm. "Come on, Justin. Does it really matter? It's not like you didn't suspect. Mom knows and she's okay with it."

"She's what?" Justin whirls around to face her. "How do you know?"

"She talked to Alfonso about it last night. She came back to my room late. I pretended to be asleep, but I heard them talking in the hall."

Mom knew? But does his father know, and what will he do when he finds out he's been fed a pack of lies? Justin rubs his eyes. His world is quickly slipping out of focus.

"The quality of the final product is top notch," Pancho says. "Alfonso has high standards. The powder is pure and uncut. That's why it's white."

"I guess ... " Justin hesitates. "That's a good thing?"

"Sure is," Pancho says. "Harvest is beginning. We took the first batch to the beach in the helicopter the day you got picked up. It went out in boats. Timing of the attack sucks for them. We've hardly got any smack here. It's been going out regularly. C'mon. I want to put the guns away. We should be safe now."

Pancho turns out the light and waits for Justin and Katy to exit.

Justin looks at the steel door and down at a trail of what looks like powdered sugar. "Is that heroin?"

"Yeah, that's smack. There must have been a rip in the bag, because Alfonso insists on keeping the lab clean."

"Why?" Justin asks.

"To avoid contamination. For security too. The stuff is valuable with a capital *V*. Like I said before, it's uncut. There's a temporary storage area in the adjoining warehouse. There's another door that has outside access to the helipads. Even I don't have a key. The stuff's worth millions. More than you can even imagine," he says in a conspiratorial way.

"So let me get this straight, the heroin is what they're looking for?" Justin says, putting an arm around his sister. Under the weight of his arm, he feels her shiver.

"That and to take over. Put us out of business. Take us out of the running. Today, Alfonso went out with your mom and the dudes knew it. They've been watching us for a while. He should have just banged her here."

Justin pulls his arm from Katy's shoulder and pushes Pancho's chest. "What are you saying about my mother, asshole?"

"Just jerking your chain. Guess they went to look at the old junker of yours or some shit excuse like that."

Justin knows that a fight with Pancho would be suicide, and now that he has survived an armed attack, he'd like to stay alive as long as possible.

"Over there," Pancho gestures to a weighing station, "that's where the farmers bring the crude extraction, and the weight is recorded. And this is really cool." He points to a box of syringes with thick needles.

Katy grabs Justin's arm. "Those needles would kill."

"They're not for shots," Pancho says. "The farmers milk opium from the pods using syringes. Suck out the sap up to four times before they get it all and the plant's destroyed. Increases our production by nearly sixty percent. The 'milk'"—he makes air quotes—"gets poured into these vats, where it's boiled down to its morphine base. This is where it's dried." He points to several ovens. "Then it gets ground into powder," he points to an industrial grinder, "and packaged."

Justin doesn't want to hear any more. In fact, he's sorry he asked in the first place, but Pancho keeps talking. "There's a lot of cash made with street drugs. Don't think we're anything other than businessmen. It's not like we'd use the stuff ourselves or anything. We're not stupid. As long as there's a market, there'll always be someone to supply it. It might as well be us. Besides, Alfonso is fair. He pays the farmers good money for the extract and gives back to the community from the profits."

The door opens and Chato's shadow falls over them.

"Pancho." His face reddens and his skin tightens, an inflated balloon stretched to pop. "What the hell you doin' here?"

Cowering under his uncle's wrath, Pancho shrinks down as though to make his presence less conspicuous. "They were here during the attack and wanted to know what this place is. It's not like I went out of my way to show them."

"You thought this was a good place for them to hide? Are you insane? This is the worst place in the entire compound. Do you think you can just bring anyone here?"

"They can't do anything. They live here." Pancho's eyes dart back and forth. "They can't even leave the compound without an escort."

"Don't matter. This is nobody's business." Chato turns to Katy and Justin. "You two better not go squealing."

"We won't," Justin promises. "Besides, who could we tell?"

Chato glares at him. "Your mouth stays shut if you know what's good for you and your family."

Justin's heart pounds. He recognizes a threat when he hears one. "We won't say anything."

Chato scowls. Justin expects him to turn and leave, but he doesn't. He appears to be thinking. In all the time they've known him Chato's hardly said two words to them, so it's hard to know what could be going through his mind.

Justin pulls his little sister closer for combined strength. Cold sweat trickles down his back.

"Damn kids. Been poking around since day one. Dunno why Alfonso brought you people here in the first place. It won't end well," Chato predicts. "Oh, and you two'd better get on back. They're asking about you at the house. And remember what I said."

When Chato steps aside, Katy and Justin push past him and race toward the villa.

CHAPTER
THIRTY-THREE

Supper is a tense affair, after which Justin retreats to his room and throws himself on the bed. As he sees it, they've been willing convicts—and in a dangerous prison. Things are becoming more and more difficult. His mother isn't even hiding her preference for their host any longer. Even if Phil were to insist on leaving, he isn't sure Alfonso would allow it. Just today, the villa was attacked, and, even though Pancho kept them safe, they could have been trapped for days. Pancho had locked them in. If the bad guys had come looking for the heroin, it would have been all over.

He turns on the television and flips through hundreds of channels, not stopping anywhere for more than a moment or two, his mind racing. He stares at the remote, hardly able to believe he can't find a single thing to watch.

What will happen when his father learns the truth—that Alfonso's not growing opium for medicinal purposes but to sell on the streets of America? What will Alfonso do with him then? He leaps up, goes down to his parents' room, and knocks. No answer. Where is Dad? Adrenaline surges through him before he realizes that his father is probably downstairs working on tomorrow's sermon.

Justin wishes he'd never asked about the laboratory. His curiosity has placed them all in danger. Knowing for certain makes it so much worse. He returns to his room and flops down on his bed. Why has Alfonso—rich, handsome Alfonso—decided to steal away his mother when the guy could have anyone? Is he just trying to replace Marisol?

He picks up the remote once more and distracts himself with a marathon night of *Lost*. He stares at the screen; the similarity with their own situation does not escape him. Surrounded by danger, and they just want off the fucking island.

He falls asleep with the television blaring and the light on. As sunlight streams through the window, he jerks upright in bed.

Sunday. A glimmer of hope. They'll be allowed out of the compound to go to church. Could they somehow escape?

He puts on his Sunday clothes and is on his way toward the stairs when his mother steps out of Katy's room. "Morning, sweetheart. Wait for me and I'll walk down with you."

She rests her hand on his shoulder as they go downstairs. At the breakfast table, Phil wears an expression of resignation. His eyes brighten as his wife joins them at the table. She hasn't shared a table with her husband since the day they returned from the poppy field.

"I'm not going to church, Phil."

His jaw drops open. "Why not?"

"I can't praise God and pretend everything's okay between us when it isn't. I may be many things, but I'm not a hypocrite. You go with the kids. Tell whoever asks that I'm sick. Tell them whatever you want. I really don't care."

"Do I have to go? Can't I stay home with you, Mom?" Katy begs.

"Come with me, Katy," Phil says.

"C'mon, sis. Let's keep Dad company," Justin urges. If the three of them are together, maybe he can somehow get his mom to come, too.

The three of them leave the table and start toward the door. Horacio drives up and stops at the front to wait for them.

"We don't mind walking," Phil says.

"No walk. Ride."

At his insistence, they get into the car, and he drives them to the half-finished church. They expect him to leave and return later, but he parks, gets out, and leans against the vehicle.

"You're staying?" Justin asks.

Horacio nods as he pulls out a cigarette. "Orders."

Doña Rosa comes over and gives Justin a big hug. "You okay? Where you mother?"

"She's home. Doesn't feel well," he lies, and wonders whether the community heard about Alfonso's blossoming relationship with his mother and about what happened the previous day. Probably everyone knows.

"You give her my greeting."

He nods, fairly sure she is indicating that the villagers will be supportive and won't judge Katherine for her decision. At least as far as Doña Rosa is concerned.

As people arrive, Phil struggles to compose himself. His half-smile does little to hide his agitation. He greets members and visitors and thanks them for coming.

When the sermon begins, Phil pleads with God for his congregation, preaching compassion and forgiveness. His sermon is dedicated to his wife, but she isn't there to hear it. He tries not to focus on her absence and puts his heart into his speech. His inner turmoil injects the words with passion. The crowd is mesmerized.

"The Lord spoke while he was dying on that rugged cross. He said, 'Father, Father, why have you forsaken me?' But the Lord Jesus hadn't been forsaken. God, the Father, watched while His Son carried the sin from you and from me. He was the perfect lamb, the sacrifice for all of us. The Father let it happen, then He brought his Son back home, back into His arms when the passion ended. The Lord is looking out for us all. There may be times when you don't feel His presence, when He seems to have left you all alone, but He's waiting. He's waiting to take you in a grandiose hug for all eternity. I know with certainty that the Lord is looking out for us all. Every one of us."

Drenched in sweat and drained of energy, Phil strums the guitar. The congregation joins the now-familiar Christian tunes, a discordant choir.

A gravelly voice with garlic breath from behind Justin says, "*Tu papá*, he not well?" He turns. Prune-faced and dark, the woman behind him is ancient, but probably hard living has made her seem older than her years. He feels like he's seen her before, like somehow, she's been at the periphery of their world. Then he remembers. She is the woman he saw at the ceremony in the ruins. The one who smiled when he caught her eye.

"Who are you?"

"They call me Pelancha. *Esperanza.* Hope. Which I come to give you. Maybe God have mercy on *mi familia.*"

She wants to give him hope? He ponders for a moment and shakes his head. Whatever she wants to sell him, he isn't buying. "Who is your family?"

"*Mi hijo es Chato. Mi otro hijo* gone. *Solo está mi nieto, Francisco.*"

Then he remembers the errand they ran with Chato to the

328

hut. His mother. Who would believe Chato even had a mother? This must be Pancho's grandmother, the one he mentioned that day on the beach.

"I praying for you." She rests her gnarled hand on his, and Justin wonders how to politely escape this crazy person.

"And your mother? Does she trust him?"

Justin doesn't grasp the significance of the question and isn't sure if she is speaking about her trusting God or Alfonso or maybe even Chato. "I – I guess."

She nods in satisfaction and sits back in her seat.

MIDWAY THROUGH THE CLOSING HYMN, Horacio's phone rings. He barks some orders and slams the car door, heading to the front. All eyes are on him as he shakes his right hand and snaps his fingers together. "Come fast. There is *problema* at the villa. *Emergencia*."

They see a helicopter leave the villa and several of Alfonso's vehicles rush down the road.

Phil calls his kids, and people rise from the seats, murmuring to each other. Horacio revs the motor impatiently. Startled, the three of them stumble into the car. The vehicle peels out, and gravel spins and sprays toward the parishioners.

"What kind of emergency?" Justin says.

"I don't know," his father answers, "but I guess we'll soon find out."

KATHERINE STANDS at the door and gazes after her family as they leave for church. Is she doing the right thing? She can't tell anymore. The attack on the villa brings attention to what is both attractive and repellent about Alfonso. He's a man who thrives on danger, who lives on the edge. Is that the kind of man she and her children should settle with?

As though summoned by her thoughts, Alfonso embraces her from behind. "Things are especially dangerous now. We may have to leave for a while. Go to my home in Mexico until things settle down."

She stiffens. What things are dangerous, and who is he including when he says *we*? She turns to him with the questions on her face.

"I want you to come with me."

"What about the children? What about Phil?"

"Justin and Katy can join us, but Phil will have to stay. Do not worry, he will not be in any danger."

"How long is a while?" she asks, thinking he might be speaking of only a few days.

"It could be as short as several weeks and it might be as long as a year or two."

She stares at him.

He says lightly, "It is always best to say your farewells keeping in mind they might be permanent."

Prickles form on the back of her neck. How can she possibly justify taking her children away from their father and flying off to Mexico with a drug dealer? No matter how she might try to change his job description, she must accept the truth. What has she been thinking?

Just then, Chato shows up and motions to Alfonso. He points toward the helicopter as it fires up. Servants load duffel bags and the copter lifts off.

Katherine senses the urgency in the air. What to do, what to do? Options race about in her head, but realistic choices are disturbingly few. She can fly off with him, or she can tell him no and stay with her family. She doesn't know if the latter will incur his anger, and if he is angry, is he likely to be dangerous? Did they already know too much to be able to stay?

Filled with anxiety, she races to the computer room and sends a quick message to her parents, saying her farewells just in case.

Brusque and businesslike, Alfonso comes in. "I received a call. We must leave now or it will be too late."

"Now?" She panics. "Too late for what?" Her eyes dart around the room, wondering how she might forestall the decision and still get her family out of this mess intact. If Alfonso and Chato leave, will the Whitehalls be free to go, or would Alfonso force her to come along? And what about her children? What if they all stayed and the villa was attacked?

The time for her decision has arrived. The problem is, she isn't sure what repercussions that decision might have.

"We need to be in the air in thirty minutes. Phil, Justin, and young Katherine are on their way back." He turns and walks out the door. How can she figure out what to do in thirty minutes?

The house bustles with activity as people run from room to room. She hears the whacking of a chopper and hurries outside in time to see Pancho wave a brief goodbye and throw in the last of the duffle bags. The second aircraft lifts off just as the first returns; Chato is at the controls. The front gates are flung open, and Horacio drives in with her family.

Horacio takes them to the side where the helicopter waits. Bewildered, they jump out of the car. "What's going on?" Justin shouts over the roar of the departing chopper. Katherine and Alfonso meet them as they get out.

"We must leave," Alfonso says.

Phil's face clouds. "What? I don't understand."

"You will soon enough," Alfonso assures him.

Katherine stands near the chopper in a quandary. She can't live like this. She will have to tell him no. She will wait until the last minute, and they will all hide in the house. Safely together.

Alfonso puts his hand on her shoulder. "It is time to go, Katherine." Then addressing Phil, he says, "We are going away for a while."

Phil's eyes are drawn to where Alfonso touches his wife, and his eyes widen. "What about us?"

"The children are welcome to join us, but you must stay here. I do not know how long we will be gone."

Suddenly Katy appears with an overnight bag. She must have slipped away while they were talking. "I'm ready to go." She races to the helicopter and climbs in. Alfonso follows her and straps her into the back seat.

"You can't go, Katy," Justin cries in astonishment. "We aren't leaving."

"Get out of there!" Phil yells and starts toward the aircraft. No way is he letting his daughter run off on her own. His wife can make her own decisions, but Katy stays with him.

Alfonso blocks Phil's path. "Stay back. It is her choice." He turns to the boy. "Justin, are you coming?"

Justin turns toward his sister. This could be a nightmare if it weren't so awful. He would have woken himself long before it came to this. Separation from his little sister, from his mother, or his father? Inconceivable. Katy is annoying, but she is still family. "Let Katy out. Let us stay together."

Alfonso shakes his head and his expression is angry. Gone is the eloquent, patient friend and in his place is someone ruthless, someone with whom they are not acquainted. "The question is, are you coming with us?"

Justin stares at Alfonso. Who is "us"? Is his mother also

going? No! Could this nightmare get any worse? He wants to go home to Indiana. To the way things were. "I ... I can't go. I have to stay with Dad. He needs me."

Icy tentacles squeeze Katherine's heart. "Let Katy go," she repeats to Alfonso. "I will go in her place."

"You are coming as well, my dear, and young Katherine has also decided to join us."

The hint of cruelty in his voice frightens her, and she fears she has no choice in the matter. She has been playing with fire and now she will be burned. Will she be able to escape at some future time? Hasn't Poppy already taught Alfonso a lesson about freedom?

She can't choose between her children, but she can't let Katy go alone. She needs to ensure her daughter's safety. She turns to Justin. "Are you sure, son? You know the life Alfonso could offer you—the best of everything."

"That's not the life I want," he says.

She sees from his expression that he has already decided. "I don't belong here. I don't belong in Mexico either." Don't go, his eyes say. Don't let him split up our family.

"Katherine." Alfonso touches her hand. "It is time."

Katy reaches her arms out, and they can't make out the words as she shouts, "Come on, everyone! Mommy, hurry! They can't wait."

Katherine looks from her husband to her son, and then back to Katy and Alfonso. Lord, help me. A desperate plan unfolds in her mind, a way to keep them all together—risky, but the only option that comes to her. Stalling for time, she says, "I haven't packed."

"It is not necessary. I will take care of everything."

She hugs her son, her darling boy. She needs to say goodbye in case the plan doesn't work. At least Justin will be safe with

Phil. "Take good care of your father. I love you more than anything. Don't doubt that for a minute. I'll be thinking of you every day."

His eyes find hers. "Don't leave," he pleads.

Her eyes try to send hope back, hope that everything will be all right in the end.

Alfonso reaches over and puts his hand on Justin's shoulder. He produces a passport and gives it to him. "I thought you might be coming with us. I was not sure."

Justin looks down at the passport, then up at Alfonso. It was all a setup. Alfonso planned this from the very beginning. He slips it into his back pocket.

"Your mother and sister will be fine with me. I will take excellent care of them. You need not worry."

Justin stares at his feet, not daring to show anger toward their host.

Alfonso turns to Phil. "Your passport is upstairs with some cash. I am sorry it has to end like this."

He holds out his hand, but Phil backs away. Reality seeps in. Why had he been unable to see it earlier? "It was all planned. You had our passports the entire time. You arranged the break-in! Set things up to steal my wife! Why would you do that?" His face mirrors his disbelief. "I trusted you!"

Over the roar of the rotors, he shouts at Katherine. "Don't leave. Alfonso had this all planned. He's seduced you with his money."

She shakes her head and says quietly, "No, Phil. You were the one seduced by his money. If we hadn't gotten close to him, this never would have happened."

He stares at her blankly as she climbs into the helicopter next to Katy. Chato and Alfonso are in the front.

Katherine has no choice, she tells herself. She can't let Katy leave alone. Then she readies herself mentally for the opportunity to turn things around. Will she have the nerve? Alfonso straps himself into the copilot's seat and prepares for takeoff.

As the aircraft begins to rise, Katherine unbuckles her daughter's seat belt and her own and pulls her out the door. They tumble to the ground and regain their footing. Running for cover, Katherine drags Katy by the arm.

One of the guards aims a weapon toward them, but Chato circles back and emphatically shakes his head. No shots are fired. Alfonso mouths her name, his face a mask of anguish, but the chopper doesn't land. It angles west and, in a blast of wind and to the roar of rotors, it thunders toward Mexico.

THIRTY-FOUR

Phil opens his arms to embrace her. A second chance! He won't mess up again and he will forgive. Forgive and forget. A tender half-smile lights his face. "Katherine, we can start over. Pretend this never happened. I will make it up to you."

She shakes her head and backs away. "This isn't about you forgiving me. This is about me needing space." She twists off her wedding band, thrusts it in his hand, and closes his fingers around it.

He stares at her, unbelieving. She had an affair with Alfonso, but the fact that she didn't run off with him must mean something. Maybe she didn't hear him the first time. "Katherine, I'm willing to forgive whatever you might have done."

"But I'm not willing to forgive you."

Helicopters buzz from a distance, coming from a different direction. "They're returning," Phil cries.

Wondering if Alfonso has circled back, Katherine's heart skips a beat. Dread, excitement, and anxiety compete.

As though willing Alfonso to return, Katy watches the sky. Justin shakes his head at his sister. Katherine grabs her daughter's hand and races to the house. The choppers are landing outside the villa's walls, and she expects an attack. This isn't Alfonso and Chato returning. They'd gone in the opposite direction. Alfonso wouldn't have left if he thought it was safe to stay. Could she have convinced him to take them all? It all happened so fast and now it is too late.

She herds her family up the stairs and, from Justin's bedroom window, watches the front gate through sheer curtains, ready to find the nearest closet.

The guards at the gate pace nervously. One calls on the radio while others look down the road, shifting their weight from one foot to the other. Horacio has been left in charge. Radio in hand, he races toward the front.

"Look!" Justin points down the road.

A dozen men in military fatigues rush the entrance. Armed with loudspeakers, they announce, "This is the U.S. Drug Enforcement Agency. Open the gate. Do not make any sudden moves and put your weapons down. You are surrounded."

The guards back away from the gate and lay their guns in the grass, then raise their arms. Horacio steps forward and unlatches the gate.

Tall, muscular, and weighted down with full protective gear, the military men jog into the compound.

Phil turns to Katherine, head tilted as he absorbs the information. "Wait. The DEA? There must be some mistake."

"There's a mistake all right, but they aren't the ones who've made it."

The soldiers split up. Two of the men round up outdoor workers and circle toward the back, toward the pool and the laboratory beyond. Two of them approach the front door. The remainder crouch down as backup.

A Spanish speaker announces over the loudspeaker, "*Yo soy Agente González.* Everyone who is inside, come out with your hands up. We're coming in. Repeat. We are coming in. No one needs to get hurt."

The four members of the Whitehall family march downstairs and fall into the queue behind the kitchen staff, the housekeeper, and several domestic helpers. The soldiers check each one for guns as they leave the house.

"What have we got here?" an agent says as Phil approaches. He pokes his back with an automatic rifle and steers him to the side. "You aren't going anywhere." He radios a colleague. "Got one."

"Wait a minute. You can't do this. I'm a U.S. citizen," Phil protests.

"I don't care if you're a Martian. I have my orders." He inspects Phil from head to shoes. "Weapons?"

Phil shakes and sputters, "I don't carry a gun. I'm a missionary, not a murderer."

He studies Phil's slouching frame. "You'll have a chance to tell your story soon, and it had better be good."

"We are only guests here. Alfonso is our landlord."

A mustached agent walks over to see what this family of unlikely prisoners has to say. "We'll be verifying your story. If it checks out, you'll be free to go."

He pushes Phil to one side, but Phil continues, "I don't understand any of this. You must be mistaken. Alfonso has a permit to process poppies. He sells the morphine base for pharmaceutical purposes."

The mustached man exchanges a glance with his buddy and

drawls, "That what he told you? Are you stupid or just playing dumb?"

For months, Katherine has waited for the moment Phil would realize the truth, but she had never expected to see her husband the way he is now, pale and shaking as if he'd stepped out of a morgue.

Phil's face fills with horror as he realizes he's been duped. He shakes his head. "I've been such a fool," he says.

"Alfonso Cardenas is a principal processor and trafficker with the Sinaloa cartel."

Phil meets his wife's eyes and mouths silently, "Forgive me."

She feels an unexpected pang of pity, but her resolve hardens. The danger they are in is a direct result of his blundering and single-mindedness.

Katherine, holding Katy's hand, joins the employees gathered on the lawn. Justin remains with his father. The soldier guarding Phil points toward Katherine and Katy. "You. Wait over there."

She hears Justin say, "Can't I stay with my dad?"

"Justin!" she calls.

"Do what you're told," the soldier says.

When she has him by her side, she clasps his hand in a fierce grip.

"Mom!" Katy pulls her own hand loose. "Don't squeeze so hard."

An officer who has been going down the line of employees finally reaches them. "Do you speak English?"

Katherine nods.

"Can I see some identification?"

"We don't have any," Katherine says. "Alfonso took our passports."

The agent looks at Justin. "How old are you, son?"

"Fifteen."

"U.S. citizen?"

Justin pulls out the passport that he'd slipped into his back pocket less than an hour earlier.

The officer scans the first page and calls his boss over. "He's a minor, but not the one we're looking for."

"Why do you have your passport, son? Didn't you say Mr. Cardenas took your passports?" He looks at Katherine.

"I didn't want to go with him," Justin says.

"And my mom dragged me out of the helicopter when it was three feet off the ground," Katy adds. "I thought we were going to die."

The officer in charge is a tall man with glacial eyes and close-cropped hair. He is dressed in khaki pants and a polo shirt. He exchanges glances with his colleague. He mouths, "Possible kidnapping?" He turns to face them. "Folks, I'm Special Agent Tyler," he says with a slight Texas drawl. "You all had better come in for questioning. We'll fly you back to Guatemala City, have a friendly interrogation, and then send you on to your home in the States, wherever that might be. All things considered, you're lucky to be alive."

Katherine feels Katy looking up at her, then blurts out to Agent Tyler, "Alfonso would never hurt us!"

Katherine holds her gaze steady with Agent Tyler. "We were captives, yes, but of our own choosing. It was all a big misunderstanding."

"I'm looking forward to hearing this story."

Across the yard, she sees a soldier patting Phil down again, and hopes he will shut up for once. The man motions for Phil to hold out his hands. Phil obeys, and the soldier cuffs him with fluorescent plastic ties. "But, I didn't do anything wrong," Phil wails.

The soldier brings him back, and the four of them, with Agent Tyler, wait off to the side of the other detainees.

A helmeted soldier in camouflage, still carrying his assault rifle, comes around the corner of the house and crosses the lawn. "We found the lab," he tells the agent. "Spotless. Not a trace of drugs. It must have been cleaned out this morning."

"You folks really had no idea what was going on here?" the agent asks.

Katherine shrugs and Phil stares at the ground.

A soldier steps out of the villa holding Phil's passport. "I found this in the master bedroom. The safe is empty. I found no weapons."

The agent takes the passport. Katherine sees that Alfonso has stuffed it with hundred-dollar bills.

"Thank you, Jim," the agent says, putting the money in his pocket and opening the passport. "Phillip Cameron Whitehall," he reads. "What were you thinking in coming here, Mr. White-hall?" He motions for a soldier to cut the ties on Phil's wrists.

While Horacio explains in broken English that they are only workers, Alfonso's men are checked for identification and licenses to carry weapons.

"And the bosses?" Jim asks.

"Gone." Horacio swipes the back of his hand over the other palm.

"The house is clear, and the remaining folks seem to be employees," Jim calls to the DEA boss. "Must have been tipped off. Could have had up to an hour's lead."

Agent Tyler takes Katherine's elbow. "Let's go."

"Where to?" she asks.

"Guatemala City."

"Can we get our things?" Phil says.

"What things?" the agent asks.

341

"My Bible," Phil says. "My son's duffel bag, and ... "

"Shut up, Dad," Justin says. "Just leave it."

Phil slouches between two burly men as they lead the way back to the helicopters. He holds his wrists together as if they were still bound.

The agent falls in step beside Katherine. "What's your name, ma'am?"

She tells him.

"How did you end up at Alfonso Cardenas's house, Mrs. Whitehall?"

"It's a long story."

"We'll need to go over the details when we get there," the agent says. "We'll be taping the interview."

They climb into the rear of a military helicopter. As they travel the hour back to La Aurora International Airport, the noise is deafening.

Katherine stares out the window, watching the treetops not that far below and the ash-covered peaks of the approaching volcanoes. What kind of story is she prepared to tell? The truth? How innocent is she going to look if the agent asks why she and Katy were onboard Alfonso's helicopter? And what if they'd gotten injured when they jumped? Or the guard had shot them? Her actions, much more than Phil's, had put them all at risk and may still put them at risk, even when they're back in the States. If Alfonso truly is with the Sinaloa cartel, then he's one of the kingpins of the Zetas. Alfonso has Katherine's and Katy's passports. He knows where they're from.

Upon landing, they are whisked to a private hangar, then loaded into the back of a van. They pass several security checks and are ushered into the basement of a bleak, gray cement building, the United States embassy. While the children are excused from questioning, Katherine and Phil are told to follow Agent Tyler.

"Where are we going?" Katherine asks.

"Providing your answers are satisfactory," Agent Tyler says, "the embassy will make arrangements for you to return to the United States." He added that provisional passports for Katherine and Katy would get them through customs.

Fine, she thinks, but between now and then, they're going to have to come up with some kind of story, and if she and Phil give conflicting versions of what happened, they could be stuck down here indefinitely. Hesitating, she looks down the hall. Justin and Katy are following a woman with a pencil skirt and buttoned-up white blouse down the corridor. Justin looks back and makes a meaningful zip across his lips. She nods and gives him a furtive thumbs up.

Agent Tyler takes them to a windowless office with a gunmetal-gray table and a box of Kleenex in the center. Another tall man in a suit and tie steps into the room, followed by a woman wearing a black uniform and white apron. She brings cups of water for the four of them, places the water in front of the chairs, and excuses herself. The tall man looks like an accountant—mousy brown hair, wire-rimmed glasses, and a receding hair-line—but introduces himself as the consul general. After seating them on one side, he asks, "Will you excuse us for a moment?"

"Of course," she says.

When the two leave the room, Phil reaches in his pocket and takes out her wedding ring. She slips it on and clasps his hand. When the embassy men return with a manila folder and a tape recorder, the couple's clasped hands are propped on the edge of the table.

When the men are seated, Agent Tyler nods at the tape

recorder and presses play. Then he opens a manila folder and rifles through the contents.

The agent questions them about how and why they'd come as missionaries and wants to know how they got involved with Alfonso. Phil talks about the church. Katherine speaks of their small house, about the break-in. Neither volunteers more than what is necessary. What can they safely say? They don't know how far the Zetas' reach extends or what might implicate them as accessories.

"How did you end up renting that particular house?" Agent Tyler asks. "Out of the hundreds of places you might have gone, why there?"

"It was arranged for us," Phil insists. "We fronted the money to our contact and he made all the arrangements."

"We know nothing about a man named Jerónimo. Could he have been on Alfonso's payroll?"

Katherine and Phil exchange glances. "I, I guess it's possible," Phil stammers. "But why would Alfonso want us nearby? We could have been a threat to his business."

"But clearly you weren't. It just doesn't add up." He chews the pencil's eraser. "How did he lure you into his house?"

"Our home had been broken into. Phil was away. Our car wasn't running. I had little choice. I couldn't believe he was a threat to us." She looked down at her wedding ring. "The kids had stayed at the villa on several occasions and nothing happened. It wasn't until he was leaving that we found out he had arranged the break-in and that he had our passports."

"Mr. Whitehall, did you know Alfonso Cardenas was in the narcotics trade, and did you actively participate in that trade with him?"

"Of course not! My family suspected, but I refused to believe." His face crumples and he begins to cry.

The agent hands him a tissue. "I trusted him," Phil continues. "Such a refined person. A man who has done beneficent projects in the community. But he wasn't a friend, after all," Phil says. "He stole my wife. He tried to take her and the kids with him. He almost got Katy."

Special Agent Tyler stops and his eyes fall on Katherine. "That must be why he took your passports. You'd better explain, Mrs. Whitehall." He turns the page on his notepad. "This is nowhere in my intelligence."

She stares at the table. "It wasn't quite like that. Right as he was leaving, he asked me to go. I think he expected me and the kids to leave with him. I was planning to turn him down, and then Katy got into the chopper, assuming that we would all be going. After Alfonso strapped her in, he wouldn't let Phil take her out." Her voice falters. "I had to join her. I couldn't let my daughter fly off with those men alone. As the chopper lifted off, I unbuckled our restraints and we jumped to the ground."

"Mr. Whitehall, seeing that Mr. Cardenas was so taken with your wife, didn't you fear for your life? It would have been very convenient for him to get rid of you."

"You mean murder? Never. I wouldn't believe it of him."

"What about you, Mrs. Whitehall? Did you have any doubts?"

"He mentioned an accident involving Phil, but he phrased it as a joke. He told me I needed to make a choice."

He scribbled on his notepad and looked up. "You two have been very helpful. Do you have any idea where they went?"

Phil shakes his head. "They seemed to be heading toward Mexico."

"Do you have any means by which to contact them?"

"No."

"Did they mention if they'd be contacting you later?"

"No, it all happened so fast," Katherine says.

As he puts his papers into the briefcase he says, "You people have no idea how lucky you are. Alfonso Cardenas is wanted on multiple felony counts of drug trafficking. He's also wanted for murder."

"Murder?" Katherine says.

"You're lucky you didn't end up just another name on a long list."

"I can't believe he murdered anyone," she murmurs.

"You can't stay on top in his profession without killing people, Mrs. Whitehall. It's a fact of the game. Mr. Cardenas is smart and a formidable adversary."

Agent Tyler closes his folder. The consul turns off the tape recorder.

"He's a damned convincing liar," Agent Tyler says. "We've been following his career for years."

Katherine sits back in her chair and releases Phil's hand. He flexes his fingers and looks down in his lap. She takes off her wedding ring and slips it into his pocket.

When the interview finally ends, evening blankets the city in a diamond-studded quilt. They are transported to the Westin Camino Real, a contrast from the hostel where they stayed upon arrival. A guard is posted outside their door.

THIRTY-FIVE

They depart on the eighth of November. As the plane makes a circular turn toward the north, Katy stares into the smoky cauldron of the Pacaya volcano. Katherine watches her daughter carefully. Is the girl regretting Katherine's decision to jump out of the chopper? Katherine, like Katy, will always wonder what their lives might have been like if she hadn't.

Alfonso was right, Katherine decides after reviewing the past few days. She couldn't be with him just because she wants to leave her husband; a failed marriage isn't a good enough reason to become partners with a criminal. Her life would have been all about looking the other way while pretending not to be fearful. How could she have almost convinced herself to take up with a drug lord?

Justin looks pleased to finally be going home, but Katherine wishes the end of their stay had been different. Would Justin ever see her with the same eyes? She had had an affair with

Alfonso. There was no longer any doubt. Would he ever be able to forgive her or trust her again?

Katherine wonders what Phil would say on his family nights about lessons learned. She doubts he would want to share his thoughts. He had failed his wife, his family, and even his job. He was too interested in establishing a church to be concerned with how that came about. Too interested in Alfonso's financial aid to discern the price he would have to pay for it. Why did Phil think God was involved in every decision? Certainly, it wasn't God's plan for Phil to become involved with someone so evil. Somewhere along the line, Phil had lost sight of the meaning of God's will. But, she tells herself, when they get home, there'll be time enough to sort this out.

The aircraft skims the clouds over the Caribbean coastline of Belize and then heads north, following the Yucatán Peninsula. Below is a blanket of green. Somewhere over Mexico, Katherine wonders how she got caught up in the idea of a life that was so exciting and dangerous. Where was Alfonso now? What would their lives be like if she hadn't jumped? Justin had told her the previous night about Alfonso's former wife, Marisol. That she had been killed in an attack, an attack that must have been like the recent one. Would Katherine have lived in fear for her life or for that of her daughter?

She takes Katy's hand and traces her lifeline. When Katy smiles up at her, Katherine is grateful once again that they made it out of that helicopter alive, but even so, she can't help but wonder which Alfonso is the real one: the one the DEA believes is a drug lord and murderer, or the man who cares for the downtrodden—the man she knew. Is the DEA's version of the truth the only one that matters, or, for a brief time, was there some version of Alfonso that longed for redemption?

If this experience has taught Katherine anything, it is that she doesn't need a man to define her: not Phil, not Alfonso. She is just Katy and Justin's mom. From now on, she will fight to do what's best for her children; they will be her priority, and she will never again put them in harm's way. She breathes deeply and, like her husband who sits behind her, thinks about what she's gained from this experience. Life is all about forgiveness and self-improvement. Phil's insistence on reflection has never seemed so relevant. For the valuable lessons they take home, she will always be grateful to Guatemala and the poppy field, but what a way to learn. What a heck of a way to learn.

ACKNOWLEDGMENTS

Many people have given their insight and encouragement for this novel, especially my husband, Eduardo Godoy. Most of all, I need to thank my mother, Ann Gates, who labored with me tirelessly through the many revisions.

ABOUT THE AUTHOR

Caroline Kellems is the author of *The Coffee Diary*, a novel about a woman who returns to Guatemala and discovers her deep connection to the land and to her roots. A native of California, Kellems joined the Peace Corps in 1985 and was sent to Guatemala, where she met her husband, Eduardo Godoy. She and her husband, parents of two grown daughters, own a coffee plantation in Moyuta, located in the Guatemalan department of Jutiapa. They also have a coffee roasting and export company in Guatemala City.

facebook.com/caroline.kellems

goodreads.com/Caroline_Kellems

ALSO BY CAROLINE KELLEMS

Please remember to post a review of *The Poppy Field* in the online bookstore of your choice. Now, are you ready for another great novel by Caroline Kellems? Autographed copies of *The Coffee Diary* are available from Godoy's Gourmet Guatemalan Coffee (www.godoyscoffee.com).

"...a love letter to modern-day Guatemala, to the rich chiaroscuro of the beauty, violence, and cultural complexities—straight from the heart of someone who clearly knows this world well."

—Julia Glass, author of *Vigil Harbor* and *Three Junes*

GRAND CANYON PRESS

If you enjoyed this book, please drop by the Grand Canyon Press
website and discover more exciting books.

...

www.grandcanyonpress.com

Grand Canyon Press

Made in United States
Troutdale, OR
01/21/2025

28152239R10224